BRIDGET MIDWAY

LICORICE WHIPS

Licorice Whips

Bridget Midway

Published by Stark Bright Entertainment
By Bridget Midway

Your Love Is King - Book 2 in the Royal Pains Series

Dedication

Thank you to the readers, who, surprisingly, have never forgotten about me and asked to see this book again.

A big thank-you to the late and always great Mistress Dama de Noche, into, Lady G, Master Wes, Susscrofa Tarr, East Bound, Ash Pacific, Stephen, kris, Madame Shadow, slave aaron, Sir Knotz, and the whole T.I.E.D. and Virginia Dommes and male submissives group in the Tidewater area of Virginia. As always, I hope I don't let you down with anything I've written. You all inspire me more than you know.

To The Jimmy, my soul mate and true love. Thank you for giving me my space and allowing me to write like a mad woman, which meant that sometimes you didn't get dinner or get to go out to see a movie. I recognize your sacrifice to be with a writer. I am bound to you in more ways than one. I love you.

Chapter One

Sweet Hawkes stalked through the aisles of his Decadent Treats candy store, probably looking harder than he should considering the sweet treats he and his brother sold.

"We own a candy shop, for God's sake," his brother Masaun would say. "Act like you like it."

Sweet had to stop mixing his personal drama into his professional successes. Just like he had to stop thinking that playing with someone in a dungeon meant that she would pledge her allegiance to him.

Sweet would have to fill that empty pit inside himself with more work. He used to love seeing the initial reaction to anything: the first taste of a luscious treat, the first sexual encounter with a woman, the first gasp from experiencing the stinging tip of his whip. Those primary responses became his drug of choice.

The sugary scent of candy wafted in the air. Aromas of cherry, grape, and chocolate tickled his nose and senses. To Sweet, it smelled like money... and power. No one would be able to understand that feeling but him.

The rows and columns of candy reminded him of Willy Wonka's chocolate factory and an amusement park all rolled in one. Light pop music played throughout the store.

God bless Katy Perry and her candy outfits. Thanks to her, teenage girls bought large lollipops and cotton candy to make Halloween outfits to look like the pop princess. If people knew what he could do with his confections, they wouldn't allow their children to step into the store again.

The looks he got from many of the female patrons as he walked down the aisles didn't escape his notice. He couldn't forget that he and Masaun had a business to run. With enough work, he would eventually forget his past and last heartbreak.

"Did you read the article about them?" a young woman whispered to her friend.

Sweet pretended not to hear her, but from her low tone and suspicious glance in his direction, she managed to catch his attention.

"He and his brother are part of that place down at the beach. You know. The Playground or The Schoolyard or something like that."

Unafraid of his association with the whispered establishment or the things he'd done in there, Sweet stopped, strolled over to the women with a scowl, and said, "The place is called The Dollhouse. It is a dungeon." He split his attention between the two of them.

The two women stared at him with their mouths gaped open. The one with curly strawberry blonde hair seemed frozen in her spot. While the other, an African-American woman in a matronly flowered dress that seemed to conflict with her youthful face, covered her mouth and split her attention between her mouthy friend and Sweet.

"If either of you want to know what really happens behind that red door, I'd be more than happy to take you there." Sweet stared at the two women. "What? No takers?" He tsked. "My loss."

He continued toward the office, which sat behind the kitchen area. Ever since the news broke about Masaun, his district attorney fiancée, and Sweet's involvement in BDSM, the whispers started around him. Although he didn't care for the clucking tongues, he wanted to control his public image.

He'd been begging Masaun for years to come clean about their proclivities. Masaun being Masaun, the safe, by-the-book one, wanted to keep that part of their lives quiet.

"No one needs to know about our private lives," Masaun used to say. Now it seemed everyone knew. To Sweet's surprise, the news had increased their business. Sweet assumed people came there now to ogle at the freak brothers. The thought of that boiled his blood.

Sweet glanced down at a row of chocolates in the front case. Before he could even weaken himself to reach for one of the pieces to ease his nerves, he continued to the kitchen area. Baking relaxed him. Playing at The Dollhouse used to take away his frustrations.

Before stopping at the kitchen, Sweet continued to the office. As he opened the door, he said, "Hey, we could use a hand out here."

Sweet caught Masaun sitting behind his desk with Masaun's fiancée on his lap. Sweet had a feeling that had he come just five minutes later, he would have seen a lot more than his brother with his hand up Kindle Langston's top.

"Whoa!" Sweet turned his back on the scene, not to give them privacy. He didn't want them to see the anger on his face.

Sweet never thought that his business-minded, square older brother would be this risqué. Had Sweet been caught doing the exact same thing, Masaun would have never let him live it down.

"Hell, don't you knock?" Masaun damn near growled the question.

"At my own business in my office? No." Sweet turned around and walked inside.

At this point, Kindle had her shirt tucked back into her skirt. Her coffee-colored smooth skin hid her obvious embarrassment. Her panting breath couldn't disguise the steamy activity that had occurred just moments before.

"How are you doing, Kindle?" Sweet kissed her cheek.

"Fine. I was just—"

Sweet held up his hand. "No explanation necessary. I get it." He split his attention between her and his brother. "Young love." He stared at his brother. "Well, maybe young-*ish* love."

Masaun picked up a notepad and threw it at Sweet. Expecting the reaction, Sweet managed to catch the bound pad of paper and toss it back to his brother.

"I'm going to freshen up a little before I go back to the office. I still have so much stuff to pack up before my last day." Kindle kissed Masaun.

Sweet felt a ripple tickle the back of his neck when he saw the expression. Although he loved that his brother found happiness with a woman who matched him in every way, Sweet knew a relationship like that wouldn't work for him. Nothing lasted beyond the spark.

Kindle ducked into their private bathroom and closed the door. As soon as the latch clicked, Masaun wasted no time in lighting into Sweet.

"You know with me and Kindle together, some things are going to have to change around here." Masaun ran his fingers through his dark, wavy hair.

"You're right. I think you should have more sex in the office."

The glare from his brother's green eyes didn't scare Sweet. Although he had a darker side, Masaun looked too conservative to be considered menacing. The illusion definitely helped him in the BDSM world.

Sweet sat on the couch next to the desk. "By the way, you need to put your dick in your pants before Connie or Hanson come in here."

"Asshole." Masaun twirled the swivel chair so that his back faced Sweet.

Sweet watched him squirming in his chair before he returned his attention to him.

"You're in here because you wanted something, right?"

Sweet blinked. "I need a reason to come into the office? Last time I checked, I'm still part owner of this establishment."

Masaun released a long sigh. "Didn't mean it that way. Usually you don't come back to the office until the end of the day."

"That means if I'm in here now, I must have something to say." Sweet planted his feet on the floor and leaned forward so that his brother could see the full intent in his eyes. "It's time for Decadent Treats to expand."

Masaun blinked. "Really? As in another location?"

Sweet shook his head. "Not exactly. I mean delving into something that we really know about." He wiped his hands over his jeans and took a breath before he continued speaking. "I'd say we open up a Decadent Treats Two and sell fetish toys and clothing." As soon as Sweet saw his brother shaking his head, he continued his pitch before he got shut down. "Our current location is good."

Masaun nodded. "Yeah. Plenty of parking. Close to the mall. Near restaurants so we get the patrons who want something different for dessert."

Sweet bit his tongue, knowing what Masaun wanted him to thank him for finding the spot.

Sweet gritted his teeth before continuing with his pre-planned speech. "I found a better spot in downtown Virginia Beach. Actually two side by side. I was thinking we get them both, close this location, and set up at the new place. Then we'll use the other location to stock our toys. You know. The whips, chains, handcuffs, corsets." Sweet felt tingles over his body.

He loved sharing his ideas. This one would put their business on the map as the top candy *and* fetish shops in Virginia Beach.

Masaun shook his head. "No."

Sweet's heartbeat slowed but he tried to remain encouraged. "Why not? If it wasn't for you, people would care less what we do on our spare time. Now we have customers whispering about us in the store. People know. So why not profit from it?"

His brother leaned back in the swivel chair. "That's not fair. How everything got revealed was an accident. Kindle and I didn't plan for our--"

Sweet cut him off. "It doesn't matter how it got out. The fact of the matter is that it is out. *I* wanted to shout it from the rooftops for years."

"I know. That's the impetuous side of you that I so enjoy."

"We're Doms, for Christ's sake. We should be masters of our own destinies. Nothing should happen by mistake. We should have said something first." Sweet sat up taller.

"It didn't happen that way. We had to improvise."

Sweet cleared his throat with a low growl. "I improvise all the time. It works during play."

Masaun shook his head. "Play? You haven't done that in a while."

Sweet swallowed hard as he glared at Masaun. After releasing his last submissive, he had no desire to resume all his Dom duties, a strange response considering how much he loved playing. He loved seeing the shocked expression on a submissive's face as soon as he inflicted the first hit.

Before Sweet could defend his actions, or lack thereof, Masaun continued. "Let's finish talking about your plan."

"What I'm proposing would make sense. Have a Decadent Treats original and a Decadent Treats Two next door. The kids will get candy while mommy and daddy explore the strap-on aisle."

"There are several problems with your plan." Masaun rested his hands on his stomach.

Sweet glared at his brother. "What are those?"
Masaun chuckled. "Are you serious? We're doing fine here because we got in at a good time and our rates have been reasonable. We're beyond profitable now. It wouldn't be a great time to get rid of this place and get on the hook for not one but two new spots in a pricey area of the Beach."

Sweet's eyebrows furrowed. "It would work if you would see the bigger picture."

Masaun's eyes widened. "If *I* saw the bigger picture? You're kidding, right?" He gripped the end of the desk as he faced Sweet. "I'm the one crunching the numbers, making sure to check the prices on our suppliers and balancing the books. *I'm* seeing the big picture. I know if we continue at this rate, we'll be an even bigger success than what we are now. You have to stay the course and not be so quick to change scenery when the mood hits you. I offered to show you our numbers, but you never want to see them."

"I'm busy at the front of the house. Since business is up, I've adjusted my schedule to work more during the day." Sweet pointed to the store area. "When I'm not there, I'm in the kitchen creating more candies and chocolates for us to sell. Throw on top of that *our* time at The Dollhouse, my day is full." Sweet raised his eyebrows to his brother who understood what the BDSM dungeon meant for the two of them.

Masaun shook his head. "Don't even mention that place like it matters to you anymore."

"What are you talking about? I'm there three or four nights a week."

Sweet felt his temperature rising. He balled his hands into fists, trying to contain his anger.

"Yes, you are there. But when was the last time you threw a whip at someone? I think it was a couple of years ago when you were with–"

"Don't you mention her name." Sweet's heart thudded in his chest just thinking of Melinda and her pale skin that marked up so easily. "As far as I'm concerned, that was a clean break."

"Bullshit." Masaun snickered. "Any other man would have gotten right back on the horse. You didn't. Any other Dom would have played with a willing submissive or slave. You haven't."

"At least I'm at The Dollhouse."

"Did I hear someone mention The Dollhouse?" Kindle, looking more like a commonwealth attorney now rather than a video vixen, sauntered out of the bathroom.

She pulled her dark hair up into a sleek bun. The pink color of her silk blouse popped against her understated gray suit. As soon as her gaze fell on Masaun, she lit up like Las Vegas.

Sweet loved seeing that initial glint of lust. Too bad the feeling never lasted...at least for him it didn't.

"Are you working late tonight?" Masaun kept his stare on Kindle.

"Not if The Dollhouse is on the table." She framed his face in her hands. "I'll be sure to be home for that." She planted a sensual kiss on his lips.

When the kiss seemed to be leading to other wanton acts, Sweet cleared his throat. Kindle pulled back but kept her stare on her man. Masaun definitely trained her well.

"See you tonight." She picked up her purse and briefcase, then strolled to the door.

"Can't wait." Masaun beamed as he watched her leave.

"Lust looks good on you." Sweet stood.

"It's more than lust. It's love. It could look good on you, too, if you let Kindle hook you up with some of her single friends."

Sweet shook his head. "I'd like something permanent. I want a lover *and* a submissive. I can't seem to get those two together. Owning a submissive or slave isn't enough for me."

"No, you don't think you can keep any type of permanent relationship. There's a difference." Masaun pointed at Sweet. "You can own again. You can love again."

Easier said than done. Some breakups couldn't be overlooked.

"You and Kindle don't keep a twenty-four/seven relationship?" Sweet stared at Masaun, who rutted his eyebrows in confusion.

"What do you mean?" Masaun regarded his brother with his standard judging stare.

"I know your playing style. I know what you demand of your slaves and submissives." Sweet eased back on the couch. "Why didn't Kindle come back into the room on her hands and knees? Why didn't she call you by your scene name? Was she wearing underwear?"

"You're out of fucking line." Masaun pointed at Sweet.

Had his brother's finger been a gun, Sweet would be dead.

"If I had someone, I would want her to call me Master Sweet all day, every day. I would want her to show her obedience to me."

Maybe if Melinda had done that, she wouldn't have wanted to be released. Then again, maybe if he had recognized the fact that she hadn't shown any obedience to him, he would have released her sooner.

"Fine. You find your own submissive. You treat her how you'd like. Stay out of my relationship." Masaun drummed his fingertips on the desk. "Let's get back to talking about business before this conversation goes too far. I think what you're proposing is a stupid idea, but I'll entertain the notion."

Sweet wiped his brow in an exaggerated motion. "Whew. Glad I got your blessing."

"Funny. Do you have a business proposal for your idea?" Masaun faced his laptop and started typing. When Sweet didn't answer right away, Masaun brought his gaze back up to him. "You did write one up that shows the cost benefits of expanding, right?"

"Of course there will be benefits to having another type of business. You talk to the people at the club. You've heard them all complain that there's not any place around here to buy good, quality toys and not gimmicky crap that breaks after one hard play session." Sweet braced his hands on his knees. He felt grounded that way.

"You think the world is in the lifestyle. They're not. Some people may want those less-expensive toys for parties. The real thing may intimidate people." Masaun exhaled. "I don't see where spending money to, one, get two new spaces, then two, stock one with quality fetish materials, and three, put employees in there to run it for us is a good move for us right now. Contract time is coming up for lease renewal. Let's hope they don't jack up our rates."

Sweet felt the headache coming on as he marched toward his brother. He slammed his hands on the desk as he stared at him. "We've been called the 'Best at the Beach' for three of the five years we've been in business. We've been featured in *The Virginian-Pilot* and on the local news a few times. Things are looking up for us. Trust me. This will work."

Masaun rolled his eyes. "A candy store and a specialty fetish store are two separate things." He shook his head. "If you had proposed a candy store and a full-on bakery, I would be more on board with that." He rocked back and forth in his swivel chair. "Yes, we're out now as far as our lifestyle. But you damn near dangle the fact that we're in the Lifestyle in front of people almost daily."

Sweet stood tall. "I'm not ashamed of being a BDSM Dom. I didn't think you were, either."

Masaun could be considered more of a dungeon master than just a Dominant who played at The Dollhouse. For the past fifteen years, he trained almost all the new Doms and Dommes in the establishment as well as many of the new submissives. From aftercare to whipping and everything in between, Masaun taught it all. Sweet had learned about the Lifestyle along with him, but preferred playing than teaching.

"I love the Lifestyle, too. So does Kindle." A sly smile cocked at the corner of his mouth. "But that side of us is private. We don't have to label ourselves."

"What do you mean?" Sweet crossed his arms over his chest. He hated feeling defensive with the one person he thought had understood him the most.

Masaun scanned the desk and picked up a bumper sticker that Sweet had been handing out to customers. He read the front of it out loud. "Decadent Treats. Bouquets, delivery, sweets and more." He dropped his hand back to the desk and glared at Sweet.

Sweet shrugged. "What? We do all those things."

"What are the initials?"

A smile almost crossed Sweet's face knowing that Masaun had caught on faster than he thought he would. "So what? So, the initials come out to BDSM. A coincidence."

"Coincidence my ass. You are right about one thing. We have more customers in here because people want to take a gander at the Dom brothers running a candy shop."

"I have no problem playing with anyone who wants to step into a dungeon with me." Sweet shrugged.

His brother's questioning glance didn't escape Sweet's notice.

"We should be known for selling great products and having excellent customer service."

Sweet waved his hand at him. "Sure. That'll keep the customers in the store. Seeing us will get them coming into the store."

Masaun shook his head. "You're all about the immediate reaction, aren't you?"

"What can I say? It's my drug."

Masaun sat back in the black leather high-back swivel chair. "It's your excuse to not open up again."

Before Sweet got into the same argument he'd had with his brother for the past two years, since Sweet and Melinda had broken up, he turned back to the door. "I'm open. I'm going to check out what's going on in the store before I head to the kitchen."

"Hey, while we're on the subject of changes, are you still looking for a new place to live?" Masaun pointed at him.

Sweet shook his head. "I like living upstairs in the apartment." Masaun released an exasperated sigh. "You're using this place and The Dollhouse to hide."

"I'm committed to the business *and* the Lifestyle." Sweet shook his head. He had to count to ten in his head before he continued speaking. "When I presented you with the idea of us owning this candy shop together, I did it without a business plan, and you jumped on the idea, right?"

"Right, but–"

"And when I said I would make some of the candies, you trusted me, right?"

"I knew you would do a–"

Sweet cut him off again. "It seems like my instincts have been pretty dead-on as far as our business. Why don't you trust me now?"

Masaun sighed. "It's not that I don't trust you. You get these romantic notions in your head without fully thinking things through. You've entrenched yourself in this business as though you're hiding away from something. You're great with the creative, but you have nothing to keep you grounded to reality."

"Except you." Sweet pointed at him. "Is that what you were going to say?" He raked his fingers back through his hair. "I know it's going to hurt you to say it, but you can tell me that I'm right sometimes."

"Even when you're wrong?"

Sweet shook his head. "Fuck you." He grabbed the doorknob. "As always, thanks for the support. I see I'll have to do this my way as usual."

Before another word could be said, Sweet stormed out of the office and slammed the door behind himself. He tried showing a pleasant appearance before getting to the main store area but even Sweet couldn't fake the expression.

Sweet went behind the counter as his employee, Hanson, checked out the purchases for a mature African-American woman. Hanson had been an employee for the last three years, coming on when business really started booming. The tall, lanky African-American man proved to be a great asset to their business.

"Everything all right, boss?" Hanson asked without taking his attention away from the customer.

"Fine. Just me and my brother having one of our discussions." Sweet scanned the area behind the counter and spotted a shipping box filled with large, heart-shaped red boxes of chocolates. He pulled one from the box.

The pre-packaged boxes of chocolates and candies had been Masaun's idea. Sweet sold some of his creations in the store, but he could only produce so much in a day before customers bought out the stock. If he could clone himself, he would.

"Connie and I were about to stock those but it got busy." Hanson handed the customer her purchases and her change.

Sweet glared at his employee. First he couldn't get his brother around to his way of thinking, and now his employees developed minds of their own.

When Hanson caught the look, he stopped moving. "I'll get them stocked right now." He started to call for Connie but Sweet stopped him.

"I'll take care of it." Sweet swept the box off the counter and moved to the middle aisle.

As he crouched down, Sweet's thoughts tumbled through his head. He knew this business venture would work, like he knew Decadent Treats would be a hit.

Masaun may not have believed in him, but that didn't mean Sweet didn't believe in himself. He had a goal. He thought his brother would have appreciated his willingness to expand their business. Even if he didn't, that didn't mean Sweet had to stop. He hadn't forgotten he owned a portion of this business and had a voice.

"Uh-oh," Connie, the other Decadent Treats employee, said next to Sweet. The older woman covered her mouth with her hand in shock.

Sweet glanced at the woman as he stood. "What?"

"She's back." She nodded her head to the front of the store. "The lone protester."

Sweet stared out through the front glass of the store and saw a woman handing out fliers to people walking by, and talking to patrons as they entered the store. He had heard about her from Masaun but hadn't seen her yet. In the glare of the noonday sun reflecting off the glass, he couldn't see her face. That would be rectified right now.

When the front door opened, Sweet heard a portion of the woman's speech.

"...leading cause of diabetes and childhood obesity."
Then the door closed and he couldn't hear her. Sweet heard his heart pounding in his head. The crackling of his grinding teeth rumbled through his ears.

"This woman acts like we're cooking puppies and kittens in here." Connie almost raised her delicate voice. She didn't get rattled easily. If this person could get his employee riled up, he had to check her out.

Connie crossed her arms over her chest. "Where does she get off protesting a place like this? At least she's smart enough not to step one foot in here." She shook her head. "Your brother said if she shows up again for us to call the police." She turned on her heel and headed to the register counter.

"Don't bother. I'll handle this." He pointed to the box on the floor. "Finish stocking up here." Sweet marched to the front door.

His brother tried squashing his dreams. This woman wouldn't do the same. He tried going the easy route by convincing Masaun he could make this idea work. Like everything else, Sweet would have to do things his way.

Chapter Two

Nikla Dearwood paced back and forth in front of Decadent Treats. She could barely look at the pink, blue, and white neon sign advertising the establishment. With each step, she felt stronger and more confident that being there and stating her case would potentially help someone.

As a couple of women walked toward the store, Nikla held up one of her bright yellow forms that pinpointed the issues of eating too much candy and sweets.

"Ladies, look at the stats on what places like this can do to you and your loved ones."

One woman snickered. "Are you kidding? You must be at the house that gets covered in toilet paper during Halloween." She opened the door. "Tutor kids. Help homeless people. Get out of my face with that."

Nikla hoped she hid her disappointment under her forced smile. Withstanding this embarrassment would be worth it in the end.

The two women walked inside the same time a tall man strolled outside. With his shape, no way could he eat anything this place had to offer. Men with flat stomachs, long, muscular arms, and broad shoulders like this guy would turn their noses up at unhealthy snacks like what this store offered. This man probably went into this place to get his girlfriend, wife or, possibly, boyfriend a box of chocolates.

Nikla sighed at the thought that she had never received the clichéd gift—not for Valentine's Day, not for her birthday, and she hadn't been with a man long enough to celebrate an anniversary.

Before she could continue to bemoan her past, Nikla noticed the intense man's Decadent Treats t-shirt. Great. He would be out there to try and run her off like the other employees had done the few times she'd been there. From the sour look on his face, he must have been chosen because they thought he would strike the most fear in her. No chance. Growing up with Lieutenant General Lawrence Dearwood, she had to learn to toughen up.

For her actions now, Nikla knew her rights. This scrooge had better not put his hands on her.

When she looked him over, she thought about amending her last thought. Besides being tall, he had shaggy brown hair that would have been great to run fingers through, or even grab during sex.

Sex. She had to push that thought out of her head, especially since she had her man. When she glanced at this enemy in his face, she made the mistake of looking into his hypnotic green eyes. She remained transfixed to the stare until she had to look away.

Nikla chalked up her newly accelerated heartbeat to how she felt about her impassioned speeches she gave to the people she encountered outside of the store. If she kept her breathing even and her mind clear, she wouldn't get afflicted with one of her attacks.

Nikla gave her flier to a woman walking by with a small boy.

"You can't be here."

The deep voice rumbled over her. Nikla trembled a little when she heard him speak but managed to compose herself quickly. When she directed her attention back to him, she noticed him standing strong with his fists to his hips. His tanned arms looked good enough to caress.

Nikla approached him. She held out a flier to him. "Do you know what eating large amounts of sweets will do to your body?"

After an uncomfortable silence, the man accepted her literature that she'd researched and had written on her own. She'd left a copy for her father to read. Whether he did or not, she didn't know. She hoped.

"Do you know that this place affords me my living as well as some other people?" He scanned over the information then crossed his arms.

She cleared her throat. "There are other jobs out there."

"What would you know about work?" He snarled. "What? Did you stop on your way to some afternoon Pilates class? You dropped off your little foo-foo dog at the groomers and passing out these little leaflets is your way to feel like you're making a positive change in someone's life?"

Nikla felt the heat climbing up her body to her face. She balled her hands into fists, crunching the remaining fliers. "You don't know me. You know nothing about me."

"And you don't know what this place means to me. I will defend it and the people in it with every breath in my body."

His passion showed through his eyes. His breathing, though, remained even. Nikla admired his control. She had a goal, too. Some employee wouldn't stop her.

"I'm on a public sidewalk. I can be here and pass out my fliers without being harassed by you or anyone else." In her flip flops, she balled her toes.

"I'm not saying what you're doing is illegal." The man took a couple of steps toward her.

Nikla remained in her spot, determined not to buckle.

"What you're doing is futile. You act as though keeping our customers away is going to solve–" He glanced at the paper. "—childhood obesity in all of Virginia. I mean, it's great that you think this little store has that much power and influence."

Nikla wanted to ignore him. Between looking at his eyes and his large hands, and listening to the deep timbre of his voice, she couldn't break away from his command.

Then again, he worked in the type of place that, as a teenager, she wanted to visit frequently.

Even in October, the unseasonably mild weather felt good considering she wore her yoga pants, sports bra, and wraparound ballet sweater. The longer she stared at him, the more she felt her hardening nipples brushing roughly against her bra.

Damn. What was wrong with her? This was the enemy.

A man started to go into the store until Nikla handed him her paper. The customer glanced at it, looked at her, smiled, then walked away.

The fact that she stopped one person from going into the establishment lifted her spirits. She turned to the Decadent Treats employee. "If I can stop one person, I can call this a success."

"You spoiled drama queen." The man stormed back into the store.

"Spoiled?" she screamed after him. "I. Am. Not. Spoiled." Considering she stood in front of a large candy store that looked like a gingerbread house and had on her workout gear, she would leave out that she did resemble a drama queen right now.

Nikla felt victorious in her fight. N ot o nly h ad s he g otten o ut her message, but she even made a Decadent Treats employee retreat.

She glanced at her watch. As much as she'd enjoyed her small victory, she would have to get going to work.

She started to turn when she heard the store door opening again. When she returned her gaze to that area, she saw the employee coming back out this time with a heart-shaped box of chocolates in his hand.

Although she didn't want to, as soon as Nikla saw this gorgeous man carrying a box of chocolates, her heart fluttered. From his grimace, she knew he wouldn't be giving her a treat out of the kindness of his heart.

"Here. Have a heart." He handed her the candies. "Come back here again, and I'll be back out here with you. You're not going to destroy this business."

Nikla held onto the box but couldn't take her stare off the man.

"Now go pick up Miss Tinkerbelle or Lulu or whatever you call your little powder puff of a dog and let the people who want to work do just that." He turned his back on her and strolled back into the store.

Determined not to let him have the last word, Nikla approached the door. As she held her hand over the handle, she stopped. Until she looked at her hand, she didn't notice that she'd been shaking.

Nikla struggled to catch her breath.

Stop it. Breathe, damn it. Breathe.

Nikla recognized her unstable body reaction and tried arresting her out-of-control breathing quick enough before it disabled her. She wanted to chalk up the response to her simmering anger. The whole idea of her going into this place scared her to her core, so much so that she pounded her fist against the door to get the man's attention.

Through the glass, she saw him turning around along with other customers milling around in the colorful place. When she connected to his stare, she held up the box then dropped it to her feet.

She smiled—or rather smirked—back at him as she turned around and headed to her car. For the past few weeks, she'd been coming to this store and trying to get people to stop shopping there, an impossible feat considering with Halloween approaching. She wouldn't give up. Hopefully her father would see that and be proud.

Nikla jumped into her car and locked the doors in case some other overzealous employee decided to confront her. Her cell phone played the opening of Stevie Wonder's "Sir Duke."

Nikla answered the call. "Hi, Dad."

"What are you doing?"

Nikla sighed. "I'm fine. How are you doing?"

"Don't get cute." The former Marine's voice shot through the phone.

Sarcasm equaled insubordination to Lawrence Dearwood.

Nikla found herself getting more direct with her father. He hoped he would have respected her need to have a backbone.

"Are you home?"

Nikla closed her eyes and said a curse in her head. "No. Right now I'm sitting in front of a candy store and passing out fliers to get people to stop going."

Her father said nothing, a first for the normally outspoken military man.

To fill in the void, Nikla kept talking. "Now I'm on my way to work."

This time her father released an audible sigh. "If you worked with me, you and I could be together more."

Although she loved her father, and she had gotten used to his brand of tough love, she couldn't imagine working side by side with him every day. The fact that her father could be a tough taskmaster had nothing to do with her decision.

If he wanted Nikla there because he wanted that bonding relationship with her, she would want to work with her father. She knew he had other reasons for keeping an eye on her.

"You know the old saying, Dad. Absence makes the heart grow fonder." Nikla started her car.

"Are you at least coming over for dinner?" Desperation, a foreign tone from her father, laced his voice.

Nikla's heart ached, but she knew what being around him would do to her spirits. She would support her dad in any way she could. She didn't know if she could hold her ground with him.

"Can I get a rain check?" Nikla clicked her seatbelt then checked her mirrors before pulling out of her spot.

She brought her gaze down and looked directly into the Decadent Treats store. Nikla spotted the employee she'd had a confrontation with moments ago staring at her. She believed him when he said that each day she protested he would be out there with her. A part of her looked forward to the fight.

"Tell me a day you'll be by the house. Unless I pin you down on a date and time, I'll never see you." Lawrence cleared his throat.

"Dad, you know that's not true. I've been busy with work and everything. But you know I always have your back. I'm always supporting you." She hoped he understood and believed that.

"Date and time, young lady."
Her father's deep voice didn't get to her like the Decadent Treats employee. Thinking of his voice raised goose bumps over her arms.

"Fine. I'll see you this weekend."

"Friday, Saturday, or Sunday?"

Nikla backed out of her spot and gunned it out of the parking lot. "I'll have to check with—"

"With who?" her father asked, interrupting her. "No one should be more important than family, right?"

Nikla thought about the changes happening to her father, to her family, right now. She and her father had encountered a lot of disappointments recently. She had to give him something.

"Sunday breakfast like we used to when I was a kid." Nikla smiled at the memory. "I'll make you breakfast this time."

"Fine. See you at oh-six hundred."

Lawrence disconnected the call before Nikla could argue about the early breakfast time. That must mean that her father wanted to do a morning run with her. Now she would be able to keep up with him.

Before she could wrap her mind about her standing Sunday date, she had to think about work. Good thing her job relaxed her as well as challenged her.

****

Nikla placed her hand on one of her student's backs as the woman tried sitting up on her yoga mat on the floor. "Very nice, Ashley. Breathe through it."

Nikla had to keep from screaming each time it hit her that she headed up her own class. She should have told that cocky guy who thought her only value had been to be the owner of a little yippy dog and being some guy's arm candy about her job and how much she loved it. Then again, he had been right on the money when he accused her of being on her way to a Pilates class. He'd been close. Today she taught yoga.

Nikla had done a lot with her life, one thing being heading up this class. The fact that the class she taught happened in a Virginia Beach recreation center didn't have her patting herself on the back. Not yet.

Baby steps. She would have to save her money so that one day she would have her own business like her father. She even had the name. "Transformations by Nikla" had been a dream since she learned about Pilates and yoga during her freshman year of college when the pesky "freshman fifteen" packed on top of her already hefty frame.

"This is so hard." Ashley puffed. "I thought yoga would be easier on me."

A couple of other students in the class nodded in agreement. Even with the door closed to the room, Nikla still heard the squeaking of sneakers and the pounding of basketballs over the center's two basketball court floors.

Her dream studio would be quiet and private. It wouldn't have a large, open glass window that would allow people walking by to see clients working out. She understood how trying something new for some people would be a bit daunting and embarrassing.

Nikla held her student's hands. Sweat covered Ashley's pale hands, which came as an encouragement to Nikla. It meant that Ashley had pushed herself during the workout. She couldn't wait to see her client's transformation over the next several weeks.

"Yoga is gentler on your joints than, say, aerobics or traditional weight training. But it's also an exercise. Judging by your hands and shirt, it looks like you put in a good day's work. Be proud of yourself for pushing your body so hard. It's the first great step to health." Nikla had to tell herself these same positive affirmations when she decided to get healthy.

Once she reached her goal, she wanted to make sure to be everyone else's cheerleader who wanted to make a change.

Ashley pushed her red hair from her face and smiled. "If you say so, Nik. My body is hating you right now."

"Mine, too," another student chimed in with a smile.

"You won't be getting a Christmas card from my body this year." A third student flopped onto her back and put her hand to her chest.

Nikla laughed. She helped Ashley ease back down to the floor. "When you reclaim your health and get back down to a healthy weight, your body will thank you and me." Once Nikla had Ashley flat on her back, she walked over to the front of the class. "End of the class, ladies."

A few of them applauded.

Nikla turned the music up a hair. "Lie on your back. Close your eyes and inhale deeply." She enjoyed sending off her students feeling both challenged and relaxed. "I have orange oil. As I come around to you, let me know if it's okay if I can rub it on your temples." Nikla retrieved a small vial of orange oil from her workout bag, then padded back over to her students starting with Ashley.

"May I rub the oil on your temples?" Nikla asked Ashley.

Ashley nodded.

Nikla smiled as she knelt behind her client's head, then dabbed some of the slick oil on her fingertips. The refreshingly clean scent of oranges wafted up to her face.

She used to use a vanilla-scented essential oil. When her students complained that after a session with her they went to their closest cinnamon bun eatery for a sweet and sticky treat, she changed the scent to something more citrus-like.

"Deep breath in, hold it, then breathe out."

Her students did as instructed. Nikla observed Ashley's larger frame. In her, she saw herself years ago, so lost and feeling out of place in a world that had little tolerance for people who didn't carry a stick-figure frame.

"You all did an amazing job today." Nikla rubbed the soothing oil on Ashley's temples.

"I feel like I'm not keeping up a good pace with everyone else."

Nikla shook her head even though with Ashley's eyes closed, she wouldn't have seen the expression. "The great thing about yoga and Pilates is that they're not exercises that you need to do in the same pace with other people. This is all self-paced. You move your body in the way you feel comfortable."

Nikla crawled on her knees over to the next student and gave her a similar head massage. The low Indian music that Nikla had playing in the background helped foster the calming environment. She noticed that her students' breathing started to slow down from a panting breath.

After attending to all the students, Nikla returned to the front of the class. "Place one hand on your chest and the other on your stomach." She watched her students to make sure they all complied. "Pay attention to your breathing. Feel your heart beating. Remember that this class, this session, this workout is all for you. This will probably be the only time you're allowed to feel selfish."

Nikla wished she could heed her own words and advice. She thought about others first, sometimes without thinking of her own needs.

"Breathe in." Nikla took in a deep breath along with her students. "And exhale. Let go all your tensions and frustrations from the day. Let the calm wash over your body and fill your senses. Allow this tranquil feeling to last you throughout the day." When the music stopped playing, Nikla opened her eyes. "Great work, ladies. See you all on Friday." She sat up and put her hands together in prayer form. "Namaste."

The class repeated the salutation back to her and started to put their shoes back on and gather their mats and towels. Nikla turned on the lights as the students started leaving one by one. Ashley remained the last straggler in the class.

"I'm so glad my friend told me about this class. I love your workouts."

Nikla smiled. "Wonderful. Please tell more friends. I'm hoping one day to have my own studio." She knew the uphill battle in starting a new business, especially one dealing in physical fitness.

"Oh, wow! Please tell me when that happens. I'll be the first to sign up. I can't imagine you wouldn't do well." Ashley smiled. "Have you found a place to set up?"

Nikla smiled. "No, not yet. I'm still trying to find a good spot."

"You should check out the new downtown area." Ashley raised her eyebrows. "Pricey, but there's a huge apartment complex and a hotel down there. You would do amazing. Of course you're going to have to teach a lot more classes or hook up with a sugar daddy to get a place in that area."

Yes, Nikla knew that for sure. She'd gotten prices for other locations and thought they were a bit out of her range, but reachable. She would have to teach classes twenty-four hours a day, seven days a week to earn enough for downtown Virginia Beach. Nikla liked dreaming. Couldn't hurt to check it out.

She knew the calculated risk to setting up shop in a costly area of Virginia Beach. The move would either catapult her into greatness or spiral her down into extreme financial failure. The idea of the two extremes hit her like an imploding building, levels upon levels falling on her until she had to take in a deep breath to bring her back to reality. She could make this business work. No way around it.

Ashley scanned Nikla. "I can't wait to look like you one day."

Nikla laughed. "You will be the best version of you. It took me a long time to get to this point. I will help you in your journey."

Ashley shook her head. "I still think you're lying about being fat."

"I would never lie about being overweight. Trust me."

As much as she wanted to forget those years of her life, Nikla tried learning to embrace her past. Her struggles helped shaped her life now. Not the teasing from her classmates. Not the repeated rejections from guys she wanted to date. Not the look of disappointment from her father at how undisciplined she'd been.

"See you later, Nikla." Ashley walked out of the room just as Nikla's best friend bounded into it.

"You ready for lunch?" Deana trotted over the hardwood floors in her killer black leather heels.

As usual, her friend decked herself out in a black-and-white dress that looked like it came from a designer. She topped the look with a white leather crop jacket. Now *Deana* looked like a kept woman.

With great reluctance, Nikla slipped into her flip flops. If she had her way, she would live her life in bare feet.

"Let me grab my bag and we can go." Nikla put on her wraparound sweater then a jacket before she slipped the strap of her gym bag on her shoulder.

As she approached Deana, her friend shook her head. "You are so cute. Why would you walk around looking so dowdy?"

Nikla scanned her outfit. "Did you forget that I just did an hour-long yoga class? I can't come in here in some ball gown and heels."

"Are you saying that if given some time, you have a better outfit in your bag that you can change into right now?"

When Nikla didn't respond, her best friend rolled her eyes.

"Come here." Deana grabbed Nikla's arm and faced her to the wall-to-wall mirror. "Look at yourself."

Nikla scanned herself. Standing next to Deana, she couldn't help but compare herself to her. Although both black, Deana's skin tone carried a slightly darker hue than Nikla's burnt honey complexion.

Nikla kept her shoulder-length dark brown hair up in a bun whereas Deana kept her black tresses in its natural state, full of waves and curls with a white flower pinned to the side.

Even though Deana wore heels, Nikla still towered over her. In her black yoga pants and conservative top, she didn't match the style of her friend.

"So?" Nikla shrugged.

"You could be so much hotter." Deana put her arm around Nikla's waist.

"Why do I need to bother to look hot when I'm teaching a class with all women and I already have my man?" Nikla cocked her head toward her friend.

"Oh, is that a dig?" Deana tilted her head. "I like dating. But, I must admit, you sure did pick your man well."

"Yeah, well, thank you." Nikla's boyfriend, Justin, had been stable and kind.

At this point in her life, Nikla needed both. Once in a while, though, she would have liked a nice surprise from him. She would check to see if Justin would go with her to her father's house on Sunday. He would be a great distraction to keep her father from concentrating all his criticisms on her.

She knew Deana liked Justin for more than his good looks and his manners. Justin's family had a lot of money. The money never factored into Nikla's feelings toward him. She learned a long time ago to do things on her own. That didn't stop her helpful nature from peeking through.

Before leaving, a bubbly trainer bounded into the room. Karen smiled as she hopped over to Nikla.

"Hey, Nikki." Karen held both of Nikla's arms as she smiled at her.

Nikla smiled back and didn't bother correcting her coworker with the use of the nickname. "Hey. Just stepping out for lunch."

"Okay." Karen volleyed her attention between Nikla and Deana. "I won't hold you up. I was hoping you would step in for me later today in my aerobics class."

Nikla cocked her head. "I haven't done an aerobics class in years, not since I was a sophomore in college, and that was almost ten years ago.”

“Come on. You’ve seen me do my class. You could wing it.” She patted Nikla on her shoulder like a buddy.

“I don’t think students pay to have a teacher winging a class. Ask Victoria. She does that intense boxing class.”

Karen winced. “She scares me.” Then she giggled.

Nikla started to say no, when Karen took a step closer to her to gain eye contact.

“Please?” Karen nibbled on her bottom lip. “I’d help you out if you ever needed it.”

“Why do you need the time off anyway?” Nikla crossed her arms over her chest.

Karen smiled as she glanced away. “Don’t tell anyone but I have this incredible date with this really amazing guy.”

Deana nudged Nikla in her arm. “You can’t stop potential love.”

Great. Now her best friend pressured her.

Nikla thought about saying “no” and disappointing Karen. Her shoulders and chest felt tight. She knew her breathing would be the next thing afflicted. Nikla hated letting anyone down. She didn’t want to be a pushover, either.

“Why not just cancel your class? You’re allowed.” Nikla hoisted her bag onto her shoulder.

“You’re right. But you can only do it three times in a four-month window. I’ve already done it three times. If I cancel a fourth class–” Karen swiped her hand across her throat.

Nikla regarded the petite blonde for a moment. “I’m not saying yes yet. Let me get some lunch in me and think about it.”

“Thank you!” The woman drew her into a bear hug. “I know you’ll say yes. You never say no.”

That had been the story of Nikla’s life. She’d become the person who couldn’t say no.

After her coworker ran out of the room, Nikla released a long breath.

“You’re a nice person.” Deana wrapped her arm around Nikla’s shoulders.

Nikla didn’t feel like a nice person. She felt like a doormat. Before relaying those thoughts to her friend, she smiled. “Let’s go. I’m starving.” Nikla headed to the door with Deana trailing behind her.

Deana followed Nikla to their favorite eatery, one with a well-stocked salad bar and a lot of fresh items on the menu. Nikla worked hard to maintain her body. She wouldn't be putting anything fattening or sweet in her mouth.

"Are you still trying to get this workout studio off the ground, Jane Fonda?" Deana snickered as she placed her drink on the table.

"Cute. Of course." Nikla took a bite of her salad, then chased it with ice water. "I'm saving as much as I can."

"You've been saving for forever and a day. You probably have enough now to get a place somewhere." Deana chopped off a hunk of her steak and chewed it like a wild animal.

"I don't want to get a place *somewhere*. I need to set up in the right spot. I want to be in the middle of it all." Nikla smiled as she thought about the possibilities of getting a spot in the middle of downtown Virginia Beach. "I don't want to settle."

"Fine. You want the best. Why not get your man to help you? You know he has the means."

Nikla shook her head. "I'm not using Justin or anyone else. I'm doing this all on my own."

Deana pumped her fist in the air. "You go, girl. Once you do open your place, I'll be so proud of you. I hope I see that happening within my lifetime."

"Very funny." Nikla hoped for the same thing, too.

"When are you and Justin going to double with me?" Deana called the waitress over to get a refill on her sweetened iced tea.

"When you pin yourself down to one man."

"Or woman?" Nikla's friend winked at her.

Nikla dropped her fork onto her plate, making a loud, clattering noise that alerted the patrons around them. "Are you switching teams?"

Deana shook her head. "Just exploring options. I've never been with a woman before, but with the way things are now with guys, I'm tempted to try."

"If it's not in your nature, don't do it. You don't want to lead anyone on and get their feelings hurt." Nikla sighed.

"Jesus, you are so serious. It's just sex. It doesn't have to be love."

"For me it does. Me? I need to be with a *man*, capital M kind of man." Like the guy who tried scaring her away from the front of Decadent Treats.

Justin approached that category, but his kindness and generosity made up for the fact that his slight frame didn't qualify him as the type of man Nikla really wanted.

Damn. Had she admitted to herself that she had settled?

No, Justin treated her well. No surprises.

"When you pick your man *or* woman, let me know and we'll arrange for a nice dinner." Nikla left half of her food on her plate, another habit she developed when she started her weight loss journey.

"Why does it have to be one or the other? I could come with both." Deana laughed.

"What in the world am I going to do with you?" Nikla couldn't help but join in the laughter.

"Just love me." Deana leaned forward. "Now let's get to some juicy topics. Sex still good with you and your boy?"

Nikla kept smiling while her insides crumbled. Too bad she couldn't lie to save her life. "It's been a while since we've been together."

Deana cocked her head.

Before her friend could inquire further, Nikla supplied her with more details. "With his busy schedule and mine, it's hard for us to get together."

She would leave out the fact that sex had become humdrum and dull. Always the same missionary position. He would climax before Nikla could reach her orgasm. Being the nice guy, he always handed Nikla her trusty vibrator so that she could finish herself.

"You need to find time or get adventurous."

"Adventurous?" Nikla wrinkled her nose.

"Yeah, do it at work. Go to a building you two don't work at and do it in the elevator." A secret smile rose on Deana's face. "One time I did it in a post office."

Nikla chuckled. "Liar. You didn't do anything like that in front of a lobby full of people."

"No. Not during business hours. After hours when the office is closed and they leave the lobby open for people to go to their post office boxes."

Nikla shook her head. "That's a little reckless. You know they have cameras all around there. You could have been arrested."

"Haven't been yet."

Nikla requested their checks. "Thanks for the advice. I think I'm doing okay."

"And you're happy with 'okay'?"

Nikla didn't answer. If she were honest with herself, she would have broken up with Justin when they couldn't make time for each other. How could she justify leaving a man who hadn't done anything to deserve it?

"Between my work, Justin, and my other activities, I don't have time to plan out-of-the-box sex events." Nikla placed her debit card in with her check for the waitress.

"What other activities are you talking about?" Deana stared at her for a moment before she put her hand over her eyes. "Oh, God. Please don't tell me you're still doing that whole protesting thing?"

Nikla handed her check and Deana's to the waitress walking by their table. "It's not a thing. I'm really passionate about childhood obesity and the number of people, especially among African Americans, who get diabetes."

"Yeah, so does Michelle Obama. But you don't see her going to Hershey, Pennsylvania and knocking on the factory door to demand they stop making their chocolate bars. I'm sure there are more constructive ways for you to get your point across without attacking one small business." Deana fluffed up her already big hair then slathered her lips with a deep berry color.

"I'm not attacking a small business." Of course the one guy there would have disagreed with her. "I'm passing out literature in front of a candy store."

"I'm sure there are other ways to show your stance on this."

"You're probably right. They even turned some guy loose on me today." She licked her lips and hoped her friend thought Nikla had gone after some leftover sauce.

"Really? Did he rough you up?"

The waitress came back and handed each woman back their cards and change.

Nikla rubbed the back of her neck. "He was a good-looking guy. Big, tall white guy. If he would smile, he could be a true heartbreaker. He gave me a box of chocolates." When she saw a smile spread across Deana's face, she hit her with the rest of the story. "He told me I needed a heart."

"Ouch." Her friend shrugged. "He's right. That's that man's job. If you lose business for them, where is he going to work? Are you going to hook him up at the rec center?"

"He's very assertive." Her clitoris throbbed when she thought about his hands. "I'm sure he'll be fine if Decadent Treats happened to close."

"But you're not worried about him or the owners or the other employees losing their jobs, right?"

Nikla shook her head. "They didn't worry about putting anyone else out of business when they opened, right?"

Deana put her hand on top of Nikla's. "You can't save the world."

She regarded Deana for a beat before removing her hand and standing. "I can save myself, though. I've also been thinking about going back to school."

Deana gave her an obvious eye roll. "Why? You have a Bachelors, right?”

"Masters, actually." Nikla smiled. "I just want to expand my mind. I want to start my own business. I think it would be nice to have a business degree."

"You're a nerd who likes learning new things."

True. Except Nikla wouldn't have called herself a nerd. She liked the challenge of picking up on a new concept.

Nikla walked with Deana to their cars. Desperate to talk about anything else but her personal life, she quickly started a new topic. "So when are you going to sign up for one of my classes?"

"What? Do the yoga thing?" Deana shook her head. "I'll do it when my ass starts slipping down my legs."

Nikla peered at her friend's backside. "So you'll be in my class Friday?"

Deana poked her friend's side with her elbow. "Bitch."

"Love you, too." Nikla's cell phone rang in time before Deana could zing her with another insult. "Talk to you later." She glanced at the screen and saw Justin's name. She put on a smile so that she would sound cheery. "Hi, honey."

At first Nikla didn't hear anything on the other line. She pulled the phone from her ear to see if the call had dropped. When she saw it hadn't and she put the phone back to her ear, she finally heard Justin's voice.

"Baby," Justin said in a muffled tone.

"Hey." Nikla never heard her boyfriend use a pet name for her before. Maybe this was him trying something new. "Justin? Hello? Are you there?"

It sounded like he had pocket dialed her, but from the moans, it sounded like he might be hurt.

"Can't take it." Justin's squeaky voice couldn't be mistaken.

"Justin!" Nikla screamed.

All sorts of scenarios raced through her head. Had he been kidnapped and being tortured? Hell, was he having a heart attack?

"Feels so good." Then Justin growled.

Feels good? Since when did torture feel good? That statement froze Nikla. Her man growled? He didn't even do that when they had sex.

Nikla stopped next to her vehicle and listened to Justin's mumblings. With each moan, grunt, and growl, her blood boiled. After staying by this man's side, admonishing herself for wanting to leave him, he had betrayed her trust and had the nerve to accidentally call her to witness it.

"Nikla has never done it like this." Justin punctuated the statement with a chuckle.

When she heard him say her name, Nikla's spine stiffened. Before the top of her head could fly off, she unlocked her car and sat inside as she listened to the rest of this horrible mistake.

The call seemed to last for hours but truly had only been a couple of minutes more before she heard him do his standard squeal and groan before coming.

"Oh, God. Can't believe you just did that. Nikla would never swallow."

This time Nikla growled. "You arrogant, self-centered, cheating, lying son-of-a-bitch!" She screamed in the phone, hoping he could hear her. "I gave you everything! I put up with your shit! And for what? If I needed sex, all I had to do was reach into my nightstand! You're worthless! I hate you!"

Nikla hated herself more for not following her initial instincts. Her instincts had never failed her before. She should have never questioned herself now.

She heard a rustling on the other line before she heard an "Oh, shit," then a sheepish, "Uh, hello?"

Nikla disconnected the call and threw her phone in her open purse that sat on the passenger side seat. The conversation she needed to have with Justin had to be done in person, not over the phone. He needed to see her rage. Once she got that off her chest, she would move on with her life and get on with her goals.

Hell, she should have been mad at herself. She'd wanted Justin to surprise her. This did it.

As she drove to her home, Nikla noticed how her hands shook. Anger coursed through her body until she thought the blinding rage would cause her to crash into another vehicle. She needed to stop for a bit to calm herself down.

At her first opportunity, Nikla pulled over into an empty parking lot except for one light blue eyesore. As old as the truck looked, despite it being so clean, she assumed someone must have left the vehicle for the city to acquire. No matter. She needed to time to wind down.

Nikla hopped out of her car, a head full of steam. With arms folded, she stomped up and down the empty sidewalk. She'd lost so much time being with Justin.

Not one for wasting time, it truly pissed her off that dealing with this Justin drama derailed her from her plans for that day. Like with her meals, planning her day gave her a sense of structure and control.

Nikla tried taking a couple of deep breaths to ease her jangled nerves. As a yoga instructor, she knew that technique should have helped. Ordinarily it would have. The lies and the betrayal hit her hard.

She balled her hands into fists. The devil on her shoulder whispered in her ear to get something sweet to ease her pain. When she was younger, eating had been her go-to to cope when aspects of her life became too tough to handle.

Nikla had to stop and push those thoughts aside. Once she halted her march, something caught her notice. A large "For Lease" sign in the window of a corner unit in the shopping center snagged her attention.

She scanned the area where she parked and realized she had stopped in the heart of downtown Virginia Beach. Nikla brought her gaze back to the empty storefront. That spot would have been perfect for "Transitions by Nikla."

With that in mind, Nikla started to calm down. She strolled up to the glass and pressed her face against it to get a sneak peek into her future. In the empty space, she could see her complete studio. She would keep the hardwood floors. She knew exactly where she would put each reformer. She would cover the back wall with mirrors like in the studio in the recreation center. On the front glass, it would have the name of her business.

She thought she would have shared that moment with Justin. Thinking of his name enraged her again.

Nikla released a long, loud, blood-curdling scream that she hoped with traffic and the general noise of the area wouldn't be noticed.

"Justin, you bastard!" Nikla wrapped her arms around her body to try to still the shaking.

She wanted to face the asshole. Knowing him, he would be waiting at her place with his sorry, hang-dog expression. Nikla wouldn't fall for it. Clean slate. With no man in her life, she would have time to truly concentrate on herself.

Nikla took a step back to return to her vehicle and finish whatever she had had with Justin when she bumped into a tall, solid mass. She yelped before righting herself and turning around to see a towering man with shaggy brown hair and the most hypnotic green eyes she'd ever seen. Damn it. The man from Decadent Treats.

For a split moment, she imagined what it would be like to fuck him. This stranger would be a perfect rebound sex subject with his large hands, muscular thighs, and those kissable lips. She could use a sex-only type of relationship. Deana would be proud of her for that decision. Too bad this guy hated her guts.

"You again." He shook his head. "I heard a scream. Can I help you?"

If he only knew.

Chapter Three

Sweet hadn't expected two things when he heard a scream that he didn't help produce. He didn't expect to see the lone protester standing alone doing the shouting, and he didn't expect to be hit with that familiar tingling feeling in his fingers that itched to spank her.

In his vision of disciplining her, he would be doing it out of pleasure, not to cause her pain like she wanted to inflict on him and his brother with all her protesting.

As much as Sweet hated to admit it, for as many times as he had gone to The Dollhouse, like Masaun had said, he hadn't played with anyone since Melinda. Until he could get back to his normal self, he couldn't think about anyone in that way right now.

"I'm fine." She ran her hand back over her hair in front of her ponytail. "No, I'm not actually." She looked at him like she wanted to unload her life story. Then she clamped her mouth shut.

Sweet scanned her body. Her tightly wrapped sweater, her clingy black pants, and flip flops showed off her fit body. She hadn't changed from the outfit he saw her wearing a few hours ago.

Out of curiosity, he glanced over at the vehicle next to his truck to see if a small dog existed inside. Although he didn't see or hear a dog in her car, he still held onto the idea that she spent her life doing the bidding of some rich man.

He didn't mind the catering part. The idea of her being attached to someone sent a strange tickle over the back of his neck.

What the hell was he doing? He didn't know this woman to feel jealousy or any kind of attachment. Being the object of her hatred didn't garner her any sort of connection.

The more he stared at her, the more he realized his quick assessment didn't hold water. Although pretty—hell, gorgeous—Sweet noticed she didn't have a stitch of makeup covering her flawless caramel-colored face.

A trophy wife, girlfriend, or mistress wouldn't leave the house without her face firmly in place for the world to admire. How brave of this woman to not only wear body-conscious clothing but to let her natural beauty shine. The sight had him giving her kudos in his head.

"People who scream like that normally don't do it without reason." He stepped into her pacing path to stop her movements.

When she halted in front of him, Sweet caught a strange aroma, a mixture of jasmine and oranges. To him, she smelled refreshing.

She peered up at him, her brown eyes looking so innocent and full of wonder. "I had a reason. I don't need to tell it to you."

Sweet glared at her, hoping to intimidate her from the location. "You're right about that. I'm certainly no Dr. Phil." He cocked his head as he stared at her. "You didn't accept my gift."

She wrinkled her nose. "What?"

"The box of chocolates."

She tilted her head. "You weren't serious with that. And you really didn't think I could accept that."

"You're right. I didn't. But I did expect you to come into the store and throw them back into my face."

She shook her head. "So that you could sue me for assault or something? Not on your life." A look of realization crossed her face, and she squared off in front of him. "Are you following me around now? I hand out a few fliers in front of your job, and now you're tailing me?"

Sweet shook his head. "I have better things to do with my time than to follow around some lunatic."

"Lunatic?" She glared at him as she reached into her cavernous brown purse and pulled out her phone.

He breathed a sigh of relief when he didn't see her retrieve a gun or Mace.

"Your assessment of people is unbelievable." She punched in numbers on her phone with her thumb.

"What can I say? You bring out the worst in me and this is only my second encounter with you."

He would leave out the fact that after their initial meeting, she sparked a deep desire in his body that he hadn't felt since Melinda. Although he'd dated African-American women before, one who came off as a kept woman usually didn't appeal to him.

The way she stood her ground and kept her stare on his eyes drew him into her. Her body also captured his attention. Considering she made it clear that she didn't appreciate him or what he did, he had no business thinking of anything else besides getting this woman away from himself and his store.

Sweet, seeing her concentrating on her call, saw the move as a sign that she wanted the conversation to end. He turned his attention back to the two empty suites. In his mind, he could see the larger space being used for the candy store, and the relatively smaller space next door to be the fetish store. He turned around and took notice of the abundant traffic.

He could see his plan working and making him and Masaun a ton of money. Masaun had been an unexpected obstacle.

"Hello?"

Sweet heard the woman on her phone, but he kept his attention on the suites.

"Yes, I'm calling about leasing a space here at the downtown building, the one on Center Main Street."

When she said that, she snagged Sweet's attention. First Masaun and now this unknown woman tried halting his dreams not once, but twice that day. Of course she didn't know what obtaining this spot would mean for him. He had to let her know where he stood.

"You can't have this space." Sweet spoke to her as he shook his head.

She furrowed her eyebrows as she glared at him. "Excuse me?" She covered the mouthpiece. "I'm on a call." She turned her back on him. "Yes, I can hold."

Sweet nodded toward the building. "I want this space. That's why I'm here."

"How would I know that? I thought you were following me." She scanned him from his eyes down to his feet. "There are two suites. You can have one and I can have the other, if they're still available."

Sweet shook his head again. "No. I want both."

"What? Did you mark them as your territory or something?" She punctuated her query by looking at the ground around him and the sidewalk in front of the two storefronts as though he had pissed on the doors to claim his spots.

Sweet blinked. "Did you just compare me to a dog?"

She shrugged. "That would be the only way to explain why you would think you can have these spots." She turned her back on him and continued her phone conversation. "Yes, I'm still here." She paused for a moment before saying, "Yes, I can meet at your business office next Monday. May I have the address?"

She reached into her purse again and pulled out a pen and a scrap of paper she managed to find.

Sweet had to hand it to her. The woman, whoever she was, knew what she wanted and was hell bent to achieve her goal. Too bad he would have to put a stop to her dream.

"My name?" She shoved the items back into her purse but continued to keep her back to Sweet. "Nikla Dearwood. N-I-K-L-A."

Sweet let the unique name roll around in his head. He thought his name was unusual. He would have to remember hers as one of possibly many adversaries.

"By the way, do you have any other appointments for someone asking for both units? Someone by the name of–" She stared pointedly at Sweet.

If he wanted to mess with her, Sweet would have left her on the hook, dangling, waiting for him to tell her his name. He liked the game they played with each other.

Sweet took a step closer to her. At this point, it didn't shock him that she remained in her spot.

"I'm Sweet." He watched Nikla swallow hard. "Sweet Hawkes."

Nikla's mouth hung open as she stared at him. As much as he didn't want it to happen, Sweet felt his heart pounding, a feeling he hadn't experienced since he first played with Melinda. It looked as though Nikla's breathing increased. She licked her bottom lip.

The sight of her delicate, pink tongue almost made Sweet growl. What the hell was happening to him? A second before, he wanted this woman to disappear and give up trying to get *his* space. Now his mind wandered over thoughts of having her use that tongue on various parts of his body.

Damn. Masaun had been right. It had been a long time since Sweet had been with anyone if he thought this woman had potential.

Someone on her phone must have snapped her out of her concentration. "Yes, do you have an appointment for someone named Sweet Hawkes?" She remained silent before directing her attention back on him. "You don't?" Nikla shook her head. "I'm not surprised. Thank you. I look forward to meeting you." She disconnected the call. "I thought you really wanted it."

Sweet put his hands to his hips. "I do *really* want it."

Nikla cleared her throat. "If Sweet Hawkes is really your name, it was interesting meeting you...again." Nikla headed to a gray sedan that sat next to his truck.

"I am Sweet." He had to say something to her to keep her there longer. As soon as Sweet spied her firm ass, he forgot about reason.

She turned to him. "Every man thinks he's nice...including my soon-to-be ex-boyfriend."

She mumbled the last part of her statement, but Sweet had heard every word. This mysterious woman planned on dumping her boyfriend.

Sweet's accelerating heart propelled his feet to move in closer.

"No. My name really is Sweet." He extended his hand.

She peered at his hand then up at him. "Are you serious? Your mother named you Sweet?"

He continued holding his hand up to her. "No. It's a nickname. I've been called Sweet since I was a baby. Just stuck."

"And what's your real name?" She crossed her arms over her chest, still wary of accepting his gentlemanly gesture.

"I only reveal that to special people, Miss Dearwood."

She blinked, looking taken aback when he used her real name. Never accepting his hand, she said, "Thank you for letting me know you are my competition. You know I'm not the only one checking this place out. You'll have other people to compete with for this spot. You need to be ready to fight for what you want."

"I'm ready to divide and conquer." Sweet stared at her pointedly so that she understood his true underlying meaning.

Images flashed through his mind of him pressing her firm ass against the glass of one storefront, spreading her long legs, and fucking her hard enough to imprint his name in her mind forever.

"I hope you have a good day."

As soon as his gaze connected to her sultry brown eyes, his body came alive. Sweet normally got that tingly feeling before playing with someone new.

As much as he wanted to invite her to The Dollhouse, Sweet didn't want to play with someone he couldn't be with romantically. Masaun would have hated his need to connect the two lives. Sweet knew what he wanted.

"Are you going to tell me about the scream?" Sweet turned to the empty storefront. "And why here?"

When Sweet stood too close to the beauty, he noticed her toned arms and tapered-in waist. She could probably withstand a vigorous play session. The thought of that had his cock throbbing. Shit, he would have to leave soon if continued talking to her.

"I can't reveal that to someone I really don't know." She gave him a sweet smile.

She must have felt clever referring to his previous statement in her response.

Nikla turned to leave him again. When he glanced down, this time at her slender legs, his mind went directly to his Dominant side. Sweet wanted to see if her darker skin tone would show red streaks from heavy play. Hell, would she be even interested in playing? Would she let him cane her?

Sweet wanted to kick himself for even thinking about playing with her. Nikla would probably be so disgusted knowing that he imagined strapping her down to a St. Andrew's cross and whipping her to submission. His brother would be disappointed to know that Sweet would want to fuck her afterward, even though Masaun probably did the same thing with Kindle.

"Will you be at Decadent Treats tomorrow?" Sweet followed her to her car and leaned against the passenger side door of his truck as he stared at her.

Nikla turned to him. She opened her mouth like she wanted to say something. Then she blinked, cleared her throat, and turned to her car door again.

"Why do you want to know? Want to have the police there ready for me just in case?" She stared at him pointedly.

"You think I need someone to help me handle you?" He wanted so much to run his fingers through her hair that she had in a ponytail.

"I don't know what you need." Nikla stared at him for a bit. When the electricity between them must have been too much for her, she broke the connection and touched the driver's side door handle, which caused a chirping sound, then she opened her car door.

"I'm always there. If you show up again, I promise to be out on that sidewalk with you." Sweet snapped out of his haze to bring his full attention to her. "You won't win."

Nikla used the car door as a barrier between their two bodies. "I wouldn't make that bet if I were you."

"I'm not a betting man." Sweet pushed himself away from his truck. The longer he stared at her the more his heart pounded. "When I know what I want, I go after it. Hard."

Nikla cocked her head making her wavy, chocolate brown ponytail sway to the side. "Mr. Hawkes–"

"Sweet," he quickly corrected.

"Mr. Hawkes, I appreciate your concern when you heard me releasing a bit of steam." Her smile tightened as though he had pushed her to the edge. "I don't know what your end game is, but trust me, I'm not interested."

"Good. I'm glad you're okay. And trust me. You are definitely interested."

Nikla ran her hand over her stomach, but remained silent like she didn't know how to respond. Or maybe she didn't want to admit what he said had been right.

"What do you do to fill your time?" Sweet lowered his voice.

"Work." Nikla sat in her car. "I have to work tonight as a matter of fact."

"But you don't want to." Sweet caught the put-upon tone in her voice when she spoke about her job.

"Filling in for a coworker."

"Wow. Not even a friend. The pressures you put on yourself." He knew exactly how to relieve those pressures.

Nikla stared at him for a moment before she averted her gaze. "I have to go. Thanks, again, for your concern."

"I'm only concerned about if I'll see you again." Sweet wanted to know what would bring her to the brink of ecstasy.

"Why would you think I would be interested in you?" she asked before closing her door.

Sweet watched a rosy color cover her cheeks. Even that made her alluring.

"I can see it in your eyes. When you look me up, and I know you will, you'll see what I have to offer." He closed her car door.

Sweet strolled to the front of his truck to give her room to maneuver out of her parking spot.

He kept his gaze on Nikla until she got out of sight. He knew she would research him online and run across the article about him and Masaun. He would have to wait to see if she would come into Decadent Treats.

Speaking of the store, Sweet had been away from it long enough. He hopped in his truck and went back to work with a renewed spirit.

He bounded into the store as he thought about their exchange.

"You look to be in a better mood than when you left earlier." Connie stocked the licorice shelf as she spoke to him.

"I just needed my second wind." Sweet stopped next to his employee. "Connie, if a woman comes in looking for me, come and get me, okay?"

"That's every woman that comes in here. They all ask for you or your brother. How am I going to tell the difference?" Her demure demeanor really reminded him of his Nana.

Sweet patted the plump woman on her back. "Trust me. You'll know. This one is special."

"Aren't they all?" She chuckled and tucked a strand of her graying light brown hair behind her ear. "Are you at least going to tell me what she looks like?"

"It's the lone protester."

"Oh." Connie blinked. "Does Masaun know?"

When Sweet's scowl deepened, Connie rethought her line of questioning.

"I'd better get back to work." She turned back to the shelves.

"That's my line. Get back to work." Sweet strolled toward the kitchen area to create more candies.

The baking would help ease his mind. Besides BDSM play, he found the creative process of developing new candies and sweets for people to enjoy relaxed him.

The conversation with Nikla put him in a mood for something rich, chocolaty, and smooth. Sweet placed the ingredients on the long stainless steel table.

Sweet wanted to know more about the beauty with the great set of lungs. He also wanted to know what man, or men, had hurt her. The fact that he had a bigger interest in her beyond her desire to ruin his business worried him. Until he could get back to his normal self in all aspects of his life, he knew he shouldn't be thinking of any woman as potential. He had to push himself, and he knew where he needed to go to do that.

Chapter Four

Nikla couldn't deny the butterflies fluttering in her stomach as soon as she parked her vehicle in front of Decadent Treats the next day.

Despite Sweet's assertion that she would check him out, Nikla had refrained. She'd dumped Justin. She didn't need his spot filled. Not right now. Not when she had other things to occupy her time. Too bad Sweet filled most of her waking and unconscious thoughts.

On her drive back from downtown, she thought about Sweet's eyes, his mouth, his hands. Oh, God, those hands. When he'd extended one for her to shake, Nikla couldn't take it. She knew that if she'd touched the man that her somewhat tame thoughts would turn into something pornographic.

She imagined him taking off her clothes and making her get on top of him to ride him. She would do that to stare into those sparkling green eyes. Too bad only his eyes sparkled. With his dour expression, no way could he have a girlfriend...or boyfriend. She'd never established whether his pendulum swung toward the ladies or men.

Nikla got out of her car with a handful of her fliers. As she paced in front of the candy store, she tried not to glance into Decadent Treats, looking for that tempting employee.

In her attempt to be shady about her observation detail, she nearly ran into a customer trying to go into the store.

"Sorry. Um, I have this if you, uh, well–" The more she fumbled with her speech, the faster the woman walked by her to get into Decadent Treats.

Thinking about Sweet had her flustered enough for her to forget her spiel.

"Damn." Nikla leaned her head back and squeezed her eyes shut. "I have to get it together."

"No, you don't."

The deep voice shook Nikla enough to right herself and spin on her heel. Behind her stood Sweet. Today he wore a pink Decadent Treats t-shirt and jeans. Only a man like Sweet could get away with having a name like "Sweet" and wear a pink t-shirt.

"Don't you have work to do?" She turned her back on Sweet and chewed on her lower lip, praying in her head that he remained outside with her.

Sweet looked good enough to eat even though he didn't smile. "You mean I should keep working until your little protests shut down this business?"

Nikla brought her attention back to him. In an unexpected move, he held up a frosty bottle of water. Nikla spied the offering suspiciously before returning her gaze to his face to gauge his sincerity.

"I figured you would be thirsty doing all of your marching." Without a smile, Sweet still seemed sinister despite the generous gesture.

Why did Nikla's stomach still flip at a simple bottle of water? She knew it had nothing to do with Sweet's olive branch gift. It had everything to do with the man behind it. Why did he intrigue her so much?

"No thank you. Besides, I don't know if you've poisoned it. You probably injected a syringe full of something to give me diarrhea." Nikla continued her pacing, waiting for someone to approach her to cut the tension between her and Sweet. When she turned back toward him, she found him staring at her.

Sweet opened the bottle and tipped it back into his mouth to prove to her that he wouldn't hurt her. She bit the inside of her cheek to keep from smiling.

"You look different today." Sweet scanned her from her head to her feet.

"Different how?" She put her hand to her stomach.

Sweet nodded. "Nice."

With it being Saturday, Nikla had had two early morning classes. At the end of them, she decided to go home, shower, and change into a simple pair of skinny jeans, a loose-fitting top, and flats. Because her lips felt chapped, she did put on some lip balm and a little gloss. She didn't do it because she thought she would see Sweet. If she kept thinking that story, she might believe the lie.

Deana would have been proud of her. Nikla at least did change her outfit from her work clothes.

"You made comments about what I wore yesterday, I thought I would switch it up a little." Nikla had told the truth there.

Sweet must have recognized it, evident from his demeanor. "You adjusted your behavior because of me."

Sweet said his statement as a declaration, not a question.

Nikla opened her mouth to refute him, but he had her. "Not entirely for you."

He shook his head. "I didn't say it was a bad thing. Had I known you listened to me, I would have told you to wear your hair down."

Instinctively, Nikla put her hand to her head. The bun she styled her hair in allowed her freedom to not think about the style the rest of the day and kept her tresses out of her face.

Knowing that Sweet wanted her hair down had her thinking about his motives. Was he just saying that to throw her off her game or did she grab his interest? If she did, why did she care?

"You really don't have to stand out here with me." Nikla kept marching back and forth in front of him.

"No, I really do. I told you I would do whatever I could to protect this place."

"I'm not going to burn it down." She turned her back on him and strolled away, hoping for a distraction.

"I don't know you. I don't know that. But I did do a little research on you."

Nikla froze in her spot. With her back still to him, she asked, "You did? What did you find?"

When Sweet didn't answer right away, she turned to him.

Sweet's stoic expression made the man hard to read. Nikla liked the mystery.

"You don't have much of a web presence." Sweet finished off the water, then crossed his arms over his chest. "You aren't on any social media sites. You don't have a website, blog, or vlog. For someone so passionate about your stance, it surprises me that you don't have a petition site."

Nikla shied away from putting herself out on the web for several reasons, one mainly because of her father. Since Sweet didn't mention her association with Lawrence, she assumed he didn't know about her father.

"Maybe you weren't looking in the right places." Nikla tried to keep up the mystery but felt Sweet could see right through her.

"Unless you are hiding a side of yourself, I like that you aren't caught up in letting the world know what you ate for breakfast."

Nikla paused before she let out a laugh. "There's something about me that you like? I'm shocked."

"You're still a pain, but you're an interesting puzzle to figure out." Sweet started to move toward her.

Nikla started her pacing again.

"How long have you been doing this? I get the impression that you've been at this for a while."

"Just a few weeks."

"How is it that I've never seen you before?"

"I don't know." She brought her gaze up to meet his. "Maybe I never captured your interest."

When he didn't speak, she thought he would burst into laughter soon. His heavy-lidded gaze told her that he didn't find anything she said funny.

"Why do you want to have your own business?" he asked.

"Why do you care? I'm just some woman with too much time on her hands and a small dog, right?" Repeating the statement tied her guts into knots.

"I was wrong about that assessment about you." He put his hand to his chest in a show of sincerity.

Before Nikla started to thank him for his subtle apology, he continued with his speech.

"It's obvious you couldn't care for another living thing."

With it being so soon after her breakup with Justin, the comment hurt more than she thought it would. Nikla felt her heart starting to pound. Even in the mild seventies temperature, sweat started to erupt on her forehead.

Keep it together. Breathe. Breathe.

"I've met some pretty hard women, but you have to be the coldest." Sweet rubbed his hand across the back of his neck. "What person, man or woman, would picket a candy store?"

When she glanced at Sweet, on the surface, she could tell he'd said the truth. Behind his eyes, he looked like he kept a secret hidden. Looked like they both kept secrets close to their vests.

"I'm passionate about a lot of things." Nikla balled her hands into fists. "Did you ever think that women were cold around you because *you* make them that way?"

For that question, he answered her with a single flex in his jaw. Nikla must have struck a nerve.

Nikla didn't know what type of women Sweet dealt with in his life. She wouldn't be some cowering woman willing to roll over for him even though her nerves started to betray her.

She took in a deep breath, held it hoping it would sustain her, then released it. Why was her heart still racing?

"Tell me about the boyfriend." He strolled next to her.

Nikla couldn't speak. Her throat felt constricted, not like she wanted to cry, but rather scream, only nothing would come out of it. Her pounding heart drummed out of control.

She stopped her march long enough to realize that the world started to blur in her vision. Squiggly colorful lines replaced distinct figures.

Oh no, no, no, no!

"Uh, I'm not going to talk about him." She glanced up at the light blue sky and hoped to be able to get herself together.

"Did you break up with him already?"

"How did you know–"

"You mentioned before that he would be your soon-to-be ex."

Damn, this man had listened to every word she'd said even when she hadn't said anything to him directly.

Although Nikla liked that trait, she couldn't think about him right now. She clutched the papers she held until they wrinkled and crinkled under the grip. She started breathing in and out of her mouth, panting so hard she started to feel lightheaded.

"Oh, God." Nikla hadn't expected to feel a hand on her shoulder. She turned her head and caught Sweet staring back at her.

"You're having a panic attack." His tone was slow, low and easy.

Even though he delivered the message in a calm, matter-of-fact way, that didn't prevent Nikla from exclaiming, "No shit!"

She didn't normally curse at strangers, but she felt her world spiraling out of her control. Nikla put her hand against her chest and tried to remember all the tricks her doctor had told her.

"Come inside and sit down." Sweet turned her shoulders and tried heading her into Decadent Treats.

Even without being able to speak, Nikla shook her head and instead moved toward her car. She managed to unlock the car door before she collapsed onto the parking lot next to it.

Her lungs burned the more she gasped for needed breath. She wanted to scream for allowing herself to lose control.

Nikla felt an arm go around her waist. Someone pulled her up and placed her limp body in the back seat of her car.

"Just...want...to...go." She stammered her statement as her hands shook.

"Not in this condition." Sweet seized her car keys from her hands. "Stay right here."

He ran off, leaving her to wonder where he went and what he'd planned on doing to her. Her luck, he would take embarrassing pictures of her and post them over the Internet.

Faster than she could think the worst, Sweet came back with a brown paper bag.

"Sit up."

With his commanding tone, she felt compelled to do whatever he requested. She sat up as she gripped the door and car seat.

Sweet opened the bag and squeezed around the top portion. "Over your mouth and nose and breathe in and out."

Without question, she placed the bag in position and took in a deep breath and breathed out. She'd been through this before. It did surprise her that Sweet recognized the signs and knew what to do.

"Is there someone who can pick you up?"

Nikla thought about her father. He'd been with her many times when these attacks had crippled her. He would have just told her to stop being a baby and suck it up. She didn't need that right now.

Deana would have paid more attention to Sweet than her. Who would blame her? Despite him being a part of a place she wanted to see shut down, he had been kind to her and really didn't have to be.

Nikla shook her head at Sweet's inquiry.

"I'll call for an ambulance."

Sweet started to stand when Nikla grabbed his wrist to still him. She looked over the rim of the crumpled paper bag and shook her head.

"Okay, no ambulance." He wriggled out of her grip. "You can't stay here like this. I can take you home. I'll drive you and Uber back." He held up her keys, a reminder that he had taken control of this situation.

Nikla found her voice to remove the bag from her face to answer him. "No. You can't."

"Yes, I can. Your only choice is whether you want to be taken there sitting up here in the front seat or lying down in the back seat." He hovered over her, awaiting her answer.

"Please, I can drive my own self home. I'm okay." Nikla started to hand him back his bag that offered her salvation.

Sweet refused to take it. Instead, he bent over, wrapped his arms around her legs, and stood so that she rolled onto her back. When he got her legs into the car, he closed the door, then hopped into the front seat.

Although she would never admit it out loud, Nikla breathed a sigh of relief to be in the reclined position.

"You can't do this." Nikla took a deep breath. "Kidnapping."

Sweet glanced at her in the rearview mirror. "Taking you back to your home is not kidnapping." He leaned over and looked in her glove box. He picked up a receipt she'd had in there for her last oil change she'd had done about two weeks ago.

"Cat O'Nine Tails Drive is where you live?"

Nikla hesitated before finally nodding her head.

Sweet started her car. "Interesting. Okay, buckle up. I'm taking you home."

With the devil in her house, what the hell would Nikla do?

****

Sweet hadn't intended on helping Nikla or even offer to take her home. As soon as he recognized the signs of her attack and had seen the sheer panic in her eyes, he saw so much of himself in her and knew he couldn't leave her.

In that moment, Sweet felt bad for all the times Masaun had to lift him up when life had gotten too much for him, just like it had happened to Nikla. For Sweet, he figured out his root issues and solved his anxiety problems. Each time he glanced in the rearview mirror and spied on the weakened yet defiant woman, his heart melted. That didn't mean he wanted her in front of his store.

Sweet pulled up in front of her apartment building. It looked like a nice area. He noticed a lot of cars missing due to residents being at work. The few cars left looked like upper middle class foreign cars. Nikla looked like she lived in a pretty nice section of Virginia Beach.

He parked, then went to the back door and opened it.

"I can make it from here." Rebellious as always, Nikla got out of the car and held out her hand for her keys.

Sweet backed up and stood in the middle of the sidewalk in front of her car. "Walk to me and get the keys, and I'll leave you alone."

Nikla slammed the back door and shook her head. As soon as she took one step, he noticed her eyes getting wide as she struggled to stand upright.

When Sweet saw her going down, he ran to her and managed to catch her before she touched the ground. He'd caught plenty of submissives during some hard play. Catching Nikla proved to be an absolute pleasure.

He pressed her soft body against his. "I got you." Her jasmine scent wafted up to his nose.

Sweet wanted to bury his face in the side of her neck and kiss it, lick it, drive her crazy with passion. As soon as that thought hit him, he pushed it away.

"Just a little unsteady on my feet." Nikla held onto Sweet's arms as she tried to walk.

"No shit."

Nikla glared at him.

"You said that first."

Sweet watched Nikla screw up her kissable lips as though trying to suppress a smile. A warm tingle went over his body as he walked her to her door.

"I shouldn't have used profanity. I usually never curse." Nikla's low voice forced Sweet to listen to her.

Through deduction, he figured out which key went to her front door. Once inside, the alarm chirped. Nikla disabled it.

"Get me to a couch and you can go." Nikla tried heading toward one, but Sweet held her waist tightly.

"Not so fast." He kicked the door closed with his foot. "I'm getting you to bed."

Sweet felt a hard jab into his side before he felt Nikla trying to squirm out of his grip.

"You are not going to rape me! I know who you are and where you work. People know where I've been today."

The wild look in her eyes let him know that she would do whatever she could to defend herself. It also gave him insight into the amount of passion she could bring to the bedroom...or a dungeon.

Sweet had to push those thoughts out of his head to calm her fears. "I'm not going to attack you, and not for the reasons you named." He started walking her through her brightly lit and tastefully decorated apartment.

He stopped at one opened door and noticed a bathtub in the bit of light that made it through the doorway. At the next doorway, he saw a large blue exercise ball, rolled up mats lining the walls, and hand weights. Nikla had made her own workout room. Good for her.

The last doorway held her bedroom. As soon as he saw the queen-sized sleigh bed with the slats in the headboard, he imagined tying her to it and playing with her until he got her to the brink of an orgasm, then fucking her to get her all the way there.

Sweet felt his cock getting hard. He had to get her in bed and get out or he would make a huge mistake. He sat her down on the high bed. "Lie back and rest."

Nikla kicked off her flats. Then she sat up without moving or even looking at him. "Thank you."

"You shouldn't be thanking me." When Sweet noticed her confused expression, he explained. "I caused your attack by asking questions you weren't prepared to answer."

Nikla closed her eyes and finally reclined back on her stack of pillows. "I didn't think I would react that way. I didn't care about him that much. I haven't had an attack like that in years, since college I think. God, I feel so...so...helpless."

Sweet went to touch the top of her head to stroke her as soon as she looked down, but he stopped himself. He couldn't get this close to this woman. Not this woman. It had been bad enough that he'd shared any kind of conversation with her.

He scanned her bedroom to see if he could find signs of this mystery man. He didn't see any men's clothing. The room smelled like Nikla, all jasmine and flowery. He didn't even see any pictures. When he returned his attention to Nikla, he found her staring at him.

"He didn't live here," she said as though answering a question he'd asked.

"What did he do?" Sweet felt every hair on the back of his neck stand up as he waited for her answer.

Nikla shook her head. "Nothing I want to talk about." She sighed. "How did you know?"

"Know what? That you had issues with your boyfriend?"

"No. The panic attack."

Sweet's insides tickled as he stared at Nikla for a beat. He hadn't opened up to anyone about that issue. A woman hell bent on taking down his establishment defined the wrong person to confide in that kind of secret. In that moment, she seemed just as vulnerable as him, maybe more so.

"I used to get them when I was younger." Sweet kept his stare on Nikla. Looking into her eyes, he couldn't be anything but honest. "That rubber band trick never worked for me."

She smiled as though realizing he'd told her the truth. "I don't know. I got used to the pop against my skin. I liked it. It gave me something to concentrate on." She chuckled and shook her head. "Call me crazy, but I like focusing on the sensation, the little sting. It made me feel–"

"Normal," Sweet said, completing her thought.

"Yes."

Blood coursed through Sweet's body. His dick throbbed at her admission. She would do so well as a submissive. He could tell he could bring her body to pure ecstasy. Sweet took a step back toward the door. If he didn't leave soon, he would be telling her to get undressed and claiming her body for himself.

"If popping the bands against your wrists helped, why did you stop?"

He needed to get her off topic.

"My father thought it was silly. He thought me going to a psychiatrist was a sign of weakness."

Sweet hadn't met the man, and he already didn't like him.

Nikla rubbed her forehead. "My head hurts."

"Do you have any aspirin here?" Sweet darted to her nightstand and opened the drawer.

"No!"

When he did, he found more than just some little, white pills. A large, pink vibrator sat on top of miscellaneous papers and pens. His mind conjured an image of Nikla's nude form on her bed, writhing in pleasure as she drove her faux phallus in and out of her pink channel. He almost emitted a growl just thinking about it.

Sweet didn't close the drawer right away. He stared at Nikla for a moment.

She kept her gaze down before finally connecting her stare to his. "Aspirins are in my bathroom." She pointed to an opened doorway across from her.

Sweet closed the drawer and walked into the bathroom. As soon as he opened the right side of the medicine cabinet, he saw a bottle of aspirins. He grabbed it and a cup from a dispenser next to her sink and filled it with water.

As soon as he walked into the room, Nikla found the strength to talk.

"I don't use that all the time." She laughed nervously.

"You don't have to explain anything to me." Sweet hated lying. He wanted to know everything about the toy.

When did she buy it? Did she buy it or did her stupid ex-boyfriend? Did the ex use it on her? Did Nikla use it on herself while he watched? How often did she use it? The next time she used it, would she think of her ex or Sweet?

Sweet handed her the cup of water, then opened the bottle.

"I didn't want you thinking that I'm some sort of repressed freak or something, one cat shy of being a shut-in."

He deposited two pills into her hand and placed the bottle on the nightstand. Nikla downed the medicine and followed it with the water.

Sweet accepted the empty cup. "I happen to like repressed freaks." He slid his hand into his pocket.

From the way Nikla looked at him, she appeared as though she thought he would be pulling out a string of condoms. Even though he hated himself for even thinking it, he wanted them because he really wanted her. Every time that thought hit him, it scared the shit out of him.

He pulled out her keys and handed them to her. "Hope you feel better. I'll let myself out."

"You know I'm still going to come to Decadent Treats and hand out my fliers."

Sweet turned at the doorway and stared at her. "I'll be out there with you. Will that stop you?"

Nikla stared at him pointedly before she shook her head. She licked her lips, then brought her hand up to undo her hair bun. She fluffed out her long, wavy, chocolate brown hair, then brought her attention back to him.

The sizzling electricity that zipped between the two of them couldn't be denied. With every part of his being, he wanted this woman. If she didn't want every part of him, both his vanilla and his kinky side, he didn't want to chance opening his heart again.

Before another word could be spoken, Sweet walked out of her apartment. He hated that his body craved her already without really touching her. Somehow, she managed to worm her way to his soul. Now he needed to figure out a way to purge her from his system.

Chapter Five

Days after his encounter with Nikla, Sweet couldn't get her out of his thoughts. Her lips, her eyes, her smell, the way her body felt next to his—he couldn't get enough of her. He now ached for a woman's touch more than before, more than when he and Melinda had been together.

Considering Nikla had come back after her panic attack to hand out her hate propaganda in front of the store every day that week, and—as he promised—he went out to confront her each day, he assumed she had wanted to see him. He also knew how brave she had been to admit—and confess—a lot of personal items to him.

Although her panic attack and her relationship with her father came as a surprise to him, he couldn't stop thinking about her vibrator and how she used it...and how often. He also wondered if she had used it after their encounter in her bedroom.

Her closed-off yet determined nature intrigued him. Maybe he'd gotten too used to the women at The Dollhouse.

Women who had just met him did whatever he requested. Nikla saw through his looks. That turned him on more than anything else. She stood her ground. Not only did she have plans to dump her man, she had plans to start her own business.

Damn. He had too much energy to burn now. Sweet made sure the store had been secured before he went upstairs to his loft apartment over the store. The expansive space held his essentials. He had a couch, a coffee table, and a big-screen TV that he rarely used. In the raised corner of the apartment sat his king-sized bed, sadly another rarely used item. The interesting piece in his home had to be the vintage, open, egg-shaped chair that hung from the ceiling.

Sweet could care less about the bedroom and living room areas. His main focus when the place had been constructed, and even now, had been the kitchen. Sweet made sure to have only the best appliances, plenty of cabinet space, and lots of counter room. This part of his home became his sanctuary, so much so that when Melinda dared to cook him something as a surprise, Sweet snapped.

The memory of the moment made him feel like a jerk all over again.

After showering and changing clothes, Sweet headed to The Dollhouse. Tired of viewing everyone else having fun, Sweet sauntered to the bar area. No one could get liquid courage at The Dollhouse. Masaun made sure no alcohol got stocked there, even though the establishment carried a liquor license. Masaun didn't trust that good Dominants wouldn't slip up and take a drink that would alter their playing style, or that new slaves or submissives would drink and become too numb to feel the pain until beyond the point of repair.

"Juicy, give me an iced tea, please." Sweet stood at the bar, not paying attention to the patrons around the place.

"Yes, sir, Dom Sweet." The tattooed woman gave him a sloppy salute and poured him a drink. "Think you can talk your brother into relaxing his stance on alcohol? Tips are lousy when people aren't buzzed."

"Not going to happen." Sweet took a sip of the cool, refreshing drink.

"Dude, he doesn't even *own* the place. Why does Zach even listen to him?" Juicy scrubbed the stainless-steel counter down with a black terrycloth dish towel.

"Because Hawk makes sense." To show support of his brother's level-headed decision and to keep the rumbling down to a minimum, he slipped a one-hundred-dollar bill into her tip jar.

He took another drink, a nice relief even during the warmer fall temperatures.

Sweet felt a hand on his back, a foreign feeling in The Dollhouse. After placing his drink on the bar, he turned around. The shorter African-American woman he found behind him looked familiar. Her nervous, twitchy smile melted, and she chewed on her lower lip. When she did that, Sweet recognized the woman as one of the customers in his store earlier in the week who had whispered about him and Masaun.

"Where's your friend?" Sweet kept his stare directly on her.
"Um, I came alone. This is my first time here." She released a giggle that displayed her nervousness. She fidgeted in her spot.

"Brave." Sweet leaned back against the bar to observe her for a moment.

She wrung her delicate hands. Then she tugged on her shirt sleeve. Her nervousness fueled his interest. Sweet would have to play with someone sometime. Why not this woman to break him out of his rut?

He propelled himself off the bar and leaned down to her ear. In a whisper, he said, "You know you're not supposed to touch a Dominant unless given permission."

Sweet heard her gasp before he pulled back from her.

"I'm so sorry. I didn't know. I don't know the rules of this place." She covered her mouth.

Sweet took that moment to observe her outfit. She wore flat black shoes, a blue and black color block dress, and a black sweater. She looked like a fucking librarian. Perfect.

His heart pounded with the idea of breaking this newbie in to the lifestyle. Sweet felt his palms itching. He couldn't wait to get a toy in his hand and work over her voluptuous body.

"Why are you here?" Sweet kept his stare directly on her eyes to make sure she told him the absolute truth.

"You invited me and my friend. I was curious about, well, you know." She dropped her gaze.

"Curious about what?" He moved in closer to her. Taking a deep whiff of her black hair, she smelled like old books.

"Curious about what it is that you do here."

Sweet regarded her for a moment before he moved. "Follow me." He turned toward the play area.

As Sweet strolled down the long hallway, he saw his brother coming toward him. Masaun held Kindle's hand as they walked together. Sweet watched his brother's gaze peer around him to spot the woman walking behind him.

"Dom Hawk." Sweet nodded to his brother.

To his surprise, Masaun grabbed Sweet's arm.

"We need to talk." Masaun glared at him. He turned to Kindle. "Go to our room. I'll meet you there."

Kindle, now wearing a black mini leather dress and black stilettos, nodded and strolled down the hall.

"I'm with someone right now." Sweet nodded to the woman who kept her frightened stare on the two of them.

Masaun looked directly at her. "Wait for Dom Sweet at the end of the hall."

"Oh, okay." She padded down the darkened hall, occasionally looking back at Sweet.

When she got far enough away from the two of them, Sweet yanked his arm out of Masaun's grip. "What the hell are you doing?"

"I was about to ask you the same thing. I know you're trying to get back into the swing of things, but she's pretty new to the lifestyle." Masaun nodded toward her.

"Yeah, so?" Sweet shrugged but he knew where his brother headed with his inquiry.

"Why aren't you taking her to the common area to get to know her first?"

"How do you know I haven't already?"

"Cameras."

Sweet smirked. "Big Brother truly is watching, huh?" He moved in closer to Masaun and lowered his voice. "She's one of the ones whispering about us in our own fucking store. I'm just going to show her a little about the BDSM lifestyle."

"By doing it the wrong way. See, this is what I was talking about earlier. Do you even know her name?"

Sweet hadn't asked for her name. He didn't want to get that attached. He just wanted to give her the experience she came to find at The Dollhouse. Above all, he needed some release. He needed something to help push Nikla Dearwood out of his mind. He hadn't even touched the woman intimately and she consumed his thoughts.

"In the scene, I'll rename her." Sweet nodded toward his plaything.

"Don't do this." Masaun shook his head. "You want to talk? Let's talk. I can pair you with a more experienced sub if you're really ready to play. Have you really gotten over Melinda and the breakup?"

At the mention of his ex's name, Sweet shut down. "Song Sparrow is waiting for you." He walked away. "I'll see you at work tomorrow." He turned but continued to walk backward. "I know what I'm doing."

Sweet reached the young woman. She appeared confused and almost scared. When he caught the fear in her eyes, he had to avert his gaze.

"Let's go in here." He opened the door to a corner playroom filled with toys.

Sweet slammed the door behind her, causing her to gasp and jump. Just the sound alone pumped blood through cock.

"Since I have not mastered you yet, you will address me as Dom Sweet." He strolled around her.

"My name is–"

Sweet cut her off. "No. In here, I name you. You're here to play, right?" He heard her breathing increase. As he stood behind her, he watched

her shoulders rise and fall with each harried breath.

"Answer me." He touched her shoulder.

The simple touch transformed her body as though her bones had turned into jelly. Her knees buckled and she had to reach her hand out to the black leather padded platform to stay upright.

"I don't know. I don't know what to expect."

"Breathe." Sweet massaged her shoulder. He felt her trembling under his touch. He stroked his thumb over the back of her neck, not to ease her fears, but to ramp them up so that she responded even more. "You're shaking."

"I'm scared." Her voice shook with each word.

Sweet should have said or done something to assuage her fears. He felt no obligation to give her the cookie-cutter experience she may have seen on TV or movies. "I'm going to call you Leaf just because you're shaking like one." He removed his hand from her. "Get undressed."

"What?" Leaf clutched her sweater around her neck.

Sweet strolled over to a wall of toys and turned on an overhead light. Rows of paddles, floggers and whips hung from the wall. He pulled down a deer-hide flogger along with a rabbit fur-lined paddle.

"If I'm going to offer you sensations, I need for you to really feel it." He placed the two items on the counter. Sweet loved seeing her stare at the toys as though they would come to life like some Disney cartoon. "Leaf?"

The woman put her hand over her mouth as she kept her stare on the two toys. After a beat, she brought her attention to him.

"Do you want to still play?"

She stared at him as though weighing a pros and con list in her head. Leaf swallowed then placed her purse on a nearby chair. Her black sweater came off first.

With each garment shed, Sweet felt his temperature rising. He didn't find this woman that sexually appealing. She seemed pleasant. She probably would be classified as reliable or maybe loyal by her co-workers and friends. He bet that she probably owned a cat or two...or three, and that seeing a mainstream movie that contained a lot of well-respected actors playing strippers had been the raciest thing she'd ever done.

Leaf pulled her dress over her head. Sweet admired her womanly body. He had a lot of playground to use on her.

He approached her. Sweet watched her take a few steps back from him the closer he got to her. When he held out his hand, she took a breath before accepting it. Her cold fingers gave him the quick reminder that she didn't match Nikla. At least Leaf went blindly with him in a dungeon, whereas Nikla didn't even want him in her apartment.

Sweet led her to the platform and helped her onto it. He should have explained safe words to her. He should have done a lot of things. Too caught up in his own head, in his own agenda, Sweet proceeded with his play on Leaf.

Sweet leaned down to her ear. "Understand that I control this room. I control everything that happens."

That added pressure on himself caused his head to pound. He hadn't played with anyone since Melinda. He'd watched some play. In his heart, Sweet wanted to resume his old life again. This would have to be the first step.

"Yes, Sir." Leaf balled her hands into fists.

Sweet stomped over to a wall of toys and scanned the inventory again. When he reached for a whip, he noticed that he didn't get that familiar tingle like he used to when he'd played before. Where had his love for this lifestyle gone? Had it disappeared along with Melinda?

He took a deep breath when the thought got to be a bit heavy. Before Sweet got to the point of being out of control like Nikla, he pressed a spot on his inner wrist, closed his eyes, and focused on the end result of a successful play session.

"Is everything okay?" Leaf asked.

Sweet released his wrist. He turned to her and saw that she'd raised her head from the platform. "What did I say earlier? Don't speak unless I address you."

Leaf nodded and lowered her head.

Sweet knew what he had to do first. In a drawer underneath the counter by the wall, he pulled out a black leather blindfold. He returned to Leaf and covered her eyes.

He expected her now standard shocked response. "This is part of the mind games. You won't know what's coming."

She also wouldn't see Sweet looking like he didn't care, like this play meant nothing. Although he had pulled down a flogger and paddle, he returned to the wall and grabbed the first thing he could get in his hand. That implement happened to be a purple dragon's tail suede whip.

The toy gave him the feel of a long single-tail whip but the response of a flogger, the best of two worlds. Before he used the whip for its intended purpose, he first dragged the tip over her foot, up her shin, to her ample thigh and her hip.

Leaf moaned from the touch. Her initial reaction accelerated his heart.

Sweet continued to drag the tapered tail up her side, to which she released a girlish giggle.

Her smile slowed his heartbeat. She didn't take him or this play seriously. Sweet continued dragging the tail up her arm to her chest. Once there, he circled her already hardened nipple.

Leaf moaned. Her body writhed. She chewed on her lower lip again.

Sweet brought the tail up to her face. He brushed the whip over her forehead and traveled down her nose to her screwed-up mouth. He swirled the whip around her mouth until Leaf released her bottom lip and relaxed her face.

Sweet gave the other side of her body the same treatment, brushing the whip down her body until he got to her feet.

"Mmm, nice." Leaf curled her toes.

"Time for something new." If Sweet wanted to get back into playing as a Dom, he would have to start now.

Standing at the foot of the platform, Sweet parted her legs. Taking a step back, Sweet swung his arm to get used to the feel of swinging a whip again. He planted himself and stared at her tuft of black pubic hair with sprigs of gray through it.

Sweet flipped his wrist over and landed the tail squarely on her pussy.

"Oh, God!" Leaf gripped the sides of the platform.

Watching Leaf's face go from relaxed to shock had been the ultimate payoff building up to this moment. Inside he felt nothing. His heart didn't pump. He didn't sweat. The play today felt like a job than a joy.

Sweet continued whipping her, keeping his stare on her face and hoping beyond hope that something clicked. Masaun would have told him that, like baseball, he needed to keep his gaze on his target. Her reaction proved to be too alluring.

Leaf kept her mouth open, making an "O" with her lips with nothing coming out except for an occasional squeak here and there.

"Breathe," he instructed.

His first time back playing as a Dom, he really didn't need his plaything passing out on him.

Leaf exhaled and turned her head.

Sweet let his mind wander thinking about Nikla. Would she like this type of treatment? Why did it even matter? She made it obvious she had no interest in him.

"Ow! Ow! Stop! Please!"

Sweet snapped out of his haze and focused on the woman in front of him, who had now propped herself up on her elbows and had removed her eye mask.

"I know it's supposed to hurt, but that was a bit too..." Leaf trailed off and covered her mound with her hand.

Sweet put the whip on the counter. He would have stopped sooner had he given her the safe words. Damn. Sweet could almost hear Masaun saying, "I told you so" in his ear.

He ran his fingers through his hair. "Session over. You can get dressed."

"Wait. That's it? But what about–"

"You have a good night." Sweet stormed out of the room.

His first time back into playing didn't go the way he wanted. Maybe he had lost his touch. He had to stop torturing himself by thinking about doing this to Nikla. If he couldn't get past doing it to a stranger, someone he didn't want, how could he do it to someone who had snagged his interests?

Chapter Six

Nikla hoped her night would have been more eventful than her packing up Justin's shit. Her night could have been interesting had she pressed Sweet to outdo her vibrator after he had spotted it when he helped her home. He definitely ticked off all the boxes in her checklist.

She found herself eager to pass out fliers at Decadent Treats just to see him. True to his word, he came out each day to confront her. His type of confrontation consisted of asking a long list of personal questions and ending it with a box of chocolates and candies, which she never accepted. That didn't mean she didn't look forward to the offer.

Nikla couldn't stop thinking about those green eyes. At five-foot-nine, Nikla sometimes found it difficult to find men taller than her. Sweet stood a good half of a foot over her. His broad shoulders looked perfect for gripping during sex.

Sex. She didn't want or need to think about that now. Nikla's doorbell chimed. At this time of night, she didn't have to guess who stood on the other side. Nikla picked up the box she'd just packed and carried it to the door. It took him a few days to come crawling to her since that unfortunate phone call.

Balancing the box on one raised leg, she unlocked and opened her door. Justin. Poor, thin, busted Justin, stood on the other side with his head hung low. His jet-black hair swung down over his face. He adjusted his glasses over his slender nose then pulled his brown jacket together to cover his chest.

"Your stuff." Nikla held up the box for him.

"Nikla, let me explain."

When he didn't accept the box, Nikla let it crash to his feet.

Justin jumped back. "What the hell! Not mature."

"I guess finding out your boyfriend is a cheating scumbag from a pocket dial is really mature and smart, right?" Nikla crossed her arms over her chest and shook her head. "I really tried to make us work."

Justin bent over to pick up his items. "Maybe that's the problem. We shouldn't have to work that hard to be together."

"And the other problem is that you need to like me." Nikla had to truly concentrate on not screaming at him. She would not appear as a hysterical woman. He didn't warrant hysteria.

"Sometimes you make it so hard. Hell, you wouldn't even hold my hand in public. I liked you. I just didn't–"

Nikla slammed the door in his face before Justin could say what she always suspected. He didn't love her.

With her hands balled into fists, she stormed over to her kitchen and stood in front of the refrigerator, staring at it. She knew what she had hid in the freezer—her emergency stash, her coping mechanism. The king-size frozen Snickers bar would hit the spot right now and ease her pain.

"No. I'm better than that." Nikla turned her back on the refrigerator and took a huge step out of the kitchen. "I don't need food to cope."

Like on autopilot, she walked into her living room, retrieved her yoga mat from behind the couch, and rolled it out in the center of the floor. Nikla stood at the end of it and did her sun salutations, raising her hands straight into the air, then doing a swan dive, swinging her arms down to her feet and flattening her back and bringing her head up to look out the front window. She did a couple of these motions before she took a powerful step back and assumed the warrior pose.

Fuck Justin. Forget that damn Snickers bar taunting her in the freezer. She lowered her arms and turned toward the kitchen to get rid of that temptation. When she got one foot away from the kitchen, her doorbell rang.

"Oh, no he didn't." Nikla turned on the ball of her foot and stomped back to the door.

Knowing Justin, he probably scanned the contents of what she'd packed and wanted to argue with her on some missing item.

Nikla pulled the door open. "Now what?"

Deana held up her hand. "Whoa. Did the FedEx guy piss you off or something?"

Nikla exhaled. "No." She took a step aside and opened the door wider. "Come in."

Her friend took a tentative step inside, keeping her stare on Nikla the entire time.

"You don't have to look at me like I'm crazy." Nikla slammed the door behind her and padded back to her living room. "I'm fine, or I will be fine."

After they sat on the couch, Nikla shared what happened after their lunch that day, and what she did just five minutes before Deana arrived.

"That son-of-a-bitch!" Deana slammed her hand on the coffee table. "And here I thought he was a nice Filipino boy who would treat you right." She unzipped her small purse. "I have folks. I can make a call and have him hurt."

Nikla shook her head. "Not even necessary. Having to hear him cheating on me gave me the permission to wipe my hands clean of him. I was never really one-hundred percent happy in the relationship." To admit it out loud wrenched her gut.

"If you weren't really feeling him, why were you with him?"

Nikla promised herself to always be authentic and honest. Letting her relationship with Justin last longer than it should made her feel like a liar. "Probably fear of being alone. But now I can worry about my business."

Deana winced. "Without Justin's money–"

Nikla stopped her friend before she could finish her thought. "I don't need Justin's money. I don't need anything from him." If she ever thought she would need to stoop so low as to ask him for anything, she would jump from a bridge first. "I found a great location for my new place."

"Awesome. Where?" Deana placed her purse on the coffee table and leaned back on the couch.

"Downtown Virginia Beach." Nikla smiled, a first in hours. Then she thought about the mysterious stranger who tried staring her down for the spot. Her smile became even broader.

"A penny for your thoughts." Deana nudged Nikla's knee.

Nikla shook her head and waved her hand to her like she wanted to erase the memory. "It's nothing. I had, um, a little incident during my–"

"Protest?"

"Yeah."

"Did you get arrested?"

Not in the way Deana meant it. Certainly, Sweet had arrested her attention. "No. I didn't feel good. A guy from Decadent Treats helped me and took me home."

"A guy took you home? And you're still cheesing like that? What did you do?"

Nikla smiled at the impure thoughts she had about the man after he left. "Nothing happened." She regretted that. She wanted him to take her body and make it his. "He's the same guy who tried running me off from in front of Decadent Treats the other day."

"Really? So? Did you exchange numbers or just bodily fluids?" Deana inched closer to Nikla.

Nikla felt her nose wrinkle after the inquiry. "Are you kidding? I just met the guy. I didn't even shake his hand."

Despite that, Sweet had no problem picking her up when she'd fallen. He helped carry her into her apartment and put her to bed. She still remembered how hard his body felt when he pressed her against him.

Her clit throbbed and she had to cross her legs.

"You don't have to shake his hand. Let him work your body." Deana stood up. "You still have that wine in the fridge?"

Nikla nodded.

Deana turned and headed to the kitchen as she slipped off her jacket.

"Did you at least get his name so you know who to look out for?"

Nikla heard the refrigerator door opening and closing, then heard her friend going into her cabinet for glasses.

"Yeah, it was a weird name." Nikla would never forget it.

"Like what? Hannibal or something?" Deana giggled as she walked out of the kitchen and toward Nikla.

"I wish."

Deana's eyebrows shot upward.

"With a name like that, you can see evil coming."

Deana sat down and opened the wine, pulling out the temporary cork and emitting a popping sound in the process.

"No, this guy's name was Sweet."

"What? It was something cutesy like Yogi or Boo Boo?" Deana poured a glass and handed it to Nikla.

Nikla took a needed sip of the fruity, red wine before continuing. "No, his name was actually Sweet. Sweet Hawkes to be exact."

Without a word, Deana pulled out her phone and started typing into her screen. When something populated in front of her that she liked, her eyes widened. "I knew it! I thought I had heard that name before. He and his brother own that candy shop in Virginia Beach. Decadent Treats."

"He's an *owner*?" Nikla shook her head. "I thought he was an employee, a scout for the owner." In all the time he'd encountered her, never once did Sweet tell her that he owned the store.

Deana made a grunting sound deep in her throat. "With the way this guy looks, I think I would be eating, licking, and sucking on something Sweet." She winked at Nikla.

"Let me see." Nikla snatched the phone from her friend's hand and looked at the picture. The shot had Sweet standing next to another equally handsome man, but Sweet grabbed her attention. Both men carried the same mesmerizing green eyes, but Sweet's gaze seemed to bore right through the picture and into her soul.

"Yeah, that's him." Nikla handed the phone back to Deana. "As soon as he heard me on the phone with the real estate company, he actually had the nerve to come up to me and say that he wants the place."

"I think I know why." Deana smiled as she continued to play with her phone. She turned the large screen around to Nikla. "Your boy dabbles on the dark side."

Nikla squinted as she looked at the tiny news article on the phone. "Does that say something about BDSM?"

Deana nodded. "Looks like he and his brother are into that."

Nikla carried her glass of wine to her office and fired up her computer. She needed to see this on a much larger screen. She felt Deana's hand on her shoulder as she did her own Google search.

The first link contained the article about his and his brother's candy shop. In the brief caption by the link, it looked like the place had been a resounding success. Their success, or rather someone else's failure, forced her to action.

The next couple of links had her interested. She clicked the first article that came from their local newspaper comparing the two brothers to the fictionalized character in that wildly popular book series about a woman's first foray into the world of BDSM.

"I told you." Deana patted Nikla's shoulder. "It's no wonder the man acted like he already owned the place. That's his nature."

Nikla started to tune out Deana as she became engrossed in the article, which mainly focused on Sweet's brother, Masaun, and Masaun's assistant commonwealth attorney fiancée, Kindle Langston.

She read every word of the article. The little bit that focused on Sweet, she read over and over again. The one thing she had hoped to have found in the article the journalist never revealed, Sweet's true name. The writer continued to call him Sweet or S. Hawkes throughout. Maybe the man had his name legally changed to Sweet.

"That guy brought you back to your apartment?" Deana asked.

Nikla nodded and kept her stare on the screen.

"And you two didn't hit it?"

Nikla turned to her friend. "I guess you missed the parts where I said I wasn't feeling well and that this guy is a stranger." She could categorize him as public enemy number one now that she knew he co-owned Decadent Treats.

"As fine as he looks, I would let him string me up and spank my ass."

Deana finished off her glass of wine and headed back to the living room.

Nikla stood and followed her friend. "Be careful of what you wish for."

"Don't act like you don't want it." Deana poured herself another glass of wine.

"I don't. He's the enemy."

Deana nearly let the glass fall from her hand. "Fuck that shit. Sleep with the enemy." Deana fanned her face.

Nikla had to play it a little cooler than that. She smiled at her friend, but her insides started heating up thinking about touching his broad chest and taking in his masculine scent. "Sounds like you're interested in this guy. Why don't you test the waters?" Nikla cocked her head. "That type of relationship wouldn't work."

Deana picked up her phone and showed the picture of Sweet again. "He is fine with a capital F. You two didn't have to talk business. Talk pleasure." She winked.

Nikla winced. "Yes, the man is attractive."

"And you got an up close and personal view of him."

"But he's not my type."

"Oh, honey, he's everybody's type. Black, white, gay, straight. Besides, he's your rebound man. Do things with him that you never thought you would do just to do them."

"You mean like let him put a collar around my neck and walk me around like a dog?" Nikla laughed.

"Don't laugh at it until you try it." Deana took a sip of her wine. "You never know. You might like being subservient."

"Doubt it. I've worked too long and hard to be independent and stand on my own two feet to just forget all that and call some guy Master." Nikla shook her head. "Nope. I hope our encounters at his shop will be the only bit of interaction that we'll have. I allowed one man to distract me. I'm not going to let some other guy in to do the same."

"It's just about sex. Don't get too deep."

"Sex would be great. I don't know if it should be with him." Nikla wanted to believe what she'd just said. Ever since meeting him, she had pretty explicit dreams about Sweet Hawkes.

She envisioned him stalking toward her completely naked. He would grab her, strip her out of her clothing, and take her—against a wall, on the floor, on any and all surfaces possible. Unlike with Justin, he would not only make her come, but he would do it over and over and over again until her body became limp.

Nikla had to cross her legs when her throbbing clitoris became too much for her. She couldn't wait for Deana to go home so that she could relieve herself.

"Now that's your father talking. He wants you to be that good girl. I'm surprised he hasn't gotten you to agree to work with him."

Nikla wouldn't admit that her father never stopped trying to get her back into the family business. She couldn't do it. She had to make her own path, but she showed her support in other ways.

"Oh, yeah. Thanks for the reminder. I have to go over to his house in the morning."

Deana nodded. "It's good that you're close with your father."

Nikla did love her father. In recent years, he had changed.

After polishing off the rest of the wine and another full bottle, Nikla tucked her friend into the bed in her spare bedroom. No way would she allow Deana to drive home after drinking. She closed the bedroom door and padded back to her office.

After reactivating her screen, she went back to the article on Sweet Hawkes. She discovered that he and his brother had been a part of the local BDSM scene for most of their adult lives. A shot of their storefront sat next to a picture of The Dollhouse, a nightclub Nikla had heard of, but she thought only drinking and dancing happened in the place. She never knew Virginia Beach had its own BDSM club. Talk about decadent.

She stared at the picture, studying the outside until it implanted in her memory. Could she ever step into a place like that? Would she let a man like Sweet Hawkes discipline her like she had seen in movies?

For now, she had to keep her head in the game and focus on her meeting. It could be the start of her new life.

Chapter Seven

Just as Nikla had suspected, as soon as she arrived at her father's home, he had her stretching her body before they took off for a five-mile run. Thank goodness Nikla had kept up her cardio as she did everything else dealing with her physical health.

"Glad you're here," Lawrence said between breaths.

"I told you I would be here Sunday morning for breakfast...and the run." She smirked at her father, who kept his face straight and tight as always.

The more she stared at him, the more she saw her brother. Her poor brother followed in their father's footsteps and joined the Marines after college.

It never bothered Nikla that her father declared that she wouldn't be military material and shouldn't join the Marines. Nikla had other plans. She did envy her brother for getting away from their father. She felt obligated to be by her father's side as much as possible.

"Did you get permission to come here?" Lawrence chuckled.

"No." Nikla hoped her clipped answer would end that line of questioning.

"And where is your young man? Couldn't get up this early?" Her father glanced both ways at a major intersection before he jogged across it with Nikla following him.

"We're no longer together."

Lawrence glanced at Nikla. Instead of offering fatherly compassion, he shook his head. "I don't understand young people nowadays. Used to be you date for a short while, you get engaged, and you get married. You were with that guy for almost a year. Why couldn't you hold on to this one?"

"Let's not go there, Dad." Nikla kicked up her jog to move beyond her father.

When she brought her gaze up, she saw where her father must have been aiming for in this run.

"Damn," she muttered under her breath.

Healthy Bites sat off in the distance. Her father's health food store had been his dream for years. It had done well as soon as he opened it. Then Decadent Treats opened about two miles away from his store.

"Are we turning around and going back to the house now so that we can eat breakfast?" To prompt her father, Nikla turned and started heading back.

"You really are avoiding this place like the plague, huh?" Lawrence continued toward his store.

"Damn. Damn." Nikla turned around and followed behind her father.

When Nikla had started the run, she wondered if Sweet would drive by and see her. For that reason, she ran taller with her stomach in, her chest out, and her back straight.

Once at Healthy Bites, Lawrence unlocked the door and ushered her inside. Thankfully Healthy Bites didn't open on Sunday, so Nikla knew her father wouldn't be asking her to work.

Inside, Nikla glanced around at the familiar surroundings. Glass cases lined three sides of the intimate space. The pure white walls didn't give the place a cozy feeling. It almost came off like a pharmacy.

Three tables sat in the main area for customers who wanted to eat in the store that made seemingly calorie-laden treats into something healthy.

Shredded beets filled the chocolate cupcakes. Her father used zucchini in his yellow cakes. The homemade granola bars and muesli had been the fan favorites there.

When Decadent Treats opened, loyal customers started slipping on their need for healthy snacks and decided to go for the full fat.

Lawrence made his way behind the elevated front counter. Already a tall man, the position made him look like a giant. He glared down at Nikla.

"My dream is dying," he declared.

"I know, Dad." Nikla took in a deep breath and strolled up to the counter to let her leg muscles relax. "That's why I'm out in front of Decadent Treats every day talking about the benefits of eating healthy and how consuming so much sugar can–"

"Eh! No one reads anymore. No one cares. They leave. They just..." Her father trailed off and Nikla knew exactly what he meant in his complaint.

"I'm here. I'll do whatever I can to help you." When she saw his father opening his mouth, she quickly interjected, "I can't work in the store with you."

Although her father made healthy foods, he had to use something to make them taste appealing to a sweet tooth. For the same reason she couldn't go into Decadent Treats, Nikla had to stay out of Healthy Bites. She couldn't trust herself not to slip.

"If you can figure out a way to get customers into this place, I would appreciate it. Right now, it's dying on the vine, and I don't know how to stop it. It just kills me that people would rather drive the extra mile or two for crap when they can have the good stuff here."

Nikla had never heard her father sound so desperate. "Dad, why not sell and retire? You need to–"

"Need to what?" he snapped. "Crawl off and never be seen again?" He shook his head. "I have a life. I want to keep working." He stomped from around the counter. "If you can't help, just say so. But don't stand there and tell me what I need to do with my life." He headed to the door. "Let's go back home. It was a mistake to bring you here."

Nikla shook her head. She felt the familiar stirrings of the start of another panic attack. She felt the supreme obligation to save her father's store, to save his life.

Before she could move her feet, she took a deep breath.

"Nikla, let's go!" Lawrence shouted from the door.

Once her body settled, she turned to him. "Coming."

Feeling stuck between a rock and hard place, Nikla didn't know how to solve her father's problems. She just knew she had to try. Someone had to be in his corner.

****

Sweet stood in the Decadent Treats kitchen, staring at the ingredients before him and feeling like he had no idea what to do with them. The sugar and honey sat next to his left hand. By his right sat flour, brown sugar, and chocolate. Nothing spoke to him.

Used to be he could gather any ingredients together and make something spectacular. He'd even made desserts with bacon.

"Hey."

Sweet snapped out of his trance to see his brother standing across from him. "How long have you been there?"

"Long enough to see that you don't look good. What's going on with you?" Masaun planted his hands on the counter.

Sweet shook his head. "I don't know. Everything I used to know and that used to make sense to me don't anymore."

"Are you talking about here and making candies?" Masaun knocked his knuckle against the bag of sugar.

"Not just that. I played with that submissive the other night, I couldn't get into it. My mind wasn't there." Sweet hated to admit that his brother had been right, but he couldn't lie to him. "I'm losing it, man."

Masaun lowered his gaze and breathed out before he spoke. "You need to take some time off. After you and, um, after your breakup, you kept working and buried your head in this place. You have to take care of yourself. Hell, I don't think I've seen you smile in forever."

Sweet let his brother's words roll around in his head before he spoke. "I'm thinking about stepping back from The Dollhouse, not doing that anymore."

Sweet didn't want to admit that his true passion for disciplining seemed to have disappeared.

"You don't mean that. You've been a Dom for a long time." Masaun came around the counter to stand next to Sweet. "You remember you used to make those chocolate chip cookies all the time and we all loved them but you hated them?"

Sweet recalled that memory of himself as a teenager trying his hand out in the kitchen. "Yeah."

"We all told you how great your cookies were, but you couldn't see that, or taste it. You kept saying something was off, and you were right. You tweaked the recipe."

"I added coffee." Sweet remembered smelling the beverage one day and thinking that the taste would enhance the flavor of the chocolate in the cookies.

"You were right. You turned something great into something spectacular."

"What are you saying?" The pep talk so far sounded awesome, but Sweet didn't know how it would solve his problem. How could Sweet find his love of cooking and disciplining again?

Masaun poked his finger into Sweet's chest. "You know yourself better than anyone. And only you know how to fix this problem. Whether it's time away or taking a cooking class somewhere or going to a BDSM bed-and-breakfast–"

Sweet blinked. "Does a place like that exist?"

Masaun shrugged. "Thought I heard about a spot down in Virginia Beach. Someone made an old school into one. If that's what's going to bring back your passion, do it."

Sweet thought about his suggestion and rubbed his hands across the back of his neck. "I met someone."

This time it was Masaun's turn to blink. "Really? At the club?"

Sweet didn't answer. He didn't want to tell his brother that the lone protester had somehow managed to capture his interests.

"Whatever, man. That's great. Vanilla?"

Sweet nodded. "That might be part of the problem. If she doesn't know..."

"Then you teach her. That'll get you out of your rut." Masaun patted Sweet on his shoulder. "Your solution is right there. Figure out the relationship and maybe you'll discover something about yourself." Masaun walked off with a laugh. "I can't believe you finally put yourself out there." He nodded. "I'm happy for you. Hope she can make you happy."

Masaun walked out.

Sweet just hoped that he could get Nikla out of his head. He couldn't be any good to her or any woman right now until he could straighten himself out. Despite what Masaun suggested, time away from work wouldn't do it. Sweet would have to keep going with his plan to open another store. He had his appointment in the morning. He would be able to focus then.

Chapter Eight

Sweet, dressed in black slacks with matching jacket, a crisp, white shirt and a red power tie, walked into the Zuberi Commercial Real Estate Company office. He could never be a submissive or slave. The tie wrapped around his neck felt too much like a collar. He hated the feeling. He kept pulling on the inside of the collar to give himself some air to breathe. He wondered how the hell Masaun could wear a tie all the time. For this meeting, Sweet would look his best.

The small building existed near the Oceanfront and sat sandwiched in between two tall buildings. He imagined the owners bought the small dwelling years ago before all of the construction happened down at the Oceanfront area, and they refused to give up their spot. He had to respect their fortitude.

Sweet smoothed his hand down his tie. As long as he kept the events that had happened with Nikla and Leaf out of his head, he would remain calm.

Sweet's thoughts had gone back and forth between his encounter with Nikla Dearwood and his sorry performance at The Dollhouse. He couldn't keep his mind on Leaf while he thought about business, losing Melinda, and Nikla Dearwood, both a headache and a distraction.

After taking a needed deep breath, he gripped the doorknob to the white building and pulled the door open. The creaking hinges welcomed him more than the venomous glare he got from Nikla who sat at the edge of a chair like she wanted to jump up at any moment.

"You actually did make an appointment, huh?" Nikla turned away from him.

"You thought I was kidding about wanting both spots?" Sweet kept his stare on her as he made his way to the receptionist desk that sat in the center of the cramped space.

Nikla never returned his look but did respond. "I thought you were trying to rattle me."

"Trust me. I have other ways I can do that." Hearing the word "rattle" had him thinking of Nikla handcuffed to an overhead bar. He could almost hear the sounds handcuffs would make as they clanged against each other.

He cleared his throat to snag the attention of the woman with the gray beehive hairdo. When she looked up, he said, "I have an appointment. Sweet Hawkes."

The prim, slight, mature woman adjusted her invisible frame glasses on her slender nose, then ran her hand down her neck like she wanted to smooth away her wrinkles. "Please have a seat." She indicated the chair next to Nikla.

Although Sweet wanted to be disappointed, his pounding heart gave away how he truly felt. He didn't like feeling this out of sorts around a woman he barely knew, especially one who wanted to shut down his business.

Sweet occupied the wooden chair next to Nikla that seemed as old as the building. It squeaked under his weight, but he welcomed being in a seated position. At six-foot-three, he felt like he had to duck his head due to the low ceiling.

He also enjoyed the aroma near Nikla. No longer smelling of oranges, she only carried a seductive jasmine scent. He took in a deep breath and his dick pulsed. *Christ*.

"I don't think I ever had the chance to tell you thank you properly for the other day." Nikla could barely look him in the eyes as she spoke. "I wasn't at my best. It was embarrassing." Her gaze connected to his. "I appreciate you giving me my dignity."

His heart thrummed at her sincere speech. "I'm human. You needed help. I did what anyone else would have done."

"I don't think so." She held up her hand to him. "Thank you."
After a beat, Sweet accepted her gesture and took her small hand in his. Her soft flesh melted in his hand. He wanted nothing more than to pull her close and seal her apology with a kiss.

Before he could humiliate himself, he released her hand. "If you really want to thank me, you'll stop protesting in front of my store."

"I can't do that."

Sweet caught her tone when she said it. She sounded like she did this task for someone else, not because it meant anything to her.

"You must be late for your appointment or incredibly early." Nikla crossed her legs.

Damn. Now in her skirt and business jacket, she exuded power. Her skirt rode up her leg, showing off more of her luscious thigh.

When she finally looked at him in his eyes, he noticed her lips carried a faint pink hue that gave them an even juicier appearance than before. The makeup around her eyes made them look even bigger. If he didn't think the chair would crack under the weight, he would have pulled the caramel beauty onto his lap.

"Why would you assume that I'm not on time?" He leaned back in the chair. When he heard a loud pop, he thought better of his decision and sat up straighter. "Aren't you way early?"

"No. I'm on time." She looked at her watch. "My appointment starts in a few minutes."

Sweet furrowed his eyebrows. "If you knew me, you'd know I'm never late."

"I've learned a lot about you, more than I should." A sly smile spread across Nikla's innocent face.

"What's that supposed to mean?" Had Nikla actually looked up information about him online?

Before Nikla could answer, the receptionist got his attention. "Mrs. Zuberi will see you now."

"Who? Me?" Sweet pointed to himself. "Or her?" He jutted his thumb over his shoulder to point at Nikla.

"Both." The receptionist stood and opened a door behind her desk.

Sweet didn't know what kind of game Zuberi played with the two of them. He planned on being on top.

He stood and held his hand out for Nikla. He had to blink hard when she accepted it. The same woman who wouldn't shake his hand days ago now had touched him twice.

Her soft, delicate fingers wrapped around his hand. He wanted so much to wrap her fingers around his cock and have her stroke him until he came.

His stomach tightened as soon as the thought hit him that this could be a diversionary tactic. Her soft touch could be a way to throw him from his game.

Nikla's velvety touch sent a shiver down Sweet's spine. He squeezed her hand as she got to her feet. Until she thanked him and removed her hand from his, he would have been fine holding her hand into the meeting...of course with her trailing behind him.

He had to get it out of his head about making her his submissive.

As a gentleman, he allowed her entrance into the office first, then he held out her chair. When he noticed the woman sitting on the flowered velvet couch, Sweet remained standing until he shook her hand. Then he sat in a matching flowered chair.

Much like the building and the waiting room, this office looked more like his grandmother's living room. Mrs. Zuberi didn't have a desk in her office. Just a flowered couch, two chairs, a coffee table, and two tall floor lamps. The Oriental rug under his feet brought home the familial feel.

Sweet didn't expect to be meeting with this older woman, the namesake behind the successful local commercial real estate company. Looking at Nikla's surprised expression, she looked a bit taken aback as well.

"You two want something to drink?" Mrs. Zuberi pointed to an avocado-colored full-sized refrigerator that sat in the corner.

"I'm fine." Sweet smoothed out his business plan on his lap.

"Nothing for me. Thank you." Nikla shook her head.

The older white woman, who he estimated to be in her seventies, reminded Sweet of one of his free-spirited aunts on his father's side of the family. Graying blonde dreadlocks adorned Mrs. Zuberi's head. She kept them contained under a brown-and-tan paisley scarf. The scarf matched the flowing caftan she wore. Her tan sandals sat on the floor in front of her. She kept her feet curled up on the couch. Very limber for a woman of her age.

Sweet decided to take charge of this meeting. "Mrs. Zuberi, I want to thank you for taking time to meet with me." He started to open his folder.

"And with me." Nikla pulled out her paperwork from her purse.

"I understand your time is valuable, which is why you must have scheduled our meetings at the same time." Sweet nodded his head toward Nikla.

"No. I realized that lots of people would like those two storefronts I'm leasing downtown." She shook her head. "That's the one thing my dear departed husband did right while he was alive. He recognized an opportunity and took it. He also loved what he loved, like this building." She raised her hands in the air like a retired showgirl. "He could have torn this place down when he had the two office buildings beside this place built, but he couldn't give up the first office building he ever owned."

Sweet nodded. To anyone else, Mrs. Zuberi sounded like a woman who respected her husband's dying wishes. To him, she sounded like a well-trained submissive who complied with her husband's instructions.

"To be honest, the day-to-day business dealings bore me. I have ignored all requests, and trust me, I've gotten plenty." She picked up her coffee mug and took a healthy swig.

Sweet didn't even know if she had coffee or tea in the mug. From her demeanor, he guessed that she probably had some sort of liquor in it.

"If you had no interest in leasing the spaces, why advertise?" Sweet started to feel like the woman had wasted his time.

"That was my son's idea. He wants to take over the business one day. I told him I wanted to take over the leasing of the spaces as my last deal."

"Good. Let me make it easy for you. We want both spaces. If you allow us to have both spots, you will only have to deal with one customer." Sweet placed his business plan on the coffee table in front of her. "If you want to look over my numbers—"

"We? Us?" The woman pointed to Sweet and Nikla. "Are you two going into business together?"

Sweet didn't even look at Nikla. "No. When I said we, I'm talking about me and my brother, Masaun. He's my business partner."

"How nice. I wish my boys would get along like that."

Her statement confirmed what Sweet already knew. He had an incredible relationship with his brother. He just hoped that once he got this deal that Masaun wouldn't be too upset with him for going behind his back.

"Mrs. Zuberi, I just want one space. The smaller one." Nikla glared at Sweet. She started to place her plan on the table on top of Sweet's.

The elderly woman waved her hand. "I don't want to see your business plans. You two tell me what you want for both spots. And please, call me Bobbi. At my age, I want to feel young in any way possible."

"Bobbi, I would like to run my own yoga and Pilates studio. I've been teaching classes for ten years." Nikla sat up taller and even smiled as she shared her plan.

"Really? I didn't know that." Her admission made Sweet regard her differently. That explained her workout gear the first time he'd met her and her exercise room in her apartment.

"And you thought I was someone else." Nikla finally acknowledged him.

Her diplomacy and tact prevented her from saying that Sweet had damn near called her a trophy wife or mistress. She could have buried him in Bobbi's eyes by casting him in a bad light. He would have deserved it for his assumption.

"I thought you had come from working out. I should have known that—"

"What?" Nikla cut him off and glared at him, preparing for a fight.

"I should have guessed with a body like yours that you took working out seriously." Sweet stared at her for a long beat, long enough to notice a shade of deep shade of crimson flooding Nikla's face.

Nikla dropped her gaze. That expression revved up his engine more than her scent and her touch. He shouldn't have wanted this woman so much. He had to keep his head into business.

When he turned his attention back to Bobbi, she looked impressed by Nikla's plan. He should have known this former hippie would have liked this touchy-feely business.

"I'm old enough to remember when yoga became big in the States. People thought that only hippies did this exercise." Bobbi glanced at Sweet as though reading his mind. "I don't think there are any other exercise studios in that shopping area."

"There aren't. I checked." Nikla beamed as she showed how much she researched this venture.

Even though she seemed to be ahead with Bobbi, Sweet still had a chance.

Sweet glanced at Nikla before returning his attention to the woman who probably wanted amusement more than business. "My brother Masaun and I run a candy shop called Decadent Treats. I'd like to expand our current business."

"You want to get both units so that you can knock down a wall to make some sort of mega store?" Bobbi asked.

"No. I would make one unit our Decadent Treats store, and I'd make the other unit one where I would sell merchandise."

"What kind of merchandise? Baking supplies? Party items?"

"Fetish toys and apparel." Sweet made the declaration with confidence and kept his stare on her hazel eyes.

Bobbi blinked. "Oh. I know there's not a store like that there now."

"No, there isn't." He turned to Nikla.

This time she stared at him. She couldn't break away, fascinated by the idea of what he had to offer.

"Tell me more," Bobbi said.

Sweet broke his stare from Nikla to address Bobbi. "I'm involved in an alternative lifestyle. I've noticed that there aren't any places around here that sell quality equipment and toys to use within that lifestyle."

"What kind of equipment, Mr. Hawkes?" Bobbi held onto her mug as she regarded him.

Sweet peered to the side and noticed Nikla hanging on his every word as well.

"Whips, floggers, dragon's tails, crosses, hobblers, chastity devices."

He noticed Bobbi's eyes widening at that admission.

While he had her on the hook, he might as well keep going. "Cock-and-ball torture devices, dildos, vibrators, anal-play training kits, nipple clamps.

I haven't even gotten to the clothing like corsets and collars."

Nikla dropped her purse to the floor.

"Yes, shocking indeed." Bobbi fanned her face. "I can honestly say that there's not another store like that in that shopping center."

"Or anywhere else." Sweet leaned back.

"And no concern about selling items like that next to a family-friendly store?" Nikla asked.

Sweet sat up. Now Nikla sounded like his brother. "Any concern about having a candy store next to your yoga studio?" He turned to Bobbi. "There's a real possibility that Bobbi could lease one place to you and the other to me, am I right?"

Bobbi placed her mug on the coffee table. "Don't put words in my mouth. You two have definitely given me a lot to chew on. I'm glad the 'For Lease' signs have been removed from the windows now. I think I've found my final candidates."

Nikla beamed. Sweet couldn't share in her joy.

"I want both units." Sweet stared at Bobbi so that she could catch the intent in his eyes.

"And people in Hell want ice water. You can't have it all, Mr. Hawkes." Nikla crossed her arms over her chest.

"Yes, I can." He stared pointedly at her.

Nikla never crumbled. Never looked away. He found her strength attractive.

"Since it looks like you two can't compromise, I'd like to try something. Since you both do what you're intending to sell, I'd like to try out what you do."

"Really?" Sweet tried imagining himself disciplining a woman old enough to be his grandmother.

Masaun would never let him live that down. Of course he would have to admit to Masaun that he'd gone behind his back to pursue something Masaun had told him to forget.

"Let me amend that." Bobbi pointed to Nikla. "I'd like to attend one of your classes if that's possible."

"Of course!" Nikla beamed. "I'll make sure to make room for you in one of my yoga or Pilates classes."

"Yoga. It would be great to get back into that again. Any way possible I can attend a session tomorrow?"

"Absolutely. I have one that starts at seven at night. You could sit in. Or if you would like a private lesson, I can do a class with you at eight."

Nikla crossed her legs and kicked it back and forth in front of Sweet's legs.

Sweet found the sight almost distracting. He couldn't break his stare from her bare legs. In her heels, he imagined her long limbs around his body.

"Eight would be better. I love to watch my 'Wheel of Fortune' and 'Jeopardy' shows." She cleared her throat. "Mr. Hawkes?"

Sweet snapped out of his imagination and brought his attention back to Bobbi.

"May I come to your candy shop?" Bobbi asked.

"Absolutely. So as not to take too much of your time, you can come to the shop after your, um, workout." Sweet tried hiding the smirk but he knew it showed on his face.

"Have you ever done yoga?" Nikla glared at him. When Sweet didn't answer immediately, Nikla answered for him. "It's a lot harder than you think."

"So is making candy."

"I never said what you did was easy." Nikla pointed at him.

"I didn't say that yoga wasn't a real exercise." He leaned closer to her. "Sounds like we have a plan. We'll go to Ms. Dearwood's class."

"We?" Sweet felt his face go tight.

"Me and you, Mr. Hawkes." Bobbi laughed. "You should check out your competition. At this point, I'm only going to consider these two proposals."

Sweet shook his head. "It's all or nothing. If you lease one space to her, my plan won't work and I wouldn't be interested in acquiring the second unit."

"Then I guess you had better impress me when you teach us how to make candy, which will happen promptly after Ms. Dearwood's class."

"Us?" Nikla questioned.

"Just like with Mr. Hawkes, you should learn what it is that he has to offer." Bobbi nodded her head toward Sweet.

"Getting to Decadent Treats after nine would work. The place will be closed so it'll be all ours. Does that mean you want to check out my second business venture, too?" Sweet kept his stare on Bobbi.

Bobbi cut her gaze at him. "One step at a time. I'm still pondering over the idea of having a business like that."

"I can understand the fear." He'd seen trepidation in the eyes of people who walked through The Dollhouse doors plenty of times.

"The only fear I have is whether or not I'll make money. I could care less if people object to what you do or sell. To the disappointment of my children, I live off controversy and love fighting against the status quo. I might go for your business just to have something to do."

Sweet heard Nikla gasp. He couldn't look at her now. Although he'd like to get both units, he wanted a fair fight.

"But that's not how I work." Bobbi brought her feet down to the floor and stood up faster than he expected.

Sweet stood up with her with Nikla following suit.

"Leave your pertinent addresses and contact information with my assistant." Bobbi held out her hand for Nikla. "I will see you two tomorrow." After shaking Nikla's hand, she shook Sweet's hand.

As instructed, Sweet and Nikla left their business addresses with the receptionist. Once they got outside, Sweet didn't want to see Nikla go. Not just yet.

"I'm not used to doing business like this." Sweet loosened his tie and undid the top two buttons.

"I don't know." Nikla shrugged. "I think it's a great way to check out your competition without being sneaky. I don't like to play games."

"Don't judge. Some games are fun." Sweet's gaze dropped down to her ass hidden underneath her sensible suit.

She snickered. "I suspect that your definition of games may involve a little more than a Monopoly game board."

"I use some of the typical implements for games. Paddle, rope, handcuffs."

For the last item on his list, Nikla flashed a confused expression.

"Cops and robbers. Can't play that without handcuffs."

Nikla laughed. "Good to see a guy like you can have a sense of humor. A woman has to be on her toes to be with you."

"You have no idea." As much as Sweet didn't want to, he started to like Nikla. Although she still kept her walls up around her, he noticed she started to relax around him. "I'd like to take you to lunch." Sweet stood in her path. "We both have to eat."

Nikla regarded him for a moment. "Why should I have lunch with you?"

Sweet felt relieved she didn't immediately say no. "Because you have a lot of questions for me. I can tell."

"And you don't want to know anything about me?" Nikla stepped around him and headed to her vehicle.

When Sweet didn't answer her right away, she stopped in her trek and turned to him.

"I want to figure you out." He moved toward her, stalking her like a prey. "I want to discover you."

Nikla's breath caught.

"You, um, can find out more about me."

Sweet stood nearly nose to nose with her. The cool air coming from the beach blew between their bodies. He'd already told his brother and the staff that he would be out most of the day. He could definitely see himself taking Nikla to The Dollhouse for an afternoon play session to break himself out of his rut.

"You can discover all you want about me in my class. Tomorrow night." She unlocked her car door and opened it. Before she got inside she said, "That's if you show up."

Sweet started to enjoy his interactions with Nikla. He planned on being in her class, but he only wanted to watch her. He couldn't wait to see her possibly hurt the seventy-something-year-old building owner and have Bobbi happily allow Sweet to get both suites.

Let the games begin.

Chapter Nine

Nikla wanted to string out her class more; that way she didn't have to think about Bobbi Zuberi showing up and doing downward dog with her. When her students started dropping like flies and leaving, she finally had to end the session.

When she thought about Sweet possibly being in her class, her heart pounded so hard she had to stop moving and take a couple of deep breaths to collect herself.

"He's just a guy. He's no better than Justin." Nikla rolled up the extra rec center's yoga mats and put them back in the storage closet.

She would have believed what she told herself if Sweet hadn't proved himself in leaps and bounds over Justin. For one thing, Sweet didn't seem content with being safe. He and his brother had a successful business. He could have been happy with that one location. Sweet wanted more.

He treated her like a gentleman. When he caught her releasing her tension at the empty storefronts, he checked on her. He opened doors for her. He helped her to her feet and held chairs for her. He didn't seem like what she imagined a Dominant would act like, although he had the confidence down.

She would never forget how he responded to her when her panic attack dropped her to her knees. His reaction to that incident made him look seriously attractive and sexy, mainly because he hadn't judged her.

If Deana knew Nikla thought about Sweet more than she should have, her friend would have told her to jump on that man. When Nikla turned down his date request, she could hear Deana screaming in her head to tell the man she didn't mean it.

Nikla couldn't lose her head. Justin had already distracted her enough. She had to keep focused. Getting involved with a Dominant sounded like time-consuming work.

Nikla padded over to the iPod player at the front of the room and made sure to have her music ready for when Bobbi arrived. She'd already planned on taking it easy on her. She didn't need to hurt Bobbi and ruin her chances at getting this one unit.

Nikla stood in front of the wall mirror, raised her hands in the air, stretching as high as she could, then bent over and pressed her hands flat on the floor. Although she had led a class, Nikla still needed something to relax herself.

In her bent over position, she heard the door opening.

"Welcome to yoga, Bobbi." Nikla peered up in the mirror.

The reflection she saw shook her to her core. She never expected to see Sweet. In his t-shirt and loose-fitting pants, he looked so damn good. Damn the devil.

Nikla also spied him staring at her ass. Ordinarily she would have admonished him for being so sexist. The hunger in his eyes as he watched her had her remaining in the position longer than she should have.

"Didn't expect to see you." She stood up straight and smoothed her hands down the front of her shirt.

"I never said I wouldn't show." He strolled toward her.

"Did you see Bobbi anywhere out there?" To keep away from the tempting man, Nikla headed to the door as though she expected the woman to walk through it at any moment.

"No. I thought she would have been here by now. I envision her as an early bird." Sweet stood in the center of the room while Nikla looked out the door.

"I'll give her another five minutes."

"Do you have her phone number?" Sweet asked.

Nikla looked back at him. "I have her office number. Do *you* have her cell phone number?" When Sweet didn't respond, she got her answer. "Oh, you have it. You're not going to share it."

He shook his head. "I told you that games aren't my thing. I have her office number just like you. I'm surprised that you would ask me for help."

"Why would you say that?" She padded back over to the music system.

"Just my impression. You're very closed off."

She glared at him. "And, what, you're some open book?"

"Little more open than you. You know what one of my pastimes is. I don't know what you do outside of work."

"You forget that we just met?"

"Yes."

Nikla glanced at him when he gave his one-word answer. She knew exactly what he meant. After a few meetings and run-ins, she felt connected to him, more than when she'd first met Justin.

"So ten years."

"What?"

"You've been teaching yoga and Pilates for ten years?" he asked.

"Yeah. Started during college." Nikla glanced at her watch. "Five after. Maybe give her another five minutes." She thought about that decision and remembered that in less than an hour, a boxing class would be in that room.

Nikla certainly didn't need to give Bobbi a full hour class. She could show her what she could do in thirty minutes. She didn't want to be stuck in the room with Sweet.

"You do have a student here." Sweet's deep voice rumbled.

"What?"

Sweet pointed to himself. "I'm here. Teach me something. It wouldn't hurt my feelings if Bobbi shows up and you start the class over again. Besides, I don't think this class will wear me out."

Hearing Sweet knock the physical effort in doing yoga raised the hairs on the back of her neck. "You think this workout is going to be easy?"

"Did you call yoga a workout?" Sweet's eyebrows knitted together.

Nikla strolled to the storage closet and grabbed a yoga mat. "I see you came to the class unprepared." She shoved the thick, rolled blue mat against his chest. "You should have brought a towel, too."

"For this?" Sweet rolled the mat on the floor.

Nikla nodded. "When I make you sweat."

"Good. Make me sweat here. I'll be sure to do the same when we go to my shop later."

The look he gave her after he made his statement caused her nipples to harden. She had to get this class going to calm herself down.

"Take off your shoes." She headed to the wall and lowered the lights. When she turned around, she saw Sweet still standing in the same spot with his shoes still on his feet.

Before she could repeat her request, he said, "Say please."

She took a deep breath. She had to remember that in this environment, she was the teacher. She wouldn't be this short with another student.

"I apologize. Please take off your shoes."

Sweet nodded. "Much better." He sat on the mat and removed his sneakers and set them on the side. "For this one time, I'm in your hands."

Nikla started the music and stood on her mat in front of him. The soothing Native American music filled the room. "I start my class with everyone on the floor on their backs. Please get down on your mat."

Nikla sat on her mat and watched Sweet as he positioned himself on his back. Looking at his long, strong body, her mind went to an image of her riding on top of him, impaling herself on his cock.

Knowing Sweet, he would want to take over. He would put her on her back and pound into her. With him, she probably wouldn't need a vibrator to finish herself off like she did with Justin.

Sweet lifted his head from the mat. "Nikla?"

"Oh, yeah. Relax. Stretch your hands over your head like you're reaching for the back wall, and close your eyes." She reclined back on her mat and did the same thing. "Now breathe in deeply, hold it, and release."

Nikla led him through several floor exercises, starting off easy before getting Sweet to his feet. She had him go into warrior pose. On him, with his feet apart and his long arms up and parallel to the floor, he truly looked like a warrior.

Like any other student, Nikla approached Sweet. She stood behind him. "Hold your arms up higher." She put her hands under his arms.

The muscles she felt opened the waterworks from her vagina. She smelled a woody aroma from him. She took a deep breath.

Her hands coasted down his waist. "Drop deeper into the pose and hold it."

Sweet cleared his throat.

"Please," she added.

"Thank you." Sweet sank deeper into the position.

Nikla gazed down at the sight of his thigh muscles bulging through his pants. What in the world was going on with her? She'd had male students in her class before. She'd positioned their bodies. She'd never had the overwhelming feelings of desires for a student, for a man, like she did with Sweet.

Before she made a fool of herself, she backed away and resumed her spot at the front of the room. "Okay, let's go into downward dog." Nikla watched Sweet go down into the position. Just seeing his ass in the air had her licking her lips. "If the pressure is too much for your wrists, you can go down to your forearms. If it's too much on your back, you can rest on your knees."

"How do I challenge myself?" Sweet asked.

Nikla liked that he didn't take the easy way out of this exercise. "If you can put your heels to the floor, do so. Doing that will stretch out your calves and hamstrings."

She heard Sweet grunt. Nikla tried not to laugh. So much for yoga not being called a workout.

Forty-five minutes later, Nikla had Sweet go into cool-down mode. "I like rubbing oil into my students' temples at the end of the class. May I do that with you?"

With a panting breath, Sweet said, "Yeah. Sure."

She smiled as she retrieved the bottle from her bag. Just like in her other classes, she rubbed the slick oil on her fingers, then approached Sweet.

"I was so wrong about this." Sweet took a deep breath as he kept his eyes closed.

"What? Was this a workout after all?" She rubbed his temples.

When he moaned, she imagined him in bed with her, holding her with those big hands and kissing her with those amazing full lips.

"I'm a man who can admit when I'm wrong."

"Good."

"It just rarely happens." His mouth twitched like he wanted to smile but he didn't.

"I should have known you would say something like that." Thank goodness Sweet kept his eyes closed. He wouldn't have seen Nikla smiling, although he probably heard the lightness in her voice.

"You're pretty amazing."

Nikla stopped the temple massage when Sweet made his statement.

He opened his eyes. "Didn't you just run an hour-long class already?"

She nodded, afraid her vocal cords would betray her.

"And then you did this class. You don't even look winded. And here you are catering to me."

Nikla never thought of herself as catering to anyone when she rubbed oil on them after each class. She just saw it as creating an all-around yoga class experience.

"I do yoga at home so it's nothing for me to do more than one session a day." She stood up and padded over to her bag. "Thanks."

Sweet sat up. "What are you thanking me for?"

"You didn't have to do this. Bobbi never showed up. You could have turned around and gone home. You did a full class, and you didn't take the easy way out. You challenged yourself. I should have had you standing on your head, but I didn't want to hurt you."

He slipped on his shoes. "If I'm not mistaken, it sounds like you're impressed with me, too."

Nikla smirked. "Impressed is a strong word."

"What about in awe?"

She laughed. "You're cute."

Her laughter subsided as she connected her gaze to his.

"The deal is that I do something of yours and you do something of mine." Sweet stood and loomed over her as he rolled up his mat.

Nikla swallowed. "Bobbi's not here." Her voice came out in a whisper. "Doesn't matter. I did a whole class, and she didn't show. The plan is that you all were supposed to come to my candy store afterward."

Nikla exhaled. "Oh, yes. Decadent Treats." Then she thought about the implications of being in a candy store.

Worse than being alone with a sexy man, Nikla feared going to a place with lots of sweets and temptations.

"Maybe another time when Bobbi can be with us." She slipped on her shoes and rolled up her mat.

Sweet shook his head. "A deal is a deal. You don't want to look like a coward, do you?"

Nikla took a deep breath. Before she could answer, the door opened.

"Nikla, you done?" Big Tom, the part-time boxing coach and full-time manager, asked as he bounded into the room. He turned on the overhead light.

In the bright light, Nikla saw Sweet clearly. He carried the rolled yoga mat to her.

"Yes, I'm done." She took the mat.

"Meet me at the store." He walked out of the workout room.

Sweet had her intrigued and excited. She would have to push those feelings aside and only think about business. Then again, being inside of a candy store, she would feel so anxious to think about anything else...she hoped.

Chapter Ten

Sweet tried not to look in his rearview mirror to make sure Nikla followed him, but she seemed reluctant to come to Decadent Treats.

He thought maybe she didn't want to be alone with him. He'd been alone with her in her apartment. Being with him in a business should be easy.

When she repositioned him during the workout, he thought he would come right out of his skin.

If she had touched him at The Dollhouse, he would have given her the speech he'd given to Leaf. Her gentle hands soothed him. He wanted to direct her to caress him in other ways. He had to keep the line drawn. He couldn't mix business and pleasure.

Sweet pulled into the Decadent Treats parking lot and drove around to the back of the building. He waited in his truck a beat before he caught a set of headlights turning into the lot. He breathed a sigh of relief. Nikla had followed him.

He got out of his truck and went to the back door. After unlocking it, he disarmed the alarm then waited for Nikla.

Nikla got out of her car, turned to the car door as though regretting that decision, then walked toward Sweet so slow he thought she would stop at some point and turn back around.

From what he could tell of her, Sweet knew she wouldn't retreat.

She stopped in front of him, keeping her stare into the store.

"Welcome to Decadent Treats." Sweet lifted his hand to usher her inside. "Did you ever think with all your protesting that you would even step foot inside?"

"I haven't walked in there yet." Nikla took a deep breath.

"Take the step."

She glanced up at him. "Are you sure you want me in there? You were pretty adamant each time I handed out my fliers that you didn't want me in front of your store."

"Are you scared?" Sweet had to think about her perspective. He hadn't exactly welcomed her into his space.

"Would you blame me if I was? What if you called ahead to your folks to ambush me?" She stared at him pointedly.

"Not my style."

"You're never late. You don't play games. And you wouldn't set anyone up." Nikla paced in her spot. "If you weren't trying to take away something I want, I would say you're a pretty cool guy."

Nikla's sweet laugh struck him in his heart, more than he thought it would. As he watched her, he got the impression that she did believe everything he'd told her about himself. Knowing that, his skin prickled. When he glanced into his store, another realization hit him. They would be alone.

"I would have to be crazy to do this." Nikla shook her head.

"And I would be crazy to bring you into the place where I make my living. But I'm a man of my word." He moved aside. "I'd like you to come inside."

Nikla swallowed, closed her eyes, then took a big step into the back of the store.

Even watching her take that crucial first step sent a chill over the back of his neck. "See. Nothing bad or scary happened." Sweet closed the door behind her and reactivated the alarm.

"Are other employees here?" She clasped her hands in front of her body and waited for him to move.

"No. They've all gone. It's just me and you." He walked toward the kitchen area.

Once there, he flicked on the light. The place remained spotless from when he'd cleaned it earlier.

"You all make of your candies?" She scanned the kitchen as Sweet pulled down a small pot hanging above the gas stove.

"Not all of them. I wish I had time to do that." He placed the pot on the stove. "I make fudge and chocolates and other treats when I can." Sweet grabbed sugar and other needed ingredients. "Cooking relaxes me. It used to." He glanced up at Nikla. "Did you take up yoga to help with your anxiety?"

Nikla nodded. "My college offered yoga classes in our fitness room. I took a couple of classes and liked them. I found that concentrating on myself and on my breathing helped center me. When I lose that focus, I can get myself wound up."

Sweet didn't want to interrupt her explanation. He liked hearing her talk. Her light voice came across as melodic and soothing.

"You said cooking used to relax you. It doesn't now?" she asked as he set out jars and lids.

He glanced at Nikla. The longer he stared into her eyes, the more he wanted to reveal his truth, the side he couldn't reveal to his own brother.

"Food meant something to me when I was a kid. Mom wasn't a great cook. She tried though. I learned to cook to make what we had taste good. I was obsessed with flavors. After a while, once we started the business, I don't know." He shook his head.

"You're not as hungry?"

Sweet brought his attention to her. "Yeah, something like that."

Nikla nailed his issue clearly.

"Shouldn't you be happy that the thing that keeps my business running is in jeopardy?"

Nikla cocked her head. "I'm really not as evil as you think I am. I think it's terrible that you can't hold onto the thing that you love."

Sweet's heart started pounding hard in his chest. He had to get onto another topic. Right now he started to find Nikla irresistible. "What do you do for fun?"

"Would you believe it if I said I rock climbing?" She smiled.

"Yes, I would." He put out the ingredients needed to make a small batch of caramel.

She smiled at his honesty. "I do it in a controlled environment."

"In a gym?"

Nikla nodded.

"You have the basics of it down. You need to put the practice into action. Go somewhere and actually do some rock climbing." Sweet fired up the heat as he kept his stare on her.

"Maybe one day. No rush to plummet down the side of the mountain." She laughed but Sweet heard the nervousness in it.

"As long as you're with someone trained, you'll be okay." He wanted to reach out and brush a stray curl from her face. Sweet had to keep his hands to himself. At least for now. "Come on. Let's wash our hands before we get cooking."

"We?" Nikla asked as they made their way to the big, industrial-sized sink.

"That was the deal. I do yoga. You make candy." Sweet turned on the water and tested the temperature. Then he pointed out to her where the location of the soap dispenser.

"And you did do yoga." Nikla laughed.

When Sweet looked down at her, she tried covering up her laughter.

"Hey, I did do it." He stared at her. "I wasn't afraid to try new things."

"No, you weren't." She washed her hands along with Sweet.

Her hip brushed against his leg. Instead of pulling away from him right away, she stayed. It hit him in that moment that she didn't move away from him, like when she'd held his hand at the rental office.

Damn Melinda for making him doubt other women, potential submissives.

Sweet couldn't help but notice her delicate fingers, the same fingers she'd used on him in class when she adjusted his body. When he remembered her easy but controlling possession of his body, his cock started throbbing.

He turned off the water in the deep stainless steel sink and handed her some paper towels. As soon as his gaze connected to hers, Nikla smiled. This time her smile erected the hairs over his body.

Sweet had to get away from her and talk about something else before she noticed his inappropriate reaction to her, to her proximity. "Nikla. Unusual name. Where did that come from?"

Nikla tossed her wad of rumpled paper towels in a trashcan in the corner. "It's a combination of my parents' names. My mother's name is Nicole and my father's name is Lawrence. They combined the two and got me." She pointed to herself. "Their only daughter."

Sweet nodded, surprised at the fact that Nikla shared that personal story with him. "And how's your relationship with your parents?"

Nikla cleared her throat. "What are you making?"

The shift in conversation happened in a not so subtle way. He saw her walls going up again. Not content to let her hide, he pressed on with his questioning.

"I'm making caramel." He explained the process and then continued with his questioning. "What's the deal with you and your parents?"

Nikla lowered her gaze. "You're not going to let this drop, are you?"

"That's not how I roll." He shook the pot of sugar over the stove. "Speaking of rolling, you want to get the ingredients in the pot to a boil and continue shaking it to move the sugar around. No spoon. Sometimes you want to agitate things. Other times you don't. You have to let things do what they're supposed to."

Nikla looked into the pot and nodded. "How did you learn how to cook?"

"You're avoiding my question."

"I'll answer your question if you answer mine. I can't be the only one exposed here." When she said "exposed" Nikla hugged her arms around her body.

The position brought her succulent breasts together. Sweet imagined her naked in front of him, on her knees and sliding his hard dick in between her round orbs. When his imagination moved on to her deep throating his cock, he let out a groan that he tried covering with a cough.

Sweet cleared his throat before he answered. "I learned to cook when I was a teenager in school. I think it was my need to control even back then." He would leave out the real reason he started to cook and bake. Sweet had to learn about portion sizes and eating a balanced diet out of a need to take control of his body. "In cooking, you control everything. The temperature, the ingredients. You have the basics down. The recipe." He kept his stare on the gradually changing sugar from granules to liquid. "Then you can make subtle changes. You can add spices."

When Sweet glanced at Nikla, he noticed her wide smile.

"You light up when you talk about cooking. You can tell you really love it." She moved in closer to him.

"I do love it. It's the only thing that makes sense to me." He raised the pot from the flame and moved the sugar around the bottom of the pot. "What I love the most is the transformation, changing something from one thing to something completely different."

This time when Sweet looked at Nikla, he noticed the shocked expression on her face.

"Did you look at my business plan?" she asked.

Sweet shook his head. "No. Why would you ask that?"

"Because that's the name I want to call my business, Transformations by Nikla." She crossed her feet as she stood in front of him and didn't wobble at all. "I enjoy helping people get to their best health. For me, it has nothing to do with being a certain weight or size. It has everything to do with getting to know your body and loving your body."

"Is that why you're so hard on me and my business?"

Nikla's smile disappeared and she dropped her gaze back to the melting sugar.

Sweet recognized that her wall had gone up. He had to keep her talking. "You and your parents."

Nikla released a long breath. "You're not letting that one go."

"Answer."

"My parents divorced as soon as I graduated from high school. I'm the baby. I think they hung on just for me."

Sweet took a step aside and held up the pot off the heat. "Here. Take this and swirl it around in the pot."

Nikla hesitated. She stared at the caramel the same way she looked at the store. He wondered where the confident woman who marched up and down in front of his store had gone.

"It's going to burn if you don't swirl this." Sweet presented her with the pot again.

This time, Nikla took it and made a circular motion over the flaming blue eye.

Sweet noticed her tentative method but at least she tried. "Faster."

When she paused, Sweet took matters into his own hands. He stood behind her and placed his hand over hers. He gripped the handle and moved the pot around.

To keep from touching the stove, and a great way to get her body closer to his, Sweet wrapped his free arm around her and put his hand on her incredibly flat stomach.

Nikla stiffened under his touch at first before she relaxed into him. Her back brushed against his chest. Her ass pushed against the front of his jeans. In response, Sweet bore down on her.

Nikla spoke as a way to break up the tension in the air. "And this is nothing but sugar? No water or anything else in there?"

"That's right. It all melted." Sweet enjoyed feeling her toned arms as she moved the pot under his manipulations. Before his mind continued to wander, he pressed on with his questioning. "Finish telling me about your parents."

Sweet brushed his thumb over her stomach to ease her fears.

"My dad owns his own business. My mom, as soon as the ink dried on her divorce papers, moved back to Maryland to be with her family." Her last statement seemed to hurt her to even say.

Sweet's heart thudded at her admission. "But you're her family."

She snickered. Through her laughter, she sounded like she agreed with what he said and like she'd made that same argument to herself. "She wanted to stay close to her parents and siblings."

"You hated her for that."

Nikla whipped her head around to glare at him. "Why would you say something like that? I don't hate my mother."

"But you didn't appreciate what she did. Instead of saying she wanted to be close to your grandparents, aunts, and uncles, you said she wanted to be close to *her* parents and *her* siblings. You're disassociating yourself from her like she was a stranger."

Nikla dropped her gaze back down to the pot. "She didn't even ask me to go. She just...left."

Sweet watched her. His heart broke for her, for her sadness and disappointment. Instinctually, he held onto her tighter as she continued swirling the hot sugar.

He thought she would have shrugged away from his touch. Nikla held onto his arm that he had around her body.

Her vulnerability struck his heart, a place he'd kept closed off after Melinda had torn it to shreds.

"What about you and your father?" Sweet asked.

Nikla straightened up. "Work in progress."

Sweet nodded. He'd pushed her enough. Despite her wanting his rental property, he didn't want to see her broken.

He peered into the pot. "Okay, we want the caramel dark but not burnt. If you notice it getting too dark for your liking, pull it off the stove eye onto a cool surface and keep moving it around."

Nikla nodded and did as instructed. What a good student. The way she took direction, the way she folded into his arms, she would probably make an exceptional submissive.

Sweet liked the color he saw in the pan. "Excellent."
"I do know how to cook, by the way. I have never made candy." Nikla looked in the pot to observe her creation.

With great reluctance, Sweet released his hold on her. He turned off the flame on the stove and set the pot on an unused eye.

He reached behind himself to the counter and picked up some butter. "Now it's time to drop the butter into the sugar and let it cool it down until we have caramel."

Nikla glanced at him. "And that's it?"

"We'll add one more ingredient after that." He nodded. "Then that's it."

She blinked as though she thought the whole process would be a lot harder.

Now Sweet understood why Masaun liked teaching. Sweet enjoyed seeing that little connection to the lesson he taught. "Why were you afraid to come in here?"

Nikla started to say something but stopped herself. She released a nervous giggle. "The alternative is worse than this."

Sweet rutted his eyebrows. "What do you mean?"

"You proposed two businesses. I wouldn't want to be in your other world with you." She laughed and shook her head.

"What other world?" Sweet knew what she meant but he had to hear her say the words.

Nikla's shoulders dropped as she stared at him. "I Googled you and found out your other life, unless that journalist was a liar."

Sweet regarded her for a moment, wondering how to proceed with her. Honesty had been helping him the entire time. No reason to stop now. After pouring in some heavy whipping cream, he had Nikla stir the concoction together before having her set the light brown liquid to the side.

"The article didn't lie." Sweet leaned against the counter and crossed his arms over his chest. "I am a BDSM Dom when I'm not working."

"Oh." Nikla's bottom lip trembled. "I see. And you do your thing–"

Sweet cut her off. "At a place called The Dollhouse down at the Oceanfront. Have you heard of it?"

She nodded as though afraid to admit out loud that she knew the place.

He pointed to her. "You look scared. Is it because it's unknown to you?"

Nikla shook her head. "It sounds like you hurt people."

Her statement made him bristle. "Far from the truth. I give what my submissive wants. Sometimes what they want is something intense."

Nikla released a nervous snort. "Submissive."

"Or slave."

At that moniker, she glared at him. "It makes you feel like a big man to–"

"To give a woman what she wants? Absolutely." He kept his stare on her, not wanting her to break down, but trying to see if she would challenge him. "But I don't only play at The Dollhouse. And I don't have to use the standard whips and chains that you see." He scanned the kitchen. "I could play with you in here. There are enough implements in here to make a woman submit and bring her to an intense orgasm."

Nikla regarded him for a moment before she burst into laughter. "In a candy store? Yeah, right. I'd like to see that happen."

Sweet shrugged. "Your wish is my command. Stay right here."

He darted into the main candy store and grabbed a small hand basket for his goodies. He loaded some licorice strings, a few large lollipops, a couple of candy rings, a candy necklace, and some jellybeans.

When he returned to the kitchen area, he found Nikla looking like she wanted to head to the door.

"Are you quitting?" He'd worded the question to challenge her.

Nikla turned back to him and took a deep breath. She shook her head. "No."

He smiled. "Good. Take off your clothes and get on the table."

Chapter Eleven

What the hell had Nikla gotten herself into with this situation? Had she actually dared Sweet Hawkes to show her some of his BDSM moves in his candy store? The fact that he came back to her with a basket full of goodies and in a quick amount of time really made her nervous.

Nikla felt the sexual tension between them while she helped make the caramel. Sweet didn't hide his erection when he stood behind her to help her swirl the sugar. It took a lot of strength not to fall to the floor when he wrapped his other arm around her waist.

When he touched her as she talked about her mother, she melted. In her mind, she wished—no, prayed—that he would kiss her neck or the side of her face. With her body pressed against his, she took in his incredibly masculine scent. His essence combined with the smell of the caramel made for a very decadent treat indeed.

Even before meeting Sweet, Nikla had fantasized about having a man taking control in the bedroom. Having the real thing in front of her scared her to death. Nikla didn't think he would hurt her. She would have to admit to herself that she wanted this life, wanted this treatment.

"I don't think this is a good idea." Nikla inched toward the back door.

Sweet set the basket down behind himself. "Why is that? You came in here so you must not be afraid of me."

"It has nothing to do with being afraid of you." Not all of it, she wanted to say.

"You have a great body so you can't be ashamed of that."

Nikla had no words for that compliment. She swallowed. Based on his statement, she took a step toward him.

"Let me show you what I can do." Sweet patted a waist-high butcher block table.

The idea of being on something meant to carve meat on struck her nerves again. "Why do I have to be naked?"

Sweet peered into the basket of goodies. "There are things I have that would only work on bare skin." He went into a drawer and pulled out a long white tablecloth. He draped the table. "Let's take this slowly. Come here."

"What if you have cameras in here and you use the footage to blackmail me against getting that space?" Nikla posed the argument so that she could run through her pros and cons list in her head on why she shouldn't take this crucial step with Sweet.

"For one thing, I told you I don't play games. Second point, I would be in this alleged video footage so I would be implicating myself. Besides, people already know that I'm in the Lifestyle."

"Yeah, but they don't know I'm not."

"Not yet."

With Sweet's two-word reply, he said what Nikla had been thinking. She balled her hands into fists and wondered why she couldn't move from her spot.

"This is crazy." Nikla shook her head.

"It's only crazy if you don't like it and you have me continue. But before you can establish that you don't like it..." Sweet patted his hand on the table again.

Nikla volleyed her stare from the table to Sweet. Her heart raced as she tried making up her mind on what she wanted. Did she want to take this crucial step? Did she want Sweet to be a part of that decision?

Sweet took a deep breath and squared off in front of her. "Take off your shoes and stand in front of the table."

Nikla gazed up at him as though looking at a complete stranger. The tone of his voice before had always commanded her attention. Now she felt powerless to do anything else. Yet her feet still refused to budge.

"Now!" Sweet barked.

Nikla blinked. After a beat, she padded to the table, turned around so that she faced him and slipped her feet out of her flip flops.

Sweet held Nikla around her waist and, in one smooth motion, lifted her in the air and placed her on top of the table. "Lie back and relax."

"Hard to do when I know what's coming." Nikla complied, reclining back and keeping her arms fixed to the sides of her body.

"No talking unless I tell you to do so, understand?"

Sweet took this dominating thing seriously. With each command, though, Nikla felt a tingling throughout her body.

"Okay," she replied.

"No. You will not answer me that way when you speak." Sweet went over to his basket and started pulling out items. "When you address me, you will call me Dom Sweet. When I have mastered your body, you can call me Master Sweet."bAs soon as Nikla jackknifed up at his statement, Sweet quickly added an addendum. "Or you may call me Sir. One of the two. Understand?"

Nikla reclined back. "Yes, Sir."

"BDSM is not all about pain, although there are people within the Lifestyle that enjoy that intense feeling. The Lifestyle is about sensations. Some people like it harder than others. And some people who inflict the discipline like to work on people who enjoy it rougher than some."

"Where do you fit in?" Nikla asked.

Sweet circled the table and stood behind her head. She drummed her fingers against the table until he spoke. When she felt his warm breath over the side of her face, she knew he had knelt down beside her head.

"I enjoy the reaction. When I get the response I seek, no matter how intense, I get a rush."

Nikla swallowed. She stared up to see if Sweet would stand directly over her head. He did for a moment before he moved off to the side of her. Without a word or permission, Sweet started undoing her wraparound sweater.

As an automatic response, she held his hands to stop him. Sweet stared into her eyes. In the silence of the kitchen, only the hum of the enormous refrigerator as the background noise, he shared a whole dialogue with her.

Deep down she knew he wouldn't hurt her. He would push her. Sweet had been pushing her all night, getting her to confess her feelings about her parents. She hadn't shared that information with Deana.

Sweet also shared a side of himself that she suspected he hadn't shown a lot of people. While he cooked, he became vulnerable. He allowed her inside of a world that he felt the most comfortable.

Nikla returned her hands to their position next to her body and allowed him to open her sweater. Then he placed his hand on her chest between her breasts.

"Breathe."

Until he made that command, Nikla hadn't realized that she'd stopped breathing until Sweet made his next move. To prove to him that she had heard him, she took in a deep breath, arching her back in the process, then exhaled.

"Good. Another part of playing is the names." He moved back to her head. "I've asked you to call me Dom Sweet or Sir. Conversely, you get a name, too."

Nikla started to open her mouth to argue to keep her unique name until Sweet cut her off.

"In keeping with the candy theme, I think I'll call you Sugar Baby."

She glared at him. "Why is that?"

Sweet reached for something in the basket he'd brought. "I have a feeling you're going to be very sweet." He removed a large blue cup. "Close your eyes."

Again, she stared at him with suspicion before complying.

"People imagine that to control someone, it takes brute strength and force. Not true."

At that moment, Nikla felt something light on her eyelids. From the sensation she felt under her eyebrows and below her eyes, the item seemed to be circular.

"Keep your eyes closed and keep those chocolate coins on your lids, understand?" Sweet instructed.

Unable to nod or move her head, Nikla smiled before she answered. "Yes, Sir."

It took all her strength for Nikla not to knock the candies from her face. She wanted to watch Sweet, see his every move. Right now, he had her set up to experience something delicious. Her heart started to race just thinking about his next move.

"Normally, I would start with some light sensations like this."

Nikla braced for what Sweet considered as light. It didn't take long for her to feel something tickling the bottoms of her feet. She flinched at first, jiggling the coins on her eyes, then settled into the sensation.

Sweet moved the item from her heel to her sole and over each toe. "How's that feel, Sugar Baby?"

"Mmm, good."

"Now would be a good time to tell you about the safe words."

Nikla's smile slipped down her face. "Safe words?"

"Yes. If I do something you like, you should say 'green.' That tells me I can keep going."

Nikla didn't say anything. She would have thought saying she liked something would have given him the green light to keep going. She had to respect his lifestyle and the rules within it.

Sweet continued. "If you like what I'm doing but it's getting to be intense, I want you to say 'yellow,' understand?"

"Yes, Sir."

Sweet moved the fluffy item up her ankle to her knee where her yoga pants stopped. Then he moved down her other leg. "And if what I'm doing is too much for you to handle, you say 'red' and I'll stop."

"If you hurt me—"

"I won't hurt you."

"—if you do, I can say 'red' and you'll stop."

"Yes."

Nikla relaxed a bit, knowing that she now had an out in case things got out of hand.

She felt Sweet's hand on her bare belly before she felt the soft item he'd been using caressing it.

"What is that?" she finally asked.

"I've given you a lot of leeway just now, but I was very clear when I said you cannot talk unless given permission."

The harshness of his tone grabbed her attention. Nikla had to know.

"Sir, may I speak?" She swallowed as she awaited his answer.

"Speak." Sweet continued feathering the item over her skin.

The tickling sensation almost had her forgetting her question. "What is that? Tell me, please."

"Do you really want to know? Can't you just enjoy the feeling?" He swept the item up her arm, over her chest and down the other arm.

"I want to know in case I want to do this to myself at home."

That got a big laugh out of Sweet. Nikla wished her eyes could have been open for that. Since encountering Sweet, she had yet to see him smile or show happiness of any kind. It made her wonder if his chosen lifestyle made him so surly or if someone had broken his heart.

Sweet ran the item over Nikla's face. "Smell."

Nikla took in a deep breath. She immediately smelled something sweet and sugary yet felt soft. She turned her face slightly to the left and right to experience more of the sensation.

"It's cotton candy."

Nikla smiled. "Wow. I thought it was a feather."

"That's the idea. I can make anything kinky."

And sexy. She imagined him running a fluffy pink ball over her skin. Had she been sweating, the sugar would have melted on her. If it had melted, would Sweet lick it from her body?

She balled her toes, and her belly compressed into a knot. As soon as she felt her clit twitch, she exhaled.

Nikla started to like the mystery as well as the fun of using unconventional items on her. Justin would have never thought outside the box like this.

When Sweet ran the candy over her lips Nikla flinched, nearly knocking the coins from her eyes.

"Don't put the sugar near my mouth. Please." She started to raise her hand, but Sweet arrested the motion and brought her arm back down to her side.

"Why?" he asked.

She still felt his heat next to her body so she knew he hadn't gone anywhere. "I don't eat sugar or anything–"

"Sweet?"

Nikla didn't answer. She balled her hands into fists. "You wouldn't understand."

She felt him hold onto her arm and brush his thumb over her skin. "You don't have to tell me if you don't want to. You asked me not to do it, so I won't."

Nikla breathed a sigh of relief. She started to like this BDSM thing if following and making requests summed up the activities.

"I'd like to see your breasts."

The whispered request in her ear sent a shiver down Nikla's body. One side of her brain screamed for her to let this man see all of her. The other side, the sensible, business-minded side reminded her that this man competed for a coveted spot in downtown Virginia Beach.

Sweet also epitomized the type of man she wanted, needed. Her pussy ached for his cock. Without a second thought, Nikla sat up while keeping her head back to prevent the coins from falling off her eyes.

Suddenly she felt some assistance in removing her sweater. Sweet helped pull one sleeve off, then allowed her to settle before pulling off the other sleeve. He took the garment from her hand. Then she pulled her sports bra over her head with such care and precision that the chocolates covering her eyes never moved. Sweet removed that item from her hand as well as she lowered herself back down to the table.

"Why am I doing this?" She balled her hands into fists. "Tell me why I'm doing this? Please."

Sweet didn't answer verbally. He continued brushing the cotton candy over her skin as though telling her that she removed her clothes because she liked the feeling. Without saying a word, he simplified her reasoning.

Nikla remained still, shocked at her brazen behavior. No way Deana could say she took the safe route with Sweet. He had her topless in the middle of his kitchen and using candies over her body. Her nipples hardened at the thought of what Sweet would do to her.

"Nice," he whispered.

She felt a large hand cupping her breast. Nikla sucked air between her teeth at the connection. With that one touch, Sweet possessed her entire body.

Sweet's large thumb circled her nipple. "Normally I would use a nipple clamp on big, firm nipples like these. Instead, I'll use these."

Nikla wanted to see what Sweet had in his hand. She swallowed hard as she waited for his next step. She'd heard the crackling of a wrapper then a slight pinch to one nipple. The pinching didn't hurt. The pressure remained constant.

After the first one had been affixed to her, Sweet attached a second item to her other breast.

"How do you feel?" he asked her.

"Green." Nikla smiled at her use of the safe word.

"Good."

"What do you have on them?" She fought the urge to reach up and touch the items. She had to trust Sweet.

True to his word, he hadn't hurt her. "Do you remember ring pops, the lollipops on rings?"

Nikla smiled and laughed a little. "Chocolate coins, cotton candy, ring pops. I will never look at candy the same way again."

"And I'm not done yet. But first…"

Nikla heard a pause before he continued speaking.

"Open your mouth."

Hesitating for a moment, Nikla thought of all the items Sweet could have put in her open mouth. Candy? Alcohol? His cock?

At the thought of the last item, she parted her lips and waited. Nikla felt something thin, wooden and hard going across her mouth.

"Bite," Sweet said.

Nikla bit down on something that felt like a stick.

"This wooden spoon should keep you quiet. Try and talk again, and I'll punish you."

Nikla wanted to ask how he would punish her, but with the spoon in place, she could only grunt. She heard him rustling around behind her, probably retrieving something else from his basket of tricks.

"Open your hand." Sweet tapped her left hand.

Considering he'd asked her to open her mouth and he didn't do anything salacious to it, Nikla felt comfortable opening her hand. She splayed her fingers and waited. She felt something hard and round in her palm. Had he given her a croquet ball?

"A Jawbreaker," he said as though she'd asked the question out loud. "If the session gets to be too much, since you can't talk, I want you to drop it to signal me to stop, understand?"

Nikla nodded.

"Has anyone ever told you how beautiful your skin is?" he asked.

Before Nikla could answer, she felt something light touch her shoulder.

Whatever item Sweet had placed there remained, then she felt another item placed a couple of inches below that.

Nikla turned her head in the direction of where Sweet worked.

"Your skin tone reminds me of the caramel we just made. So smooth and rich." Sweet placed what felt like pebbles down one arm then the other, then he put one in her navel. "Don't move. I've placed jellybeans over your body. If you move and knock any of them off, I'll have to punish you."

Sweet made it very clear that he controlled this environment. With his second promise to discipline her, Nikla wondered what he would do. Would this man spank her or whip her like she'd seen in movies?

In her head, Nikla laughed. Whip her? With what? They were in a candy store. So far he'd used nothing but candies on her. He had been true to his word so far. No pain.

"You want to know how I would punish you?" Sweet continued covering her with jellybeans.

Nikla nodded. She bore her teeth down on the spoon as she waited for him to respond.

"I would spank you. Old fashion. Right over the knee."

Nikla smiled as much as she could with the spoon in her mouth, hoping Sweet would soon laugh to show he had been kidding. When he didn't, she stopped smiling.

She started to ball her free hand into a fist again and felt one of the jellybeans by her wrist start to move. She made sure to leave her hands motionless on the table.

Nikla couldn't imagine a rational, grown woman would subject herself to being treated like a child, to have all responsibilities taken away and have her life boiled down to doing what she was told and being a good girl.

As that idea rolled in her head, Nikla's breathing slowed. Her true happiness had been when life had been simple, when someone told her what to do, what to wear, what to eat, how to be.

God, did she really want this life? Could she be subservient? More importantly, could she be happy that way?

Sweet put his hand on the bare skin under Nikla's breasts and above her navel.

She grunted, then nodded.

"Are you trying to talk again?"

She shook her head. If Nikla could have answered with a definitive "No, Sir" she would have.

Nikla felt a slight tug on one of the ring pops. It pulled on her nipple but didn't detach from it. The sensation caused her to arch her back slightly, careful not to jostle the beans or coins.

Funny how these small items now ruled her being right now. Her only job, her only responsibility had been to keep her body still. She had to remain silent. She had to keep her eyes closed. She had to be the guardian of the jellybean soldiers lining her body. The simplicity of that comforted her.

She felt him let go of the ring and heard him moving around the kitchen. She heard what sounded like a jar being placed on the counter. Then she heard something pouring into it. What did Sweet have in mind for her now?

Nikla heard his footfalls come back toward her. She heard a metal-on-metal scraping sound, Sweet blowing on something, then a warm sensation hitting her stomach.

Nikla jerked. She released a scream around the spoon in her mouth while keeping her jaw clenched.

She didn't care if she knocked any of the candies from her body. She hadn't expected to feel something hot and searing touch her skin.

"I can't do wax play on you here," Sweet said as he made a swirly design over her stomach. "This is the closest I can get. This is the caramel you and I created. The color blends so well with your skin."

After she caught her breath, Nikla settled her body onto the table.

The room remained quiet for a moment before Nikla felt Sweet's finger brush above her lips. He slathered caramel around her mouth.

Nikla shook her head, then raised her hand to release the Jawbreaker. She had expected Sweet to arrest her hand to stop her. If he had, the whole idea that she had power to stop this would have been lost.

"I'm not putting the caramel on your lips. Just around them." True to his word, he'd kept the caramel from her mouth.

Nikla smelled the buttery topping and she so wanted to take a swipe of the gooey liquid with her tongue. She swallowed and clamped her mouth shut as much as she could.

"Good, Sugar Baby."

Sweet slowly licked the caramel from her skin, taking long, languid swipes. The sudden connection caused Nikla to draw in a sharp intake of breath. Then she settled into the masterful expression.

His skillful tongue teased her lips with playful flicks in between the long licks. The treatment had her thinking about how he could use that tongue all over her body, over her nipples that now started to feel sore from the consistent pinching, over her stomach, and down to her pussy.

She didn't care if he got caramel in her mouth, a strange reaction considering how diligent she'd been on staying away from foods made with sugar. Sweet had been good about keeping it from her mouth. He'd listened to her. That meant more than anything. As soon as Nikla heard him moan and felt the vibration against her mouth, her juices oozed from the apex of her thighs.

She wanted every part of this man who had given her a brand new appreciation for everything decadent.

Nikla swallowed and tried catching her breath. Since he hadn't told her what the physical equivalent of the command "green" looked like, she nodded to let him know he could continue. To show she wanted more, she held up her hand with the Jawbreaker. She had no plans of letting it go anytime soon.

She felt the warmth of Sweet's body pulling away from her. Then he gripped the sides of her yoga pants. This time she didn't gasp. She didn't seem shocked. She wanted to be completely naked in front of this man, a man who days ago she didn't like. Now she wanted all of him.

"I'll remove your pants." Sweet pulled her pants down her legs.

Without prompting, Nikla lifted her hips to help him remove her thong panties to be completely naked. To be so nude, so exposed, Nikla thought she would have been more self-conscious. She wanted to show Sweet her body. She wanted more from him.

"Spread your legs."

Nikla didn't hesitate. She opened her legs, allowing Sweet to see all of her. She heard some paper tearing and a bit of rattling before she felt Sweet parting her nether lips with his fingers and the sudden introduction of something sprinkled on her vagina that popped in various spots.

"Pop Rocks." Sweet licked up one side of her labia to remove the candy pieces.

Nikla wanted to scream and moan and jerk her body. The feeling of tiny explosions occurring over her pussy made her feel like Sweet had declared war on her sex and only he could defeat the enemy.

Sweet continued licking her, using his skilled tongue in a way that she had imagined. She couldn't tell if he swirled his tongue around her clitoris because a lot of the candy had landed there, or if he wanted to give her extra pleasure. Either way, she didn't want him to stop.

As soon as she started gyrating her hips, Sweet stopped. Sweet torture.

"That was good." Sweet kissed Nikla's inner thigh. "I'll have to remember to do that one again."

Nikla smiled. She wanted to respond to his statement, but couldn't.

She felt Sweet pull back from her. Her body tingled waiting for the next treatment, his next trick.

She felt something light, like a spider web, against her inner ankle that crept up to the apex of her thighs. Sweet brushed something that felt like strings against her skin. Damn, did he really have a whip with him? Had he lied to her when he said he didn't have any true BDSM toys in there?

The item went away and, within seconds, she felt it smacking against her pussy, igniting her clitoris.

Nikla jackknifed up from the table. She heard a couple of the jellybeans roll off her arms and onto the table and floor.

"Drop the Jawbreaker if you want me to stop," Sweet advised.

From the depths of her toes and with every fiber of her being, around the wooden spoon Nikla screamed, "Green!"

In a regular motion and with some intensity, Sweet flicked the item over her aching vagina. Nikla gripped the edge of the table with her free hand. Between the combination of the clamps on her nipples and the swatting motion, Nikla felt something she hadn't felt in a long time from a man, an orgasm.

Her stomach tightened. Her clitoris throbbed. If she didn't have a release soon, Nikla thought her heart would pound outside of her body. Her legs thrashed as she chomped down on the spoon. As she sat her upper body up on her elbows, she leaned her head back and took the treatment.

"Remember the rubber band on your wrist?" Sweet asked.

Nikla nodded. The chocolate coins rolled off her face, but she still kept her eyes closed.

"Concentrate on the sensation. Think about the connection to your pussy. That's all you need to think about."

Nikla balled her toes as she concentrated on every sensation she could feel, from the few remaining jellybeans on her arms, to the smoldering heat from the caramel on her body, to the sweet sting of this whip or flogger Sweet wielded. Nikla thought of nothing else.

Nikla screamed as she came harder than she'd ever felt before. She couldn't remember the last time she had an orgasm without the assistance of her trusty vibrator or the fact that she had no penetration at all. Sweet had managed to lower her resistance enough to infiltrate her mind, body, and soul. She couldn't get enough of this treatment, of this man.

The stinging hits to her pussy stopped.

"Open your mouth."

Nikla felt a slight tugging on the spoon. She obliged his request and heard it land on the counter by the sink.

"Open your eyes. Look at me," Sweet demanded.

With her eyes opened, Nikla struggled to regain focus as she sought out Sweet. She ignored the soreness around the corners of her mouth where the spoon had been. She kept her stare on his dark green eyes. She licked her lips and found no trace of the caramel. As she peered down, she saw he held a thin dowel with white, pink, and purple columns of rock candy at the tip, and taped around that tip had been red, thin, long licorice strings.

Yes, Nikla would never look at candy the same way again. For that matter, she would never look at Sweet Hawkes in the same way again. From the way he stared at her, he looked as though he wanted to do more than just show what he could do with some licorice and lollipops.

Chapter Twelve

While panting like a beast, Sweet picked Nikla up in his arms and carried her to another room. From a quick scan, it looked like an office. He placed her on a couch that sat next to a desk. Then Sweet turned to the desk and searched through the top drawers.

Nikla's body tingled as she watched him. To keep from touching her now sensitive flesh, she gripped the couch. From the little bit that Sweet had done to her, he made her body feel more alive that she'd ever felt, even after doing yoga or Pilates. Nikla wanted more, craved more.

"Yes!" Sweet turned with a string of condoms in his hand.

Yes, indeed. As he made his way toward Nikla, he removed his t-shirt with one hand. His muscled chest with its light dusting of sandy hair begged to be touched, licked, and teased.

Standing in front of her, she started to undo his workout pants after pulling off the toy nipple clamps. She threw the plastic rings to the floor, careless of where they landed.

Sweet pushed down his pants and boxers, kicked off his shoes, and slid on the condom. With his cock in her face, she got to see his full length jutting from a tuft of light brown hair. It sat up long and strong with enough width that she knew would bring her to the pinnacle of ecstasy.

Sweet didn't take her on the couch. Instead, Sweet lifted her so that her legs wrapped around his body. Then he impaled her on his cock.

The sensation of the penetration rendered her breathless for a moment. He plunged himself so deep in her that her body stiffened from the intrusion.

"Jesus H., you're tight!" Sweet braced her back against the closest wall and thrust deep in her.

Nikla gripped his shoulders, holding onto him like she'd imagined, like she wanted. Her coiled legs around his body tightened. The caramel that covered her stomach glued their bodies together. The way he made her feel no way did she want to separate from him. Not now.

In the semi-lit office, she found his lips and devoured his mouth with a hungry kiss as he kept his thrusts even, steady, and deep.

Sweet broke from the kiss long enough to say, "Don't come."

Nikla blinked. "What?"

"Don't come until I tell you. If you do, I'll discipline you."

Sweet cupped her ass in his strong hands as she clawed his back. The length of his impressive erection stroked her inner walls and hit her sweet spot.

Although she'd never tried not climaxing before during sex, Nikla chewed on her lower lip and embedded her fingernails into his hard skin to stave off the impending orgasm.

Her body trembled. Nikla dragged her tongue over his shoulder, tasting his salty flesh. She managed to meet him stroke for stroke by undulating her hips. She'd never experienced a connection like this during sex. Ever. His carnal need matched her own.

Nikla's slick inner walls tightened around Sweet's shaft. She held him closer. Her abdomen compressed like she'd done ten thousand crunches. She could deny herself no longer.

"Feel so good." Tears stung Nikla's eyes. "Fuck it! Spank my ass. I can't! I can't! Fuck! Fuck! Fuck!"

Nikla's legs and arms constricted around Sweet's body. She released a long, low moan that turned into a scream.

"Did you just–"

Hungrily, she kissed his mouth, the side of his face, his neck, wherever she could reach. "Don't stop. Please. Let me come again."

Sweet pulled out of her long enough to help her gain her footing on floor, turned her around, and had her place her hands on the wall. "Bend over."

Just as she did so, he held onto her hip and slid the length of himself into her eager pussy.

"Yes!" Nikla brought one foot up from the floor as she clawed the wall.

After a couple of thrusts, Sweet delivered on his promise. Nikla felt a pop on her ass. She looked over her shoulder expecting to see Sweet's hand in the air. She did see that. Then she saw he had one of those large red lollipops in his hand, paddling her with it.

Nikla smiled and faced the wall. She arched her back more to curve her ass in the air for him. When the sting subsided, she wanted another hit, another way to feel truly possessed by Sweet.

"You dropped the coins from your eyes." Sweet paddled her again in a new spot.

"Yes, Sir."

"You dropped the jellybeans." He surprised her by switching sides and smacking the candy against her other cheek.

"Yes, Sir," Nikla said a little louder this time.

"And you came not once but twice."

Nikla smiled. "Hell, yes!"

"You like being disobedient?"

"No. Teach me." Nikla hated to admit her friend had been right about out-of-the-box sex, but she had a point.

She never thought she would have had sex with Sweet Hawkes, a BDSM Dominant and the co-owner of a business that had had a hand in slowly drawing business from her father's store. Nikla didn't know which concept made her more nervous.

She didn't want to think about that right now. For once, Nikla liked being selfish.

"Green!"

"What do you need?" he asked in a harried breath.

"You." She turned her head to view him. "All of you."

Sweet gripped her hair. She felt him removing her ponytail holder to allow her hair to move freely over her head before he fisted her hair and pumped harder and faster into her channel.

"Christ. Not supposed to happen," Sweet said between gritted teeth.

Nikla felt his legs shaking. The hold he had on her hair tightened. He pulled her head back enough to kiss her neck and lick up to her ear. He used his other hand to press against her stomach.

Some caramel remained on her skin as he traveled his hand down her body to her pussy. He slid her clit between his fingers, rubbing it until she couldn't help but come again. Sweat covered her body as she screamed.

"Oh, my God!" Nikla's legs buckled from under her body.

Sweet caught her and managed to pull out of her and lift her in his arms. This time he laid her on the couch and covered her body with his. He spread her legs open and eased himself in her until down to the hilt. He held himself there as he stared into her eyes.

"Mine." Sweet planted kisses over her face, nose, chin, and eyes.

The almost delicate treatment seemed contrary to the man who had whipped and spanked her. Nikla didn't question it. She wrapped her legs around his waist and reveled in him.

Sweet cupped her breast. He lowered his head and licked her nipple. His skilled tongue made her body jerk with each pass, like an electric current existed on the tip of his tongue.

She shouldn't have wanted this, wanted Sweet. After almost a year of mediocre sex, Nikla earned the right to have an orgasm or two from a really hot guy.

Nikla arched her back. She ran her fingers through his thick hair, liking the way his soft hair tickled the pads of her fingers.

Before moving over to her other breast, he said again, "Mine." Sweet licked her other nipple, sucking it into his mouth and grazing the hardened pebble with his teeth.

Nikla gripped the back of his head and gyrated her hips in concert with his thrusts. Their bodies moved as a unit, as though they had done this before with each other.

Sweet brought his face up and reconnected his stare to hers. "Mine." His thrusting became faster. "Mine." He gripped the arm rest behind Nikla's head. "Mine."

Nikla nodded, unable to speak, unable to verbally agree with him.

Sweet's body froze as he drove in deep. "Mine!"

He collapsed his body on top of hers. The only thing Nikla could think of to say was, "Yes."

Sweet brought his face up and looked more serious than she'd ever seen him. In an unexpected move, he cupped her chin and stared at her as though studying her face. Or maybe he couldn't believe what they had done and he wanted to validate her authenticity. Nikla thought about running her own test to see if Sweet had been real.

When he pulled out of her, a chill covered her body. She drew her knees up as she sat up on the couch. She watched Sweet stumble to his feet and move back against the wall away from her.

Once he regained his bearings, he proclaimed, "You're going to learn about the Lifestyle from me."

Sweet's declaration made Nikla feel like she had no choice, no voice. A tickling sensation filled her belly as she thought about the ramifications of accepting his twisted offer. Hell, she had told Deana she wanted to learn something new, to get an education. Learning about BDSM could be it. She could no longer deny after this short session that she wanted more, wanted more from Sweet, wanted to see how far she could push herself.

Nikla stood, but she kept her place by the couch. "You opened a whole new world to me. I don't think I want to stop the education."

Sweet stared at her. He crossed his arms over his chest. Even naked, he looked powerful. "You understand that you'll be disciplined using real toys and not just candy? Real whips. Real canes. Real floggers." Sweet peered down at Nikla's breasts. "Real nipple clamps."

The idea of being in an authentic dungeon made Nikla wring her hands together and fidget in her spot. When she drew in her lower lip into her mouth, Sweet approached her and pulled it back out.

He moved his head in close to her like he wanted to kiss her, but he pulled back. "Come to The Dollhouse with me."

Nikla shifted in her spot. "I'm scared."

He shook his head. "Then you haven't been listening to what I've said. BDSM play is what you want it to be. All you have to do is concentrate on me and concentrate on yourself. You have the basics down. You need to put it into real practice. As long as you're with someone trained, you'll be okay."

Nikla recognized that he'd used that same argument when he talked to her about rock climbing. If she could do that, surely she could do this, right?

Nikla blinked. In her desire to serve her man, she brushed his hair from his face.

Sweet flinched back from her as though afraid of her touch. "If I touch you or if you touch me again, I'll want to fuck you. BDSM is not all about sex."

Sweet's abrasive delivery only made her want him more. The fact that she could cripple the man with her touch made her feel pretty powerful.

"You say that like it's a bad thing."

"If you want to train as a submissive, I mean really get into the Lifestyle, I can help you with that. But the fact that you're competing against me on a spot I want, and you're protesting my establishment, anything else we would do wouldn't work."

"I get that." Nikla put her hands to her hips. "It's just..." She trailed off, unable to find the words on how she felt.

Sweet regarded her for a moment before he pointed to something behind her. "Bathroom is right there."

As she headed to the bathroom, she thought about her challenges. How would she explain this new relationship to her father? Did she really want to be a submissive? How was she going to get the caramel off her body?

****

No matter how he justified it in his mind, Sweet couldn't excuse what he'd done. As a co-owner of Decadent Treats, he shouldn't have had sex with the woman who had been protesting his establishment for months. As a trained Dominant, he knew better than to have sex with a submissive in training.

As soon as Nikla made herself open and available to both cooking with him and for the play, he saw her on a whole different level. She became the woman he truly wanted. He couldn't have her.

With his mind warring with his senses, Sweet paced in the office area, giving Nikla time in the bathroom. He needed the time to think.

He wanted so much to trust her, but he couldn't. Not yet. At this point, he didn't know if he would ever be able to trust her. One thing he knew for sure. He hadn't lied when he said he would want her again if either he touched her or if she put her hand on him.

Thinking about her long, slender fingers had his cock throbbing again. Sweet padded to the bathroom. Even through the closed door, he heard Nikla starting the shower.

Sweet opened the door. Through the frosted shower stall glass door, Sweet admired the outline of her luscious body. Her curves drew him. Yes, he definitely had to be careful around her.

He opened the door. Nikla didn't flinch. She turned her face up under the shower spray and rubbed her hands over her stomach.

Nikla turned and glared at him. "I don't do this kind of thing, you know. I don't sleep with guys I just met." She covered her eyes and shook her head. "I can't believe I did this."

Not content to let her shoulder the full burden, Sweet joined her into the stall. "I don't do this, either. My last relationship was a couple of years ago."

Sweet came up behind her and wrapped his arms around her slender waist. Nikla paused for a moment before she continued showering.

"Sounds like we're both pretty raw from our past relationships." Nikla touched his forearm as he held her.

Sweet shouldn't have touched her. As soon as he saw her wet skin, he couldn't resist her.

"We'll keep it kinky."

Nikla shook her head and turned to Sweet. "What?"

"We'll keep it to playing and nothing else." Sweet turned Nikla around so that she could look directly at him. "We agree to no more sex, especially since I'm going to be training you."

That would be the most difficult relationship he could ever have with a woman. Now that Sweet had had sex with her, he wanted more. Resisting her would be detrimental to his body and soul.

"You're introducing me to this lifestyle of yours. I can't say that I would only want to play, as you call it. I do know that whatever it is that I do in this arrangement, I only trust you to do it with."

With that confession, Sweet almost broke a smile.

"You're probably wondering about my vibrator in my nightstand." Nikla's tanned skin tone carried a rosy color on her cheeks. "My ex-boyfriend you heard me talking about, whenever we would have sex, he would always come before me. He wouldn't worry about getting me there. Wait. That's not exactly true. He would hand me my vibrator so that I could finish myself." Nikla smoothed her wet hair from her face. "When you said for me not to come, I couldn't do that." She released an uncomfortable laugh. "Do you know how long it's been since I had an orgasm from a man being inside me? When I felt it coming on, there was no way I was going to let that go."

Sweet ground his teeth after hearing her story. What asshole didn't want to live or die to see this woman have an orgasm? Sweet would never forget her gorgeous face when he'd made her climax. Nikla carried a pure almost angelic expression. She kept her eyes closed and her mouth open like a baby bird looking for sustenance. Sweet wanted to feed her need.

"If I tell you to not come, it's because when it's time to come, it'll be so intense." He told the truth, but knowing what her ex had put her through, Sweet wondered if he should push her that way again.

"I'm giving you my history so you'll know how to come at me in the future."

Sweet didn't think about the ramifications of infusing himself into Nikla's life. He knew that now that she'd opened up about her life that he couldn't let her go.

"Might as well start now." He picked up the container of body wash and handed it to her. "I need for you to wash me, Sugar Baby."

Nikla looked at the bottle before taking it from his hand. "Yes, Sir." She poured a dollop in her hand, got it a bit wet, then slathered the white soft soap over his chest.

Her velvety but skilled hands felt like heaven on his flesh. As she rubbed him down, coasting her hands over his shoulders and moving down his arms, Nikla maintained eye contact with him.

Sweet could have drowned in her brown eyes.

Nikla slid her hands down to his hips, then brought them forward to his dick. One hand wrapped around the base of his cock. She used her other hand to cradle his balls. As she drew her hand up on his shaft, her other hand massaged his sac.

Blood pulsed into his growing erection. Nikla awakened all of his senses. Her touch brought his body back to life. Her stare made him feel like only the two of them existed in the world. She smelled like a meadow full of exotic flowers. His mouth watered to taste her.

"I'm breaking the scene."

"What?" Nikla asked.

Sweet brought his head down and captured her mouth in his. He slid his tongue into her mouth. Nikla touched her tongue against his before sucking the tip. Damn, he hated himself for being so weak.

To satisfy his need to touch her, Sweet massaged her breasts. Nikla broke from the kiss to lean her head back and release a loud cry. She tightened her grip on his dick and stroked him faster and faster. Her other hand massaged his steadily tightening balls.

If she continued, Sweet would come all over her. After what she shared about her last boyfriend, Sweet wouldn't be content to receive all of the pleasure.

He held onto her wrist to stop her.

"What are you doing?" Nikla licked her lips.

"I need to–"

She cut him off. "I need to satisfy my Dom Sweet." She smiled as she lowered herself to her knees.

"How do you know that I want this?" Sweet stared into her eyes as she held his now erect dick.

Before she answered, she licked the underside of his penis, from his balls to the tip. Sweet sucked air between his gritted teeth.

"If you don't want me to do this, tell me to stop."

Damn, she was clever.

Nikla covered the tip with her mouth and pressed her tongue against it. Her warm mouth couldn't compare to her tight, hot pussy. The things she did with her tongue had him reeling. She lowered her mouth down to the base and held him there.

"Yes!" Sweet put his hand to the back of her head.

Her wet hair formed a slippery web over his fingers. Nikla gripped his thighs and let her mouth do all the work, moving her head back and forth over his dick. She moaned. The vibration shook his body from his wet hair down to his feet.

Sweet couldn't help but gyrate his hips, fucking her hot mouth as he fisted her hair. As soon as he clutched her hair, Nikla moaned again.

"My Sugar Baby."

Nikla continued licking him and sucking him. She pulled her mouth back to the tip, held him there, then dropped back down to the base.

Sweet couldn't take this wonderful torture for much longer. He didn't care that the water had turned cold. He could endure that and more for more of Nikla's oral treatment.

Sweet's body shook and he felt his balls tighten just as he came in her mouth. He held his breath as his full essence emptied and she devoured every drop.

Sated, he fell back against the shower stall wall. Nikla rose to her feet. Before she could do anything else, he pulled her into his arms and held her so tightly, he thought he would squeeze the air out of her.

"Nikla."

She peered up at him. "Not Sugar Baby?"

Sweet gazed down at her. "Are you still going to protest in front of the store?"

Nikla regarded him with seriousness before she nodded.

"Then we can't keep doing this." Sweet waved his hand between their two bodies. "However this ends, we're only going to disappoint ourselves."

****

After a real shower, and thanks to a brand new toothbrush Sweet had given her, Nikla cleaned up and got dressed. It still seemed so surreal that the same business she wanted to see shut down gave her some fond memories.

Sweet's dose of reality hit her harder than she thought. She had the same argument running through her head as well about them continuing to have a sexual relationship. Not willing to cut herself off cold turkey, and curious about his chosen lifestyle, she agreed to continue learning to be a submissive. She hoped she hadn't made a huge mistake.

When she reemerged from the bathroom, she didn't see Sweet in the office. She went into the kitchen area and found him in only his pants. Facing away from her, Nikla saw the claw marks across his back that she'd inflicted on him. Good. She wanted a reminder on him of what he would be missing.

Nikla touched his skin. "I left my mark on you."

When Sweet turned around, he still carried a serious expression on his face although his eyes seemed softer when he looked at her. In his hand, he held a jar filled with the caramel they'd made.

"Here." He held up the jar to her.

Nikla didn't want to turn him down, but she shook her head. "I can't take that."

He turned the jar around to show off a special label that he'd attached. On it, it read "Sugar Baby's Topping."

Nikla laughed. "Cute. I still can't take this."

"I want you to keep this." He placed the jar in her hands. "Always remember what we did."

"Why not keep this at your place?"

Sweet's mouth hung open. He waited a beat before he answered. "I'd rather you keep it. I know how to make this again."

His answer sounded good, if not guarded. A tickle crept up the back of her neck when she suspected that he hid something from her. Maybe he had a wife in his place. Could he be just like Justin?

Before Nikla could ponder other possibilities, her cell phone rang. "One second." She reached into her purse and pulled out her phone. The number didn't look familiar, but she answered it anyway. "Hello?"

"Ms. Dearwood? It's Bobbi."

Nikla glanced up at Sweet. As she stared at him, she said, "Hi, Bobbi."

Sweet blinked and crossed his arms as he stared at her.

"I'm so sorry for missing our appointment. I hope I didn't ruin your evening plans." Bobbi sounded strong and lively considering she had stood up Nikla and Sweet.

"I did miss you this evening, but I managed to fill in my time."

When she said that, Sweet leaned against the counter.

"Unfortunately, I won't be able to reschedule. I'll be able to give you an answer about the unit after Halloween." Bobbi asked.

"After Halloween? That's a month away." Nikla watched Sweet's expression change to confusion as she spoke to the elderly owner.

"If my schedule is not convenient for you, you're more than welcome to look for other locations. I will be tied up through October." Bobbi released a sigh.

Nikla glanced at Sweet and wanted to agree with Bobbi on being tied up. She dropped her gaze to the floor.

"I don't want to make any commitments until I return. But I have your proposal. I will review it carefully. My office will contact you again in a couple of weeks to see if you're still interested."

"Yes, Bobbi. That would be fine. Feel free to call me anytime if anything changes." Nikla tried to suppress her anger until she could disconnect the call. With the call ended, she turned to Sweet. "Bobbi is going to leave us on the hook. She'll be tied up for a month."

"Then the two of you will have something in common." Sweet started to approach her just as his cell phone rang.

"Bet you it's Bobbi." Nikla beamed.

Sweet answered phone. "Yes?" He looked at Nikla. "Hi, Bobbi."

Nikla aimed to distract the hell out of Sweet. As he spoke to Bobbi, getting the bad news himself, Nikla did a little dance in front of him. To entice him more, she teased him by pretending to pull down her pants, tugging on one side then the other.

When Sweet seemed to not break as he continued talking, Nikla upped the stakes. She pulled her pants down and bent over in front of him.

"Look forward to seeing you again, Bobbi." Sweet ended the call and tossed his phone to the side as he went after Nikla.

Before she could right herself, he grabbed her and pulled her back against himself. Through his thin pants, she felt his hardness.

"You will learn very quickly never to tease a Dom." Sweet gave her a rough kiss as he backed her against the same butcher block center island table, the same one he disciplined her on using only candies.

"What happened to us not having sex anymore?" Her body begged for Nikla to shut the hell up.

"One last time." Sweet reached into his pants pocket and pulled out a string of condoms. "I had a feeling I would be able to use this before you left."

He pulled down her pants and turned her around. Nikla braced her hands on the table as she felt Sweet pulling down his pants. She heard the sound of him ripping open the wrapper.

Nikla managed to remove one foot out of her yoga pants to give her more freedom. Sweet placed his hand on the small of her back. She felt him sliding the tip of his cock up and down between the folds of her nether lips.

"You are so sexy." With that declaration, Sweet eased himself inside of her pussy and held himself there.

His shaft filled her completely. Nikla pushed her ass back against him to get him in deeper. The pounding of her heart sounded in her head, but she heard Sweet's panting breath.

He kept his thrusts slow and even. He controlled her body, her every emotion. Nikla loved the spontaneity. Damn Deana.

In keeping with the surprises, Sweet pulled out of her, turned Nikla around, picked her up, and placed her on top of the table. Grabbing her legs, he pulled her forward. When he entered her again, Nikla had to grab his broad shoulders.

Sweet grabbed her top and pulled it up above her breasts. As he cupped one, his mouth latched onto the other. His skilled tongue circled her nipple, getting it hard enough to be both painful and pleasurable.

Nikla wrapped her legs around Sweet's body. When her pants dangled from one ankle, she felt silly that she hadn't removed them. She had no idea that Sweet would take her like he did, especially since he seemed dead set against touching her at all except to discipline her.

"Don't come." Sweet stared into her eyes, challenging her.

Nikla felt her vaginal walls closing in around his thick cock. Sweet must have felt it, too. He slowed his thrusts and kept his stare on her.

"Trust me." Sweet stroked the side of her face and placed a kiss on her lips.

Nikla wanted to trust him. Throughout the night, he'd been a man of his word. He hadn't hurt her. He did teach her how to cook at least one thing. He also gave her the best pleasure she'd had in a long, long time.

The annoying voice in the back of her head questioned why Sweet hadn't revealed his real name to her. When a man fucked this well, did she really need to know?

Yes.

Nikla rotated her hips. The motion felt too good to her. Sweet hit spots inside of her that she'd never hit with her vibrator.

As soon as Nikla felt Sweet shaking, she knew he couldn't hold out for much longer. She brought one hand down and squeezed one of Sweet's hard nipples. He groaned and gripped her ass.

"Now! Now!" Sweet screamed.

Nikla released her pent-up feelings and with it, an intense orgasm that made her legs tremble.

As the two of them tried to regain their breaths, Sweet broke the ice.

"I want you tomorrow night." Without disengaging from her, he kissed the side of her face. "I'll pick you up from your apartment."

"Really? I don't get a say so in that?" Although Nikla wanted to sound like she hated him for taking over her life, she actually loved it.

Sweet shook his head. "If you want this, you need to give me control. I'm going to tell you what I want you to wear."

Nikla felt her heart starting to pound. She took a deep breath.

Sweet must have recognized her uneasiness. "Breathe." He held onto her wrist and pressed his sizable thumb against her inner wrist. "Trust me. I will take care of you."

The concentrated feeling allowed her to regain control of her breathing and anxiety.

Nikla nodded. "I would probably feel more comfortable if I knew your real name."

Sweet pulled out of her and pulled up his pants. "You know my name. It's Sweet."

"Right." Nikla jumped down from the table and got dressed. She grabbed her jar of caramel. "Thanks for the gift I can't use."

"I guess you're willing to wait to see if Bobbi will allow you to have the other unit, right?" Sweet glared at her.

"And you're still going for both suites, too, right?" She clutched the jar. Right now the jar felt warmer than Sweet. "You thought I would give up my dreams for a man who won't give me his real name?" Nikla shook her head. "I'll see you tomorrow night, Sweet."

"Good night, Sugar Baby."

With her newly anointed scene name, Nikla now wondered who the hell she was. How could she explain this life to her friends and family? How could she tell her father that not only had she slept with the enemy, she would be following his every word?

Chapter Thirteen

Sweet bounded down from his apartment and strolled into the Decadent Treats store with only Nikla on his mind. Although he hadn't expected to have sex with Nikla, he knew he couldn't allow that to happen again. As a Dom, he had to keep in control. With Nikla, he only felt out of control.

Before he headed to the kitchen, he went to the office. Sweet had cleaned up the kitchen before he retreated to his apartment after Nikla went home. He hadn't expected to see Masaun in the office so early.

"Morning." Sweet looked through some mail piled in the inbox on the desk as he scanned the floor. He thought he had picked everything up, including his discarded condom wrappers.

Knowing Masaun, he could find one small piece of evidence that proved what Sweet had done in their office.

"Did you forget to tell me something?" Masaun asked as he sat behind the desk.

Sweet cut a glance at him but continued looking at the mail. He wondered for a moment if Masaun had found out about his side deal to acquire the two suites in downtown Virginia Beach. A tickle crawled over his belly as he thought about his arguments for what he wanted to do.

"Hanson requested to get off early on Halloween." Sweet shrugged.

"I knew about that. Anything else I might have missed?"

Sweet didn't like Masaun's fishing expedition. "Nope." He headed to the kitchen to start on some fudge.

"Okay. Hey, you're welcome."

Sweet stopped at the doorway and turned around. He felt his eyebrows draw together. "What am I supposed to be thanking you for?"

Masaun opened his desk drawer and pulled out two unopened condoms. "Supplying you with protection when you were in the office fucking your brains out last night." He threw the condoms at Sweet, who caught them in midair.

"Don't you dare come off as innocent." Sweet closed the door just in case Connie or Hanson showed up early. Then he shoved the condoms in his pocket. "You're the one who put them in the drawer in the first place. You were going to fuck Kindle in here had I not caught you."

"I didn't. I only had the condoms in the desk because they happened to be in my pocket. Kindle and I had gone to a party, and there were bowls of them all around. Coincidentally, she said that we should grab some for you. She put some in my pocket. I was emptying it out and put them there."

"Yeah, because your car is so far away. Oh, wait. They were for me, right? Damn. If you only knew where I lived. You are so full of shit." Sweet thought about what Masaun had said. "How did you know I had someone in here? I cleaned up. Do you count your condoms or something?"

Masaun cocked his head. "Don't be silly. I forgot some paperwork here last night. I showed up and saw you in the office with a woman. Against the wall. Nice touch."

Good. Masaun hadn't seen Sweet with Nikla on his desk or, especially, on the couch, the shower or in the kitchen. Sweet hadn't even heard the door opening or the alarm being disabled. He had used every bit of his will and concentration on Nikla and her satisfaction.

He swallowed, waiting to see if Masaun knew that he'd been with the lone protester.

"I am at least happy to see you getting over Melinda. Is this the woman you said you just met?"

Sweet nodded.

"You know I get that when you get the urge, you have to act on it." Masaun stood. "What I don't get is why you didn't take her to your place. It's not like you had far to go."

Masaun could never understand Sweet's need to keep his sanctuary his own. Opening up his home would be like opening up his soul. Sweet could do a lot of things. Being that vulnerable couldn't be one of them.

"Like you said, the need hit, and we had to act on it here. It won't happen again." Sweet started to leave again when Masaun's voice stopped him.

"You're not going to tell me about this mystery woman? Is she vanilla or is she interested in–"

Sweet cut off his brother. "I don't know. Too new to tell. Probably a one-night stand type of thing."

Masaun regarded Sweet for a while before he spoke. Sweet knew his brother knew he hadn't told the full truth. Had he been honest with him and himself, he would have confessed that, like with Melinda, he would want to take this relationship to both a romantic and kinky level.

"Okay. Be safe. I know the beating you took after your last one."

Masaun walked over to Sweet. He patted him on his chest. "Protect that and you'll be okay."

Easier said than done. Sweet made a crucial misstep by having sex with Nikla, not once but twice. Then that incredible treatment in the shower where she gave him the best blow job he'd ever gotten from any woman, or any submissive or slave for that matter. He couldn't get her out of his head.

Thinking about it now started to make his dick hard. A part of himself wanted to jump into his truck and drive over to her apartment to take her again. If he couldn't find her there, he would go to where she worked. Maybe get her in a locker room. His mouth watered just thinking about tasting her, using some of his caramel on that cleanly-shaven pussy of hers and devouring her until she came over and over and over again.

"Morning, boss." Connie barreled through the hallway.

"Morning. Be right back." Sweet had to take care of some business first before he could be any good for the day.

****

At the end of her second class of the day, Nikla still felt wound up. Sweet had given her a lot to chew on since last night. First the incredible sex that he didn't want to have happen again...even though she could tell that he did. Throw on top of that the idea of starting this lifestyle that she'd fantasized about but never thought in her wildest dreams that she would do.

Maybe a good, long swim in the recreation center pool would help ease her sexual tensions. As Nikla headed to her work locker to get her swimsuit, her phone rang.

Nikla recognized the number being from the Zuberi office. "Bobbi." Nikla drew up a smile. "I'm surprised to hear back from you so soon."

Nikla heard Bobbi giggling a little. "I wanted a quick word with you before I go. I suspected something about you and just wanted something cleared up."

Nikla felt a tickle creep up the back of her neck. "Suspected something about me? Did you get something from a background check on me?"

Bobbi laughed. "No, dear. Nothing like that. I wonder if owning and running a business is really something you want or are you just trying to prove something to someone."

Nikla gritted her teeth and counted to ten before answering. "With every fiber of my being, I truly want to have my own business. It's been a dream of mine for years." She hoped her conviction came through on the call. Then a little niggling of doubt existed in the back of her head. "Why would you ask me that?"

"Maybe I'm making that assumption in comparison to Mr. Hawkes. He showed a lot more passion for his businesses." Bobbi's conviction in her voice worried Nikla.

She almost wondered if the owner had her mind made up already, and she needed Nikla to convince her otherwise.

"I think because he's already a business owner that he's used to getting his way." Nikla pressed her phone to her ear using her shoulder as she put away the rolled mats into a supply closet. "Rest assured, Mrs. Zuberi, I want this more than you know."

Nikla didn't mean to sound so heavy handed with the pressure for Bobbi to side with her. She wanted the woman to know what acquiring this space meant for her.

"Message received." The lightness in Bobbi's voice came through on the phone. "I am still considering your proposal. I hope I haven't worried you about that."

Nikla blew out her breath.

"So did he keep his word?" Bobbi asked. "Did he teach you how to make candy?"

"Caramel."

"What?"

"We made caramel." Nikla strolled to the door. With another class about to start there soon, she would have to leave the space.

"Good. I'm proud of you. Most competitors wouldn't bother checking out one another's businesses. I'm assuming he showed up for the yoga class, right?"

Nikla smiled as she leaned on the wall next to the door. Remembering Sweet in a warrior pose had her nipples hardening harder than he'd gotten them last night. "Yes, he did a yoga class with me last night."

"It's a shame he's not willing to work with you so that you can have one spot and he get the other. I think the two of you together would be great. The two businesses I mean." Bobbi made an audible tsking sound over the phone. "I'm sure you are wonderful at what you do. I have no doubt that you can run a profitable business and have it for years and years and years."

"Does that mean you're letting me have the spot?" Nikla didn't want to sound too excited even though her heart pounded hard in her chest and she felt sweat rolling down between her shoulder blades.

"I still have to check out what Mr. Hawkes has to offer. I want to be fair. Like I mentioned in the call last night, you don't have to wait for me. There are other spots out there if you want to keep shopping around." Bobbi chuckled. "I have a feeling, though, that you'll wait. You're very compliant that way."

"You mean stubborn. Headstrong."

"Nope. I meant what I said. Goodbye, dear." Bobbi disconnected the call.

Although Nikla could have taken Bobbi's advice and checked out other spots, the woman knew she wouldn't. Why? What did she mean by being compliant? Had Sweet said something to her after they talked last night?

Nikla would find out soon enough tonight.

Chapter Fourteen

Sweet knocked on Nikla's apartment door for the second time. If he had to do it again, he would be pounding on it with his fist.

What the hell was he doing? He'd never gone after a woman—a submissive—like this. Then again, he hadn't thought about another woman the way Nikla consumed his thoughts. Early that morning, he had to masturbate to relieve his sexual tensions. He hadn't done that since his teenage years.

Sweet raised his balled fist to pound on Nikla's door when it opened. Nikla stood on the other side wearing jeans, ankle boots, an oversized stripped sweater, and the harshest scowl he'd ever seen on her.

What the hell did she have to be so upset about? She had left him waiting.

Sweet stormed into her apartment.

"What are you doing? I'm ready to go." Nikla stood by the door like she thought Sweet would turn around and march right back through it.

"You're not dressed." Sweet headed directly to her bedroom.

When he hit the hallway, he heard her close the front door and curse. He opened her closet door and found it exactly how he imagined it. Neat, clean, organized. Nikla had even arranged her clothes by color.

"What are you doing?" Nikla stood at her bedroom doorway as though afraid to take a step inside with him.

Her instincts may have been right. With her so close to a bed, he would have stripped her out of every stitch of clothing and had his way with her again. Damn, it had been less than twenty-four hours and he missed her body, missed her smell.

"Are you serious about training as a submissive?" Sweet went through her clothing as he awaited her answer. When she didn't say anything, he glanced at her. "Do you want to be trained?"

"I'm dressed. Why can't we go?" Nikla crossed her arms over her chest, which in the bulky sweater, hid her delicious curves.

"Answer my question."

"Oh, is this Dom Sweet talking to me now, or is it the guy going after my suite and will do anything to undermine me."

Sweet felt his blood boiling. "Take off your clothes."

"No." She shook her head.

"If you don't want to do this, then don't waste my time. You keep me waiting at your door, and then when you answer it, you give me attitude. I thought we were straight on what's going on between us." Sweet waved his hand between the two of them.

As much as he wanted to be mad at Nikla, the longer he stared into her eyes, the more he wanted her.

"Yeah, I thought we were straight, too. I thought I could trust you. Then I talked to Bobbi today." Nikla paced in her bedroom. "Compliant."

Sweet blinked. "What?"

"She called me compliant." Then Nikla stormed up to Sweet. "What did you say to her? You think what I did with you was something I would do with anyone? How could you betray my trust and tell her something like that?"

Sweet held up his hand. "Whoa. You think I told Bobbi what we did and the training? You think I would do that to you after–" Sweet stopped himself. "I would never do that to you or any submissive I'm training."

"Despite the sex, you and I barely know each other. How do you expect me to trust you? Other than the fact that you co-own Decadent Treats, and you're a wizard of some sort."

"Master."

"Whatever. I don't know you. When Bobbi said that about me, I felt embarrassed and…and–"

"Vulnerable."

Nikla remained quiet, but Sweet could see the frustration etched in her face. In that moment, he wanted to draw her into his arms and hold her, reassure her, let her know everything would be fine.

He approached her. It took all of his will not to frame her small face in his hands. He so desperately wanted to touch her.

"I didn't tell Bobbi anything about you or what we did."

Nikla strolled to her bed and sat on it. With her head hung low, she looked defeated. "How do you do it?"

"Do what? Run a business? Expand that business?" Not touch her in the entire time he'd been in her bedroom with her?

"Be okay doing what you do, being who you are? Don't you get angry at how people judge you?"

Sweet crouched down in front of Nikla. Despite the running argument in his head not to lay a finger on her, he held her hands. That first connection sent a lightning bolt of fire to his heart. He had to take in a deep breath before he spoke.

"When I was a kid, I worried about what people said about me all the time. If I heard someone laughing behind my back, I internalized it and wouldn't say anything. If it wasn't for my brother Masaun and for the Lifestyle, I don't know if I could survive the looks and the chitchat. Now I know who I am and I know what I am and what I have to offer." Sweet released her hands, reached down, and grabbed one foot. He removed her boot without any resistance from her. "My lifestyle got put out there because of circumstances surrounding my brother's fiancée. I'm not ashamed of what I am or that people know. You, however, don't have to say to the world that you're a submissive." Even though deep down Sweet wanted her to do just that.

She looked up at him.

"That's if you're still interested in training as one." He removed her other shoe, then her thick purple socks.

Until he had her socks off, he never noticed the beauty of her delicate feet. She'd painted each toenail a bright red color. Her feet would look so good as she dangled from an overhead bar.

"I was angry when I thought you had told Bobbi that we had had sex and that you used the candy on me," Nikla said in a low voice.

"Disciplined you," Sweet corrected.

Nikla snickered. "Because I'm so bad?"

"You did leave me waiting a long time at your front door. And you accused me of something I didn't do."

Nikla took a deep breath before she smoothed a strand of his hair from his face. "If you discipline me here, we'll have sex."

She said it in a matter-of-fact way that left little doubt what she had in mind. When she licked her lips, Sweet's heart pounded. He slid his hands up her thighs to her sweater. When he removed her sweater, he saw she had on a red lace bra.

Her dark areolas peeked through the thin lace. Sweet's mouth watered, wanting to lick her nipple through the fabric.

Sweet started undoing her jeans. When he got them unzipped, Nikla leaned back on the bed and helped wriggle out of her jeans as he pulled them down. Underneath hid a whisper thin set of red thong panties. The heart-shaped fabric in front did little to dissuade him from ripping them from her body.

So that he wouldn't be tempted, Sweet stood. Too bad Nikla didn't sit up or stand along with him. She stayed reclined on her bed. He watched her chest rise and fall with each harried breath.

It would be so easy. He could kick her feet apart, drop his pants and boxers, have that spider web of fabric ripped off her pussy, and be inside of her faster than either of them could blink.

"Where are your shoes?" He kept his stare on her eyes.

Nikla didn't answer. She sat up and rose to her feet. Like a graceful cat, she sauntered in front of him, went to her open closet door and knelt down in front of it, showing off her rounded ass.

She reached into the closet and held up a pair of black platform stilettos. "Are these acceptable?"

Sweet kept his stare on her as he shook his head. "What else?"

Nikla returned the shoes to their spot and reached deeper into the closet, which showed more of her luscious ass. Sweet growled the longer she took to find the shoes.

She retrieved another pair and held them up. "How about these?"

The tan pair of heels looked more sensible than sexy.

"Nothing red?" Sweet asked.

Nikla shook her head. "Not a red kind of girl."

"Except for your toenails."

She peered down then up at him with a smile. "Thank my friend, Deana. The color was her idea."

"Deana should have convinced you to buy more sexy shoes."

Nikla laughed. "Losing battle. I love to be barefoot." She glanced down at a pair of flip flops on the floor beside Sweet.

"Put on the black pumps." Sweet crossed his arms over his chest as he waited for her to move.

Her mouth dropped open as she looked at the shoes in her closet, then back at him. "Really?"

He nodded. "I know what I want to see you wearing. I wouldn't be a good Dom if I didn't push you. Wear the heels."

Nikla nodded, rose to her feet and padded over to her shoes, a pair that he could tell had to be the ones she only wore to job interviews and funerals. Once she slipped them on her feet, her whole body stiffened. Her shoulders bunched up around her ears. She stopped breathing for a bit before she finally exhaled. She hugged her arms around her body.

Nikla walked over to him with her head held high. "What would you like for me to wear?"

Sweet almost smiled at her look of determination. He hadn't broken her. After this night, he knew she would retreat to her yoga classes. "Let's look at your coats. Do you keep them out here?" Sweet walked out of her bedroom and headed to a door by her front door.

"Yes. Did you want to match my coat to my outfit?" Nikla followed him.

She managed to keep up with him in the high shoes although she grimaced once or twice in her trek. Nikla wouldn't have to worry. Sweet wouldn't have her on her feet for very long.

He opened the closet door and saw a small array of coats and jackets.

When he spotted a trench coat, he removed it from the hanger. "Put this on."

Nikla furrowed her eyebrows. "Over my underwear? You don't want me to wear clothes underneath?"

Sweet held up the coat, readying it for her to slip it on.

"High heels and a coat. You're serious." Nikla looked at the coat like Sweet held a straightjacket.

"And you're making us late. Come on. Put it on, grab your keys, and let's go."

Without further argument, Nikla slipped on the coat and grabbed her keys. "Do I need my driver's license?"

"Get it."

Nikla ran off to her bedroom and, after a beat, she returned with her purse. "Ready."

Sweet shook his head. "No. I only want your license." He held out his hand.

Nikla opened her purse and fished out her wallet. After a couple of hard tugs, she managed to remove her license from its protective shield. "Here."

Sweet accepted it and held it up to her. "When I hold this, I own you. You're mine."

Nikla swallowed and wrapped her arms around her body. "What does that mean?"

Sweet opened the door. "Come with me and find out."

She took a deep breath and walked outside.

As soon as Nikla took one step outside, Sweet felt his belly tremble. This would be the true test to see if this lifestyle is really for her. Could Nikla withstand discipline in The Dollhouse?

Chapter Fifteen

Nikla's heart thrummed the entire way to The Dollhouse. Bouncing around in Sweet's truck didn't help with her jittery nerves. She balled her hands into fists and kept repeating in her head that she would be okay.

For as loud as the truck had been, he kept the inside pretty pristine. The scent of lemony cleanser filled the air. It made her wonder if Sweet kept his truck clean himself or if he had some submissive on retainer. Would he expect her to do this for him?

Nikla rubbed her hands over the matching powder blue leather seats. The supple material felt smooth and soft under her hands. Would the real toys used on her feel like this? Her nipples hardened at the thought. Every time she thought of Sweet and what he had done to her and what he would do to her always accelerated her heart. That didn't mean she felt at all comfortable about this trip, about this new experience.

What provided some comfort came from knowing a little bit more about Sweet. She couldn't believe when he shared with her about his background that he used to be insecure. This sexy man had a heart and could be vulnerable. A wall still existed around him.

Maybe it had to do with his preoccupation with expanding his business. Maybe it had to do with her. She glanced at him as he drove. Sweet kept his stare on the road. As always, he looked intense.

He pulled his truck into the parking lot of a large building. Sweet parked behind the building. As soon as he turned off his noisy truck, he faced her. She regarded him while clasping her hands together. In her head she prayed he wouldn't tell her he didn't think she could cut it at this new venture. She wanted him to see something in her that no one else had. She could be strong. She could be brave.

Sweet pointed to the building. "What's going to happen in there will be different than what I did to you at Decadent Treats."

Nikla nodded, but remained quiet until he finished talking. She wanted to absorb every word.

He continued. "Once we hit the door, I expect you to follow my every word. In there, I am your Dom. You are a submissive in training. Understand?"

She waited a beat, letting his heavy words sink into her head, before she finally nodded.

"Speak to me," he demanded.

Nikla cleared her throat. "Yes, Sir." She would refrain from telling him that they hadn't gone inside of the establishment yet.

Sweet took his way of life and his role in it seriously. Her clitoris throbbed as she thought about what he would do to her behind the red door.

"I'm ready." Nikla nodded.

Sweet jumped out of the truck first. Nikla reached for her door handle but Sweet wagged his finger at her as he walked in front of his truck.

When he got to her door, Sweet opened it.

"Thank you." Nikla stepped out of the truck.

"You're a lady. Just because you're training to be a submissive, never forget that." Sweet closed the door, then ushered her to the door of the club.

The polite gesture and his explanation brought the widest smile to Nikla's face. Cool air from the ocean whipped around her bare legs until Sweet got her into the building.

Nikla stumbled into a dark hallway as her introduction to the club. The heavy steel door slammed behind her, but she couldn't stop shivering. From the dim hallways to the cries that seemed to come from all around her, even from overhead, the scene felt surreal yet scary.

She glanced up and saw a woman suspended from a large wooden X about twenty feet above the floor. Nikla gasped and clasped Sweet's hand.

"Remember. You're Sugar Baby in here, got it?" Sweet said.

Nikla nodded, but then remembered Sweet's rule. "Yes, Sir."

"You do what I tell you to do." Sweet took his hand from her grasp.

"Okay." She shook her head. "I mean, yes, Sir."

"Quick study." He patted her backside. "On your knees."

Nikla stared at him. Surely he didn't want oral sex here and now in the middle of the hallway. Would she even be allowed to do something like that in this place? Would she even do it? She swallowed hard.

Sweet blinked and faced her with his arms crossed over his massive chest. "Don't make me repeat myself. Get on your hands and knees."

Frozen to her spot, Nikla felt conflicted. What would it mean to her to drop to her knees for this man in these walls? She didn't want to appear weak.

"I knew you would chicken out." Sweet headed for the door.

After a deep breath, Nikla lowered herself to the cold concrete floor. She brought her hands down to the floor and waited. She heard the back door opening and hoped beyond hope that Sweet hadn't gone back to the truck.

Too afraid to turn around to see where he'd gone, Nikla remained in her spot with her gaze aimed for the floor. She studied the dark gray color against her bare hands. The cool material and her position had her body trembling. She swallowed.

From behind her, she heard heavy footfalls.

"Don't make me wait like that again." Sweet continued down the hall.

Nikla suspected that he wanted her to follow him...on her hands and knees. She crawled down the hall. She couldn't tell if she moved quickly over her hands and knees or if Sweet slowed his gait, but she reached his side. She crawled next to him in an eerie companionable silence like an obedient pet.

The idea of that made her heart thrum. Her knees already started to get sore from meeting the hard flooring. Nikla could do this. The fact that he had her crawling on the floor around strangers gave her a sense of pride, an unusual reaction considering the seemingly demeaning position.

Nikla brought her head up to scan her surroundings. At the end of the hall, Nikla spotted a tall man walking toward her and standing next to a beautiful black woman who wore what looked like a black leather one-piece swimsuit and high heels.

"Come over here with me." Sweet tapped Nikla on her back. He aimed her toward a room and closed the door behind them.

The cozy room reminded her of a waiting room in Hell. Red couches stood out against the painted black walls. The only great thing about the room had to be the hardwood floors. They felt better against her hands and knees than the concrete.

Nikla scraped the tips of her shoes against the dark hardwood floors. Sweet led her to a couch. He sat first, then he pointed to a spot on the floor next to himself, a space he must have wanted her to occupy.

Just like when she dropped to her hands and knees, she assumed the spot as dutifully. She sat back on her haunches. Fear gripped her before she brought her attention to Sweet. What kind of man would she see next to her? Since coming into this place, his whole demeanor had shifted. Then again, so had hers.

Nikla started to open her mouth to speak but Sweet shook his head, halting her from that thought.

"We need to go over some ground rules and some procedures." He stared at her for a moment before he pressed a button on table next to the couch.

Within a minute, a petite blonde wearing a short pleated black leather skirt, a white mesh top, and no bra sauntered in the room. Nikla peered down at the woman's feet. She'd had each toe painted a different color.

"Sweet iced tea for me," Sweet said to the woman. He glanced at Nikla. Before she could speak, he said, "She'll have an ice cold glass of water with a lemon."

The simple gesture made Nikla smile. She liked being cared for, more than she thought she would.

The woman nodded once before starting to turn to leave.

"Wait." Sweet stared at Nikla. "Take off your coat."

Blazing heat engulfed Nikla's face. "What?" She leaned close to him and in a low tone said, "You know what I have on underneath."

Sweet's scowl deepened. "I've only given you one directive since we got here. You do as I say. Take off your coat. Now."

Nikla balled her hands and took a deep breath before she removed the garment as she sat on the floor. She unfastened her coat and slipped the garment down her arms. If she felt chilly before, she now had ice water running through her veins.

With her coat off, she kept her stare on the man who'd made the demand of her. She let the coat drape in front of her body.

"Hand it to her." Sweet nodded toward the blonde.

The woman held out her hand. She smiled as she accepted the coat.

"Thank you." Sweet nodded and the woman left as quickly and as quietly as when she'd first walked into the room.

"Would you like for me to continue kneeling?" Nikla kept her hands on her lap.

Sweet said nothing as he scanned her. He put his hand to her head and stroked her hair.

Sweet looked ready to crawl out of his own skin. He balled his hands into fists and released a low groan.

"Stay where you are or I'll do something I will never regret." He rubbed his hands over his eyes.

"Yes, Sir." The address to Sweet had started to become easier and easier each time she'd said it.

The thought of that shouldn't have given her comfort. It did. She knew what he expected. She knew what would make him happy. By doing that, it had pleased her. A wave of relief showered over her body.

"Is this what you expected?" He kept his stare on her.

"What do you mean? Expected from this place? This room? You?" Nikla felt him bringing his hand down behind her head. He rubbed the back of her neck with his thumb.

Nikla closed her eyes and enjoyed the sensation. Strange that with a few words and a thumb rubbed lazily across her skin how he easily controlled her. She couldn't move. She didn't want to move.

"All of it." He removed his hand from her.

When he stopped touching her, she sobered to the situation. Nikla bit her lip. "This place is kind of what I thought it would be like. Dark and mysterious." She gained eye contact with Sweet. "It's like you. You're very closed off." Except for what he'd revealed about his last relationship. Nikla still found it impossible that a man this sexy would be without a woman for two years.

"Considering we're going to end this in a month, don't you think I should be?"

"It would be nice to get to know the man who looks so comfortable to be in a place like this."

Sweet put his finger to her lips. "Don't overthink this. It's very basic. It's just sensations."

She slipped his finger into her mouth.

Sweet shook his head and removed it. "You do that, and I'll want to do other things. In here, I can't." He nodded upward.

When Nikla peered up, she caught a blackened, overhead dome affixed to the ceiling. "Cameras."

"Everywhere."

Nikla looked around the empty room. "What is this room? Do people do what you do in here?"

"It's called playing or you can call it discipline." To give her a reminder of what he could do, he fisted her loose hair and pulled her head back.

The sensation to her scalp awakened her senses. "No man has ever touched me the way you do." Nikla remained quiet after her admission.

"You're surprised at how much you like what I do?"

She nodded. "It's different from a fantasy."

"To answer your question, this is the meeting room. It's the room we use to get to know our submissives or slaves before we play with them. We establish rules." He held up his finger. "First rule." Then he released her hair.

"Always do as you say." Nikla lowered her head.

"Second rule. No sex." When he mentioned that rule, Sweet almost looked disappointed.

Nikla wouldn't be so subtle. Despite their rule that they wouldn't get intimate again, Nikla had hoped for a repeat performance. No man had ever gotten her to come as hard and as often as Sweet in the one time she'd been with him.

"No sex–"

"In here," he said, interrupting her.

The anxiety bunching in her stomach subsided. "Anything else?"

"What is it that you want?"

Nikla snickered. "That suite downtown."

Sweet almost broke into a smile. Almost. "That's another rule. The real life, our vanilla world, doesn't exist here."

"If only it could be that easy." She sighed. "What do I want? That I don't know. I do know what I don't want." She placed her hand on her chest. "I don't want to get hurt. I don't want to be made a fool of. I don't want to be the joke of some elaborate prank. I don't want to be inconsequential or some afterthought."

"Good. Now tell me what you *want*."

As fire filled her belly, Nikla felt compelled to purge her feelings. "I want to feel. I haven't really been touched in forever. I want to be the center of someone's universe. I want to matter. How can I do that as a–"

The word "submissive" got caught in her throat.

Sweet cleared his throat. He made her look at him. "This lifestyle demands a lot from both of us. You may find that my playing style doesn't suit you. One thing you need to know for sure. As a submissive, you are powerful. You regulate the play within the scene. The focus will always be on you. You will be the center of it all. Can you really handle that?"

Nikla thought of the idea of being the focus of a man's attention, of Sweet's attention. A tingle rippled through her body.

"I want one other thing," she said. "Tell me what you'll do to me."

Sweet leaned in closer to her. "I'm going to make you feel more alive that you've ever felt. You will feel completely spent, another great reason for me to drive." He got quiet before he finished his speech. "I will push you. I can tell you're strong enough to take it. I've never met a woman like you before."

She took a deep breath. "Is that a good thing?"

Sweet stared at her for a while before he answered. "It's the best thing. You're about the most open person I've ever met."

"You're only saying that because I'm sitting here on the floor in my underwear." Nikla laughed.

"Not the only reason."

The waitress returned with their drinks. She placed them on the side table and walked out without a word. Sweet handed Nikla her drink. Feeling a little overheated, she took a couple of gulps of the lemon-flavored water. The refreshing liquid cooled her down a bit but not enough to douse the intense fire between her legs.

"Ready?" Sweet asked after he finished his drink.

Nikla nodded.

He took her drink. "Come with me."

Since he didn't tell her to stand, she crawled behind him again. Sweet led her down a darkened hallway to a room at the end. Only a sheer curtain separated the hallway from the activities that would happen in the room.

Nikla stopped in the center of the room. She scanned the space. From the stone walls to the heavy wooden furniture, the place looked like a dungeon. What really startled her had to have been the different torture devices hanging from the walls. Whips, chains, floggers, paddles. One more sinister than the next.

As she looked around from her kneeling position, she suddenly saw Sweet reaching over her head with a black band in his hand. Nikla jerked her head back and slammed against his legs.

"It's a mask, not a blindfold." Sweet covered her eyes, making sure to line up the eyeholes properly. Then he secured it behind her head.

With the mask in place, Sweet reached behind her and undid her bra.

Nikla swallowed. "Nudity is allowed?"

"Trust that I won't do anything to you that I shouldn't. With me, you're safe."

She nodded. With it off, he hung it on a wall.

"Up," he said as he walked back to her.

Nikla stood from the floor. Her knees throbbed. She couldn't think about them right now. Her focus remained on Sweet.

Keeping his stare on her, he hooked his finger into the side of her thong and pulled it down her legs.

Bracing her hands on his shoulders, Nikla stepped out of them. Sweet hung them up on the wall along with her bra.

Being completely nude in a strange place in front of this man, Nikla would have thought she would have been self-conscious. Instead, she felt free. The way Sweet looked at her, she now felt beautiful.

"Do you remember your safe words, Sugar Baby?" Sweet moved

to a corner of the room.

"Yes. Green, yellow, and red."

Nikla watched his every move, his every step. She couldn't help but feel helpless when he moved away from her and no longer looked at her. Standing nude, she felt so unprepared if something were to happen. No one knew Sweet had taken her to this place. She hadn't told Deana or her father about Sweet. If he hurt her, no one would know.

Nikla struggled to swallow. Her breathing became shallow. She balled her hands and pounded her thighs with her fists.

Sweet stood in front of her and framed her face with his large hands. "Breathe. Look at me and breathe."

Even with his soothing voice, Nikla felt the attack coming on and she didn't think she could stop it. "Take me home." She placed her hand on her chest.

"Come here." Sweet held her hand and pulled her over to a large, high-back wooden chair with black leather accents on the back and arms.

He sat down first and pulled her onto his lap.

"I can't breathe." Nikla felt her throat tightening.

The longer she stayed in this room in this dungeon, the worse her breathing had become.

"Shh." He held her arm around her wrist and pressed on a spot on her inner wrist. "Look at me and listen to my voice."

Nikla nodded. She attempted to bring Sweet into focus.

He smoothed his thumb over her cheek. "Keep looking at me. Don't stop looking at me, okay?"

She nodded again. With each movement of her head, her focus became fuzzier and fuzzier.

"Deep breath in and hold it, then release." Sweet never broke his stare. "You're stronger than this."

Nikla had hoped to hold herself together for her first trip to Sweet's playground. It embarrassed her that she came off so scared.

"You feel my thumb on your wrist?" he asked.

"Y-y-yes, Sir."

Sweet shook his head. "Don't worry about the scene right now. You keep breathing in and out. Concentrate on where my thumb is and your breathing."

Nikla struggled to take in deep breaths. "Can't believe I'm doing this. I swore I wouldn't panic."

"It's just us in here. Don't think about anything else. Nothing else matters."

Nikla kept her stare on his face to see if he had been teasing her. When his normally stoic face remained that way, she blinked. "Help me, please."

"Do you know how brave you are to come in here, crawl on the floor, and get naked? You're a lot stronger than you give yourself credit."

She smiled. "Yeah? You think so?"

Sweet stared at her for a moment. "You feeling better?"

She nodded. "Maybe we do things where I'm lying down."

Sweet shook his head. "You're with the wrong Dom if you think you're going to take it easy in here." He patted her backside. "Up."

Nikla stood on wobbly legs. Sweet helped her to the corner of the room where a cross she'd seen the woman hanging from over her head when she first walked into the dungeon sat.

"Put your hands up."

Nikla did as instructed. Sweet wasted no time in wrapping a padded cuff around each.

"Let me show you something. See this?" Sweet engaged a clip that connected the cuff to the eyebolt that attached to the cross. "This is called a panic clip."

Nikla snickered. "Sounds appropriate for me."

"If you're unable to say your safe word or if I'm incapacitated, you just hit this clip like this and it'll set you free." He showed her how to operate the clip, then he watched her do it one time. "Very good, Sugar Baby. Now spread your legs."

Sweet crouched down and gave her ankles the same treatment as her wrists.

"You know I am really, really flexible." Nikla liked this salacious side to herself that Sweet brought out in her.

As Sweet secured her other ankle, he moaned. "Good to know for future activities." He stood.

Inches away from her face, he leaned in, his lips parted. Nikla smelled that familiar musky scent that she'd grown to love. She moved her face in closer to his as he pulled back.

"You are a dangerous woman, Sugar Baby." He tapped the end of her nose with his finger before going to the wall of toys.

Nikla heard him opening a drawer. "Says the man who has me tied up to a big X." She heard the distinct sound of chains clinking together. She swallowed.

"A St. Andrew's cross." He turned back to her. "You can stop all of this if you want. You can engage the panic clips and go home." He turned around and showed off a thin chain that looked like they had clips on either end.

"You're my ride." Nikla couldn't remove her stare from the chained device as he approached her.

He shook his head. "I wouldn't leave you stranded."

"Not your style, right?"

"You're starting to get to know me."

Not enough, Nikla wanted to say. The man in the menacing black motorcycle boots, jeans, and a simple t-shirt seemed like an opened book, but he came off guarded. Each time she played with him, she discovered more about him.

Sweet brought his face next to hers. She felt his lips brush against the shell of her ear. Nikla wanted to rip off her mask and press her face against his. She squirmed against the cross. She wanted to release herself and touch this man. Letting herself go from the restraints would keep her bound in her old ways of thinking, of wanting to try to control every moment. She had to let Sweet lead.

Sweet held her breast, which made her gasp. Nikla balled her toes and pulled against her cuffs. This time when her heart pounded, she knew it stemmed from a different reason. Why the hell had she agreed to keep their relationship sex free?

In her ear he whispered, "As the Dom, I decide when we play. If I'm not in the mood, it won't happen."

His hot breath warmed her body. Nikla no longer felt the chill swirling about the dungeon.

He continued. "When we do play, you can set the pace. I decide the implements. You decide the rhythm. Understand?"

Unable to speak, Nikla nodded.

"Talk to me."

"Yes. Yes. Yes, Sir." She panted her words as he massaged her tit.

Sweet's thumb brushed over her nipple. The motion hardened it more than before. The sounds of Nikla's panting breath echoed off the walls. He stiffened it to a painful level, and she wanted more.

The kisses Sweet made down her face to her neck eventually landed him at her other breast. He drew her nipple into his mouth, grazing the hardened pebble with his teeth.

Nikla gripped the chains that held her as Sweet lovingly laved her breast. When he moaned, she did also. She felt the vibration through her body.

He kissed across her chest to her other breast and gave it the same treatment with his hot mouth. When she felt something pinch her unattended nipple, Nikla gasped. She looked down to see a clamp on her nipple and a chain dangling from it.

Sweet pulled back from her and regained eye contact. "No more candy." He grabbed the other end of the chain and showed her the other clamp. He opened the small rubber-tipped clip, held her breast, then attached it to her other nipple.

On instinct, Nikla held her breath as she allowed the slight discomfort to wash through her body, from her head down to her toes.

"Breathe. Breathe through the pain." Sweet held the dangling chain that connected her nipples and tugged on it.

The motion forced her to breathe. She released a scream and pushed back against the cross.

He released the chain and let it brush against the skin in between her breasts. The feeling of the pressure on her nipples consumed Nikla's thoughts. Her father, her desire to own and run own business, her job, nothing entered her mind except for the clamps.

"Yes. Green." The pain hadn't been too unbearable. As long as she kept her concentration, she learned to sink into the feeling.

The pain became a part of her, like a child that she helped create and pushed through her body. Nikla closed her eyes and brushed her back against the hard wood that supported her.

"Look at me."

Sweet's demand didn't surprise Nikla. She opened her eyes and brought the man into focus. In his large hands, he held several clothespins.

When he approached her, Nikla raised herself higher on her toes to brace for whatever came next.

While Sweet stared into her eyes, like an expert, he clipped one pin onto her breast beside her nipple.

Nikla sucked air in between her teeth. She leaned her head back as she adjusted to this new sensation, this new pain. Balling her hands into fists, she prepared herself for the next pin, which Sweet affixed on the other side of her nipple.

"Fuck!" Nikla exhaled. Her breathing became erratic, but she refused to activate her clips. She could take this.

"Concentrate on where the clothespins are pinching you," Sweet said as he pinned another on her other tit.

Unable to verbally respond without cursing, Nikla nodded.
Sweet continued pinning her skin for what seemed like hours but had to have been a minute or so.

"Look down."

Nikla opened her eyes and peered down at herself. She counted about eight clothespins jutting from her breasts, making her look like a freak, especially next to the nipple clamps.

From looking at the pins and clamps, Nikla became overwhelmed with pride. She had endured this. Sweet trusted that she could be strong enough to take this type of play.

Sweet had retrieved a large, heavy-looking flogger. He stood a few feet in front of her. "You don't really understand this dynamic, do you?"

Nikla chewed on her lip as she watched Sweet swinging the flogger back and forth as though warming up for the full-on assault.

"You're very impressive." He swung the flogger and allowed the heavy tails to thud against her chest and slide down her body and over the chain and pins. The impact dislodged two of the pins.

"Oh, God!" The feeling of the impact against her chest took her breath for a moment.

Unlike with the nipple clamps, she couldn't settle into this intense sensation. As she got used to the pound on her chest and the falls pulling on the chain, Sweet inflicted another hit, and another. With each hit, one by one, the clothespins popped from her body, leaving in their wake sensitive patches of skin.

Nikla turned her face away, thinking if she didn't see the hit coming that she could take the impact better. Instead, the surprise startled her more.

She didn't want to stop Sweet. She could take this.

Sweet landed the flogger on her a few more times, each time hitting her harder and harder. Nikla imagined her chest must be red from the impacts.

"Shit! Yellow." Nikla felt the sweat dripping down underneath her mask.

She hoped Sweet didn't think he had reduced her to tears.

While keeping her eyes closed, she felt one of the clamps release from her nipple. She opened her eyes to see Sweet removing the torture device. With both gone, blood rushed into her nipples and inflicted a painful, stinging sensation that, had she not been held up by the restraints, would have dropped her to her knees.

Aside from palming her breasts, Sweet offered little in relief. Then again, she didn't want him to soften the blow. She'd sustained the treatment. The feeling almost felt like a badge of honor.

Nikla peered down to see if she could see a mark. As she suspected, her chest had transformed into a dark crimson color. Her dark brown nipples had a distinct indentation on the sides. A line of dark, rust-colored blotches went across both breasts. She smiled.

Sweet returned to the wall and removed something that looked like a dowel rod. He came back to her and stood off to the side. With a swift motion, he smacked the stick against her thighs. The intense pain shifted her focus to the sensation he'd given her legs.

He brought the cane up higher and spanked it against her upper thighs. "What are you thinking?"

"How—how—how good this would feel on my ass."

Nikla didn't know if Sweet wanted to prove her wrong or right, but he continued slapping the cane against different areas of her thighs. He stood directly in front of her. He tapped the cane between her thighs, moving up to her pussy, but not touching it.

Nikla lowered herself as much as she could with her wrists bound to the top of the cross.

Sweet stopped the spanking to regard her for a moment. He went back to the wall, returned the one cane to the wall, and instead grabbed two thinner canes. He held the canes like long drumsticks. Like a drummer, he gave her alternating taps over her breasts, circling her nipple, and hitting all sides of her tit.

Nikla leaned her head back and took the pain that she wanted, that she needed. Juices flowed from the apex of her thighs. She couldn't imagine what else he could do to her that would top this moment.

Sweet continued the drumming down her body. He tapped the thin canes over her heated thighs, ignited them again.

"Oh, you're killing me." Nikla leaned her head back. She noticed that the drumming stopped.

She brought her head back up and looked at Sweet.

"Did you want me to stop?" He gripped the two canes in one hand as he regarded her.

Nikla shook her head. "No, Sir."

"And this is why there are safe words." He placed the canes on a counter.

Sweet opened a drawer and pulled a box from it. He opened it and pulled out something that looked like a silver egg. He outfitted it with a couple of batteries, then he twisted it.

Nikla heard the distinctive buzzing right away. It reminded her of her trusty vibrator.

When Sweet turned around, she saw him holding the egg. He approached her. Once he stood next to her, he fisted her hair.

Nikla could deal with her sore scalp as long as Sweet kept playing with her.

"Open your legs."

With her ankles bound, Nikla opened her legs as much as she could and squatted down to give Sweet room to work. He brought his hand down and slipped the battery-operated device over her protruding clit.

Nikla squeezed her eyes shut. The vibration shook her body, but in particular, her clitoris.

"Use your fucking safe words now," Sweet demanded.

"Green. Green, Sir." Nikla kept her eyes closed as she gyrated her hips over the naughty egg.

Sweet tortured her by circling the device over her sensitive nub until Nikla thought she would come. Knowing Sweet, he wouldn't want her to come yet. When he slipped the device inside of her, she nearly broke.

"Yellow!" Nikla tried clamping her legs together to get the vibrating toy inside of her.

"You don't like it, Sugar Baby?"

Nikla, still with her eyes closed, heard Sweet moving away from her. "I love it. I love it, Sir."

"Why did you say 'yellow'? You want me to slow it down?"

She heard his voice closer to her again. Nikla nodded, then remembered Sweet's demands. "Yes. I want to come so badly right now."

"And you know I don't want you coming yet, right?" His voice dipped down lower.

"Yes, Sir."

Sweet started drumming the thin canes over her arms, down to her breasts, and over her stomach. He did nothing to adjust the speed or intensity of the silver egg still lodged in her pussy.

Sweet's tapping migrated down to her thighs again. When he reached her vagina, he used one cane and gave her a swift swat against her throbbing clit.

The sensation left her feeling like something exploded behind her eyes. In well-spaced hits, Sweet continued hitting her clit with the thin cane until Nikla felt her stomach tighten. Her knees trembled. She knew he had to have seen the happy tears running down her eyes and over her cheeks.

"Green! Green!"

"Don't come."

Before Sweet could get out the order, Nikla felt her body constrict as the orgasm took over her. She held her breath as every muscle tensed. When she felt Sweet reach between her legs and pinch her clit, she couldn't hold back the scream.

"Sir," she said on an exhale. "Sir. Sir. Dom Sweet."

Sweet approached her. "What is it?"

"Closer." When Nikla felt his face next to hers, she said, "Fuck me. Please."

This time when Sweet growled, Nikla didn't feel his sexual frustration like she had experienced. He sounded more frustrated than anything else. Didn't he know what he'd done to her, how that made her feel?

Sweet removed the toy and threw it on the counter. Nikla released a long exhale and leaned her face against one of her outstretched arms.

"I'm going to let you be alone for a bit. I'll be right back." He squeezed, then patted her backside.

Damn. Nikla didn't want Sweet to go. She definitely didn't want to be alone with her thoughts. She hoped that Sweet didn't leave so he could figure out how to stop this arrangement altogether.

Chapter Sixteen

Sweet nearly ran to the bar area. This time he needed an ice water for himself. He wanted to fuck Nikla. He had been imagining it while he disciplined her. He had only been halfway through the scene when she broke it by coming then begging to be fucked.

"Damn!" Sweet downed the water and demanded another. He needed something to douse his overheated nature.

Sweet felt a hand on his shoulder. Hoping Leaf hadn't made a return trip, he slowed in responding. After finishing his second water, he pivoted and found someone else he didn't want to talk to right now.

"Hawk. Aren't you here with Song Sparrow?" Sweet started to walk back to his playroom.

"I was watching you on camera." Masaun followed him. "Your form looked good. Looks like you're back in the swing of things, so to speak."

"Don't you have better things to do than–"

"Watch out for my baby brother? No. Besides Kindle, you're the most important thing in my life." Masaun put his hand on Sweet's back and guided him to another room.

Sweet knew exactly where he had him going. Masaun opened the door to the security office and ushered him inside.

"I don't have time for this. I have a submissive to get back to." Sweet searched the cameras and stopped when he spotted Nikla still bound to the cross alone.

He hadn't meant to leave her by herself. He wanted to cradle her in his arms and do the aftercare that she deserved. He couldn't do that with still feeling like he wanted to take her sexually.

"The audio is incredible in this security feed." Masaun strolled in front of the wall of video screens showing off scenes of men dominating women, women making men submit, and unsure people strolling around the premises. The gawkers pissed Sweet off the most.

"Is she the same one from the other day?" Masaun asked.

"What do you mean?" Sweet shrugged but he knew what Masaun meant.

"Don't be cute." His brother stood in front of him, nose to nose. "Is that the one you fucked in the office?"

Sweet waited a beat before he answered. "I thought you were happy I had moved on. Isn't that what you told me? Glad to see you getting over Melinda."

Masaun shook his head. "I don't want to see you get hurt again and spiral down even further."

"What if she's the one?"

Masaun sighed. "You wouldn't ask me that question if she was." He moved in closer to Sweet so that the other staff in the office reviewing the monitors wouldn't hear him. "Does she know your real name?"

Sweet blinked.

"If she doesn't, I don't think she'll last."

"Fuck you." Sweet stormed out of the office and headed back to Nikla, his Sugar Baby.

He hadn't shared his real name with Melinda either until she needed to know it. That meant nothing to him. Masaun had no right to even bring that up. Sweet couldn't help but think that he had a point. Hell, when he saw Masaun coming down the hall when Sweet had been with Nikla earlier, he took her to the meeting room to get her out of view.

Masaun still didn't know the woman who had kept Sweet awake at night and consumed his thoughts during the day had been the lone protester.

If Masaun had met her and saw her passion, he would understand how Sweet could be so enamored with her.

Before Sweet got back into the room, he spotted a woman coming down the hall. Wearing a see-through lace nightie and nothing else, Sweet had to applaud the zaftig woman for wearing an outfit like that. Once he got to the doorway, he recognized her.

"Leaf? What are you doing here?" He blocked the doorway with his body.

"I liked what we did before. I wanted to try it again." She moved closer to him. "I was hoping I would see you here."

Sweet maintained his spot and glared at Leaf. "I'm here with someone else."

Leaf shrank back. "Oh. Lucky woman." She shrugged. "My loss."

"I'm sure you'll find a Dom who you can connect with." He took a step back into the room to signal that he wanted the conversation to end.

"Yeah. I don't know if anyone else can whip me like you did. It was great. You made me feel special."

Sweet heard some rustling behind him before he heard the panic clips engage. Damn.

"Have fun tonight." Sweet turned his back on Leaf and concentrated on Nikla, who now had herself down from the cross. "I didn't tell you to get down."

Nikla removed the cuffs from her wrists and threw them on the floor. "You said I decide. I choose. I'm ready to go home now. I need my coat." She took off the mask and tossed it aside as well.

"I've been in the Lifestyle a long, long time. You don't think you're the only one I've played with, do you?"

Nikla slipped on her panties, then put on her bra. "Of course not. To hear that after what happened to me tonight, it made it feel less special, like I was part of some big assembly line of submissives you've trained in the past. I felt used." She shook her head. "I never want to feel that way. Ever." She started to go by him and Sweet stopped her.

"Wait."

"Let me by. I'll find my coat."

"Hey!" Sweet didn't want to raise his voice, but he had to get this stubborn woman to stop.

Nikla halted her movements and gazed up at him.

"When I play with someone, I try to make them feel special. Right now, you're the only one I'm playing with. I'd like to keep it that way."

Nikla regarded him for a moment like she wanted to believe him.

"Wait here. I'll get your coat and we'll go." Sweet turned her head back so that she could look him in his eyes. "You have nothing to feel jealous about."

She chuckled and took a step back from him. "My last boyfriend cheated on me. I know we're not dating. I don't know what it is that we're doing, which scares me to death. But if you're interested in playing or disciplining or whatever it is you call it with anyone else, tell me now so that I don't go in this head first and break my neck. I'm tired of putting myself out there. I'm so tired." Nikla put her hand to her bowed head.

Sweet helped her to the chair and sat her down. He picked up the water she'd brought to the room and placed it in both of her hands. "Drink this. Don't move. I'll get your coat and we'll go."

Nikla nodded and took a sip of the water. As Sweet stormed down the hallway, anger built inside of him. What kind of idiot would cheat on a woman so sexy, so passionate as Nikla? He wanted to find that guy and wring his fucking neck. Then again, he had to thank the asshole because if he hadn't fucked up, Sweet wouldn't be with Nikla now.

Sweet grabbed Nikla's coat from behind the bar area. He dropped another hundred in Juicy's tip jar to keep the surly woman happy. Then he headed back to the room. When he got there, he found Nikla sitting up and looking more serene than when he'd left her.

"Sorry for freaking out on you earlier." She stood.

Sweet helped her on with her coat. "Come on. Let me take you home." With his hand on the small of her back, he walked her out of the club and to his truck. Once he got her inside and helped her with her seatbelt, he jumped in on the driver's side, and drove her home.

Nikla remained eerily quiet the entire ride back. The silence made Sweet wonder what went through her head. Was she now second guessing this arrangement? Did she want to stop training as a submissive?

When Sweet got to her apartment, he parked his truck and got out. When he got to Nikla's side, he opened her door. Instead of letting her walk out of the truck, he picked her up in his arms.

"Sweet! What are you doing? I can walk."

Sweet kicked the door closed with his foot and carried her to her door. "Yeah. And I can carry you." When he got to her front door, he told her to unlock it.

Nikla did. When he got her inside, he continued holding her as she disabled her alarm and locked the door.

Sweet carried his precious parcel to the living room. There he sat on the couch with her in his arms. With one arm still around her shoulders, he used his free hand to remove her shoes. He would leave her coat on for now. With that off, he wouldn't be able to control himself.

"This should have happened at the club." Sweet smoothed his hand over her soft hair. "This is called aftercare. After discipline, the Dom or Domme will talk to the person or people who have been disciplined and discuss the scene."

"You think I need to be talked down from the ledge?" Nikla smiled.

"In a way. Sometimes it's not all about the sub or slave. Sometimes the Dom needs to know he's not strange for doing what he's done." He stared at her for a moment. "I would never cheat on you."

Nikla broke the stare. "I shouldn't have told you that."

"Yes, you should have. It gives me some insight into what I should do with you." He started to undo her coat.

"What do you mean by that?" Nikla glanced at his hand that busied itself unbuttoning her coat.

"You wouldn't respond well if I brought in another sub to play with you."

She screwed up her face. "You would play with two women at one time?"

"I've done it before. It's challenging, but it can be fun." Sweet opened her coat and exposed her fit body. He cupped her tit, barely hidden underneath her transparent bra. "You shouldn't have asked me to fuck you back at the club." He connected his stare to hers.

"Why? It was how I was feeling." Nikla put her hand over his. "Shouldn't I always tell you the truth?"

"Yes." He liked her honesty. Sweet liked a lot of things about her including her drive to get the space he wanted. It showed that she had her own passions.

"What are we doing?" Nikla asked.

"I'm making sure that after our session that you're okay. How do you feel?"

She wriggled up so that she could sit up on his lap instead of being in a reclined position. "Like you said, I feel spent, tired but energized. I feel like I just did a marathon." She glanced down at her thighs and smiled.

When Sweet peered down at her long legs, he caught what Nikla saw. Red streaks marked her shapely legs.

She rubbed her thighs. "They're still hot." Then she looked at him. "You scare me."

A wave of disappointment washed over him. "I told you I would never hurt you."

Nikla shook her head. "I don't mean that. Ever since I met you, when you said I had no heart, I can't get you out of my head."

"I didn't mean that whole heart thing."

"No. It's okay. If the situation were reversed, I would have said and done the same thing. What scares me about you is that I want you so badly. I feel with you I have left myself open and raw. No matter what I'm wearing or what I'm doing, I always feel you can see right through me. What scares me is that I like it. What really frightens me is that I love the sex just as much as the other stuff." She put her hand over her eyes. "What's wrong with me?"

Before Sweet answered, he helped Nikla out of her coat. Then he lifted her in his arms and carried her to her bedroom. "There is nothing wrong with you." He placed her on her bed. "Let me guess what goes on in your life. You have a lot of responsibility and you feel stressed, right?"

"You don't have to guess. My father owns a business and he wants me to give up my job and work there with him. I do what I can to support him, but he pressures me way more than he pressures my brother, who had to join the military just to get away from him."

Sweet sat on the edge of her bed and removed his boots.

"I have a co-worker who always pawns off her work on me and I feel obligated to do it because I can't stand for people to be disappointed. I hate disappointing anyone."

Sweet recognized her need to please early. To hear her admit it calmed a bit of his fears. "You are a lot stronger than you think. I don't mean just physically strong. Do you know what kind of guts it takes for someone to be nude in a strange place and have someone discipline them? Every time I'm with you, you amaze me. You're willing to try something new and different."

"And you?"

Sweet took off his t-shirt before undoing his jeans. "You're making me trust. I haven't trusted a woman in a long time."

"Did a woman cheat on you, too?"

Sweet pulled down Nikla's panties. "In a way. I thought we were exclusive as far as me being her Dom. I found out that she'd been playing with every Dom and Domme who didn't know I had owned her. It didn't help that we were together intimately as well. To find out she'd given other Doms hand jobs and blow jobs didn't sit well with me." He reached under her back and unfastened her bra. "I can't take someone who isn't on the same page as me."

"Are we on the same page?" She smiled.

"I think we're in the same book. Maybe in the same chapter." Sweet pressed his body on top of hers.

"I know what you do. I know you have a brother. And I know what you want to do."

"Do you?" He kissed her soft enough to take her breath. Sweet heard her gasping when he pulled back.

"I mean as far as your business. I don't know much more about you. How old are you?"

Sweet kissed her chin. "I'm thirty-two."

"What's your favorite color?" Nikla arched her back as he continued kissing down her neck.

"Purple."

Nikla lifted her head. "Really?"

"What can I say? Prince had it right. Purple means passion." Sweet loved smelling Nikla. Her jasmine scent sent him over the moon. "What else?" She had him open enough to confess a lot of things.

Sweet never thought he would have talked about Melinda with Nikla. "When did you lose your virginity?" Nikla spread her legs and allowed Sweet to scoot down her body.

At her breasts, he massaged one as he licked her nipple. "When I was twenty."

"Now you're teasing me."

"Late bloomer." Sweet moved his mouth over to her other nipple and licked it. She tasted like honey. He wouldn't need the caramel to sweeten her body.

"Why did you start so late?"

Sweet continued kissing down her midsection. When he got to her navel, he inserted his tongue.

Nikla jumped and ran her fingers through his hair.

"Believe it or not, not a lot of women find bookish nerds who like cooking attractive. I hadn't found my place in the BDSM world until about that time. Women found the confidence attractive."

Sweet moved down the bed so that his head hovered over her smooth pussy.

"And your favorite food?" With full expectation in her eyes, Nikla peered down at Sweet.

"I like to eat a lot of things."

Before he could elaborate, Sweet parted her pussy lips and licked her from the bottom of her pussy opening to her clit. He loved listening to her moan just as much as he craved tasting her.

Sweet's imagination didn't disappoint him. Her nectar tasted sweeter than anything he'd ever use in any of his candy recipes. He pressed his tongue against her hardened nub, then flicked it over it. Her breath caught each time he touched her clit.

Sweet felt prickles go over his entire body. Nikla smelled of jasmine doused in sea water. He couldn't get enough of her salty goodness.

Nikla brought her knees up, then wrapped her legs around his body. That didn't stop Sweet from devouring her pussy. He slipped his tongue inside of her.

"Fuck!"

Sweet raised his head. "I love hearing you curse."

He continued licking and loving her core until he felt her body wracked with tremors. He knew he had her close.

"Please tell me you have condoms." Sweet should have known better than to leave the house without some with him, especially since he knew he would be with Nikla.

He'd tried convincing himself that he could be strong enough not to break his rule. Whenever he got around Nikla, he forgot about everything.

"Under the vibrator." Nikla reached her hand back, but Sweet moved much faster.

He jumped off the bed and pulled the drawer open. As she said, a string of condoms lay underneath the vibrator he'd stumbled on before. Sweet opened a package and rolled the rubber onto his erection.

"I want you on top." Sweet got on his back.

"Yes, Sir." Nikla straddled his midsection.

As she held onto his cock, Nikla stared into his eyes.

"Don't you stop looking at me." Sweet needed to feel a connection with the woman who had somehow stolen his heart in a short amount of time.

Nikla lowered herself onto his cock and gripped his chest. "Shit! So hard and—damn!"

"That's it, Sugar Baby." Sweet held onto her hips.

Her hips gyrated, grinding on top of him, moving Sweet's cock in and out of her and making him feel like a king. She kept her stare on him as she kept her undulations going.

"You feel so good inside of me."

Sweet brought his hands up and filled them with her perfect, brown orbs. When he pinched her nipples, Nikla froze. She cursed through her gritted teeth.

"Don't hold back. Come. Show me."

Nikla swayed her hips faster and faster. A light sheen of sweat covered her body. Sweet could stay like this forever.

Nikla held Sweet's hands against her chest as she came with a scream.

For her sake, Sweet hoped she had soundproof apartment walls, especially since he had more to give her.

Sweet sat up and held Nikla around her waist. He turned over to put her on her back. When she grabbed his shoulders, he took her hands and pressed them to the mattress.

"You drive me crazy." Sweet drove deep inside her.

"God! Don't stop." She wrapped her legs around him, rubbing her leg up and down over his ass.

Nikla curved her hips up to allow Sweet to plunge deeper. "Tell me what you want."

"Will you do it? All of it?" Sweet increased his thrusts. Her tight, hot inner walls pulled him in and blew his mind.

Nikla nodded. "Anything."

"Even give up the suite?"

Nikla's eyes widened. "You son-of-a-bitch!"

To silence her, Sweet smothered her mouth with kisses. When he pulled back from her, he said, "Even pissed off you're sexy."

Sweet continued moving in and out of her until he felt his body shaking. "Let my hands go."

Sweet shook his head. "If you touch me, I'm going to explode."

"Please. Let me go."

"No!" He did let her hands go, but then sat up on his knees and put her legs over his shoulders.

Nikla sat up and managed to grab his shoulders. "Never fuck with a yoga instructor."

She sat on his lap and rotated her hips. When she kissed him and ran her fingers through his hair, he couldn't take it.

Sweet grabbed her around her waist and drove in so deep, he thought he would lose his mind. As he came down from his orgasmic high, he said, "We need to revise our agreement."

"Why can't we just keep going the way we have been?" Nikla smoothed her hand down the side of Sweet's face.

He captured her hand in his. "Because in a few weeks, things are going to change between us."

"Great. Then let's do what we want. I'll continue to learn from you until a decision has been made. We'll continue to have sex until that point. Once a decision has been made, we'll stop. You'll go your way and I'll go mine. Deal?"

Sweet cupped her ass in his hands as he held her. "Will you be able to walk away? I'm not sure I can."

Nikla got quiet. She wrapped her arms around him like this could be the last time she would see him. "Stay with me tonight. Please."

Sweet held her. For now, he would have her.

Chapter Seventeen

Nikla stared at the man who took up a great portion of her bed. She didn't mind giving up a bit of comfort for the sexy giant. Sweet slept on his back with his arm over his eyes. One foot kicked out from under the covers. His other arm wrapped around her waist. Every time Nikla tried pulling away, Sweet would pull her in close in an automatic reflex.

She glanced behind her at the mess on the floor. Not that she minded the strewn clothes. She wanted Sweet's wallet. Nikla didn't want his money. She wanted to see his real name on his driver's license. It would have been nice to see where he lived.

Nikla tried pulling out of Sweet's grip again.

"Where are you going?" Sweet asked in a sleepy tone. He kept arm over his eyes.

"I have to ask you permission to go to the bathroom?" Nikla put her hand on his bare chest.

Sweet removed his arm and opened his eyes to stare at her.

The hypnotic green color rendered her speechless every time she stared into them.

"I hadn't thought of that. Maybe I can make that a rule along with some others." He rolled her onto her back and pressed his lips against hers.

For as big as he was and for being a Dominant, Sweet possessed a delicate touch. He knew how to handle a woman's body.

"What other rules?" Nikla rubbed her hand up his arm. For as long as she could have him, she loved looking at and touching his body.

"If you really want to be my submissive, I want you to greet me in a certain way." He rolled off her. "Stand up."

Nikla sat up and then stood. Now being nude in front of him didn't bother her. The way Sweet stared at her, she couldn't believe she ever let it bother her. The seriousness of Sweet's face straightened her playful attitude.

"When I wake up in the morning or when I first walk into the room, I want you to kiss me on both cheeks."

"Face or butt?" When Sweet didn't break a smile, Nikla straightened up. "Kisses on your face. Go on."

"Then kiss me on the lips. After that, stand with your hands behind your back."

"Like I'm standing at attention?"

Sweet moved toward the edge of the bed. "Kind of." Then he stood.

"I don't like that part." Nikla shook her head and crossed her arms over her chest.

"And why is that?"

"My dad. He used to make me and my brother stand with our backs against the wall and he would inspect us at the beginning of the day and before we went to bed."

"As a Dom, I could use that information to make you do that." Sweet stood in front of her.

"I thought you said a good Dom listened to his submissives."

"You didn't let me finish. I want the kisses, then get on your knees." He moved in closer. "Start."

Nikla got up on her toes and kissed his one cheek. A sandpaper grit covered his face. The spiny texture felt prickly against her lips, and she loved it. She kissed his other cheek. When Nikla went in for his lips, she framed his face in her hands and brushed her lips against his. She sank in, tasting the brininess of his mouth.

When she broke from the kiss and attempted to lower herself to her knees, Sweet stopped her. "Well done. Don't go down on your knees. I don't know if I could take that so early in the morning."

Nikla gazed down at his dick and saw what morning lust had done to him. She smiled as she reconnected her gaze to his.

"Another thing that I want. I want you naked all the time."

"Even if we go out to dinner?" Nikla thought about her statement. "We haven't had a real date."

Sweet thought about her proclamation. "You're right. Our first get together was business. Last night was–"

"Also business." When Nikla saw his confused expression, she clarified. "At the club. You were supposed to be teaching me about being a submissive. I would say that that counts as business."

Nikla looked around Sweet at the digital clock next to her bed. "Oh, no. I need to get ready for work."

Sweet peered behind her. "Yeah, me, too. You take the bathroom first. I'll make breakfast."

Nikla knew the man knew how to cook. She also knew the man didn't mind using sugar, but still managed to look wonderful.

"No, you go in first and I'll make you breakfast." She tried aiming him toward her bathroom.

"Why won't you let me cook for you?"

Nikla paused before answering. "I don't have the best relationships with food. I used to use it to mask a lot of my feelings."

"Can't tell that now."

"I know. I worked my behind off, literally, to get this body. I changed my diet and I exercise all the time. I eat a specific diet every day. I don't want to deviate from it."

"What do you think will happen if you stray from the norm?" Sweet approached her again.

"I will gain weight again. I've worked hard to take control of my body."

"Now I want to control it." Sweet pulled her into his arms.

Nikla tried pushing back from him. "If you don't think that that makes me nervous, you're crazy."

The stubborn man refused to let her go. "And yet you still come to me. You still listen. You still obey."

She didn't know how to answer that. After a little contemplation, she said, "I think the difference is that I have a choice. I choose to submit."

Admitting that out loud rendered her speechless.

"I'm going to give you a diet each day." As soon as Nikla started to open her mouth to object, he continued. "I won't give you anything out of the norm. Nothing fattening."

"Nothing with refined sugar."

"Tell me what you eat now. As my submissive, I want you to turn everything over to me. I'll control what you eat and drink every day. I want to even decide what you wear. The only thing you'll have to think about is what to do at work."

As much as Nikla wanted to object to that, she kind of liked having some decisions made for her. She had to be herself for the rest of the day. Reconciling the idea that being herself meant she would become a submissive didn't hit her as hard as she thought it would.

"Run a bath." Sweet stood off to the side and let her go by him to her bathroom.

As instructed, Nikla ran a hot bath. She submerged herself inside and waited for him. Instead Sweet sat on the rim of the tub.

"What do you normally eat for breakfast?" he asked.

"I have a twenty-ounce spinach smoothie." Nikla ran a soapy washcloth over her body.

"Change it to an egg-white omelet mixed with peppers, onions, and mushrooms. Same calorie count, more substantial.”

“It’s faster if I just–”

“What about lunch?”

Nikla sighed. “If I don’t go out, it’s usually a spinach salad and a hard-boiled egg for protein.”

“Do a grilled chicken breast, grilled veggies, and some fruit for dessert.”

Nikla blinked. “You’ll let me have dessert?”

“I’m generous that way.” He smoothed her hair back from her face. “If you happen to go out to lunch, do the salad bar but stay away from the dried cranberries, corn, and croutons.”

Nikla smiled. “That’s exactly what I do now. What do I do for dinner?”

“I’d like to take care of that for tonight.”

Nikla’s smile dripped down. “Are we going to a restaurant or am I actually going to see where you live?”

Sweet remained quiet for a while. “Meet me at Decadent Treats after nine tonight.”

Nikla rolled her eyes. She guessed it would be another meal in the store and more sex in the office and the kitchen. “No, I’ll go home.”

“I wasn’t asking. Meet me at the store after nine.” Sweet stood and walked into the bedroom. When he returned, he carried Nikla’s cell phone. “I’m putting your meal plan on your phone as well as my cell phone number and a reminder of our date tonight.” He dialed a number and Nikla heard a phone ringing. “Now I have your number, too. If you’re late, I will be spanking that firm ass of yours. Do you understand?”

Nikla moved closer to him in the tub, splashing water on him. “Understood.”

He kissed her forehead. “Now, take your bath. I’ll get your breakfast going.”

Nikla slipped down into the balmy water. “Yes, Sir,” she whispered then smiled.

Nikla liked Sweet’s take-charge attitude. Considering someone would lose out on the downtown suite deal, she should have been satisfied to only have him for a short while. He managed to open up a side of her that she didn’t know existed. She didn’t want it to stop.

Did Sweet? Did he look forward to ending their little tryst?

****

At lunchtime, Deana showed up as expected. In her jeans and leather jacket, she kind of reminded Nikla of Sweet.

"Done with your classes?" Deana glanced at her phone.

Before Nikla could answer, Karen trotted into the workout room. Nikla cursed in her head. She didn't need to see her work distraction and irritant right now.

"Hey, Nikki! How's it going?" Karen trotted over to Nikla.

"It's Nikla. Not Nikki. Not Nik. Nikla."

Karen's smile melted as she split her attention between Nikla and Deana.

"I'm about to go out to lunch. Did you need something?" Nikla hung her workout bag on her shoulder.

"Yeah, can you pick up my spinning class tonight? It starts at eight-thirty and I–"

"No." Nikla headed to the door.

"But I have a date. And you always say yes." Karen pouted.

"And now *I* have a date." Nikla looked at her friend. "Ready to go to lunch?"

"Uh, yeah." Deana walked out of the center with Nikla. "That was pretty bad ass back there. I've never heard you say no to anyone."

Nikla smiled. "It was long overdue. And I really do have a date."

"Really? Hold that thought. I want to hear all the juicy details when we get to lunch."

Nikla went to their favorite restaurant with Deana following behind her. Once in the restaurant, they got seated by the window. After they got served drinks, Deana wasted no time in grilling her.

"Spill it. Who's the guy?" Deana asked.

Nikla tried to hide her smile but she couldn't. "Sweet Hawkes."

Deana dropped her drink and spilled some of the contents on the table. "Are you shitting me?"

Nikla shook her head as she helped her friend clean the mess on the table. "No. After our meeting with the leasing agent for that unit downtown, we kind of hit it off. He came to one of my yoga classes."

"Really?"

Nikla thought about the effort Sweet put into the class. "Yeah. He did pretty good, actually."

"And did he return the favor?"

Nikla nodded. "Yeah. He taught me how to make caramel."

"And?"

Nikla waited a moment before revealing everything.

"You did it, didn't you?"

Nikla's smile must have answered her friend's question.

"Oh, my God! Girl, when you rebound, you do it right. Was he as good as I imagined?"

Nikla felt her face get hot. "I'm not going to kiss and tell. I will say that he was very good in the kitchen and his office and the bathroom."

Deana blinked. "Wow. Good to see this whole competing for the suites thing hasn't turned you two off each other."

"Not yet. A final decision will be made in a few weeks. We'll see what happens then. I think if he loses the unit, he won't want to see me again. If I lose the unit to him," she shrugged, "I don't know."

"Which means that you like this guy. Are you cool with him getting the suite?"

"I would be hurt and disappointed. I worked so hard to get something I know I deserve."

Deana cocked her head. "Are you talking about the rental space or Sweet?"

Nikla remained quiet.

"That whole BDSM thing, has that come up yet? Are you cool with that?"

Before Nikla had a chance to answer, the waitress came to their table to get their order. As instructed by Sweet, Nikla ordered herself grilled chicken and mixed vegetables, and asked for a cup of fruit.

She felt her phone vibrating in her pocket. While Deana busied herself at the salad bar, Nikla retrieved her phone and looked at the screen for the text message.

Can't wait to have you tonight. Enjoy your lunch, read the message from Sweet, or rather Dom Sweet as he had labeled himself in her phone.

By the time Deana returned to the table, she had moved on to a new topic. Now Nikla couldn't wait until that night.

Chapter Eighteen

Sweet waited at the front door of Decadent Treats for Nikla. At nine, he saw her pulling into the parking lot. His skin prickled as he pointed to the side, signaling her to go around to the back of the building to park.

Sweet secured the store then walked outside. Nikla got out of her car wearing black slacks and a pink cashmere sweater. She resembled a fluffy stick of cotton candy. Like the sweet treat, he could have devoured her in seconds.

She walked up to him. "I probably wore the wrong outfit if we're going to be cooking again."

"No cooking." Sweet held her hand and led her to a set of steps on the side of the building.

"Where are we going? What's up here?" Nikla asked.

"My place." Sweet noticed Nikla remained quiet until he opened the door. "Welcome to my home."

"You live above the store?"

Sweet couldn't tell if she liked the idea or thought it made him look pathetic. Either way, he no longer wanted to hide the truth from her. "Yes. I wanted to stay close to the action."

"Close to the action? I think it's more of your control issues." She smiled as she strolled around the place. "Why didn't you take me up here the first night we were together?"

"In case you haven't noticed, I have issues with letting a lot of people into my world." Admitting it out loud chipped away at the wall that he'd erected around him. It'd taken him years to build it up, and longer to fix it once Melinda betrayed him. In a few days, Nikla managed to get him to take down a portion, brick by brick.

"I noticed. So how did I get so privileged?"

Sweet regarded her for a moment before answering. "You haven't judged me yet for anything I've said or done."

"I've had enough of that in my lifetime. I wouldn't do it to anyone else."

Sweet scanned her body. He hated to see her in so many layers, in clothes in general. As expected, Nikla removed her shoes.

Nikla looked around the place. "So do I get a tour?"

"Only after you give me my standard greeting."

Nikla placed her purse on the back of the couch. "I almost forgot." She kissed his cheeks, then his lips. This time he let her drop down to her knees and lower her head for him.

Perfect.

"Very good, Sugar Baby." He held his hand out to her. "Now you get the tour even though you could probably see every bit of my place from where you are."

He showed her the bathroom first before showing off his loft bedroom, the small living room, the dining room that consisted of a small round table and two chairs before finally bringing her to the kitchen.

"This is my favorite room here. I love this spot." Sweet braced his hands against the counter.

"It looks like a chef's dream." Nikla beamed as she came around the counter to him.

"That's how I had it made." When Nikla stood by Sweet, he imagined taking her on the counter, driving deep into her tight core.

"I almost forgot to do one thing for you." She started unbuttoning her sweater. "You wanted me completely nude at all times, right?"

A knock sounded at the door.

"Oh, God. Please don't tell me you ordered out." Nikla stopped at the second button.

"No. Of course not." Sweet went to the door and opened it.

On the other side stood his friend and a guest who had arrived right on time.

"We're going to have entertainment first before dinner." When Nikla stood beside him, Sweet put his hand at the small of her back. "I hope you stretched."

Sweet had known Master Wasabi since working for him back in Sweet's teenage years, before he knew the man dabbled in the darker sensual arts. Sweet used to deliver food for Wasabi's Japanese restaurant. When he visited the restaurant after hours one night and caught his boss with a young woman strung up in an elaborate rope web, Sweet couldn't help but admire the work.

Now his former boss and Sweet ran in the same circles. He had to ask him for a favor for tonight. Sweet wanted to push Nikla just a bit more. Either this would send her running away from him or into his arms. He hoped the latter would be true.

After a slight bow, Sweet ushered his friend and his friend's guest into his home. "Master Wasabi, this is–" Sweet paused before he finished his introduction. How should he address this woman? "My submissive, Sugar Baby."

Nikla glanced at him before putting out her hand. Sweet captured her extended hand in his and lowered it.

"He doesn't shake hands. Bow your head," Sweet instructed.

Nikla bowed her head to him.

"Who's your friend?" Sweet nodded toward the woman behind him.

"I call her Nori." Wasabi said something to the incredibly tall, thin woman in Japanese.

She smiled, bowed her head, and brought her attention back to Wasabi. Besides her height, her striking platinum blonde hair on the Asian woman grabbed his attention.

"I didn't know you had invited guests." Nikla wrapped her arms around her body.

"They're not here for dinner. They're going to help with the entertainment."

Nikla chewed on her lower lip. She pulled Sweet back away from the duo. "I'm not a bisexual."

Sweet furrowed his eyebrows at her statement.

"I don't want to be with another woman. I don't swing." She shook her head.

"There are different types of swinging. You're going to do one of them." Sweet put his hands on her shoulders and pushed her toward the corner of his apartment where the 1970's chair swing hung. "The first thing I need for you to do, Sugar Baby, is take off your clothes."

****

Nikla couldn't believe her neck didn't snap from how fast she turned her head when Sweet had made his request. "Excuse me?"

"For what I want you to do, you need to be naked." He walked around her and removed the chair from the hook in the ceiling and set it on the side. When he returned his attention to Nikla, his expression turned to a scowl. "Sugar Baby, get undressed and don't make me tell you again."

Nikla studied him for a moment. She balled her hands into fists and took a deep breath.

"Remember what I taught you." Sweet approached her and started undoing buttons on her sweater.

"You would never hurt me." Nikla lowered her arms to her sides. "If I feel uncomfortable, I can use my safe words."

Sweet nodded as he slipped her sweater down her arms. Nikla looked over at Wasabi and Nori, and didn't feel as hungry as she thought she would. She noticed the older man placed a black bag on the floor. When he opened it, ropes of all kinds spilled out from the opening.

"Red! Red!" Nikla backed away from Sweet.

What did this stranger want to do? Hang her?

Sweet pursued Nikla and captured her hands. "Shibari."

"What?" Nikla kept her stare on this mysterious duo.

"Shibari is the art of Japanese rope bondage." Sweet grabbed Nikla's pants and started undoing them. "Master Wasabi is a true expert at this. I really, really want to see you trussed up and hung from my ceiling."

Nikla looked at the hook in the ceiling, then back at the duo who hadn't stopped removing rope after rope after rope from their bag.

"And you won't leave me with them alone?" Nikla stared into Sweet's eyes.

"Of course not." He unzipped her pants and dropped them to the floor. Sweet looked down at her body. "No panties." He released a long, low whistle. "Didn't see that coming."

Nikla hadn't expected to leave the house without underwear. She felt a little brazen enough to do it. Maybe she needed that bit of bravery to trust him in this venture.

"I will be over there in the kitchen making our dinner." Sweet turned to Wasabi.

Sweet spoke to Wasabi in Japanese. The young woman must have understood what Sweet had said. She smiled and glanced at Nikla.

Sweet turned to Nikla. He reached behind her and undid her bra. With that off, he stared at her body. "Is there a backbend move you do in yoga?"

Nikla felt her eyebrows drawing together. "Yes."

"Do it."

Nikla took a couple of steps back into a free space area. She bent backward until her hands touched the floor.

"And can you raise one leg in the air?" Sweet asked.

Without verbally answering, Nikla raised one leg straight into the air.

"That." Sweet pointed to Nikla as he spoke to Wasabi. "I want that captured."

Wasabi nodded.

Sweet helped right Nikla. Once upright, he gave Nikla a kiss. "Have fun. They'll take good care of you. I will be right over there." He pointed to his open kitchen area.

Nikla walked toward the duo. Wasabi pointed to the floor.

"The Master wants you standing right here," Nori said without a hint of an accent.

Nikla obliged, directly underneath the eyebolt in the ceiling. As she remained still, Master Wasabi arranged his ropes. He placed them next to Nikla. Occasionally he would hold a few of them up from the ceiling to her like he wanted to make sure he would have enough rope.

After a few minutes, he touched her, wrapping a thick rope around her midsection. Standing on a chair, he slipped the rope through the hook attached to the ceiling. The thin older man surprised Nikla by hoisting her body off the floor in a couple of strong tugs. He secured the rope to an exposed pipe jutting from the floor.

As Nikla hung from the ceiling, both Wasabi and Nori worked on her, wrapping ropes around Nikla's body, from her arms to her breasts to her legs. Wasabi stood on a chair again and drew her leg up in the air.

Nikla straightened it, knowing how much Sweet would have liked that. The fact that Sweet liked any of this didn't strike her as odd, mainly because Nikla wanted to do this to please him.

After about fifteen minutes, Wasabi seemed to be done. He muttered something under his breath as he gathered his belongings. Nori stood beside Nikla's head and combed her fingers down through Nikla's hair.

Nikla stared at the woman who looked like she started to bring her head down toward Nikla's face.

Wasabi barked an order and snapped the woman out of her pursuit. Nori sighed and winked at Nikla.

Sweet walked the duo to the door, then came over to Nikla. "I wish you could see what I see. You look amazing." He strolled around her. "You look like a dancer in flight. So elegant."

"Take my picture." Nikla looked at Sweet. "I want to see what you see."

Sweet went into the kitchen and retrieved a camera from the drawer. "I don't want you thinking that I would take your picture with my phone and show it off anywhere or post it online." He aimed the camera at her and took a shot.

Sweet repositioned his body, taking another picture that he aimed at her vagina. With each picture she felt his admiration of her.

Nikla felt the rope that held her up move and suddenly she started lowering to the floor. "No. Just a little longer."

"I appreciate your newfound enthusiasm for shibari. But at a certain point it gets dangerous to keep you tied up and upside down like this." Sweet held her back as he continued lowering her.

Freed from being hung from overhead, he carried her to his bedroom and placed her on his bed. With careful precision, he removed the ropes from around her body.

"Are you able to do this?" Nikla asked as she remained still.

"Not this elaborately. I can do simple rope bondage." Sweet removed the last of the ropes from her body. "I'll get these back to him." He started to massage Nikla's body.

"No!" She jumped up. "Not yet." She padded to the bathroom and turned on the lights.

The full-length mirror offered her a great view of the rope indentions left over her body. Tracks of them ran over her breasts and arms and stomach. She ran her fingers over where her skin dipped in thanks to the ropes.

Whereas others may have found her disfigured and temporarily scarred, Nikla loved it. She turned her back to the mirror and saw the same track marks over her ass and back.

Sweet walked into the bathroom. "What do you think?"

She looked at him, wrapped her arms around his neck, and kissed him. "I know I'm not supposed to ask this, but I really want to feel you inside of me now."

Sweet held her waist. "We eat first." His hands coasted down to her ass. "And then..." He trailed off. A growl rumbled in his chest.

Nikla sat on the counter and pulled Sweet in closer with her legs. "Are you sure?" She reached for his jeans, but Sweet captured her hands.

"I'm sure that keeping you waiting will make the experience even better." He helped her from the counter. "By the way, I love the way you look in and out of rope." His hands trailed over her body where the rope had been.

The feeling gave her a tickling sensation that made her wet. She held his hand and placed it over her mound. "Please." She stared into his eyes. "Please."

Nikla brushed her clitoris over the palm of his hand. She didn't want or expect him to pull away.

"Come here." Sweet held her hand and led her to the dining room. He sat down in a chair at the table. "Come across my lap."

"What?"

"Punishment. Over my knee." He patted his lap. "Now."

Nikla obliged him, lying across his muscled thighs. She held onto his ankle with one hand and braced her other hand on the floor.

"Ten hits," Sweet said. "I want you to count them out." When Sweet administered the first hit, everything in Nikla's body shook.

"One." She gripped his ankle tighter.

The spanks after that became progressively harder. Dutifully, Nikla continued counting them, afraid to disappoint Sweet.

This spanking didn't resemble the spanking he'd given her when they'd had sex. It truly felt like a punishment. It didn't help that Sweet talked her through it.

"If you want to be a submissive, you're going to have to learn to listen and obey." He gave her another hit on her other cheek. "Do you want to be a submissive?"

"Seven. Yes," Nikla shouted.

"Why?"

Nikla's answer choked in her throat. She tightened her grip on his leg.

"Tell me."

She gritted her teeth before answering. "I want to just be. No worries. Keep it simple." Nikla released a grunt. "Eight! I want you to tell me what to do." She craned her head up to look at him. "I want you."

Sweet gave her two more spanks before he turned her over and placed her on his lap. The hug he gave her let her know that he must have felt the same way.

"You're so special." Sweet repeated that until Nikla's panting breath subsided.

She hadn't cried like she thought she would. She didn't feel anger. Something else riddled her body, rattled her senses. Frustration.

Sweet pulled back from her to look at her face. With his large hands, he framed her face.

"Thank you." Nikla smiled.

"Christ." Sweet blinked. "You completely get it. It's scary."

He kissed her.

"May I serve you dinner, Sir?"

Sweet shook his head. He stood up with her on his lap and placed her on a chair at the dining room table. "I'll get dinner. You wait here."

Sitting naked at the dinner table would have seemed weird to her only a week ago. Now it seemed perfectly normal. When she heard footfalls coming back toward her, Nikla turned her head.

Sweet held something up in his hand that look like a toy bracelet. "Give me your hand."

Nikla held her hand up to him.

"Ordinarily a Dom or Domme would do something called collaring a submissive or slave they want. The collar makes it known that you belong to someone else." Sweet slipped the elastic bracelet covered in circular discs over her wrist. "I want you. I want you to know that I want you always. I figured since our first play time happened in the candy store, I wanted to give you something to make you remember that."

Nikla looked at her wrist. She smiled when she saw the candy bracelet. "I haven't seen one of these since I was a kid."

"It won't match anything in your wardrobe, but I want you to wear it always." Sweet brushed his thumb over the candy beads.

"I'll wear it. Always."

Sweet kissed the top of her head, then went to the kitchen. As Nikla watched him, she realized how far deep she'd gotten with being with him. If he'd hoped to push her away with the rope bondage, he'd been mistaken. She would have to talk to him about their future. With each test he put her through, Nikla found herself wanting him and wanting this new life more and more.

Chapter Nineteen

After dinner, Sweet happily took Nikla to his bed. He'd wanted to fuck her before Wasabi strung her up. When he'd gotten her down from the bondage, he wanted to take her on his bed. He had to be the voice of reason, the calm in the sexual storm that he'd created.

Nikla snuggled next to him, resting her head on his chest. A smile crossed her face from ear to ear.

"Did you enjoy your meal plan today?" Sweet asked as he rubbed his hand up and down her toned arm.

"Yes, Sir. Very delicious. Variety is the spice of life." Nikla rested her chin on his chest.

"We're not in scene. You can call me by my name." He smoothed his hand back through her soft hair.

"Okay, Sweet."

Sweet cleared his throat. "Swithin."

"What?"

"Swithin is my real name." Sweet smirked at the admission.

Nikla sat up. "Are you serious?"

"Swithin Bartholomew Hawkes to be exact. My mother wanted something English with some meaning. She looked up male names meaning strength. She came upon Swithin and liked it. I hated it." The teasing Sweet took as a kid never left him. "Grandma came up with the nickname of Sweet. That stuck. I'd rather be called that than Bart or Sweet Roll or Sweatin' to the Oldies."

Nikla screwed up her lips. "That would be a stupid nickname."

"Not when you're a hundred pounds overweight."

Nikla stared at him. "You? You're kidding."

Sweet shook his head. "I used food to cope and I rarely did anything athletic. Kids teased me all the time."

"I find that hard to believe. You're so assertive."

"Yeah, now. I wasn't always. Masaun, my brother, he got me into a lot of things that put me straight. He got me into karate and that gave me discipline and exercise. Then he got me into the BDSM scene. Both gave me focus."

"I'd like to meet your brother."

Sweet looked away. He'd had an opportunity to introduce Nikla to Masaun at the club. Sweet didn't want to get a lecture from his brother on his choices. He could hear him ask how could Sweet associate with the woman who actively picketed their store. Masaun didn't know her. Sweet didn't want whatever he had with Nikla ruined.

Nikla ran her fingers through the few hairs he had on his chest. "I would never picture you as a fat kid. I mean. I was a fat kid. I think my dad was disappointed in me because of it."

"I wanted to rebel against the stereotype. I wasn't going to run away from food. I wanted to embrace it. That's why I started the store. This was my way to control food instead of it controlling me."

"You never thought about having a business where you made healthy items like a vegan cupcake store."

Sweet shook his head before Nikla finished her question. "Never. I think some guy opened a place like that around here. I haven't heard much about it."

Nikla nodded but kept her gaze down.

"Besides, having a store like that would make me feel like I wasn't being true to myself. Fat or fit, I've always wanted to own a candy store. Some of my best memories came from being in a candy store." He glanced at Nikla who gave him a doubting look. "When you're an overweight kid, there aren't a lot of places you can go and not feel out of place. I'd go to a gym or a recreation center; I didn't get picked for any teams. No one wanted me because I would only hold someone back. I'd go to the old Captain Candyland." He noticed how Nikla beamed. "You remember that place?"

She nodded. "Dad drove by it, but I never managed to make it inside. I just loved the colors I could see through the glass. The kids that came out all seemed happy."

"I was one of those happy kids. I'd go in there and discovered my utopia. The older women in there would pinch my cheeks and tell me how cute I was. The owner would test out candies on me. I loved that I didn't have to be anything more than what I was. It's the reason I love The Dollhouse."

"I went the other way. I knew I couldn't control the food so I ate what I knew would work for me and I dove headfirst into a physical fitness career." Nikla laughed. "I can't believe we both have the same kind of past with food." She laughed harder. "I can't believe your name is Swithin."

"Hey, *Nikla*, I wouldn't go throwing stones."

"Actually, I like it." She straddled his lap. "Swithin."

Sweet felt his cock getting hard as she gyrated on top of him. Hearing her say his name it didn't sound dorky or odd.

"Swithin."

Sweet loved seeing her small pink tongue poking between her teeth as she said his name. He reached over to the nightstand and grabbed a condom. Nikla took the rubber from his hand and rolled it onto his cock.

Sweet held the base of his dick and helped guide Nikla on top of it. She tried easing down on him. He thrust his hips up and impaled her.

"Shit!" She grabbed his shoulders.

He held her hips. "Say my name."

"Swithin." Nikla leaned her head back. "Swithin. So good inside. Don't stop."

Sweet raised his hips, forcing Nikla to grab his headboard instead. With her face so close to his, he couldn't help but kiss her. He massaged her tits. As soon as he pinched her nipples, Nikla's body froze.

"Harder," she said. "Make me feel it."

Sweet squeezed harder, then licked her long neck.

"Say it. Please just say it."

Sweet knew what she meant. He knew what she wanted to hear. "Mine."

"Yes!" Nikla rode him harder.

He released one breast so that he could spank her. When he did that, Nikla wrapped her arms around his neck and held him close. He felt her heart pounding in her chest. Her knees pressed against his hips.

"Come. Come, baby." Sweet cradled the back of her head.

Nikla pounded her fist on Sweet's back as she came hard. He had more to give.

Sweet rolled her onto her back then got out of bed.

"Where are you going? You didn't come." Nikla pressed her back against the pillows arranged on the headboard.

Sweet ducked into his closet and found a couple of old neckties he hadn't worn in years. He returned to the bed. "Hands up."

Without question, Nikla brought her hands up and grabbed his headboard. Sweet tied one wrist to his bed, being careful to avoid her new candy bracelet. He kissed her fingers before moving around his bed to get to the other side. After tying her other wrist to the headboard, he deposited the condom he wore.

"I trust you." Nikla stared at him. "You can trust me."

He knew what she implied with her statement. "I'm clean."

"I got checked recently." She spread her legs. "I get the shot."

Sweet knew she wouldn't get pregnant. A small part of him wanted her to carry his child. Shit, he needed to stop thinking that way and think about the future.

He returned to bed. Sweet needed to receive every type of sensation possible. He placed his body on top of hers and enjoyed her warmth and softness. Before he did anything else, he ran his hands down her strung up arms, to her face, over her breasts and to her stomach.

"You feel so good. So soft." Sweet kept his gaze directly on her eyes.

He ran his hand over her hair. Nikla lifted her head to get the full experience. Sweet nuzzled his face in her hair. He picked up her usual jasmine scent combined now with a honey aroma.

When Sweet entered her this time, he felt different. The walls he had around himself came down so hard he thought he would climax at that moment. To feel her hot vaginal walls tightening around him connected him to Nikla more intimately than he thought it would.

Nikla pulled on her restraints. "Swithin."

Sweet thrust himself inside her and held himself there. "Keep saying my name."

"And cursing?" Nikla smiled.

He nodded. Sweet swept one hand back and grabbed her thigh. He positioned her leg around his body just to feel her more. This time with her, Sweet wanted to take his time.

Nikla licked his bottom lip. That move gave him the permission to capture her mouth. He drove his tongue in her mouth. Thanks to the strawberries he'd fed her for dessert, she still tasted sweet.

"Mmm." He thrust into her again, curving his hips this time.

"Swithin." Nikla's body undulated under his. She matched his movements in every way like a well-played tennis match.

With Nikla, he could go on for hours.

"I love this." Nikla gripped the ties holding her arms down. "Keep me tied here all night."

Sweet kissed her neck. "I'll just put jellybeans on you and tell you not to move."

"Or just ask me to stay."

Sweet said nothing. He continued making love to this beauty as he let the idea of having Nikla in his bed, by his side, every night and every morning, roll around in his head. If he could make it work, if he could have this amazing woman by his side, he would be over the moon.

Sweet continued making love to Nikla until she came twice. He untied her wrists. He sat on the edge of the bed and placed her on his lap. His body shook as he drove in her deeper and deeper until he exploded.

Nikla placed her head on his shoulder.

"What are we going to do? What the hell are we going to do?" Sweet stroked her back.

****

Nikla watched Sweet sleep. She brushed his hair from his face as she listened to him breathing heavily. She scanned his body, the same one that gave her endless hours of pleasure last night.

She circled his nipple with her index finger until he moaned. When he opened his eyes, his expression quickly changed to something quizzical.

"Why are you smiling at me like that?" he asked.

"You. For the first time, I saw you smiling." She brushed her fingers down the side of his face. "You smiled in your sleep. It was wonderful."

Sweet groaned and sat up. "I was dreaming about you."

"You were? What was I doing?"

Sweet remained quiet. He stared at her almost with a bit of remorse in his gaze. He must have been thinking about what had occurred to her as well. When Bobbi decided who would get the units, what would happen to the two of them?

Nikla ran her fingers down over his face to his lips. "You have a wonderful smile. You should do it more often."

Sweet gazed down at her. To Nikla's relief, he smiled at her.

"Now that I have something to smile about, maybe I will." He kissed her. Then he plopped his head back on his pillows. "What a night." He looked at her. "I never even asked, what were you thinking when you saw Wasabi?"

Nikla smiled to herself. "When I first saw them, I thought you had gotten some world-class chef to cook our dinners for us."

"I did." He pointed to himself and laughed.

Nikla even loved his laugh, a deep-bellied, full-on laugh. "Dinner and dessert were pretty amazing. When I saw the bag full of ropes, I thought you were going to hang me. I was thinking, man, this guy really wants those units."

Sweet's face went somber. "I told you I would never hurt you. If someone even thought about hurting you, I would stop them dead in their tracks."

The seriousness of his tone struck Nikla deep. She never had anyone defend her like that or even want to protect her. The notion made her feel good, made her feel safe.

"When you described what it is that Master Wasabi did, I was curious."

"Had you ever seen it before?"

Nikla shook her head. Sweet's smile widened as he got out of bed. He went over to his closet and retrieved something from the top shelf. When he backed up, Nikla saw he had a large, flat coffee table book in his hands.

Sweet got back in bed and handed the book to her. "Take a look at that."

Nikla looked at the cover. The title of *Wrapped Up* went across the top and emblazoned in red. The image of a woman's torso bound in thick rope accompanied the salacious title. She opened the cover and the first picture that greeted her contained a man and a woman both with ropes constricting their fit bodies and contorted in a way that it looked like rope connected their bodies, like intestines and arteries providing life sources to each other.

The black-and-white shots made the pictures look more artistic. Page after page, Nikla's heart pounded.

"Look at this." Sweet held up his camera and showed her the screen.

Nikla took the camera from his hands and stared at the picture of herself. Her back bend looked deeper as she hovered in the air. With her leg kicked up, she saw herself as a superhero. The picture looked surreal, but in color, it made it even more real.

"I did this." Nikla shook her head. "I got naked and allowed strangers to tie me with rope and suspend me in the air." She looked at Sweet. "And you have it immortalized."

"I can delete it if you want." He reached for the camera.

Nikla pulled away. "No. No. I like it. I like that you have it. You'll always have it." She scanned her body. The deep indentations that the ropes had made no longer marred her skin.

Nikla brushed her hands over her chest, arms and stomach. Sweet slid his hand over her hand and rested it on her stomach.

"No marks." She gazed at Sweet. "It's like it never happened."

Sweet tapped the camera. "Only it did."

Nikla nodded. "You made it happen."

He shook his head. "No, *you* did. You could have said no. You could have walked out and never seen me again. Or run to the media and talk about me and my strange ways."

"Like you said before, telling on you would be like telling on myself." Nikla rested her hand on his chest.

Sweet pulled her close to him. "Thank you for being brave. I don't know a lot of submissives who have been in the lifestyle a while who would even do this."

"But you subjected me to it. Why?"

Sweet looked serious. He didn't look her in the eyes, a first for him. "I keep thinking you're not real. I put you through tests to see at what point you'll run."

Nikla laughed. "I'm still here."

"I should have known you wouldn't shy away from this." Sweet held her hand. "You've taken training as a submissive very seriously. I want to do so much more with you."

Nikla put her hand to her wrist. "My students are going to wonder why I'm wearing a candy bracelet."

"What will you say if any of them asks?"
Nikla thought about the question before she answered. "I'll say someone special gave it to me." She glanced at the clock next to the bed. "Damn. I need to go. I didn't bring a change of clothes."

"Maybe you should the next time you come over." Sweet put his hand on her thigh and rubbed his thumb over her skin. "I want you here a lot."

Nikla beamed. "You don't want to come over to my place sometime?"

"I have better toys here."

She laughed. "Says the man who told me he can make anything kinky."

"Is that a dare?" He wiggled his fingers into her sides.

Nikla laughed hard enough that her sides hurt immediately. "No! No! No tickling! Please!"

"What's the word?" Sweet straddled her body and continued tickling her.

"Red! Red! Red!"

Sweet stopped but continued smiling at her. "You are a quick study."

"And you are an unfair competitor." She gave him a playful slap on the arm. "Here." She held up his book.

Sweet climbed off her. "Keep it." He nudged it toward her.

"Thank you. I'll give it back."

Sweet waved his hand in the air. "Don't worry about it."

"I do have to go."

"Not until I make you breakfast and set up your meal plan."

Nikla so wanted to slide back down in bed and snuggle next to Sweet, or Swithin as she now knew him. She had to go home. Even though she would be leaving with the clothes she'd worn the night before, there would be no shame in her gait.

"What are you doing tonight?" She hopped out of bed.

He gave her a salacious smile as his answer.

Nikla's clit twitched in response. "I want us to do something I'm good at."

Sweet's smile broadened.

"No. Not that. My last class is over around five. Are you able to break free then?" Nikla tiptoed back toward the bathroom.

"Maybe seven. Would that be too late?"

Nikla shook her head. "Wear workout clothing."

Sweet groaned again. "More yoga?"

She shook her head. "Not this time. But it will be very physical. Are you game?"

Sweet got out of bed and stalked toward her. "There's nothing you could do that could scare me away." He guided her into the bathroom.

Nikla held onto his shoulders as she stared at him. Before he could say anything, she kissed his one cheek, then the other, then kissed his lips. When she lowered herself to her knees in front of him, she felt the muscles in his thighs tighten.

"Call in sick. Stay here."

Nikla brought her gaze up to meet his. She shook her head. "I can't. I want to." She brought her hands up to his cock. "I have people who depend on me."

Sweet held her wrists and pulled them back from his body. "I'll see you tonight then. Let me get your breakfast going. Take your time in the bathroom." He kissed the top of her head before leaving her.

Nikla allowed her body to slump down even more once he departed. She had to figure out what she wanted, what she needed, in her life. Managing this balancing act didn't suit her. From Sweet's reaction, he must not have liked it either.

Sweet was right. What the hell were they going to do?

Chapter Twenty

"Oh, my God!" Masaun stared at Sweet with his hand over his mouth.

Sweet looked down at the fudge bars he'd just made. "What? Something wrong?" His mind had been on Nikla and her luscious body so he wouldn't have been surprised if he'd done something strange with his fudge, like adding Pop Rocks to the mix.

Masaun walked up to him. "What is that?" He pointed to Sweet's face. "Is that a smile?"

Sweet grabbed his brother's finger and shoved it back. "Asshole. You got jokes, huh?"

Masaun laughed. "I think it's great. I haven't seen you smile like that in a long, long time. What gives?" He leaned against the counter as he watched Sweet package each portion of fudge he'd cut.

"Can't I be happy about making a beautiful tray of fudge?" Sweet wrapped another piece and put it on a pile with the other ones he'd wrapped.

"They are great looking. But I know you." Masaun wagged his finger at him. "Is it the woman I caught you here with the other day?"

"You're not going to let this drop, are you?" Sweet set the empty baking sheet by the sink.

"Is she the same woman you were playing with at the club?"

"Yes."

"Huh. Really?"

The question in Masaun's tone caused Sweet to bring his attention back to his brother. "What?"

"The whole thing with Melinda. I don't want you to go through that again."

Sweet waved his hand. "Won't happen. We talked. We established some rules. We both know what we have going on is only going to be for a short time."

"But you think about her and smile. You don't see anything happening beyond just play and, uh, other activities?"

Masaun's question had been rolling around in Sweet's head for days. Did Sweet see a lasting relationship with Nikla? He wanted one. In her he'd found his dream woman, one open for both playing and sex with drive and ambition that rivaled his own. The competitiveness concerned him.

"Look, just be happy I'm getting out there."

"Trust me. I am. Where you were before worried me." Masaun put his hand on Sweet's chest.

Sweet brought his full attention to his older brother.

"I didn't want to see you spiraling down again."

Sweet knew exactly what Masaun meant. As much as he wanted to admonish his brother for being so overprotective, he couldn't.

"I'm okay." He pushed past Masaun.

"You look it. Since what you have going on is a temporary thing, does that mean I won't get a chance to meet her?"

Sweet turned back to Masaun.

"Can you two do dinner tonight?" Masaun asked.

Sweet shook his head.

"Come on. I'm not like you in the kitchen, but I do okay. Kindle, not so much." Masaun laughed. "We haven't broken bread since–"

"Since you and Kindle got together." Sweet didn't mean to sound bitter about his brother's happy love life. He couldn't deny he wanted something like that for himself. Something permanent. Something of his own. "I have plans tonight. She's taking me somewhere."

Masaun blinked. "Really?"

"Why does that surprise you?"

"I can't believe you let someone else plan an event. Vanilla or not, I've never known you to release the reins on anything."

When Masaun posed the situation that way, it struck Sweet that he'd had relaxed his standards around Nikla. What did that mean to him?

He shook his head. "I'm learning to be open. What can I say?"

"I'd say I really would like to meet this miracle worker."

"Rain check."

"At least you have something keeping you busy to keep your mind off that crazy plan to expand." Masaun shook his head. "It's not a good time. You know that, right?"

Sweet just smiled at Masaun. Now would have been a great time to share with him his idea to acquire that new spot downtown. Even though Sweet hadn't talked to Bobbi in over a week, he had a good feeling that she saw his business as a frontrunner. Not that Nikla didn't have something to offer.

As he thought about her, he imagined her having her own business. With her drive, she could do it. More importantly, it would make her happy.

Where would that leave him?

Sweet carried the tray of fudge to the main store and placed them in the case. He broke his attention from his task when he heard his name being bellowed out in the store.

"Mr. Sweet!" Connie called out.

Sweet turned to the older woman standing in the middle of the store.

Connie pointed to the front of the store. "She's back."

Sweet didn't even ask her who she meant. He darted to the door and marched through it. His heart pounded with each step until he came face to face with Nikla.

He had to bite the inside of his cheek to keep from smiling. "What are you still doing here?"

****

Nikla's stomach trembled with excitement although in front of Sweet, she tried to remain cool. "What? You think because of what has happened between us that I wouldn't still come and do this?"

Sweet approached her. He lowered his voice and whispered, "I would expect nothing less."

She gripped her fliers as she let his deep voice roll over her. If she were honest with herself, Nikla would admit that her visit today had everything to do with seeing this sexy man again.

She should have taken him up on his offer to call in sick. Nikla had never done that before. She'd never missed a day of school, either. Good ol' reliable Nikla Dearwood. Here she stood with a man her father wouldn't want for her.

His race had nothing to do with it. Lawrence would say Sweet controlled her. Nikla would have to happily agree.

"Having any luck?" Sweet circled her body.

"Not a lot of people out here today."

"They heard you were coming and they all ran."

Nikla looked at Sweet and noticed he laughed. Better than his smile, his laugh made her feel light. "Cute."

"Tell me what you were like as a child."

Nikla regarded Sweet for a moment. "Are you serious?"

He crossed his arms over his chest. "I want to know what a young Nikla was like."

She smirked. "My father would say I was unmotivated and lazy despite being my high school's valedictorian and graduating *magna cum laude* from college."

Sweet shook his head. "I have no interest in hearing how other people have defined you."

"Says the man who calls me Sugar Baby." What she did as Sugar Baby made her cheeks feel hot.

"Do you really want to go there now? If so, you didn't give me my standard greeting."

Nikla stared at him for a moment before she smiled to break up the tension. No way in public could she kiss his cheeks then his lips, then lower herself to the ground. What would people think if they saw that?

"Me as a child, right?" Nikla crossed her feet and locked her knees back in her spot. "I was curious. Where we lived, the woods backed up to our property. I would go exploring in the woods all the time. I'd catch tadpoles and snapping turtles."

She noticed that at that bit of news, Sweet's eyes widened.

"You caught snapping turtles? Wasn't that dangerous?"

She nodded. "But when you're a kid, you feel invincible like nothing can ever hurt you." Nikla lowered her gaze as she thought about herself as a child. "I can't believe how brave I was back then. I couldn't do that now."

"Do what? Go into the woods?" Sweet asked.

"The unknown."

"That I don't believe."

She brought her gaze up to meet his.

"You're wanting to start your own business, which takes a tremendous amount of guts. And you're learning about my lifestyle and have yet to flinch."

"That's different."

"How?"

"The business is my passion. I love what I do. The business is just a natural extension of me."

"And with me?" He took a step toward her. He lowered his arms down to his sides.

"You talked about your lifestyle with such passion, I believed you." Nikla meant that.

Had Sweet acted goofy or immature about being a Dom, or worse, cocky, she wouldn't have been willing to allow him to do what he'd done to her.

"Go on. Talk about your childhood." Sweet put his hands to his hips.

"You don't want to hear about my boring childhood, me catching fireflies and reading old books." She turned her back on him before she could admit anything else embarrassing.

"You act as though what you did as a child is so very different from everyone else."

After Nikla returned her gaze to Sweet did he continued speaking.

"I did the same thing." He patted his flat stomach. "Remember I didn't always look like this."

Nikla snickered. "Yeah? Who's your favorite author?"

"Back then? Edgar Allen Poe. What can I say? Even as a kid I knew I needed to be in a dungeon." His smile slipped down. "You?"

Nikla shook her head. "I'm not going to say. You'll laugh."

"Never."

She took a deep breath. "I liked Judy Blume." When it looked like nothing registered over Sweet's face, she elaborated. "I didn't like her children's stuff, even as a kid. You know. *Fudge*, and *Are You There, God? It's Me, Margaret*."

"There's a book out there titled like that?" Sweet swept his brown hair back from his face.

"Yes. It's about a young girl's foray into womanhood." Nikla smirked. "She gets her period."

"Ah, nice. Guys don't have any books about masturbating for the first time. You know. No, *Hey, God, Climbing This Rope Feels Good*."

Nikla laughed. "You're funny. No, I liked Judy Blume's adult stuff like *Wifey*."

"What did you like about the book?" he asked.

"She talked honestly about a woman, a wife, and how she dealt with everyday life. She gets to live out fantasies. It all starts with a naked man on a motorcycle wearing an American flag."

"It all started with us with some licorice whips."

Nikla stared at him. The silence that existed between them made her feel like she stood right in front him, not just a few feet away. She noticed his breathing increasing. He licked his bottom lip as he stared at her.

"Hey, Mr. Sweet. Should I call the police?" a heavyset woman asked from the store's open door.

Sweet broke his gaze from her for a moment to address her. He turned around. "No. I told you I had this handled."

"You've been out here a long time. I thought–"

"I'm fine. Go back inside." Sweet kept his stare on his employee until she retreated into the store.

"Maybe you should go." Nikla looked at her fliers. "And I should go, too."

"I'm not going to call the police on you. I believe someone told me that you had a right to stand on this public sidewalk."

Nikla went to her car. "Yes. But I shouldn't be out here doing this."

"Why did you come?"

Nikla stared at Sweet. She nibbled on her bottom lip.

"Did you have lunch already?" Sweet went toward her car.

Unable to speak, she nodded.

"Did you eat what I had in your plan?"

Nikla nodded again.

"Come up to my place."

She opened her door and threw the fliers inside. Nikla shook her head. "I shouldn't."

"Just to talk. I like talking to you."

Nikla smiled. "I like talking to you, too. But when we get together, it tends to go too far."

"It doesn't have to." He held his hands up. "I won't touch you."

"You wouldn't have to. I look into those eyes and–" Nikla stopped herself before she could admit anything else. "I need to go. Suddenly a very cold shower sounds necessary." She sat in her car and powered the window down as soon as she started her car. "I'll see you later tonight."

"Besides workout clothes, should I bring anything else?" Sweet braced his hands on her car door.

Nikla shook her head. "I'll have what you need."

"Yes, you do."

Before Nikla could crumble, she backed her car up and left. For the first time, Nikla felt conflicted about handing out fliers about Sweet's business. How could she hurt him when he'd done nothing to her but accepted her for her true self, something she couldn't even get her father to do? She glanced over at the stack and flipped them over.

Tonight she would push Sweet this time. If he cracked, she would know if she had Sweet pegged right. Something deep inside told her that she already knew the answer to that question.

Chapter Twenty-One

It took every bit of strength for Nikla to leave Sweet, especially being so close to his apartment. She had time in between classes to get in a good spanking...or more. It seemed like he wanted to know more about her than what he could do to make her climax. She smiled and had to fight herself from turning around in the middle of the street to go back to him.

When she returned to work, Nikla had to keep reminding herself to focus on her students. Her mind wandered over several topics. First she thought about Sweet. Swithin. It didn't escape her notice that in a short amount of time the man managed to get her to forget her sorry ex-boyfriend while getting her to bend to his will, to submit.

Submission. Nikla never thought anyone could get her to do that. If her father knew, he would demand that she quit her job, give up her apartment, move in with him and work in his store. Of course it wouldn't take much for her father to make that offer.

The other thing rolling around in her head had to do with her business. As each day went by, she thought about it more and more. Bobbi could tell her that she could have that small suite. Nikla would then have to get the equipment, set up bank accounts, get insurance, advertise, and more before any customers could come through the door. The idea of all that seemed daunting. She swallowed and continued her class, hoping by doing yoga she could calm herself down.

After her last class, Nikla gathered her belongings. The butterflies in her stomach existed because of her upcoming date with Sweet.

Date? No. Outing. Nothing more. She had to get her head back into the game. If only everything Sweet did to her didn't feel so good.

Big Tom strolled into the workout room. "Hey, Nikla."

"Just packing up. The room is all yours."

He held up his bear paw-sized hand. "Hold up. I have to talk to you real quick."

Nikla set her bag on the floor at her feet as she regarded the linebacker-sized man. "What's up?"

"You know we're all a team here. More than a team. We're like a big family."

Nikla nodded. "I love this place." She put her hand over her mouth. "Oh, God. Please don't tell me the center is closing."

Big Tom shook his shaved head. "No. Nothing like that."

Nikla breathed a sigh of relief for a number of reasons. Until she could get her business up and running, she needed this job. She had only herself to rely on for support. No way could she go crawling to her father to ask him for help.

"Whew. From the way you started, I thought something was going to go down with the recreation center." She wiped her forehead, then casually glanced at her watch. She didn't want to keep Sweet waiting.

Or maybe she did. If she arrived late, would he punish her? If so, how? How twisted had she become that she thought about ways for Sweet to punish her *and* she looked forward to them?

"Like I was saying, we're a family here. We support each other."

Nikla smiled. No one could ever say that she wasn't a team player as many times she came in early, stayed late, and covered for other employees.

"Of course." She nodded.

Big Tom lowered his voice. "I understand that you didn't help one of your coworkers."

Nikla's smile melted and her face heated up to a nuclear level. "What are you talking about?"

"Karen."

That one name almost forced Nikla to scream. She took a deep breath before speaking. "Do you know how many times I've covered for her in the past? I couldn't do it one time because I had plans and she ran to you and cried?"

"Brought me the concern, not cried."

"Doubtful. She cries when she asks me to cover for her. I've never asked anyone to cover my classes. I'm always here. I work my behind off." Nikla balled her hands into fists.

She hated going to this date tonight with Sweet and feeling this wound up. Not a date. Oh hell, who was she kidding?

"I'm just asking that if any of our employees ask for help that you do what you can for them."

"And if I can't, what? Am I going to get reprimanded again?" Nikla crossed her arms over her chest. She didn't mind squaring off against this giant. "You're dating her, aren't you?"

Big Tom took a step back. "Just be a team player, Nik."

"It's Nikla." She snatched her bag from the floor. "I can't believe this.

You enjoy your relationship with her."

"We're not dat—"

"I mean professional," Nikla said in a smarmy tone. "See you tomorrow for my *normal* shift."

Nikla stormed out of the recreation center and headed to her car. She wouldn't be any good for Sweet tonight, but she promised him something special. She needed something to relax her.

****

After the second pounding on his apartment door, Sweet answered it. He found Nikla on the other side looking fit to be tied. He couldn't focus on her outfit when he spotted the scowl ruining her beautiful face. She had her brown hair pulled up to a high ponytail. Even without a stitch makeup, her cheeks looked rosy.

"Are you okay?" He watched her for her reaction.

"Yeah. No." Nikla breathed out in exasperation. "Are you ready?"

"No." Sweet took a step aside. "Come in here." When Nikla opened her mouth, Sweet cut her off. "Now!"

Nikla strolled into his apartment but stood by the door. That didn't prevent Sweet from shutting it.

"What happened? Who pissed you off?" Sweet thought about his earlier conversation with his brother. "Did Bobbi call you?"

Nikla glared at him. "No." She rubbed the heel of her hand over her eyes. "I'm sorry. I tried so hard not to carry this attitude here. I promised you something special and I'm messing it up."

Sweet put his hands on her shoulders and forced her to look at him. Once she brought her gaze up to his face, she took a deep breath.

"What happened?" he asked.

"Work." She shook her head. "I have a co-worker who is the aerobics instructor. Whenever she gets a wild hair, she blows off her classes and asks me to fill in for her. I always tell her yes. The one time I told her no, she ran to our manager and complained. The manager actually got on me and said I needed to be more of a team player."

Sweet saw her eyes getting red, but it didn't get that way from sadness. Anger dripped from every word she said.

He rubbed her shoulders to calm her. "He's probably seeing her."

Nikla chuckled. "I accused him of the same thing." She ran her hand over her head. "I give and give all the time. I can't believe someone would give me crap about not filling one shift."

Sweet put his knuckle under her chin and raised her face. "You did nothing wrong. Your manager had no right to confront you about not filling one shift. If anything he should have talked to your coworker about missing so much of her job. Sounds like she's not earning her pay."

Nikla nodded and relaxed her arms.

"You want me to talk to your manager?" Not that Sweet would know what to say, but he hated seeing Nikla this upset.

Nikla blinked. "What in the world would you even say to him? 'Hi, I'm Nikla's Dom. Be nice to her or I'll beat you up'?" She laughed.

"Yes."

Her laughter died down when she noticed his face didn't break. "No. I'll take care of it." She headed to his door. "Another great reason to work for myself." When she turned to Sweet, she squeezed her eyes shut. "Sorry. I know that's one of the rules. No talk about the suites until after the decision has been made."

Nikla's innocence appealed to him. He even found it cute that she held onto this problem until she saw him.

"Are you ready now? We could always stay here." The thought of keeping her in his apartment appealed to him.

He could string her up and work her body over so that she would forget everything that happened at work.

"No. I'm a woman of my word." She scanned his outfit.

Sweet hoped his sweatpants and t-shirt fit for whatever Nikla had planned. "I'll drive."

"You don't know where we're going."

"You'll give me directions."

She nodded. "Always in control, huh?"

"You're finally getting it." Sweet closed and locked his door behind him. Before Nikla could take one step down, he put his hand on her shoulder. "You consider me as your Dom?"

Under his single outside light, he saw her cheeks transform to a rust color.

"It was the anger talking." Nikla walked downstairs.

After retrieving her workout bag from her car, Sweet helped her into his truck. Once they hit the road, Nikla gave him directions to an area of Virginia Beach he hadn't been to before. At the end of their trip, he found that she'd directed him to go to a rock climbing gym.

Sweet smiled.

"You're okay about this?" Nikla stayed seated as Sweet parked and turned off his truck.

"This is great. I was kind of doubting you and the whole rock climbing thing."

Nikla's mouth hung open. "I wouldn't lie about that."

Sweet got out of his side first before he opened her door and helped her out.

"I hope you enjoy it. When I have a stressful day and yoga can't calm my nerves, I do this."

Sweet put his hand at the small of her back. Before they walked into the gym, he leaned over and whispered, "I can't wait to see you in the harness."

Nikla giggled as she walked inside.

The bright gym showed off bodies climbing walls with various colored rock-like pegs covering the fake walls. Grunts echoed throughout the gym with sounds of rope sliding through metal rings. Make the place darker with naked bodies and it would have been like The Dollhouse.

"I'll rent you your gear." Nikla started to head to the counter.

Sweet grabbed her wrist. "No. I'll pay for it."

Nikla strolled toward him with a smile. "I invited you to this, um—"

"Date?" he quickly supplied.

She didn't acknowledge his word. "I'll get your stuff. Besides, these people owe me." Nikla moved in closer to him. She raised herself up on her tiptoes and whispered, "Let me serve you."

Nikla's words, her tone, and the proximity of her body caused Sweet's to ignite. He felt his cock throbbing even after she pushed away from him.

She peered down at his feet. "Size eleven?"

Sweet smiled. "Thirteen triple E."

Nikla blushed. "Of course. Wait right there, please. Be right back." She headed off to the counter and left Sweet to scan his surroundings.

Sweet wondered what would make a woman tackle obstacles like Nikla had done. Had growing up with a military father made her want to push herself to do more? Whatever the reason, Sweet couldn't deny that he found the trait attractive.

Sexy or not, he still questioned her intentions. Had she come over and pretended to be so upset about what had happened at her job so that he could soften his stance about the suite? She'd dropped the hint about wanting to be her own boss. Was that casual or on purpose?

Damn. He hated that he couldn't trust anyone, couldn't trust Nikla.

She trotted back to him with an armful of equipment. "Ready?"

Sweet forced a smile and accepted the gear. "Sure."

After a class on how to protect himself and the proper climbing procedure by a man who looked like he'd been climbing mountains since Jesus's birth, Sweet got outfitted in a harness. Sweet sat down to change shoes.

"Let me get those." Nikla bowed at his feet.

She undid his sneakers and removed them as she stared into his eyes. Sweet liked her need to serve. The fact that she did this in public didn't go unappreciated. His heart pounded as she removed his shoes and put on his climbing shoes.

After she outfitted him with his shoes, Sweet stood. He saw Nikla had been put into her harness as well.

Sweet grabbed her belt and pulled her forward. "Is it tight enough?"

Nikla's body trembled. "Maybe it could be secured tighter." She patted her thighs. "Around my legs."

Sweet lowered himself and pulled the straps snugly against her thighs. Being so close to her pussy, he wanted so much to drag his finger in between her legs. He loved hearing her gasp.

With helmets in place, the instructor laced ropes through their harnesses and talked Sweet through his first climb. Sweet watched Nikla scale the wall on her own with an employee at the ground holding her safety line. Once she got to the top, she sat on the wall and peered down at him.

"You're still on the ground? What? Are you scared?" Nikla laughed.

Sweet smiled at the beauty and started his own climb. He felt each of his muscles straining and trembling as he hooked his fingers and toes into each climbing holds mimicking actual rocks.

Never one to quit, Sweet had to admit that this climb kicked his ass. Each time he stopped to rest, he looked up and saw the goal on top of the wall. Seeing her brown eyes it gave him the extra boost of energy he needed to continue.

At the top of the wall, Sweet pulled himself up and sat next to Nikla. She applauded his efforts.

"I can't believe you did it." She put her hand on his leg.

"You thought I was going to quit?" Sweet tried to catch his breath.

"I have to admit. I bring guys here about the third or fourth date in to see if they'll crack. If they can't do this, they probably won't be able to take me. Probably the same thing you do with your women and The Dollhouse."

Sweet shook his head. "I've never taken a vanilla date to The Dollhouse before. You're a first."

Nikla smoothed her hand down his leg. "After what I've done, would you still consider me vanilla?"

Sweet studied her for a moment before answering. "I don't know what to consider you."

Nikla looked down. "Ready to come down now."

The instructor on the ground gave her a thumbs-up signal and held onto her ropes.

She glanced at Sweet. Before making her move, she kissed one cheek then the other before landing her lips on his mouth. "Meet you on the ground."

He watched her rappelling down the wall like an expert. When she got to the ground, he had expected her to lower herself to her knees. She didn't. Instead, she did a cutesy bow for him.

"On my way." Sweet started his descent to meet the woman on the ground who had driven him crazy. By the time he got his feet on the ground, he wasted no time in scooping Nikla into his arms. "Ready to go."

"Don't you want to climb another wall?" Nikla wrapped one arm around his shoulders.

"I wasn't asking a question."

"Okay. Let's go. But I don't want to go back to your place or mine." Nikla wriggled out of Sweet's arms. "Let's go to the club."

Definitely music to his ears.

Chapter Twenty-Two

Nikla wanted to peel off her clothes in the truck as Sweet drove them to The Dollhouse. If she didn't think they would get pulled over for Sweet's speeding, she would have.

Like last time, Sweet pulled into the back parking lot. After helping Nikla out of the truck, he damn near pulled her to the door. Once inside, Sweet didn't take her to an empty room.

"Where are we going?" Nikla asked.

Sweet turned to her. "Don't speak unless I instruct you to do so."

The game was on. Nikla clamped her mouth shut as she passed vacant rooms. Sweet brought her to a doorway and opened it.

"Go in." Sweet nodded toward the room.

With tentative steps, Nikla walked into the darkened room. The illuminated stage caught her attention first. The place looked like an old surgery observation room. A circular stage sat in the center with tiered auditorium seats surrounding it. A few people occupied the chairs.

The people who sat had to be the dominant ones. The people they had next to them either stood or remained kneeling on the floor. One man curled his body into a fetal position as he sobbed. In between his cries, Nikla heard him whispering, "Thank you. Thank you, Mistress." Sweat covered his body.

Nikla didn't know if the woman had played with him somewhere else and brought him here, or if she played with him there by her seat or maybe down at the stage.

Nikla stared at the stage and stopped moving. No. Sweet wouldn't do that to her. He wouldn't put her on display. She'd wanted to drop to her knees for Sweet at the gym, but that would have been too much.

Sweet held her hand as he walked down the steps. When Nikla refused to move another step, he stopped and brought his attention to her.

"Come with me." He tugged on her hand.

"Permission to speak." Nikla didn't want to upset him in front of his peers.

He took a step back up toward her but remained one step below so that he could be eye to eye with her. "What's wrong?"

"What are you planning?" She shifted uncomfortably in her spot.

"Do you trust me?"

Nikla leaned her head back and took in a deep breath. "Oh, God."

Sweet tugged on her hand. "Trust me."

She nodded only because her throat had closed. Sweet led her down to the stage. He had the stage slaves cover the floor with plastic before he brought her up on the raised floor.

Standing off to the side, Nikla watched Sweet go to a panel behind the stage. He flipped a switch that started a loud whirring sound. Nikla glanced up and noticed a long beam lowering. Eyebolts attached to either ends of the board. A substantial chain with heavy wire interwoven through the links connected the board to the pulley system.

Sweet lowered the beam down low enough that it reached Nikla's waist.

He took off his t-shirt. "Get undressed."

When Nikla didn't start stripping right away, Sweet stopped moving. It only took one look from him for her to feel compelled to strip down.

Nikla took off her jacket and shoes first. With each piece, she looked out into the audience and saw all these strangers staring at her. Her breathing increased into a pant.

When she got down to her sports bra and thong panties she stopped. Nikla balled her hands into fists. As a way to save her, Sweet covered her eyes with a blindfold.

"Just concentrate on my voice. Nothing else is here. Nothing else matters." Sweet rubbed her shoulders.

Nikla nodded and took in a couple of deep breaths to calm herself down. She felt his hands coasting down her arms then over her breasts. Just his touch alone sprang her hard nipples to life.

She didn't know if Sweet had removed her bra because of her newly hardened nipples. The cool air that hit her body made her shiver. He hooked his fingers into the sides of her panties and pulled them down.

When the garment hit her feet, Nikla stepped out of them.

"Crouch down," she heard Sweet say.

Nikla did as instructed. She felt him take one of her hands and bring it to the side. The softness that encircled her wrist let her know that he had attached a fur-lined cuff to her. When she noticed how her arm dangled, she assumed he must have connected the cuff to the beam.

"So that there is not so much pressure on your shoulders and wrists, I'm going to tie your arms to the beam." Sweet stroked her arm.

Nikla nodded.

"Use your safe words." Sweet cuffed and connected her other wrist so that she now had her arms outspread.

Then Nikla felt soft rope circling her arms. Since both sides had been worked at the same time, she knew more than just Sweet tied her arms. She had to think of the situation in the same way she thought of Wasabi. She had to trust Sweet. He wouldn't do anything to harm her. He would only put people around her who know what to do.

"Were you serious about being flexible?" Sweet asked.

"Yes, Sir." She turned her head to follow his voice.

"Good."

The familiar whirring sounded again. This time Nikla felt the bar going up. She had no choice but to follow the ascension. When she could stand normally the bar stopped.

A soft cuff became affixed to one ankle, then the other.

"Tell me if this hurts or is uncomfortable." Sweet put his hand on the small of her back then slid it down over her ass to her thigh.

He raised her thigh, then let his hand travel down her leg to her ankle. At it, he lifted it in the air and met it with her wrist.

Nikla had to scoot her planted foot in order to keep her balance.

"Very good," Sweet whispered to her. "Can you do that with your other leg at the same time?"

Nikla turned her face toward his voice. She felt his warm breath feathering over her cheek.

"Yes, Sir." She hoped he picked up on the confidence in her voice.

Sweet must have. He raised her other leg in the air and attached it to the bar along with her wrist. Now Nikla had her arms and legs spread open wide for all to see. Not being able to view the audience members' faces did calm her a little, which struck her as odd.

Sweet seemed determined to make her stand out.

He gave her a kiss on her cheek, then whispered, "You look like a bird in flight. Just magnificent."

That wouldn't have been the adjective she would have chosen for that moment. Maybe she looked flexible. She looked open and willing. She looked fearless.

At that description, she pumped up her chest as Sweet raised her higher. She didn't care how far he hoisted her in the air. She liked how much he wanted to push her like she'd pushed him at the rock gym.

Nikla yelped as soon as she felt the tips of thin canes drumming over her back. She didn't know Sweet had picked up canes and moved behind her. The stinging sensation crept up her back to the top of her head and spread throughout her body. Her heart seemed to beat in rhythm with his drumming.

Sweet moved the canes down to her ass, striking them lightly and in different spots, which offered her a new way to experience the pain. Nikla leaned her head back as he continued.

"Green," Nikla whispered.

"Good." Sweet's voice sounded like he'd moved to the side of her.

Just as the caning took her by surprise, so did the light, tickling feeling under her thigh. Nikla jumped, but with her wrists and ankles bound, she couldn't move that much. In her mind, she didn't see Sweet sweeping a feather over her flesh. She imagined him holding a handful of cotton candy.

The delicate touch went away and she felt a hard slap against her inner thigh. Nikla gritted her teeth and absorbed the pain.

Sweet worked her body over, alternating between caning her, rubbing her with something that felt like fur and paddling her. At some point, Nikla lost track of time. Her mind seemed cluttered and cloudy, then strangely became clear. Her body belonged to Sweet. He controlled her reactions.

Until she felt one of her legs being lowered did she realize that the play had ended.

"What's going on?" Nikla desperately wanted to see Sweet.

"Help me get her down." Sweet's voice didn't sound frantic, more excited than anything else.

Nikla felt hands working at both ends of the board in an attempt to untie and release her. With her arms and hands unbound, she fell into a man's arms. She'd hoped Sweet had caught her.

"Amazing." Sweet kissed her forehead.

Nikla realized he moved around and felt him sitting down. He finally removed her mask. A look of excitement covered Sweet's face.

"What's going on?" Nikla rubbed her eyes.

"You went into subspace." Sweet smoothed her hair from her face. "It's when you free your mind so much that you feel super relaxed. Sometimes you don't realize what's happening around you."

Nikla blinked and tried sitting up.

"Easy. Easy. Let me hold you for a while." Sweet cradled her naked body on his lap.

"Tell me what happened. What did I do?"

"You said your safe word 'green' a few times. Then you rolled your head back and smiled." Sweet leaned in like he wanted to kiss her but stopped. He glanced around their surroundings and sat back.

"So Doms, do you go to Dom-space or something?" Nikla curled closer to his chest.

"Yes, some do. You think play is only for the submissive or the slave." He shook his head. "The one administering the discipline gets something out of it, too."

"Did you go to Dom-space?"

Sweet averted his gaze. "Let's get you dressed. It's late. I need to get you back home."

The disappointment must have been easy to read on Nikla's face. As she started to get off Sweet's lap, he stopped her.

"You did amazing up there."

She offered a slight smile before she pulled away from him to dress. Her sports bra rubbed against her welts. The feeling of the sores elevated her pulse again. Nikla slipped on her thong panties and couldn't help but run her hand over her enflamed ass cheek. She craned her head around to see the red streaks that colored them.

When Nikla searched for Sweet to see if he watched her observing herself, she found him standing behind the stage putting on his t-shirt. With his back to her, she watched him shaking his head as though arguing with himself.

Nikla slipped on her shoes and her jacket and strolled over to him. She touched his back, which caused him to twist around in a flurry.

"Are you okay?" she asked.

Without answering, he walked by her and headed to the door. Nikla followed him, racing behind his hurried steps. He burst through the back door and headed to his truck. He opened the passenger side door first. She assumed that he had completely tuned her out and forgotten that she had accompanied him to the club.

The drive back to Decadent Treats, where she'd left her car, remained as tense and quiet as when Nikla had touched his back and asked about his well-being. In the parking lot, Sweet turned off his truck. He drummed his thumbs on the steering wheel before finally acknowledging Nikla.

"I used to feel it." His low voice rumbled. "The Dom-space thing. I used to get so worked up after a session that I would physically feel wiped out." He shook his head. "I don't feel that way anymore. I don't know what's wrong with me." He stared at her. "I want to. I want to feel it with you, but I feel–" Sweet struggled to find the right word until he finally belted out the word, "stuck."

Nikla breathed a sigh of relief that he'd confided in her. Justin wouldn't even tell her when he'd gotten a speeding ticket.

She put her hand on Sweet's arm. "I don't know much about this lifestyle of yours other than what I've experienced and what you've told me. It seems to me like trust is the ultimate ingredient in that type of relationship. Maybe once you truly can trust who you're playing with, it'll come back."

Sweet stared at her with astonishment in his eyes. "Why are you being so nice to me? You could just call me a weirdo loser and be done with me."

"Because I don't think a man who helped me when I had my panic attack and who was able to make me have an incredible orgasm without penetration is a weirdo or a loser."

He held her wrist and pulled her close to his body. His kiss started off soft and became forceful and eager. His tongue darted in her mouth.

"I want you," he said in between kisses.

She started to open the truck door, but Sweet pulled it closed. When he broke from the kiss, he smiled.

"Here. I want you now." Sweet reached down and pulled down his sweatpants as Nikla removed her jacket and pulled up her bra. She didn't have an opportunity to remove her pants before Sweet grabbed her and forced them down her legs.

He scooted to the center of the bench seat and brought Nikla onto his lap with her back to him. She raised her hips enough for Sweet to guide his hard cock to her pussy opening and entered her with one thrust.

"Shit!" Nikla gripped the dashboard as she ground her hips onto his lap. Sweet held onto her hips and moved in and out of her like an expert, like he owned her. He freed one hand to palm her breast. He squeezed her nipples between his thumb and index finger.

"Christ! Yes!" Nikla covered his hand with hers and kept up her gyrations.

Sweet filled her up like no man ever had. She shouldn't have cared about him. She shouldn't have fucked him or allowed him to spank her or cane her. At this point, she couldn't do without him. He'd infected her, and she had no interest in a cure.

Their heavy breathing clouded the windows. Sweet pulled her back so that her back lay flushed against his chest. He removed his other hand from her hip and coasted it over her thigh to her clit. As soon as he touched it, Nikla twitched. When he pinched it, she wailed.

"Swithin!"

Sweet growled like a bear and pushed himself in her harder and faster. Nikla felt her body shaking before the inner walls in her pussy started constricting around him. She reached her hand back and grabbed a handful of his hair just as she came.

Nikla screamed so loud she thought the sound would shatter his windows...in his apartment.

Sweet kept pumping inside of her. "Say my name again. Say it."

"Swithin. Mmm, Swithin."

He wrapped his arms around her body as he emptied himself inside of her. She felt his hot jism bathing her womb as he held her. Sweat rolled down the sides of her face.

"May I stay with you tonight?" Nikla asked.

Sweet kissed her shoulder up to the back of her neck. "You can if you promise you'll do one thing."

Nikla didn't care what he wanted–blow job, hand job, her on her hands and knees crawling up to his apartment– she would do it. "Name it. Please tell your Sugar Baby what you want."

"Have dinner with me, my brother, and his fiancée."

Not what Nikla had expected to hear, but she smiled at the gesture. If Sweet wanted to introduce her to his family it must meant that he saw more in her than a fuck buddy or a play toy, or even an adversary.

"I would love to."

"Good." Sweet kissed her back. "Good."

Nikla hoped so.

Chapter Twenty-Three

"Hey!" Deana plucked Nikla on the side of her head.

"Ow!" Nikla rubbed her temple. She didn't expect abuse like this from her friend during lunch.

Some of the diners near them in the restaurant glanced their way. Nikla ignored them.

"What was that for?" Nikla placed her fork back on her plate and rubbed her head, which still throbbed from the hit.

"I've been going on and on about my date and you look totally zoned out. What is going on with you?" Deana waved her hand in front of Nikla's face. "Earth to Nikla. Are you with me?"

"I'm right here at the table with you." She took a sip of her water, then glanced at her cell phone.

Today Sweet allowed her to have twenty pieces of baby spinach leaves for her salad, three cherry tomatoes, ten slices of mushrooms, four cucumber slices, and a tablespoon of Italian dressing. Down to the exact measurement, she prepared and ate what he commanded.

Now she kept glancing at her phone to see if he had any other orders for her. Would she be allowed a dessert? Would he want her to be his dessert? Nikla crossed her legs.

"There! You're doing it again. What's going on with you?" Deana crossed her arms over her chest and leaned back. "And why are you wearing that candy bracelet? What are you, two?"

Nikla covered her bracelet with her hand. "It's nothing. I'm fine. I'm just thinking. That's all." Nikla flicked around the remaining salad that she had on her plate.

"You're still not fucking that guy, are you?"

Nikla scanned the area around them to see if anyone else heard her crass friend. "Will you keep your voice down?"

"You are, aren't you? It's been a couple of weeks now. Please don't tell me you're hung up on him." Deana laughed.

"And what if I am?" Nikla crossed her legs under the table. "You're the one who said I should go out and meet people. Weren't you the one gushing over Sweet Hawkes when I told you about him?"

"Yeah." She nodded. "But I thought you would have hit it and quit it. You just got out of a long-term relationship."

"It was less than a year." Nikla distinctly remembered that they hadn't even reached their anniversary date yet.

"That's almost a year of being in a bad relationship. Almost a year of bad sex. Almost a year of being unhappy. Don't get hung up on one guy you've only known a week."

"Almost two weeks."

Deana cocked her head. "As fine as he is, I'm sure there are other guys out there who will go along with your vision for a sugar-free, gluten-free, fun-free America."

"Not fair." Nikla actually liked that she and Sweet differed on topics. It gave them a lot to talk about, especially after sex.

She loved that they would argue about politics and current events. No man had challenged her like Sweet had. Why couldn't he fully give himself to her? Why couldn't she show him out in public how she felt about him?

Deana interjected into Nikla's thoughts. "You know he's probably doing other women on the side. No man as fine as that is alone, not for long."

That idea haunted Nikla. She'd thought the same thing each time he seemed distant after playing. The man did invite her into his home whenever he could, so if he had someone else on the side, the other woman could only be getting a good five minutes of Sweet's time.

"And you know about his special hobby." Deana finished off her steak.

"Yeah. I know." Nikla tried to hide her smile but it came through. So did the kick that Deana administered under the table. "Ouch! What was that for?"

"Please, please, please tell me that you did not let that man spank your ass." This time Deana spoke in a whisper.

Nikla rubbed the sore spot on her shin. "And what if I did? It's not like you haven't had some guy spank you during sex. Same thing."

Deana shook her head. "It's not. You know that."

Nikla did. She hoped Deana didn't know, didn't understand about the Lifestyle.

"Those BDSM people are freaks. They're like a cult. They will force you to drink the Kool-Aid and lock you up in a basement for ten years like that dude in Ohio."

Nikla sighed. "It's not like that."

Deana held up her hand. "And you don't have to tell me anything about it. Know this. When your business is up and running, are you going to have time to cater to him like he wants? I'm sure that man wants a naked-twenty-four-seven type of sex slave."

"Submissive," Nikla whispered.

"I'm sure you working all the time will be a problem for him. He'll force you to choose. If you don't choose him, it'll be bye-bye, Nikla."

Nikla shook her head. "You have no idea what's going on between me and Sweet. You can't generalize what we have based on the little bit you know. Sweet likes that I work."

"And yet he doesn't want you to have that unit downtown."

Nikla got quiet.

Deana continued. "Don't hang your hat on this one guy. Sounds like he may be a lot of fun and someone you can check off your bucket list. At the end of the day, he's not boyfriend material. He's not even husband material. Sure, he's good looking and has his own business. But he's a Dominant. Read into that that he's selfish. He wants what he wants when he wants it. Didn't you get enough of living under someone's thumb from growing up with your dad?"

Nikla shook her head. "Jesus H. Christ, Deana. Can't you for once ever be in my corner? You see me looking happy and you just want to dump all over that."

"No, I just–"

"I know what you want to do. You want me to remain the predictable, stable one while you get to do whatever the hell you want with whoever you want. You talk about going out with women and expect me to be fine with it. I talk about a guy who's a Dominant and you think I'm ruining my life."

"Two separate things."

"No. The same thing. We're both stepping outside of our comfort zones. At least, I did. You're just all talk."

"Easy, Nikla. I'm your friend. You don't want to lose me. With what you have going on at work and this shaky thing you have going on with this guy, I have a feeling you're going to need all the friends you can get."

Nikla covered her eyes and tried to suppress her laughter. "Wow. First Big Tom and now you. The threats just keep on coming. You know the only person who hasn't threatened me? Sweet."

Nikla called for her check.

"I didn't mean to piss you off." Deana fluffed out her big hair. "I'm trying to be your friend."

Nikla handed the waitress money before she could even set down her bill. "You want to be my friend? Stay out of my private life."

She stood and left the table. With adrenaline coursing through her veins, Nikla needed an outlet. She hopped in her car and drove away from the parking lot, not wanting to confront Deana again about the ways to be a good friend.

She drove down to the empty suites. Nikla parked her car directly in front of the empty storefronts. Bobbi, being true to her word, had removed the "For Lease" signs in front of the two units.

Nikla pulled out her phone and dialed Sweet. She'd never called him. He'd always called her or they would make arrangements during their meetings, their dates, their fuck fest sessions.

"Nikla?" Sweet answered the phone with a questioning lilt in his voice. "What's going on? Are you not able to make it tonight?"

"No, I'll be there." She chewed her lower lip. "I needed to talk to someone, to you. I needed to hear your voice."

"Are you okay?"

Beyond her control, Nikla grunted and kicked her foot against the wall. Like the first time Sweet had met her at this location, she wanted to scream out her frustrations.

Sweet must have heard her.

"Where are you?" Sweet asked with panic in his tone.

"Our spot. The suites." Nikla disconnected the call.

Her day started off so wonderful, so full of promise. Then her dear friend filled her head with doubt. Nikla couldn't blame her distress all on Deana. Deana voiced what Nikla had been feeling for a while.

Why couldn't Nikla be one of those women who could do what Deana said, hit it and quit it? She and Sweet had talked about the dynamics of their relationship. Until a decision had been made on the units, they would play and have sex and that's it. Once a decision had been rendered, they would go their separate ways. Nikla started wondering if she wanted her leash to be released.

Nikla heard the rumbling of Sweet's truck before she saw it. He pulled into the spot next to her and got out of the truck. He came around to the driver's side of her car and opened the door.

"What's going on?" Sweet stroked his thumb over her cheek.

Before she knew it, he had her out of the car and into his arms, hugging her. Nikla gripped him like she needed him. He smelled like his store, sugary sweet and fruity. Right now, those scents calmed her down more than a field full of lavender.

"Bad day at work?" he asked as he held her.

Nikla shook her head. "Bad lunch."

Sweet pulled back from her and stared into her eyes.

To calm his fears, she told him about the argument with Deana. "No one seems happy for me."

"Why do you need anyone's approval?" Sweet framed her face in his hands. "My brother does the same thing to me. He's my rain cloud, although he'll tell you that he's my conscience. Don't hate your friend."

Nikla shook her head. "I don't hate her. I hate that she gets to be reckless, but I'm not allowed. I'm always supposed to be good."

"You are good. If you weren't you wouldn't have gotten so upset." He stared at her for a moment.

Nikla swallowed. "Why are you looking at me like that?"

"You were pissed and you called me."

"Do you find that strange?"

Sweet removed his hands from her face. "Strange?"

"Considering our arrangement. We're not a couple."

"There's one thing you need to do." Sweet leaned forward and whispered in Nikla's ear. "Stop defining us based on the norm. There's nothing normal about us."

Sweet had been right about that.

Nikla took a deep cleansing breath. "I'm sorry for pulling you from work. I feel silly."

"Don't. You needed someone. I'm glad I could be here for you."

"I won't hold you up." Nikla turned to her car.

"Aren't you forgetting something?" Sweet asked.

She returned her attention to him. "What?"

He glared at her long enough that she understood his unspoken message.

"Here?" She peered out at the traffic zooming by the building. "People will see. People who won't understand."

"You're telling me you know everyone driving by?" Sweet pointed to the speeding cars. "You don't know them. They don't know you or me. It's just us."

Nikla stepped closer to him. She stood on her tiptoes and kissed one cheek. She moved over to the other one and pressed her lips against it. When it came to his lips, she had no problems covering his mouth with hers. She slipped her hand behind his head to hold him there. She'd hoped the sensual expression would let him forget about her lowering herself to her knees.

When Sweet pulled back first, Nikla knew he wouldn't let her get away with not doing the last step of the introduction.

Nikla hesitated. She looked around the area to see if she could find anyone looking at them.

"I'll pick you up tonight around six." Sweet went to the driver's side of his truck.

The disappointed look on his face stopped Nikla's heart. "Wait. I didn't bow."

"And you weren't going to do it, either. Be ready when I get there." Sweet pulled away without looking back.

Damn. Nikla seemed to be pushing all kinds of people away from her today. She sat down on the curb and rested her head in her hands. Dinner tonight with Sweet's brother would be interesting.

Chapter Twenty-Four

Sweet sat in the convenience store parking lot near Nikla's apartment complex, thinking about how the evening would go. He didn't want to carry the disappointment he felt over Nikla not doing the full introduction earlier into dinner.

Since Nikla had done so much within the BDSM world with him, he tended to forget that she had so much more to learn before she could feel comfortable. Each time he thought about her calling him when she needed someone to talk to, to hold, his body became warm all over.

On the vanilla side, they clicked. Why couldn't he get her on his other side? Then again, maybe the problem had nothing to do with her.

At that thought, Sweet put his truck in drive and headed over to Nikla's apartment. He parked in front of her building and then went up to her unit. Sweet glanced at his watch. On time. Right at six on the dot.

Nikla's door opened. Sweet clenched his jaw at what he saw.

"You're not dressed," he said tightly.

"No." Nikla stepped aside to allow him into her place.

Although she had makeup on and her hair piled into a bun on top of her head, she wore a red satin robe and pink bedroom slippers.

"I was very clear when I said you needed to be ready at six o'clock." Sweet followed Nikla to her bedroom.

"You were. But I need you to do three things." She picked up two garments from her bed still on their hangers. "Which dress?"

The black sweater dress looked nice, like it would keep her covered from her neck to her knees. The cut of the dress looked like it would show off her hourglass shape. Judging by the footwear she had on the floor, it looked like she would be wearing black boots with it.

The red dress she held up would guarantee that Sweet would not be paying attention to any dinner conversation and would only be staring down into her cleavage. Next to the black boots sat a pair of red pumps.

"You do have red shoes," Sweet said and nodded toward the pair.

Nikla glanced down at them. "I just bought them."

"Then you should break them in properly. The black dress and the red pumps." Sweet pointed to the garment first before the shoes.

"Two birds with one stone. My second question was going to be which shoes I should wear." Nikla disappeared into her closet with the red dress.

"And your third question?" Sweet didn't want to play games. If he arrived late to his brother's, he knew Masaun would never let him live it down.

Nikla reemerged from the closet with her robe opened. She wore a flesh-colored bra and panty set, only the bra had nothing covering her breasts. Sweet's heart pounded as she moved closer to him.

"I think I deserve some punishment." She strolled by him. After removing her robe and tossing it on her bed, she placed her hands on her dresser and bent over. "I didn't do the greeting earlier and I wasn't ready just now."

Sweet remained cemented in his spot for a moment. He knew if he touched her, they would never leave the apartment. That didn't stop him from approaching her. Sweet planted his hand next to hers on the dresser. The other hand he let hover over her firm ass.

The heat from her body warmed his hand. It didn't help that Nikla arched her back to raise her ass up higher.

She turned to him. "Should I count out the spanks, Sir?"

Sweet connected his gaze to hers. Before he could touch her, he backed away. "Get dressed. We're going to be late."

Nikla looked like she wanted to argue with him. Instead, she righted herself and greeted him like she should have done in the parking lot earlier. She kissed his cheeks and his lips, then lowered herself down to her knees.

Sweet reached out to touch her hair but stopped himself. "Up."

Nikla rose to her feet and slipped on her dress. Just as he imagined, the sweater dress hugged her body like a second skin. She accentuated her tiny waist with a skinny red belt. Her nipples jutted forward and could be seen through the dress. That part he did like.

"Why can't you do that all the time?" Sweet asked. "When we're behind closed doors, you're fearless. When we're at the club, you can do anything as long as you're in a mask. Out in public, you freeze up. What gives?"

"I didn't grow up in a family that held hands and said 'I love you' all the time. My father was very strict. He didn't praise accomplishments. You were expected to excel." She stared at him. "I'm not used to being that expressive. I'm trying."

Sweet had to respect her honesty. He still wanted more from her.

She slipped on her shoes and grabbed her purse. "Did you tell your brother anything about me?"

"He knows some things about you but not everything." Sweet reached for the door to open it for her.

"Like what? What tidbit did you leave out?"

Sweet opened the door then closed it. He spun Nikla around and pressed her back to the door. "He doesn't know that your pussy tastes like honey. He doesn't know that when you come you scream and a single tear runs out of your eye. And he doesn't know that I want to fuck you in every way possible including up your ass."

"Oh, God." Nikla's mouth hung open.

"Have you ever had anal sex?"

She shook her head. "Does it hurt?"

Sweet smirked. "*I* wouldn't know."

Nikla chuckled. "Yeah, I guess not."

He watched her breathing increase. Nikla reached out and touched his belt.

"Can you call your brother and tell him you got a flat?"

Sweet wrapped his arm around Nikla's waist and pulled her away from the door. "No. We're going to dinner. You will apologize for us being late. Your punishment is going to be sitting through dinner thinking about what I'm going to do to you when we get back."

Nikla's face relaxed and she groaned. "Damn it."

"I told you BDSM wasn't all about the physical. It's mental as well." He opened the door. "Come on." Sweet gave Nikla a playful smack on her ass.

Nikla yelped as she walked out of her apartment.

If things went well tonight, he would be inside that tight ass.

****

Nikla had to cross her legs the entire trip to Sweet's brother's house to douse the flames at the apex of her thighs. The entire trip Sweet would mention little things he would do to her.

"You have the perfect bed to tie you down," he'd said at one traffic light.

Nikla could do nothing but sit and listen. Thankfully she wore her shelf bra that just elevated her breasts but kept them unobstructed. The soft fabric of her dress brushed over her hard nipples.

"If we have sex tonight, I don't want you to come until I give you permission."

Nikla smiled. "Yes, Sir." She put her hand on his leg.

"Did I tell you how gorgeous you look tonight?"

Nikla gasped. "Uh, no."

"You are. With makeup on..." Sweet trailed off and shook his head. "I didn't think you could get any sexier."

Sweet pulled his truck up to a large two-story brick home. Even at night, Nikla noticed the colorful flowers and rosebushes that still had bloomed thanks to the warm October weather.

"Are you sure you want to do this?" Nikla glanced at the serene house then back at Sweet. "We're breaking our own rules. Nothing more than play."

"We broke that rule as soon as we had sex." He held her hand. "Sugar Baby, I think the rule book is out the window."

A shiver went down her spine when he held her hand then mentioned her scene name. Sweet's thumb brushed over her candy bracelet.

Nikla shook her head. "It's one thing for us to do what we're doing with each other. Now we're getting outsiders involved." Getting so involved with Sweet never factored into her plans.

So much for taking Deana's advice to get with a guy to get Justin out of her thoughts. Now she couldn't get Sweet out of her head...and heart.

"You talk as though you have to explain what we are to people. I thought you learned something from the Lifestyle." Sweet connected his gaze to hers. "Only thing that matters is that you stay true to me, yourself, and what you really want."

The truth part killed her. Nikla had a crucial secret to tell Sweet. She still had to figure out how to break it to him and her father about their competing businesses.

Sweet's expression went very somber. He peered around Nikla. "Brother is watching us. Let's get in before he comes out."

Sweet got out first then opened the door for Nikla.

As they walked up to the door, Nikla asked, "Since your brother is a Dom, too, should I bow to him? What should I do?"

"This is a vanilla dinner. I'm Sweet. You're Nikla. He's Masaun and his girl is Kindle. It'll be a chill event." He put his hand to the back of her neck and massaged it. "I should have told you not to wear panties."

She had to smile. "We still have time. I can remove them now."

"See. You are learning." Sweet rang the doorbell then knocked on the red door.

When it opened, Nikla saw a striking couple on the other side. Until she focused on their faces did she realize that she had seen these people at the club. Now they wore way more clothing.

"It's my fault we're late," Nikla said quickly. "I'm sorry."

"Not a problem. Don't just stand out there. Come on in." Sweet's brother stood to the side to allow Nikla and Sweet to come into the home.

Nikla's heels clicked against the dark hardwood floor. The simple but classic decorations matched the look of the couple. Both appeared so straightlaced, but Nikla knew of their dark sides.

"Masaun, this is Nikla Dearwood." Sweet put his arm around Nikla's waist.

She extended her hand to Masaun, who resembled Sweet slightly. Masaun's brown wavy hair had some control to it, not like Sweet's longer hair. The two brothers matched in height with Sweet being a little bigger. Their eyes gave them away as brothers. From his conservative look and dress, she guessed Masaun to be the older one.

"Very nice to meet you." Nikla shook his hand.

Masaun smiled. "I wanted to meet the woman who could make my brother smile again."

"Hey. Don't tell her that. She'll never let me live it down." Sweet gave his brother a playful punch against his shoulder.

"Nikla, this is my fiancée, Kindle Langston."

After Masaun's introduction, Nikla shook the woman's hand. Even though Kindle wore a simple orange shift dress that complemented her darker skin tone and tan flats, she looked polished and accomplished. She had her black hair parted in the center with soft waves surrounding her face. She had arms that would make Michelle Obama jealous. The way she looked at Masaun, Kindle had a love that Nikla desired.

Nikla kept her gaze away from Sweet to hide her disappointment. Would she ever experience real love like that? Could Sweet love her like that?

"Let me take your purse and jacket." Sweet removed the items from her.

"Please make yourself at home. I'll get the hors d'oeuvres." Kindle looked at Masaun. "Will you help me? Maybe Sweet can give Nikla the tour."

"Yeah, keep her out of the dungeon," Masaun said.

Nikla laughed. When she saw no one else did, she looked at Sweet.

"They do have a playroom." Sweet nodded.

"Oh. Okay."

Sweet put his hand to the small of Nikla's back. Over his shoulder he shouted, "I'm going to show her the room anyway!"

Sweet brought her through each bedroom and bathroom. Each room looked understated and elegant, like the duo that lived there. At a doorway, Sweet paused.

"This is where the magic happens." He opened the door and hit a switch on the wall.

Nikla peered into the room before taking a step inside. The room looked like a miniature version of The Dollhouse. A St. Andrew's cross sat in the corner. In the center of the room hung a long beam, kind of like the beam Sweet had her handcuffed to recently. Across the back wall hung different whips, canes, paddles and floggers. Just looking at them had her clit twitching.

"My brother had to get all of his items from New York or have them made for him." Sweet strolled around in the room. "He had a local friend of ours make the cross." He picked up a dark brown flogger. "This he had made when he went up to New York to conduct some business."

Nikla ran her fingertips over a fur-lined paddle. "Is that why you want to open your own store?"

"One of many reasons." Sweet slipped his hand into Nikla's. "Let's go back out before Masaun comes back here and kicks us out."

"I heard that." Masaun stood in the doorway.

"What did I tell you?" Sweet nudged Nikla in her side.

She loved the relationship between the two brothers. She could tell they both would do anything for the other one. "You have a lovely home. I really like your dungeon." Nikla smiled.

Masaun scanned the space. "We'll have to enjoy the room now. Once we have children, we're going to have to keep our activities in the club." Masaun turned off the light and closed the door behind Sweet and Nikla.

"Kids? You two are already talking about having a family?" Sweet led Nikla to the family room where Kindle had a couple of trays of finger foods available, from crudités to stuffed mushrooms and spinach dip.

"Of course." Masaun assumed his spot next to Kindle and wrapped his arm around her. He whispered something in her ear, which made her giggle like a schoolgirl and squeeze him tighter.

"I hope you all brought your appetites. Masaun made lamb with mint jelly." Kindle kissed Masaun before heading to the bar. "Nikla, would you like something to drink?"

"Water is fine. I want to be able to play tonight if Sweet is up for it."

The room became quiet at her admission.

Nikla felt heat rising up her neck to her face. "Should I have not said that? I'm sorry."

"No. It's fine." Masaun held up his glass to her. "You're absolutely right." He pointed to Sweet. "You do have her trained well."

"I'm lucky." Sweet stared at Nikla for what seemed like an eternity.

If Kindle hadn't placed a drink in Nikla's hand, she wouldn't have broken the stare.

Nikla found Sweet's brother and Masaun's fiancée to be kind and generous. The love they had for each other came through so vividly that it overwhelmed the room.

Conversation flowed easily between the four. Nikla felt like she'd known Masaun and Kindle all her life, like she felt with Sweet.

When they sat down for dinner, Nikla looked down at her plate, then over to Sweet. She leaned in close to him. "What can I have?"

Sweet rubbed the back of her neck as he smiled at her.

"Come on. This is a regular dinner." Masaun shook his head. "No topping at the table."

Ignoring his brother, Sweet whispered to Nikla, "Have the salad, but no dressing."

She exhaled at his directives and continued listening to him.

"I'll give you your portion of lamb, couscous, and sautéed vegetables. Take a bite of each and look to me for further instructions. I'll wait on dessert to decide if you can have any."

Nikla crossed her legs. She never thought she would give up so much of her power to a man, or anyone. Something as simple as being told what to eat freed her from doing anything but being herself. With Sweet, she found her happiness.

"Are you two done? Can we get going on our *normal* dinner?" Masaun asked. "You said you wanted vanilla. What gives?"

"You of all people should know how hard it is to stop." Sweet kept his stare on Nikla. He continued rubbing her neck until she thought she would dissolve into a puddle of pudding on her chair.

"Come on. Let's eat." Kindle held Masaun's hand and smiled at him.

Only after her touch did Masaun seem like he relaxed a little. After a short prayer by Masaun, dinner started.

As instructed, Nikla took small bites from her salad and her meal. When Sweet tapped her thigh and nodded, she knew she could have more. Their unspoken bond connected her to him more intensely than when he played with her body.

"What is it that you do, Nikla?" Kindle asked toward the end of dinner.

"I'm a yoga and Pilates instructor at the recreation center." Nikla took a sip of her water, but she noticed Masaun giving Sweet an approving wink.

"Don't think I didn't see that." Kindle gave a hard but playful glare to Masaun.

"Just thinking how great it must be for Sweet to have a submissive who is so flexible. He likes putting his subs through their paces." Masaun wagged his finger at Nikla. "You were the one Sweet played with the other night, right? He had you spread eagle on the beam."

Nikla glanced down, a bit embarrassed that she showed her body to Sweet's brother. Had she known he had been sitting in the audience at the time, she wouldn't have done it.

Who was she kidding? Nikla couldn't deny Sweet.

"Yes, that was me. I was so scared doing it at first. Once Sweet started on me with the canes, I wanted more." Nikla held Sweet's hand under the table.

"She's been incredible. She picks up techniques very quickly. There's so much more I'd like to teach her." Sweet turned his hand around so that he could kiss the back of her hand.

"I'm glad you're getting out of that apartment and you've gotten into real play."

"How did you two meet?" Nikla asked the duo.

Kindle smiled. "Masaun delivered a candy bouquet to me."

Nikla melted at that story. "That's so sweet. That's almost like us."

"Really? How's that?" Kindle took a drink of her iced tea.

"Sweet gave me a heart-shaped box of chocolates while I was out in front of your store." Although Sweet had given Nikla the box as a dig against her, Nikla could laugh about the situation now.

When she observed Sweet, he didn't look as happy to recall that moment. He glared at her, his jaw clenched. Nikla swallowed wondering what she could have done to anger him. Did he not want his brother to know that they started on rocky terms?

Masaun patted Sweet on his back. "Romance is still in you, I see." He turned to Nikla. "What were you doing in front of our store? I don't remember seeing you as a customer."

The smile slipped down Nikla's face. No wonder Sweet looked so angry. He hadn't told Masaun all about her.

Nikla would rectify that right now. "I'm the one handing out fliers in front of your store."

Masaun's face became serious as he stared at her. "I thought you looked familiar. I thought it was from the club."

"And I thought you had told your brother about me." Nikla slipped her hand out of Sweet's grip.

"I told him the important items like how you make me feel," Sweet said. "Everything else is irrelevant."

"Irrelevant? Are you kidding me? Let me get this straight. You're sleeping with and disciplining the lone protester, and you had the nerve to bring her to my *home*?"

"Masaun, please." Kindle put her hand on top of his. "She is still a guest in our home."

"No, she's the enemy."

"Back that up." Sweet sat up taller. "If I brought her here, that must mean that I trust her. If I trust her, then you should do the same."

"This woman is trying to shut down our business." Masaun glared at his brother. "Sweet, have you told her how important our business is to us? To you?"

"Let's drop this subject and move on." Sweet pushed back from the table.

Without touching Sweet, Nikla could feel the heat emitting from his body. He could have thrown her to the wolves in this environment. Although she hated that Sweet never told his brother how he met her and her true identity, she loved that he defended her.

"Hell no. I'm not moving on from this." Masaun pushed himself from the table. "Decadent Treats is our life. We built that from nothing except for hope and a prayer. I can't believe you would side with her."

"It's not a matter of taking sides." Sweet started to raise his voice. "I'm not stupid or reckless. There's a side of Nikla that you don't see."

"I didn't mean to cause an argument." Nikla started to stand, but Sweet's arresting grip on her wrist stilled her in her chair.

"Get your head out of your ass." Masaun never broke his glare on his brother. "Out of all the women out there, you had to bed and spank the one who hates us." He shook his head.

"I don't hate you." Nikla tried talking over the men but between their booming voices only thunder could compete with them.

"Nikla is not what you think. I've gotten to know her."

Masaun leaned back in his chair and let out an exasperated chuckle.

"Gotten to know her? Has she gotten to know you?" He directed his attention to Nikla. "Has he told you his real name? Did he tell you about his struggles growing up? Did he tell you about the panic attacks?"

"Masaun!" Kindle put her hand on Masaun's arm.

"You son-of-a-bitch." Sweet shook his head.

Masaun kept his glare on Nikla. "It's the reason I stay on top of him all the time. When he released his last submissive, he shut down. I can't lose my only brother. That candy store gave him a goal. Gave him something to look forward to each day. I'll be damned if you or anyone else try to take that from him."

Sweet balled his hand into a fist on top of the table. "No matter what I do, you will always see me as that lost kid, won't you? I don't need you protecting me. I need you to believe in me. Be my goddamn brother and not my keeper."

Nikla felt anger, something she didn't think she would in the moment. Despite being disappointed that Sweet hadn't told Masaun about her, her heart broke for him when he realized that Masaun would always see him as a failure. She had the same feeling from her father.

Nikla stood from table. She grabbed Sweet's hand. "His name is Swithin Bartholomew Hawkes." She watched Masaun's face relax. "Captain Candyland was his favorite candy store as a kid. I know about his panic attacks because I had one in front of your store and he helped me. He's the bravest man I've ever met, willing to try anything." Nikla made sure to stare directly into his eyes. "He is enough of a man to let me be myself, even if it means picketing his baby." She leaned close to Masaun. "And I will gladly, gladly do whatever he wants me to do in the bedroom and in the dungeon." To punctuate her point, she reached under her dress, removed her panties and handed them to Sweet.

Sweet accepted them with a smile.

"Where would you like me, Sir?" she asked him.

"Get your purse and coat." He stood. "I think we're done here."

"Please, don't go like this." Kindle rose to her feet. "We barely finished dinner, and we still have dessert."

Masaun waved his hand to his fiancée. "Let them go."

Nikla strolled to the bedroom where Kindle had left her personal items. If he wanted to come in the room and take her right now, she would let him. Defiance coursed through her veins.

When she returned to the dining room, she found Sweet moving over to Kindle.

"Kindle, I appreciate dinner. Wished we could stay for dessert." Sweet gave his future sister-in-law a hug.

"You could stay."

Nikla heard the pleading tone in her voice.

"Not tonight." Sweet shook his head.

Masaun rose to his feet but stared stoically at Sweet.

"See you at the store." Sweet stepped away from the table and held Nikla's hand.

With Sweet by her side, she felt invincible. For that reason, she knew she would have to tell him about her father.

****

When Sweet got to his truck he opened the door for Nikla. Sweet jumped in and locked his door. He faced her. "I should have told Masaun who you really were."

"Yes, you should have. I felt humiliated. I felt set up." Nikla crossed her arms over her chest.

"I didn't want that to happen."

"Oh, yeah? What did you expect to happen?"

"I wanted him to see the amazing person I see." Sweet stared at her. "I wanted him to understand how I could be so crazy about you."

All air escaped her lungs. Nikla couldn't break her gaze from Sweet.

"Breathe," he said simply.

On an exhale she said, "You're crazy about me?"

He smiled at her. "You're all I think about every day." He held her hand. "When it comes to me, my brother is very protective. I'm the same with him. He wants to make sure I'm happy."

"I do, too." Nikla put her free hand on his lap. "Can we go home now?"

"Come back to my place."

"Wherever you want to take me, I'll go." She squeezed his thigh and felt his muscles flex. "However–"

Sweet split his attention between her and the road.

"If you can take me back to my apartment, I can pack a bag. I have late classes tomorrow so I can sleep in."

"Too bad I can't." He brushed his finger down the side of her face. "Duty calls. But every moment I can spend with you would be worth skating in to work on time."

Nikla smiled at his response. The real reason she wanted him to take her to her apartment wouldn't be pleasant. She didn't want what happened at dinner to happen when Sweet met her father. If she wanted a somewhat cordial meeting, she would have to break the news to both.

****

Sweet didn't take his stare off the road during the drive. From his peripheral vision, he caught Nikla's surprised expression when he passed the exit going to her home. He knew where he needed to take her. From her silence, Nikla must have had an idea of where he headed as well.

When he pulled into The Dollhouse parking lot, his stomach tightened into a ball. He parked, and Nikla waited in her seat until he opened her door and helped her out of his truck.

Sweet felt her shaking as he walked to the door. He really hoped her reaction stemmed from excitement and not from fear.

As he held her hand, Sweet led her to the room where he wanted to push himself and her body. He pulled her down a darkened hallway to the rooms with the large bondage furniture. Sweet looked in one room and found Dominant Razor whipping Lolli as he had her strapped to a wooden sawhorse.

At the next room, he found Mistress Extreme with a male sub in a stockade.

"Damn." Sweet wanted to put Nikla in that device.

At the last room in the corner, the room many of the Doms and Dommes didn't use because of its uneven temperature, Sweet found the space empty and darker than the hallway. He dragged Nikla inside and closed the door. The significantly cooler room didn't seem inviting. What he would do to her would seem even less appealing.

"Take off your clothes." Sweet looked at her to see if Nikla would hesitate.

Unlike when he took her to the voyeur room, she didn't pause. Nikla removed her thin red belt then her dress. Sweet took the items from her and waited for her to remove her bra.

When she placed the undergarment in his hand, she held up one foot as though to nonverbally ask him if she should take off her shoes or leave them. Sweet knew how much she loved walking around in bare feet.

"Take them off."

Nikla smiled slightly as she stepped out of her shoes. Sweet led her over to a piece of furniture that had four legs and a bar across the top. Two bars across the bottom braced the piece. Before he had Nikla assume the position, he had to push her.

"Stand right here and let me inspect you." He stared into her eyes.

Already he saw them turning red, either out of anger or sadness. Sweet maintained his stare. She would have to trust him in this exercise. He knew her father did this to her and her brother. He would do it in a different way.

"Yellow," Nikla whispered.

Sweet kept his hard stance. He put his hands behind his back and raised his chest, knowing that it would remind her of a military stance. "I said stand there and let me look you over."

Nikla's jaw flexed. "Please."

This time Sweet couldn't look her in her eyes. He turned his head as he said, "You know the standard safe words. Green, yellow, and red. Do you want this to stop?"

God, he hoped not.

Please trust me.

Nikla took a deep breath. She exhaled out of her mouth. She gave him one slight nod letting him know he could continue.

Sweet took a couple of steps back and scanned her body. "Hair up in a bun." He regained eye contact with her. "Perfect." He watched her shoulders relax a little.

Good. Sweet could see her resistance melting.

"Makeup. Flawless." He approached her and pressed his lips against hers. When he pulled back he said, "Not so much now."

Nikla laughed then righted herself.

"Eyes." Sweet couldn't think of a word to perfectly describe her soulful brown eyes that managed to suck him in every time he looked at them. "Mesmerizing."

He ran his hand down her neck to her shoulder then her hand. "Soft, glowing skin." Sweet cupped her tits. The firm orbs felt weighty in his hands. "Firm, wonderful breasts." He peered down. "Sexy feet."

Nikla's smile widened.

Sweet strolled around her body. He administered one hard smack to her ass that made Nikla gasp and jump. "The best ass I've ever seen." He circled back around to the front of Nikla. "I'd say you pass this inspection with flying colors."

Nikla beamed like she wanted to hop around and do a happy dance. She started to approach him and raise her hands to hug him but stopped herself.

Sweet leaned down and whispered in her ear, "You're worthy. I hope you know that. You didn't need me to tell you what's so obvious." He kissed the side of her face then took a step back from her. "Stand behind this, get on your knees and lie across the top bar."

"Yes, Sir." Nikla did as instructed. She dropped to her knees, bent over, and grabbed the legs of the furniture.

Sweet moved behind her. As soon as he spied her rounded ass, his mind filled with images of fucking her from behind. He had to snap out of those thoughts. In The Dollhouse, sex topped the list of no-no's. Funny. Cutting, fire play, needle play and oral sex could all be performed there. No sex.

Sweet went to a large, black armoire and opened the creaky doors, which triggered the light inside. He retrieved a few bundles of rope.

Now beside Nikla, Sweet dropped down to his knees and first tied her wrists and arms to the legs. He moved behind her. With little effort, he pried her legs apart. Sweet emitted a moan at the sight of her glistening pink core.

Against his better judgment, Sweet ran his finger down from her puckered asshole to her pussy opening then to her clit. This time Nikla moaned. Her body writhed.

"Mmm, good." She craned her head around. "I wish we could do more in here."

Sweet regarded her for a moment, but he didn't answer. He tied her thighs to the other table legs then stood. He observed his work, this woman. She trusted him to make herself so open and vulnerable.

Sweet returned to the armoire and retrieved a paddle. "Do you think it was appropriate to pull off your panties at dinner in front of my brother and Kindle?"

Nikla smiled, hoping that Sweet would share in her revelry. "For you? I'd do it again."

Feeling the hard smack on her ass made her rethink her decision. Did Sweet like or hate her stunt?

Then she thought about her response and quickly added, "Sir." For that, she still got another smack on her other cheek. The surface pain resonated and Nikla started to react to the immediate feeling. She balled her hands and her breathing increased.

"I still have your panties in my pocket." Sweet spanked her ass two more times, always in different spots.

Nikla winced and released small cries.

"I loved that you did that." Sweet caressed her backside. "Sexiest damn thing I have ever seen in my life." This time, instead of using the paddle, Sweet spanked her ass with his bare hand. "What made it sexy was how you defended me to my brother."

Realizing that Sweet's discipline didn't come from anger but more for pleasure, Nikla's breathing slowed. She curved her back and raised her ass in the air as much as she could for him considering her bound state.

"Why did you do that?"

Nikla heard Sweet moving away from her. He must have been getting another toy.

"Answer me," Sweet demanded. "I didn't tell Masaun about you. You should have been pissed with me."

Nikla had almost forgotten that he had posed a question. "I was angry with you." She didn't hear Sweet move. The air in the room stilled. "The more I listened to your brother, the more I realized how much he sounded like my father when he talks to me."

"You felt sorry for me?"

Nikla felt the thudding smack of a flogger against her already sensitive skin. The feeling shook her body. Her clit throbbed. Juices ran down her inner thighs.

She licked her lips and now hoped that Sweet wouldn't stop. "I didn't feel sorry for you. I felt anger *for* you."

Nikla suddenly felt the tails of the flogger hit her naked pussy. She curved her back up like she had executed a yoga cat pose once she experienced the hit.

"Green." She settled onto the sensations.

With each hit, Nikla felt connected to Sweet. She noticed that Sweet increased the intensity. She loved it.

"Green!" Nikla didn't want him to stop. She wanted to show him that she could take this punishment and more from him, only from him.

She balled her hands into fists to stave off her impending climax. Nikla wouldn't call out her safe word. Just as Sweet had taught her, she learned to embrace the pain, make it a part of her, look forward to it.

As suddenly as the discipline started, it stopped. Nikla thought Sweet paused so that she could catch his breath. Then she heard a large thud hit the floor.

Nikla tried turning her head to catch what had happened. She caught Sweet on the floor on his knees with his head down.

"Sweet! Sweet!" Nikla tried getting out of the bindings but couldn't.

Her gut wrenched, knowing that she couldn't help him. Just when she thought she would break her own arm to get out of the ties, Sweet waved his hand to her and struggled to get up to his feet. Expecting to see him looking distressed, she couldn't believe Sweet carried a smile instead.

He stumbled to her, bent over, and put his hand next to her face. "Thank you." He kissed her. "Thank you."

Nikla felt her eyebrows draw together until she really looked at him and pieced together what had happened. "Dom-space? Did you get there?"

"*You* got me there." He untied her.

With freedom achieved, Nikla stood and wrapped her arms around Sweet's neck. "Tell me how it felt?"

Sweet settled his hands on her hips. "Where an orgasm is intense, Dom-space is intense in the opposite way. At first, I was completely focused on you. I couldn't hear anything. I saw you and only you. Then everything hit me. I realized how important you are to me. Then I saw your reaction. The combination dropped me like a stone. I felt so relaxed and happy. You make me happy."

Nikla felt light inside. Then she lit into him. "You scared me. I didn't know what had happened to you. I thought you had a heart attack or something. If I have to have safe words, so should you. I need to know that you're okay."

Sweet stared at her for a moment before speaking. "Good fucking student." He kissed her temple. "I'll say 'blue' if I'm in trouble. Deal?"

Nikla nodded.

Sweet scooped her up under her ass. Nikla wrapped her legs around his waist. She grabbed his broad shoulders. He placed her on top of a waist-high platform.

Before she could adjust being on top of the platform, Sweet smothered her with a breathtaking kiss. He drove his tongue into her mouth. As he kissed her, she felt him moving his arms.

When he broke from her, Nikla noticed that Sweet had undone his pants. "Wait. We can't here. You said–"

"I fucking need you." Sweet grabbed the base of his cock and aimed the tip at her core.

He plunged deep inside. Nikla gripped his shoulders, embedding her fingernails into him. Coiling her legs around him, she pressed her breasts against his chest.

"Mine," Sweet said into her ear.

This time when he said that, Nikla believed him. She felt it. She couldn't wipe the smile from her face.

Hearing the screams and moans around their room echoed Nikla's moans and Sweet's deep breathing. To accentuate the feeling, Sweet spanked Nikla's ass cheek.

Since her ass had been made sensitive because of the spanking, Nikla squirmed on the platform but welcomed the sensation. Sweet had taught her how to embrace the pain.

Sweet lifted Nikla off the platform and cradled her ass in the air. With his strength, he managed to propel her up and down on his shaft without any support. Nikla tightened her thighs around him and undulated her hips. She felt as one with Sweet.

"Mine." Sweet licked then chewed on her lower lip.

He fisted her hair and pulled her head back. Nikla's head throbbed, but she loved it. He licked her neck up to her chin.

A knock sounded outside of their playroom. "Master Sweet."

Sweet didn't stop. He brought Nikla down to the floor and drove into her harder and faster. He palmed her breast but never broke eye contact with her. Sweat covered his face. He looked like a man on a mission. Nikla loved being his goal.

The pounding outside happened again.

"Pay attention to me," Sweet said.

Nikla nodded. She felt her inner vaginal walls tighten around his shaft. Sweet responded with a growl.

"That's it." He nodded. "That's my Sugar Baby. My Nikla." He grunted. "Mine."

Nikla gyrated her hips. "Dom Sweet, may I–"

He didn't allow her to finish her question. "Come! Now! Now!"

Nikla screamed and coiled every extremity around his hard body. In response, Sweet's body stiffened as he emptied inside of her. As he relaxed, he kissed the tip of her nose then softly on her lips.

He pulled out of her and stood. He helped her to her feet. "Get dressed." He pulled up his pants as he headed to the doorway. When he pulled back the black curtain, a young man and an older gentleman with silvery hair stood on the other side.

The older man glanced at Nikla as she put on her bra and slipped her shoes onto her feet.

"Can we talk, Master Sweet?" the older gentleman asked.

Sweet shook his head. "Not necessary."

The older man nodded. "Good." He held out his hand. "Good luck in your travels."

Nikla put her dress on and watched Sweet shaking the man's hand. She didn't know what had transpired or why there had been an urgent need to get his attention.

When Sweet returned to Nikla, he held her hand and walked with her to the door. She noticed a few angry glares aimed in their direction as they strolled out of the dungeon.

"What was that about?" Nikla asked.

Sweet unlocked the truck and helped her inside. "Nothing important. You're all that matters now."

Nikla smiled at his statement. She felt the same way. If she wanted him fully in her life, she had to do a couple of things. She wanted to introduce him to her father and come clean about why she protested his store. She also needed to talk to Masaun.

Chapter Twenty-Five

Sweet slept soundly next to Nikla in his bed. He did manage to get her over to her apartment so that she could pack a bag. Even that quick trip resulted in them having passionate sex.

He moaned as he recalled how he got her limber legs damn near around the back of her neck. After last night, his perception about their relationship changed. Everything seemed both heavier and lighter. He could make sense of things. More importantly, Nikla had gotten him to trust again.

Sweet's cock started to get hard when he thought about her. He reached over to touch her and found an empty space beside him. Sweet opened his eyes. October morning sun filled the room, an unusual look considering Sweet liked keeping his blinds closed.

Sweet sat up in bed and had a stunning view greeting him. Nikla stood naked in the middle of his small living room space. She slowly went back into a deep back bend with her smooth pussy facing him.

Damn, what a view. Sweet sat up more as he watched her do her yoga exercises.

"Good morning." Sweet drew his hand over his hard cock.

Nikla stood up and faced Sweet with a smile. "Good morning."

"Come here." He patted the bed.

"Wait one second." Nikla ran off to the kitchen.

Sweet heard glasses clinking and silverware brushing against each other. Soon he saw her approaching him with a tray of food. Sweet smiled until he noticed some cooked food on the tray. Nikla had cooked in his kitchen? *His* kitchen?

Before he could hop out of bed and look at the damage, Nikla set the tray on a nightstand next to the bed. She crawled in bed, straddling his lap, and kissed him.

"Good morning." She nodded over to the tray. "I made you breakfast this time."

Sweet glanced at the tray of food. Looked like she'd made him an omelet and a muffin with a side of fresh cut-up fruit and juice.

"You made muffins?" Sweet questioned.

Nikla screwed up her lips. "I know what you're thinking." She picked it up and placed it at his mouth. "Bite."

Sweet kept his lips shut tight as he looked at her.

"Please," she said.

He opened his mouth and took a careful bite. The soft muffin melted in his mouth. The berries burst as he chewed and added to the sweetness. The sweetness beyond the berries surprised him. What happened to the woman who refused to eat or use any refined sugars?

As though answering his thoughts, Nikla supplied, "I made this with applesauce and shredded carrots to add some natural sweetness. Good?"

Sweet swallowed the piece and glared at her before breaking into a smile. "It's very good. Delicious actually. I didn't know you knew how to bake."

Nikla cocked her head. "Of course I can cook. I learned from the best."

"I didn't teach you." Sweet laughed.

"Cute. No, my father. He taught me." Nikla cut a piece of the eggs she'd made and fed Sweet the portion.

Even that tasted wonderful, full of fresh vegetables and diced chicken.

"I don't let anyone cook in my kitchen but me." He stared at Nikla, waiting for a reaction.

"Good thing I'm not just anyone." She smiled.

His heart melted. "You're right about that." He patted her ass. "What will you do today?"

"First thing I'll do is go through your drawers and find all of your secrets." Nikla laughed. "Kidding. I'll run some errands before I go to work."

Sweet pulled her in closer to him. "In your errands, you'll need to find a costume."

"Why is that?"

"Halloween is in a couple of days. I want someone here with me to help pass out candy to the kids, and Hawk and Song Sparrow are throwing a party."

"Have I met them?"

Sweet nodded. "Hawk is Masaun's scene name. Song Sparrow is–"

"Kindle?" Nikla interrupted him.

"It's Hawk's name for her."

"It's that kind of party?"

Sweet caught the tentative tone in her voice. "Would you be ready for that?"

Nikla swallowed, looked away, then brought her gaze back to him.

"Yes."

Heat surged through his body at her firm answer.

Then she surprised him when she followed up with, "I think."

On reflex, he gritted his jaw then relaxed it. Sweet had to remember that Nikla hadn't been in the Lifestyle over a number of years like him. She didn't go into the training on her own. She had to be goaded, dared practically. What else could he expect?

Nikla cut off another piece of her dish and fed it to Sweet. "You're dressing up, too?"

Sweet chewed the morsel before he answered. "Of course."

"Will you tell me what you're wearing so that we match?"

Sweet shook his head. "Surprise me." He glanced at the clock next to his bed. "As much as I would love to stay here in bed with you, I have to get dressed and go to work." Sweet took a sip of his orange juice that tasted freshly squeezed.

Nikla released a long, exaggerated sigh. "Fine." She jumped off him and padded toward the bathroom. "I'll take a shower while you finish your breakfast."

As she walked away, Nikla ran her hands down her body. At the bathroom door, she bent over in front of him, showing off her pink opening and her ass.

"Let me help you wash your back." Sweet jumped from the bed and chased her into the bathroom.

Nikla squealed as she ran into the room.

Sweet caught up with her. With his arm around her waist, he turned on the shower and waited for it to heat up to a good temperature.

He guided her inside and closed the stall door. It didn't take him long to wrap his arms around her body and smother her in kisses. Nikla looped her arms around his neck. He loved that he could be that support for her.

Sweet slid his hand up her slick body to her breast, cupping it as he continued kissing her. He broke from the kiss long enough to say, "I need you wet."

Thinking he must have meant the shower, Nikla ducked her head under the stream of water as he licked down her chin and neck. When he got down to her tits, he sucked one into his mouth and teased her nipple with his tongue. He circled it, getting it as hard as he could.

"Swithin." Nikla raked her fingers through his hair.

Nikla would be the only person, man or woman, who could make Sweet love hearing his name mentioned out loud. Whenever his mother said it, he'd cringed. Then again, when she said it, an admonishment followed.

Sweet moved his mouth over to her other breast and gave it the same loving treatment he'd given the first. Down on his knees, he brought one leg over his shoulder. Face to face with her delectable pussy, he wasted no time in tasting her essence.

The first tongue swipe over her clitoris got him rewarded with a moan that echoed off the bathroom walls. He moved his tongue back and forth over her, teasing her, wanting her to come, to yield to him, to need him.

With the hand that held her propped up thigh, Sweet moved it down her leg to her ass. He palmed it, squeezing it hard enough for her to know that she belonged to him. Then he curved his hand under her and attempted to push his finger in between her cheeks. As soon as he felt her clamping her cheeks together, he peered up at her.

"Relax."

Nikla nodded, but her ass told a different story. Still clenched, she wouldn't allow his finger to dip inside.

Instead of commanding her, Sweet decided to coax her reaction. He twirled his tongue around her hardened nub until he felt her knee buckle. He lowered his head and slid his tongue back and forth over her vaginal opening.

"Yes." Nikla's hips gyrated in concert with his oral ministrations.

Soon Sweet felt her ass relax. He took that opportunity to slide his finger in between her firm cheeks. He brushed his finger over her asshole. For that, Nikla gasped. She fisted his hair.

Sweet didn't need encouragement to satisfy this woman. He continued licking her, dipping her tongue inside her until he felt her legs shaking. At that point, he knew he had to get her over the edge.

He slipped his finger inside her tight asshole.

"Oh, God! Yes! Yes!" Nikla gripped his hair and her body froze.

Sweet's scalp throbbed under her grasp, but he didn't care. He loved getting her to come.

When Nikla came down from her orgasm, Sweet stood. He pushed her against the shower stall wall and held up one leg as he guided the tip of his cock into her opening. He eased himself inside her tight channel.

As he entered her, Nikla's fingernails clawed his shoulders. Sweet kept his arm hooked under her leg as he made his thrusts. He also made sure to keep his stare directly on her eyes.

"So good." Sweet wanted to call the moment perfect.

Too afraid of jinxing the moment, he stopped at calling it good. As he saw what he thought could have been a tear escaping her eye, Nikla buried her face in the crook of his neck.

Hell, they stood in a shower. It could have been water. If Sweet hadn't felt her internal walls tightening around him, he would have chalked it up to the shower.

Sweet pulled out of her for moment, placed her foot back on the floor, and turned her around so that she faced the shower stall wall. Then he bent her over. "You tell me if you don't want this."

He held his shaft as he used his other hand to push her ass cheek aside. Nikla glanced back at him but didn't say a word.

Sweet rubbed the tip over her puckered hole. He slipped the tip inside and held himself there for moment.

Nikla's knees buckled more pronounced this time. Good thing Sweet had his arm around her waist. He held her up as he eased himself inside her until he got down to the hilt.

Each time Sweet pulled back, her constricting hole drew him back inside. He could live there and be happy.

"More," Nikla said in a whisper.

She reached behind herself and held the back of Sweet's head. With each thrust, his heart pounded harder and harder. He kissed her shoulder, then gave her playful nips with his teeth over it up to her neck.

With her body all wet, Sweet drank her all in, licking the water from her skin. He could sustain his life being buried deep in her and drinking in her essence.

Sweet wrapped his arm around her waist and increased his tempo. Nikla must have felt his body trembling. She wrapped her foot around his ankle as though to keep him in his spot. No way could he even break from his position until he satisfied himself and Nikla, his woman, his submissive, his lover.

"Ohh, yes!" Sweet growled in her ear.

At the same time, Nikla cried out, pressing her ass against him. "Shit. I didn't think that was even possible." She craned her head back as far as she could while bringing him in closer to kiss him.

For as long as he lived, he would love hearing Nikla's voice. If he had any chance of a long-term relationship with her, he would have to find and talk to her father.

****

After her afternoon classes, Nikla went back to Decadent Treats, but not to see Sweet. Actually she hoped he wouldn't be there. What she had to do, she had to do without Sweet's knowledge or approval.

At the door of the candy store, Nikla would have normally paused there, too afraid to go inside. She would have probably had an anxiety attack at this point. Feeling confident of her decision, she opened the door and stepped inside.

"Welcome to Decadent Treats." The robust, older woman who had threatened to call the police on her before stared at Nikla for a moment before her smile disappeared. "I'll call the police on you if you try anything." She patted her pockets and pulled out a roll of red ribbon, something she would probably use on their gift baskets. "I'll tie you up until the police arrive."

Nikla tried hard not to laugh. She liked how this woman protected Sweet and the store. "I'd like to talk to Masaun."

The woman, whose ID badge named her as Connie, blinked but remained in her spot. Connie shook her head. "Oh no you don't, Missy. Mr. Hawkes is with a beautiful attorney. If you're looking to break up their relationship, I'll–"

Nikla held up her hand. "Please. I'm not looking to break up any relationship." Not intentionally, she wanted to add. Nikla had a feeling that with her introduction at dinner last night that she may have ruined Sweet and Masaun's relationship. She couldn't have that happen.

"Connie."

Nikla and Connie both looked behind the counter where the voice emanated. Masaun stood by a doorway as he looked at the two women. Still wearing a suit, he looked official...and mad.

"Nikla, come on back to my office." He opened the door for her.

Although she knew the location of the office, she allowed Masaun to lead her. He closed the door behind the two of them and directed her to sit in a chair in front of the desk as he occupied a seat behind it.

"To what do I owe the pleasure of this visit?" Masaun's soured expression didn't scream that he wanted to see her, now or ever.

Nikla took a deep breath. "I know you don't like me, and you have a good reason not to."

Masaun remained quiet as she spoke.

"I would be upset with anyone who wanted to crush my dreams, too. But I had a good reason."

"People who set off bombs at abortion clinics believe they have good reason, too. Terrorists think that what they're doing is right and just."

"You think I'm a terrorist?" Nikla hadn't thought of herself that way but obviously Masaun had.

"What you're doing is designed to drive business away."

Nikla nodded. "You're right. Before we get into that, I'd like to discuss the real reason why I'm here."

"And why is that?"

"Sweet. Swithin." Nikla sat at the edge of her seat. "Sweet is the most stubborn and determined man I have ever met." She smiled at some of his antics and had to cross her legs when she recalled times at the club. "He loves this business." She stared at Masaun. "He loves you. He wants you to be proud of him."

"I am." Masaun leaned back in his chair and turned to the side. "He doesn't think I'm proud of him?"

She shook her head. "He thinks you're holding onto his past mistakes and won't let him get beyond that to see the amazing man he is now. He's smart and resourceful and, yes, sometimes difficult."

At that revelation, Masaun chuckled.

"But he's a lot stronger than you think. He managed to train me in a lifestyle I knew nothing about."

Masaun whipped his head around to look at her.

"Sweet has made me fall in love with it. He could have done exactly what you wanted to do, have me arrested or run me off your property. He didn't. He went out there and talked to me. When I didn't feel strong, he helped me, literally carried me. Even after the dynamic of our relationship changed, he told me to continue picketing his store. He wanted me to stay true to myself. That's part of the reason I, uh, respect him so much."

Masaun turned his chair around and faced her. "Are you sure you aren't doing this to worm your way into our business and try to break it down from the inside?"

Nikla sighed. She understood some of Masaun's skepticism. She wished he could have been a little more open like Sweet.

"I don't want to do that. Like I said, I respect Sweet. I would do anything for him."

"I know. I saw. That whole panty stunt shut me right up."

Nikla felt the heat flooding her cheeks.

"You made it very obvious that you care for my brother. I don't know if I've ever seen him this happy. I don't think I had even met Melinda, his last submissive, until toward the end of their relationship." Masaun sighed and bowed his head. "Don't break his heart."

She shook her head. "I won't." She put her hand to her chest. "And I'm done passing out fliers. I did it initially for love, and now I have to stop for that same reason."

"Love?"

Nikla didn't want to reveal too much to Masaun, not until she had a chance to talk to Sweet. "Nothing romantic. Family, actually. But I'm discovering that grand gestures aren't going to solve the problems between us." Like with Masaun, Nikla would need to sit down and talk to her father. That conversation should have been done a long time ago.

Masaun stood and held his hand out to her. Nikla shook it.

"I appreciate you coming in and talking to me face to face. It takes a lot of guts for you to do that." After shaking her hand, he walked around the desk. "I can see why Sweet would like you." He nodded.

Nikla stood and walked with Masaun to the office door.

"Has he met your family yet?"

She shook her head. "My brother's in the Marines. My mother lives in Maryland."

"And your father?"

"A hard nut to crack, but I'll get him to see what I see." She hoped.

"Good luck. I understand about obstacles that can hold up a relationship. I hope you two make it."

Nikla couldn't help but give Masaun a kiss on his cheek.

"You stop that right now!" Connie called from the aisle. "I told you he's getting married."

"I'm not trying to–"

"Let it go." Masaun patted Nikla's shoulder. "I'll take care of this one."

Before any more drama could escalate, Nikla hightailed it out of the candy store. Now she had to get a costume for Halloween. She never liked the special day because of the candy involved. She had a feeling with Sweet, she would find a new way to appreciate the event. Plus, she had a great idea of what to wear for him that would fit their relationship.

****

At the end of the day, Sweet just wanted to go back to his apartment and crash. After cleaning up the kitchen area, he went to the office to talk to Masaun. They hadn't spoken all day. After dinner last night, the air had to be cleared.

He stepped into the office, finding Masaun in his usual spot behind the desk. Sweet closed the office door to keep their conversation private from their eager employees.

"I had an interesting visitor today." Masaun leaned back in his swivel chair and propped his ankle up on his other knee.

"Who? Mom and Dad?" Sweet sat on the couch and stretched his arms across the back.

"Nope. Nikla Dearwood."

That name got his attention. She'd called him and said she couldn't see him tonight. Sweet wondered if his brother said something to upset her. No, Nikla would have shared that with him. He found her to be an open book.

"What was she doing here?" Sweet braced his hands on his knees.

"She defended you very, very fiercely."

Sweet's breathing slowed at that news. "She did?"

Masaun nodded. "Then she said she would stop the picketing."

Sweet started to yell at his brother if he intimidated her to stop.

His brother raised his hand. "It was her idea, not mine. She said the reason why she started is the same reason why she stopped. She didn't explain. I'm hoping she talked to you already."

Not yet. Sweet suspected their conversation would happen soon.

"By the way, I had a very lonely night after that dinner. Kindle thought I was too hard on you and Nikla during dinner." Masaun cleared his throat. "I apologize if I made either of you feel bad, but I love you. I won't apologize for being overprotective."

"Big shock." Sweet stood. "God forbid you actually admit that you were wrong at anything."

"It's so rare that I am wrong." Masaun laughed. "Seriously, are you and I good?"

Sweet moved to the door. He brought his attention back to his brother. "Getting there. Glad Kindle put your ass out of the bedroom last night. I knew I liked her."

"Yeah. She likes you and Nikla together. By the way, I'm assuming you did a Google search on her, right?"

Sweet groaned. "Come on. Give me some credit."

Masaun lifted his hands in defeat. "Okay, I should have figured you would have done a search on Nikla and her father."

Sweet didn't want to pause too long and let his brother see that Sweet hadn't done any research on Nikla's father. He had her parents' names. Why hadn't he thought of that before?

"I'll see you in the morning." Before Masaun could bring up anything else, Sweet rushed up to his apartment. He had some research to do.

Chapter Twenty-Six

Nikla would have rather spent the evening with Sweet than with her father at Healthy Bites. With a week in between the last time she saw him, she knew she couldn't get away with avoiding him for much longer.

At closing time, Lawrence locked the doors then turned to Nikla. "Thanks for helping out today."

Nikla plastered a smile on her face. She managed to glance at her watch to see if Sweet would still be available. She still couldn't believe he had gotten her to try anal sex. It shocked her even more that she came from it. Her bottom still tingled as she thought about it.

No, she had to stay focused. Although she missed Sweet's body, she had to give her full attention to her father.

"You're not even listening to me."

Busted.

"I am, Dad. You said you wanted me to work with you full-time." Nikla hoped her guess came close to what her father had said. She avoided looking at him, concentrating on cleaning off the tables and counters, so that he wouldn't look into her face and see that she had lied to him.

"You can't do that yoga stuff forever."

Nikla sighed that she had assumed correctly. "Dad, you haven't been listening to *me* now. I've been telling you for the last couple of years that I've wanted to have my own studio."

Lawrence shook his head. "Too dangerous. Too risky."

"Dangerous? I do yoga for a living."

Her father glared at her. "Depending on where you set up your business, some crazed lunatic may come in and try to rob you or worse." He broke his stare to remove the cash from the register. "No, you need to be here with me. Your brother is protecting our country. You need me to protect you."

"What? I'm not a child. I've managed to go to college, live on my own, get my own job, buy my own car and take care of myself for years. I don't need–" Nikla started to say she didn't need him when she got a death stare from him. "I don't need you to protect me. You remember all those self-defense classes you enrolled me in before I graduated college? I really did go to them."

Lawrence locked the money in the safe in his office before he turned off the light and locked the office door.

"I do have to talk to you. We can do it over dinner. My treat." Nikla smiled.

Her insides tickled thinking about telling her father about Sweet and her feelings for him. She would reveal that before admitting what her new man did for a living.

Lawrence snickered and plopped down in a chair. "You want to get me out in public so I won't embarrass you?"

Nikla shook her head. "No." She approached him but didn't sit. What she had to say she really wanted to be grounded. Standing would give her some power. "I thought after such a long day that it would be nice for someone to serve us for a change."

Just saying the word "serve" brought memories of the times she'd served Sweet. She would leave those stories out when talking to her father about Sweet Hawkes.

"What do you have to tell me? You're going to say that I don't listen to you and that I'm preventing from you living your life? You're going to say that being here with me would be like being a prisoner? You think you know everything, Nicole?" He stopped and quickly said, "Nikla."

What Nikla had suspected finally reared its head. She sat down across from her father and held his hands. "I love you, Dad."

Lawrence, proud as always, kept his head turned as she spoke.

"Mom left us both. But you stayed. You made sure Junior and I focused on what was important." She squeezed his hand. "You're a great man and an amazing father." Nikla thought she noticed her father's eyes transforming to a cherry color. He still refused to look at her. "You have to trust that if I'm not by your side that that doesn't mean that I'll leave like Mom did." She took a deep breath. Since they delved into deep topics, she would continue. "I still want to open my own business. If it wasn't for you, I wouldn't even think about it. As a matter of fact, I should hear about a pretty nice space in a few days."

Her father glanced at her and cocked his head. "Opening a business is hard. It's not all roses and light."

She nodded. "I know. I'm hoping if I have any questions that you'll be there to help me."

Lawrence remained quiet.

Nikla barreled on with her other news while she had his attention. "A couple of weeks ago, I met a man." She smiled as she thought about him, his incredible hands that seemed to transform her body whenever he'd touched her, and his eyes that saw down into her soul.

Lawrence pulled his hand away from her. "Who is this man?"

Nikla cleared her throat. "His name is Sweet Hawkes." She watched her father's eyes narrow for a moment before he widened them and bolted up to his feet.

"Traitor!"

Nikla stood. "It's not what you think, Dad. I was handing out fliers in front of his store and I had one of my attacks."

Her father shook his head. "Weak. You've always been so weak. You're just like your mother."

That dig ordinarily would have crumbled Nikla. Her normal kneejerk reaction would be to tell her father that the reason his son joined the military had everything to do with getting away from him. Nikla could have also revealed that her brother had a wonderful relationship with a man.

Nikla kept her word with her brother. Despite what her father thought, Nikla didn't want to cut him out of her life. She didn't see herself as someone who couldn't be loyal, someone who would run. Thanks to what she learned from Sweet, she felt strong enough to take his slings and arrows.

"Sweet is very special to me, Dad." Nikla went behind the counter and grabbed her purse and sweater. "I'd love for the two of you to meet." As she walked toward the back door to leave, she felt her father's vise-like grip around her upper arm.

"I forbid you to see him." Her father's booming voice echoed off the walls.

Nikla concentrated on the constricting feeling around her arm. Her father grabbed her, not out of anger, but more out of desperation. He dropped his gaze when he noticed the candy bracelet around her wrist. As he reached down to touch it, Nikla wriggled away from him.

Again, she took a deep breath and connected to his gaze. "He's an amazing man who likes your daughter for exactly who she is. That should make you happy." She opened the door but stopped to address him. "I'll call you in a couple of days when you're calmer."

Nikla managed to make it to her car and all the way back to her apartment before she let what happened tonight settle into her thoughts. She had always suspected that her father wanted to keep her close to ensure that he didn't lose her. His type of bondage didn't appeal to her.

Nikla always found it odd that being tied up by Sweet gave her the most freedom that she'd ever felt. She hoped she offered something to him as well.

After the tense conversation with her father, she wondered how admitting that her father owned Healthy Bites would go over with Sweet.

Tomorrow. She would have to tell him tomorrow. Maybe in her costume he would be more receptive to listen to her.

****

Sweet took a few sips of his coffee as he stared at the man working behind the counter. After talking to Masaun last night, Sweet immediately went to his apartment to do an online search on Lawrence Dearwood. After finding one Lawrence Dearwood who looked to be about his age and in the military, he found another one in the Virginia Beach area who happened to run his own bakery in town.

He stared at the man to see if he could find any of Nikla's features. She certainly got her height from him. Otherwise he found no resemblance. His darker skin tone didn't match Nikla's butter caramel tone. Nikla must have gotten her cute button nose from her mother. The man's thin lips gave him the appearance that he hadn't had a happy day in his entire life.

After finding the story online about Lawrence and the store, she wondered why Nikla hadn't admitted to him what her father did. Then it hit him. She did everything she did to support her father. Did that mean that she really didn't care about Sweet? Was she playing him?

Sweet shook his head to get rid of the doubt. He hadn't talked to her since yesterday, and she had planned on seeing him tonight. Right now he had to do this.

Sweet stood from the table and approached the front counter. "Mr. Dearwood?"

The man with a shaved head met his gaze with Sweet's. "Would you like another muffin?"

Sweet had purchased the coffee and pastry to buy him some time to think about what he would say to this man. After eating the muffin, he could definitely tell that Nikla learned to cook from this man. Hers tasted better. Maybe he thought that because he desired her.

"No, I don't need another muffin." Sweet waved his hand.

"It's good, right? Made without fattening eggs or milk or butter. Just applesauce and honey and one secret ingredient." The man looked around like he would be sharing government secrets before he blurted, "Shredded zucchini. That's what makes them moist. No one can ever taste it. It's a great way to get your kids to eat their vegetables without telling them. You have children?"

"Not yet." Sweet did imagine what a child between him and Nikla would look like.

In his lifestyle, they couldn't fit a child. He wondered the same thing when Masaun said he and Kindle thought about having children. How could they make that work?

"Wait to have kids." The man behind the counter snickered and shook his head. "They only end up breaking your heart."

"Hopefully not all the time." Sweet threw away his cup and paper plate where his muffin once sat. He wiped his fingers on his jeans. "Mr. Dearwood, you don't know me."

"Are you the I.R.S.? I paid my taxes. Yeah, they were late, but I paid them." He placed his fist on his hip. The white t-shirt he wore accentuated his darker skin tone.

"No, I'm not the tax man. Although, with my business, I have to worry about them, too."

Lawrence gave Sweet a suspicious glare.

Before Lawrence could make any assumptions in his head, Sweet quickly filled in the blanks. "I know your daughter, Nikla."

Lawrence's eyes started to widen.

"My name is Sweet Hawkes. I'm co-owner of Decadent Treats, and your daughter and I have been spending a lot of time together recently."

Lawrence threw the towel he had in his hand down and came from around the counter to square off against Sweet.

Sweet didn't budge. He would treat Nikla's father with respect, but he refused to be intimidated or bullied by him.

"You've got some nerve stepping into my establishment. It's because of you that I don't have any business." He raised his hands in the air to show off the empty space. "As soon as our doors opened, we did great business. Then Decadent Treats opened with their full-fat candies and crap. Customers ran over to you all. Then about a couple of months ago, business really dropped."

The article appeared about that time. Sweet didn't realize the effect it would have on people outside of their circle. For that, he felt sorry for Nikla's father.

"You certainly don't think my brother and I opened our business to specifically hurt your business, do you?" Sweet stood a few inches over the man and had to look down slightly to talk to him.

"I don't care why you opened it. For all I know, you did it to pick up women." When Lawrence made the statement, he pounded his fist on the counter.

It probably registered to him what Sweet had said a moment ago about Nikla.

"I respect your daughter." Although right now he had to question her decision about not telling him about her father and his business.

"She and I argued last night and you show up the next day. Boy, she couldn't wait to run home and tell you about it, huh? Used to be she told me everything."

Sweet shook his head. "Nikla didn't tell me you two talked last night. Was it about me?"

Lawrence regarded him for a while as though gauging whether he'd told the truth or not. "Yeah. She felt the need to admit her feelings about you to me after she worked in my store yesterday."

That's what Nikla had to do. The fact that she had told her father about him took away some of his niggling doubt buzzing in his head.

"I don't want her with you." Lawrence shook his head.

Before Sweet could argue that as a grown woman, Nikla had the right to choose or refuse him, he went another route. "What kind of man do you see with your daughter?"

Lawrence put his fists to his hips. "You think I'm going to discount you because of your race. You're wrong. I want my daughter to be with a man who has integrity."

"Good. I am a man with integrity. As soon as I found out who you were, I made the decision to come here to meet you. Nikla doesn't know I'm here."

"What do you mean, found out about me? Didn't Nikla tell you?"

"She told me your name. She said you owned your own business but didn't tell me what it was. She said she was picketing Decadent Treats because she wanted to warn people about the risks of eating too much sugar. She didn't tell me that she did it to please you."

Lawrence took a step back. "I didn't tell her to do that. She did it on her own."

"To make you happy." Sweet ran his hand over his hair. "Nikla said her relationship with you is tense."

Lawrence blinked. "She did?"

"I'm not trying to get in your business, Mr. Dearwood, personally or otherwise. I run an honest business and I can tell you do the same. I'd like to invite you and Nikla to dinner so that we all can get to know each other and clear the air.”

Lawrence scanned Sweet before he retreated behind his counter. “Happy Halloween. Feel free to grab one of our menus on your way out. Pass it along to your friends.”

Sweet didn’t think anyone could be any more stubborn than him. Lawrence had him beat. Maybe Lawrence’s reluctance to listen to anyone had pushed Nikla in her decision to keep her father’s identity a secret. It didn’t matter. Sweet would have to get the truth out of her tonight.

Sweet passed a tall, thin Filipino man at the doorway as he left without further argument. Lawrence didn’t care that Sweet could make his daughter very happy. Did Nikla believe that?

Chapter Twenty-Seven

"Eight o'clock. Time to close up shop!" Nikla clapped as the last of the trick-or-treaters left with bags full of candy courtesy of Sweet, Connie, and her.

Usually, Nikla never handed out candy. Her father said that begging didn't become anyone. Tonight, she felt like a kid herself handing out candies and treats to little goblins, princesses, and superheroes.

"You want me to help you clean up, Mr. Sweet?" Connie asked as she kept a suspicious gaze on Nikla.

Wearing a long trench coat as she handed out candy probably made Nikla look distrustful. She didn't want to show her outfit to Connie. The view would only be for Sweet.

"No, I got it, Connie. Thanks for staying." Sweet patted the woman on her back.

"Anytime, boss. I know how important these occasions are to you and this business." She glared at Nikla.

"Connie–"

Nikla held up her hand. "No, I have this, Sweet." She stood in front of the overly protective woman. "Yes, I'm the one who handed out the fliers in front of the store. I'm not doing that anymore. I'm not trying to take Masaun from Kindle." She turned to Sweet who had a confused expression on his face. "I'll explain later." She returned her attention to Connie. "I care deeply about Sweet, which is why I'm out here handing out candy and in an outfit that's suitable for his eyes only. I appreciate how loyal you are to Masaun and Sweet, but please see me as an ally, not an enemy." Nikla held out her hand to the matronly woman.

Until Sweet nudged his employee with his elbow did she finally extend her hand to shake Nikla's.

"Don't be fooled by my accommodating demeanor. You hurt Sweet or this business I will come after you." Connie light voice didn't match her fierce intentions.

"Never. Won't happen."

Connie nodded. "See you in the morning, Mr. Sweet." She walked out the back door and Sweet locked it.

Nikla scanned over Sweet. In his dark blue suit with red power tie, she wondered if he dressed like the president or maybe he wanted to look like his brother as a joke. His hair threw her. He had a deep part on the side and swept over his head.

"Okay, I give. What's your costume?" she asked as he led her up to his apartment.

"You can't tell?" Sweet opened the door for her. Once inside he closed and locked his door. "Let me give you a hint. You're fired!" He pointed at her.

Nikla couldn't help but laugh. "Donald Trump. Really?" She reached up and touched his hair. "The hair should have given it away."

"Let me see your costume."

Nikla opened her coat and let it fall to the floor. Underneath hid her genie costume complete with the harem pants, curled-toed shoes, and belly-baring top that would make Barbara Eden blush.

She put her hands together in prayer form. "I figured this would be the only costume I could wear where me calling you Master wouldn't be a big deal."

"I should have guessed from the shoes. I imagined a getup like that underneath your coat." Sweet smiled, but she had expected him to laugh or be extremely turned on or something. All night and now, he seemed deflated for some reason.

"I met someone earlier today." He strolled into the living room area.

With a line like that, no way could Nikla let that go. "Who? Another woman?"

"Lawrence Dearwood."

Shit, she said in her head. She'd hoped he meant the younger Lawrence, but she knew better than that.

"How? When?"

"I did a search online and, to my surprise, I saw he owned Healthy Bites." He stood in his kitchen. He braced his fists on the counter. "Why didn't you tell me?"

"I was going to. Today, actually."

"You told me your whole picketing act was to promote health. That was a lie."

She shook her head. "No, it wasn't. And it wasn't an act. I was promoting health, but I was also trying to support my father."

"By taking down my business."

"You don't understand." How could Sweet know how Nikla had to compete with the memory of what her mother did? How could he even guess that no matter what she did, it would never be enough for her father?

Sweet shook his head. "I do." He finally dropped the barrier between them by coming around the kitchen counter. "After talking to him, I get it. Your father asks so much of you." He pointed at her, placing his fingertip on her chest below her clavicle. "When are you going to do something for yourself?"

Nikla took a deep breath. "I should have told you about my dad. I feel like I've been jumping up and down in front of him to get him to see me and notice that I'm here for him. He thinks I'm going to leave him like my mother did. I shouldn't have tried to make a point with him by using your business."

"Nikla." Sweet grabbed her shoulders and made her look at him. "You're going to have to find what makes you happy before you can please anyone else."

She started to say something when she heard a knock at his door. "Master Wasabi again?"

Sweet shook his head. "I didn't invite anyone over." He went to the door and opened it.

Masaun stood on the other side. He took one step into Sweet's apartment. "You and Nikla still coming to our Halloween party?"

Sweet regarded Nikla for a moment. "We're going to have to skip it this time."

Nikla held his arm. "No. I'd like to go if you're in the mood. This is my first full-on Halloween celebration." She smiled. "I want to celebrate."

Sweet covered her hand with his. "We'll see you at your house."

Masaun nodded and closed the door.

"Are you sure you want to go?" He faced her. "This might be our last night together. After we find out about the spaces, we may not want to be together anymore."

Nikla said nothing. She strolled over to where she dropped her coat to the floor and picked it up. After slipping it back on, she said, "Or maybe we will."

This time Sweet remained silent as he buttoned up her coat and secured the belt around her waist, pulling it tighter and tighter and eliciting a strange response from her.

Nikla liked feeling the pressure around her body. It reminded her of the times Sweet strapped her down. When he pulled her close to him, wetness oozed into the panty of her costume. Good thing she purchased the garment instead of renting it. She had a feeling that by the end of the night she or Sweet would be ripping it off her body.

"We had better go or we'll never leave." Sweet pulled her to the door.

Nikla welcomed the cool October air as soon as he opened the door. She knew tonight would be a hot night.

****

Sweet took his time getting to Masaun's. As he had mentioned to Nikla back at his place, he didn't know how long they would have together. If he got the spaces and she didn't, would she want to stay with him? Then again, if she got one of the spaces, he didn't know if he could handle losing.

As he walked Nikla up to the front door, he placed his hand at the small of her back. "Don't be afraid."

Nikla turned to him. "Why would I be? I'm with you."

Her honest response pumped his cock. He would have to corral those feelings until the end of the night.

Party noises of music and laughter permeated through the house even with the doors and windows closed. When Sweet opened the door, a burst of colors met his gaze first. People in various costumes wandered in his view.

Sweet recognized many partygoers from The Dollhouse. The ones who knew him greeted him and Nikla. She smiled cordially at them but only after she glanced at him first as though waiting for approval.

Until Sweet reached the kitchen did he finally find his brother and Kindle. He had to blink when he saw what they wore, or rather what they didn't have on their bodies. Nearly naked Masaun simply wore a fig leaf over his genitals. Sweet didn't want to look behind him to see if had on a pair of flesh-colored Speedos or if he had his bare ass on display.

Kindle had a string of fig leaves around her hips to cover her private parts. She had a fake stuffed snake around her neck that she used to cover her naked breasts. As soon as Masaun spotted Sweet, his eyes widened.

"Glad to see you two made it." Masaun lifted his hand in the air to give Sweet a high five.

"What in the world are you in?" Sweet laughed. After he gave Kindle a kiss on her cheek, he asked, "Did you come up with this Adam and Eve idea?"

She shook her head. "All Dom Hawk's idea." Kindle peered up at her man. "I hope no one has a camera."

"Who would have thought that I would be the one in a full suit and you would be the one nearly naked?" Sweet patted his brother's shoulder.

"You're a bad influence on me." Masaun winked. He looked over at Nikla. "You look lovely tonight." He leaned down and kissed Nikla on her cheek. "Enjoy yourself at the party." He brought his attention back to Sweet. "The dungeon is open."

Sweet nodded. He helped Nikla out of her coat. "Put this in the back bedroom and come right back here."

"Yes, Master Sweet."

When she called him that, it didn't sound like she did it because she wore the costume. Christmas would come early for him if she meant it.

"Nice subby." Tough, a Dominant from the club, nudged Sweet in his side. "You had her long?"

Sweet shook his head. "Not long." Although he felt like he'd known her forever.

"You two playing tonight?" The African-American man pulled the leash on his submissive who apparently had made the mistake of not paying enough attention to Tough. The blonde rolled her eyes before lowering them.

"I hadn't planned on it." Sweet looked through the crowd to see his beauty sauntering through it to get back to him. "But I might."

Tough leaned close to him. "Mind if I played with her?"

A pang of anger zipped through his body. "Yes, I would. Don't let that Superman costume get to your head."

Tough raised his hands. "Got it. She's yours." He walked away with his submissive. As he passed Nikla, he stepped in front of her, leaned down, and whispered something in her ear.

Before Sweet could get to him, Tough walked away without a second look. Nikla made her way to Sweet without any more interruptions.

"What did he say to you?" Sweet asked as he put his arm around her tiny waist.

"He said how lucky I was to have you as my master." She put her arm around him.

Sweet nodded.

"But said that if things didn't work out between us that I should look him up."

Sweet gritted his teeth. Tough had broken the code between Dominants. Although he wanted to admonish the man for his brazen behavior, how could he when he'd defied the number one rule at The Dollhouse when he had sex there on the property?

Because of that, he would have to limit his play to his home, at another

Dom or Domme's house, or drive to D.C. or North Carolina for some club action. Maybe he needed to find that BDSM bed-and-breakfast.

"Would my master like something to drink?" Nikla asked.

Sweet nodded. "Iced tea if you can find any, or anything diet."

She bowed her head and it made Sweet wonder how in the world he'd gotten so lucky to find her. Find her? She practically delivered herself to his doorstep.

When Nikla returned with his drink he directed her to follow him. In the corner of the dining room sat a large dog cage with a naked man inside lying on a fleece-lined dog bed. Sweet sat on top of the cage and brought Nikla onto his lap. The slave continued sleeping, a feat considering the noise level in the house.

"Am I doing okay?" Nikla asked and adjusted herself on his lap.

Sweet placed his hand on her ass to steady her and to feel her firm cheek. "I'll tell you if you do something wrong." He took a sip of his drink.

Iced tea. Good submissive.

He placed the cup to her lips to give her a sip. Nikla drank whatever he gave her.

Sweet sat the cup on top of the cage, then pulled Nikla close to him. "Let me introduce you to some people."

She nodded and smiled.

Sweet stood and held Nikla's hand. He introduced her to a few Dominants and a couple of club submissives. He found that Nikla would only nod to acknowledge them until he gave her a couple taps on her side.

Damn, she was good.

After a pleasant conversation with Madame Le Freak, a prim Englishwoman with a penchant for cock-and-ball torture, Sweet pulled Nikla aside. "Let's go to the dungeon."

Sweet pulled her toward Masaun and Kindle's playroom. The room already overflowed with party guests. As Sweet pulled her through the room to the back corner, Nikla noticed another door, one that had a man wearing a police costume standing next to it.

"Raspberries are delicious," Sweet said, knowing the code phrase to get into the dungeon.

The man nodded and opened the door for him. The additional room remained illuminated only by a purple-tinted light bulb. Although a large area rug covered the cherry hardwood floor, plastic sat on top of it.

Sweet found Razor with Lolli strung up on a cross and whipping her. Sweet assumed he worked on Lolli. The woman wore a full hood. With her back to him, he couldn't tell if zippers covered her eyes and mouth. From her audible cries, if a zipper existed over her mouth, then Razor must have had it opened.

Red welts marked up her pale back and ass cheeks. A small crowd of admirers gathered around the duo.

In one corner of the large room, a Domme had a naked male submissive on the floor under a mechanic's light that she used as a spotlight. She had pads from a TENS unit attached to the underside of his penis. When she engaged the electric current, the man twitched, winced, and eventually moaned. Pre-cum dripped from the tip of his penis.

Between panting breaths, he uttered, "Thank you, ma'am."

Nikla squeezed Sweet's hand. "Whatever you want to do to me, I'll do it." She smiled. "I want this. I want you."

Sweet longed to hear those words, not just from anyone, from Nikla. He led her to another area of the expansive dungeon, which housed a bed and it looked like an attached bathroom.

A Domme sat in a chair in the center of the room. In her ornate Marie Antoinette-like costume, Sweet nearly missed the man underneath her chair. Only his feet appeared from under her large ball gown of a dress.

"What is he doing?" Nikla asked without taking her stare off the woman whose eyes rolled to the back of her head several times.

"Queening." Sweet pointed. "The seat of the chair is gone." He leaned down and whispered. "So are her panties."

Nikla split her attention between him and the queen on her throne. "Oh." She stared at the woman longer until an audible slurp sounded in the open room. "Oh!"

"Good boy." The woman snapped her white lace fan open to cool down her face. When she opened her eyes and spotted Sweet, she smiled. "We'll be done soon."

"Take your time." Sweet put his hand to the small of Nikla's back. "We'll use the bed."

Nikla followed Sweet over to the bed. From the excited look in her eyes, he believed that if he had told her that they would be having sex that she would have done it.

"Take off your top."

Nikla didn't hesitate. She started to undo the buttons on her crop top as Sweet went to a dresser. Considering he helped Masaun stock this room, he knew where he kept some of his toys. Sweet found six glass therapeutic cups. He picked them up and headed back to the bed.

Sweet found Nikla without her top standing for his next order. As she stood frozen to her spot, he leaned down and whispered, "Your tits are amazing." He bent his head down and licked one nipple, which made Nikla giggle.

"Only you could make Donald Trump sexy." She covered her mouth with her hand.

After placing the six curved cups on a side table he put his index finger over her lips. "Don't speak unless I give you permission."

Nikla nodded.

"Good. Lie on the bed on your stomach."

She obeyed his directive, turning her head to watch him. Sweet ducked into the bathroom to retrieve a bottle of rubbing alcohol, cotton balls, and a cup of water. He sat on the bed next to Nikla's body.

"Ever heard of cupping?" Sweet smoothed his hand over her skin.

Not only did he want to touch her, but he also had to check for any blemishes, scratches, or scars.

Nikla shook her head.

"Good. I like introducing you to new things." He removed his jacket and rolled up his sleeves. How Masaun could wear a suit day in and day out baffled Sweet. Then again, the man showed up to his own Halloween party naked except for a strategically placed leaf.

"Cupping may have come from an ancient Chinese practice to draw toxins from the skin." Sweet dipped a cotton ball into a cap full of alcohol. "I also heard it may be used as a cancer treatment." He lit the white puff ball until he saw a slight light blue flame. He dropped it into one of the glass cups for a couple of seconds before turning over the cup and dropping the cotton ball into the cup of water. "I don't believe any of that." He placed the open mouth of the cup onto Nikla's bare back. "I love the way it alters a person's body."

Nikla jumped a little when the jar touched her. Then she drew air in between her teeth as her skin sucked into the cup.

Nikla tried reaching behind herself to touch the cup but Sweet arrested her hand and placed it back on the bed.

He held one of the cups in her face. "I'm using this on your back. I put a lit cotton ball in it for a second before I put it on you. The residual heat draws your skin into it like a vacuum. Permission to speak. Does it hurt?"

She shook her head. "No. It just feels strange, like getting a hickey from a bigmouth bass."

"Strange is good. I'll take strange." Sweet continued the same process of lighting cotton balls, dropping them into the glass cups, removing them before affixing them to her skin.

It didn't take him long to have two rows of the glass domes down her back. When she took a deep breath, the circular glasses rose and fell.

Sweet pressed his hand on her back and smoothed it all the way down between the rows to her ass.

Not able to resist her, he kissed the side of her face. "You are so incredible."

"Yes, she is."

Sweet turned when he heard the familiar voice coming from behind him. He had to stand when he spotted the speaker.

"No hug for me?" Melinda asked with her arms outstretched.

"What are you doing here at Dom Hawk's party?" No way would his brother betray him and invite her.

"I came with someone else." She took a step closer to him. "I don't have to leave with him, though."

Sweet remained grounded in his spot. "I'm with Sugar Baby."

"Just for play though, right?"

Sweet shook his head. "You have a good time at the party. I'm going to continue to play with my submissive. I'm sure the person you came here with wouldn't appreciate you offering yourself to other Doms."

Melinda snickered. When Sweet didn't break her smile disappeared.

"That was always your problem, Sweet. You took things too fucking seriously. It's just play." She reached out to touch him. "It's just sex."

Sweet grabbed her wrist. "It's Master Sweet to you. Don't touch me unless I give you permission." He released her hand. "You're more than welcome to watch me play with Sugar Baby."

"Fuck you."

"Not ever again." Sweet turned his back on her and resumed his spot next to Nikla. He listened to Melinda's pounding steps as she stormed out of the dungeon.

Although he'd instructed Nikla not to say a word, her expression spoke volumes. He couldn't have this conversation now. Not there.

While gently tugging a patch of skin by a glass dome, he broke the seal and released it. As he knew it would, it left a raised, bubbled, circular red mark on her back. He pressed his lips against her warm flesh. He did the same process after releasing each cup.

"Let's go." Sweet stood and helped Nikla to her feet.

She picked up her top and wrapped it around her body. When Sweet noticed her wincing, he turned her around. He saw that her top rubbed against the center of where he had two of the cups.

Sweet removed the top and helped her put on his jacket. He buttoned it but it still gaped open in the front. "Good thing we're going home."

Sweet started to head to the door when Masaun's arrival stopped him.

Masaun looked around Sweet at Nikla. "Nikla–"

"Sugar Baby." Sweet wanted his brother to adhere to his own rules.

"Will you wait for us in the main house?" Masaun asked Nikla.

Sweet turned to her. "We're going home anyway. Go get your coat and meet me by the truck." He kissed her temple.

Nikla walked out of the room.

When Sweet felt she couldn't hear their conversation, he lit into Masaun. "You couldn't warn me about Melinda?"

Masaun glanced behind himself. "She's here? I didn't know."

"She said she arrived with someone you invited." Sweet planted his hands on his hips.

"You okay?"

"Yeah." He thought about the brief encounter and nodded. "Better than okay."

"Good. Now we need to talk. Why the hell didn't you tell me you got kicked out of The Dollhouse?"

Sweet exhaled. "Because I didn't want a lecture. I knew what I was doing at the time was wrong, but damn it, it felt so right."

"You have to think about consequences for your actions. You can't do what you want because it feels good."

"Yes, I can. And I can open a second business if I want." Sweet attempted to walk by his brother, but he knew with a statement like that that Masaun wouldn't let it fly.

"What do you mean? What did you do?"

"Nothing yet. But I should know something soon."

"God damn it, Sweet! You don't exist in a vacuum. Your decisions affect other people. If you go through some deal without involving me, then I want to buy you out of Decadent Treats and you can go down on your own."

Sweet stared at his brother like he saw a stranger in front of him. "Thanks, man. Good to know I can always count on you."

Sweet went outside, relieved to see Nikla by his truck. He should have told Kindle goodbye, but he didn't feel social right now. Masaun sucked the life out of him.

His only salvation, the only bright spot, stood next to his truck. Holding her coat in her arms, she smiled at him as he made his way to her.

"Everything okay?" she asked as he unlocked the passenger door.

"It will be as soon as I get you back to my place." Sweet helped her inside.

He would have a lot of decisions to make over the next few days. For now, he would enjoy being with this woman.

Chapter Twenty-Eight

"Who was that woman to you?" Nikla asked as soon as they headed to Sweet's place. She wanted to ask him when he talked to her, but she couldn't.

"Melinda," Sweet said simply.

"Your last submissive."

"Yeah, and more." Sweet glanced at her. "She's also my ex-wife."

Nikla wanted to hide her shocked expression, but she knew from Sweet's reaction that it must have shown all over her face.

"Masaun doesn't even know we were married. I never told him. We did a justice of the peace thing. We were together for a couple of years before she wanted to explore other options, which for her meant not only playing with other Doms but sleeping with them, too. I liked playing, but I didn't want an open relationship, not like that." Sweet cleared his throat. "Since we didn't have kids or property, we got divorced as quietly."

Sweet pulled into the Decadent Treats parking lot. Before either one could get out of the vehicle, Nikla held Sweet's hand.

"Her loss is my gain." She smiled to reassure him.

"How does your back feel?" He rubbed his thumb across the back of her hand.

"Sensitive."

Sweet nodded. Without a word, he got out of the truck then helped her out on her side. He got her up to his apartment. As soon as he locked the door, Sweet directed her every move.

He undressed her and made her undress him. Sweet lifted Nikla into his arms and carried her to his bed. Nikla never noticed how soft the comforter felt until her now sensitive back made contact with it.

"How's it feel?" Sweet asked as though knowing what ran through her head.

"It feels like I can feel each and every thread. It's so weird." Nikla curved her back to feel more of the sensation.

"Be right back." Sweet hopped off the bed and headed to the kitchen.

Nikla heard him opening up a cabinet, then the freezer. The distinct sounds of clinking in a glass clued her in that the man had gone after some ice, maybe for a drink.

Sweet returned with a tall, frosty glass filled with ice and nothing else.

"What's that for?" she asked.

"You'll see."

Before any more conversation could be had, Sweet pressed his mouth onto hers, but he possessed a gentleness this time that she hadn't experienced before with him. His hand coasted down her body, cupping her breast and massaging it as though he wanted to permanently imprint this moment, her body, into his memory.

Sweet moved his hand down to her ass and held it. He used his other hand to cradle the back of her head. Had they had a future together, she would have loved this treatment. Now it felt like a parting gift. If he wanted this to be their last hurrah, then she wanted it her way.

Nikla pushed against his shoulder with all her force to roll him onto his back. He barely moved.

"What are you doing?" he asked between kissing the side of her face.

"I want you on your back." Nikla continued pushing him as though he would eventually budge.

"Nope. I'm running this. You enjoy the ride." Sweet started kissing down her body.

"But–"

He stopped long enough to glare at her. "If you move again, I'm tying you to the bed."

"Really?" Ready for some kink, Nikla wiggled from under him but he held her still.

"What are you doing?"

"Fuck me." She licked his bottom lip. "Take me. Make me yours."

Instead of acknowledging what Nikla had said, Sweet continued dragging his lips down her body. At her breasts, he circled his tongue around her nipple, forcing it to a hardness that offered her both pain and pleasure.

Nikla ran her fingers through her thick hair and gripped it. Sweet moved over to her unattended tit and gave it the same treatment. By the time he moved down her body to between her thighs, every inch of her flesh went on high alert. Tingles ran through her body. The blood that pumped through her back heightened her already sensitive flesh.

Sweet pushed her legs apart. When the tip of his tongue touched her clit her body became electrified. When she writhed, her back brushed against the covers.

"Yes," Nikla hissed.

Her hips undulated courtesy of his oral ministrations. She never felt so alive, so needed, so precious.

Sweet reached up and grabbed an ice cube from the glass. He placed it in his mouth and went down on her again.

"Oh, God!" Nikla cried out and arched her back.

When she blew her breath out, she could have sworn she could see a puff of frosty exhalation floating in front of her face. The cold sensation Sweet applied to her clit seemed like it froze her insides in the best way.

Sweet slipped a finger inside and Nikla felt herself break.

"No." She didn't want to come yet.

Nikla didn't want to experience an orgasm at all. In her gut she knew Sweet wanted this to be their last moment together. She couldn't reconcile that in her head. Coming to her meant the end.

"Am I hurting you?" Sweet growled from between her legs.

"Please stop." She attempted to close her legs but Sweet kept them pried apart.

He sat up on his knees, scooped her up, and sat on the edge of the bed with her on his lap facing him. "What are you so afraid of?"

When Sweet reached down between their bodies, Nikla held his wrist.

"Don't. Please don't."

Ignoring her pleas, he positioned his erection at her center and slid himself inside. Both exhaled as though their bodies had fused into one.

"Damn it!" Nikla felt a tear rolling from her eye.

"You came." Sweet wrapped one arm around her waist while the other cupped her ass.

Nikla shook her head.

"Don't lie."

"Spank me."

"No." Sweet easily captured her mouth in his, smothering her in a passionate kiss. "Look at me."

Nikla rested her head on his shoulder as he thrust in and out of her. She couldn't look in his eyes and see her loss.

"I said look at me." Sweet tried leaning forward like he wanted to tip Nikla back.

Nikla held onto him tightly, keeping her face turned away from him. She wrapped her legs around him, trying so hard to prolong this feeling.

In one smooth motion, Sweet stood while holding onto her. His strength always amazed her. He turned and placed her on her back in the bed.

Shit. There she had less leverage to avoid his gaze. That didn't mean she wouldn't try. Nikla kept her head turned as Sweet moved in and out of her so slowly it felt like the world had stopped.

Sweet held her chin and turned her head. "Look at me."

Nikla pressed her eyelids shut and shook her head.

"Open your eyes."

"No!" She tried wriggling from under him. "Take me from behind."

Sweet held her wrists down on the bed. "Look at me. Why won't you look at me?"

"Because I know if I do that it'll be it. It'll be the last time. I'll come. I always come when I look into your eyes. I want to make this last." Nikla balled her hands into fists but couldn't move them from under Sweet's iron grasp.

With her eyes still closed, she felt his lips on hers again.

"Open your eyes."

Unable to defy his orders any longer, Nikla opened her eyes. As she said, Sweet's gaze met hers and she melted. Sweet let her hands go.

"No matter what happens, hold onto this moment." Sweet kissed her. "Swithin, I hate you." She didn't mean it, but she didn't know what else to say. "Why did you make me feel anything for you? Why couldn't you just have me arrested? Why did—"

"Don't talk." Sweet drove into her deeper and harder. While maintaining eye contact with her, he said, "Come with me."

Nikla nodded.

Sweet reached over and grabbed another ice cube. This time he rolled onto his back, carrying Nikla with him. As she rode him, he rubbed the ice over her inflamed flesh. It felt so good where her skin had been raised because of the cupping. Where the melted ice dripped to her unaffected skin, the feeling made her wince and twitch.

"Fuck! Fuck!" Nikla gyrated her hips.

She felt her body stiffen as she let the climax take over her body. Coming down from her high, she peered down at Sweet.

"I still expect you to come with me." He smiled.

Nikla wanted to smile with him, but in her heart, she couldn't. "Yes, Sir."

To prompt her to move, Sweet lifted his hips. Nikla's gyrating hips caused Sweet's eyes to roll to the back of his head. He held onto her hips. Once in a while, he would administer a hard smack to her ass.

"Yes! Fuck!" Nikla rested her hands on his chest.

Sweet felt both hot and hard. She leaned forward and pressed her body against his as he held her. His large hands swept over her sensitive back. Each spot he touched sent an electric current through her body, to her hardened nipples, down each finger, and to her toes.

Sweet turned Nikla over onto her back, then pulled out of her. He turned her to her side so that her back faced him. Like a master, he swept her upper leg over his and entered her again from behind.

"Is this what you want? You don't want to see me?" Sweet's thrusts increased in speed.

"Stop." Nikla grabbed Sweet's hand, which rested on her hip.

"You think if I fucked you that you would forget?" He kissed the back of her neck and her shoulder. "I'll never forget you. Never."

"Shut up, please." Tears stung Nikla's eyes.

Although she tried holding his hand still, Sweet moved his hand between her thighs and rubbed her clit.

The touch broke Nikla. She undulated her body, pressing her ass against him to get the most pleasure. Sweet wrapped his free arm around her body as his body stiffened.

"You are the best thing that ever happened to me," Sweet said as he came down from his orgasmic high.

Nikla kissed his arm but remained quiet. After tonight, things would change. He would be Swithin Hawkes, business owner going after the unit she wanted. She would no longer be his Sugar Baby. It would hurt too much to stay.

****

The night of lovemaking couldn't make up a lifetime with Nikla. Sweet wanted to kick his own ass for making that initial deal with her to stop their arrangement by November first so that they could concentrate on their businesses.

Sweet peered down at the woman lying on his chest. Her hand rested on him. Damn, she felt so good on him, next to him, in his bed. He smoothed his hand over her bare arm.

Nikla moaned. "I'm not sleeping."

Sweet hugged her and kissed the top of her head. "I'll make us some breakfast."

She wrapped her long leg around his. "No, no, no. Stay here. Let's not move at all today." She laughed. "Maybe I'm suggesting that we don't move because I can't move." Nikla stretched like a cat. "You wore me out."

"I think you gave as good as you got." Sweet loved being with Nikla. If he could extend this one moment, he would.

"I could go again." She licked his nipple.

Sweet held onto her shoulders. "As much as I would love another go 'round with you, we do need to talk. Zuberi is going to make her decision soon." He rubbed his hand over her arm. "We did make a deal."

Nikla sat up. "Are you saying that if you don't get both units that you wouldn't want to be with me anymore?"

Sweet regarded her for a moment before he responded. "If you don't get the unit, will you hold it against me?"

Nikla threw the covers off her and hopped out of bed. "You have an established business already. I want to put myself out there. This is my life, too." She stomped her foot. "All of this is you. You have your career. You want to expand. I'm twenty-eight. I want to jump start my life."

"I'm not holding you back. But I have dreams, too. I want more than one storefront. I want to be a chain. I also want to make my mark in BDSM. I want it all, too." Sweet sat up against the headboard. "I'm losing it all."

That revelation hit him harder than he thought it would.

"What are you talking about? You have your business. It's a success. It's crushing the competition."

Sweet glared at her. The dig about how Decadent Treats took business away from her father's place didn't get lost on him.

Nikla continued. "You have the lifestyle you're comfortable in. And you have your family."

Sweet snickered. "Last night when you went to get your coat, I finally admitted to Masaun that I'm moving through getting a second location for Decadent Treats. He's against it. Says it wouldn't make good business sense." He grabbed his stomach. "In my gut, I know this would work. He told me he's going to try and buy me out of my share of the business. I'm not going to sell, but I know he won't make it easy on me." Sweet exhaled before revealing the next piece of the news. "Like I told you before, it's against The Dollhouse rules to have sex in the establishment." He looked at Nikla.

Her mouth hung open. She padded toward him until she stood next to the bed.

"As a result, I'm no longer welcomed back. I think it's a stupid rule anyway. We're grown, consenting adults. The place should have the same rules as a hotel."

"Why didn't you listen to me when I tried to remind you about the rule?" Nikla smoothed her wild curls from her face.

"You had just stood up for me with my brother. I trusted you fully at that moment. I wanted you. I could care less about their rules."

"I care." She balled the comforter in her fist.

"Really?" He cocked his head.

"Yes. In case you haven't noticed, I do really well with following rules." She shook her head. "I like the instructions and rules you give me, but I didn't expect you to change your life because of me."

"I know what's best. I can work around this."

"And you don't need any input from me, right?" She stared at him for a moment when he didn't respond immediately. "You still don't trust me, do you?"

Sweet lowered his gaze.

Nikla cursed under her breath. "Unbelievable. I opened myself up to you. I told you about my past. You still have that wall up around you." She stormed over to main open area where she'd left her clothes and shoes.

"Don't leave. We need to discuss this." Sweet got out of bed.

"We have." Nikla slipped on her pants. "You're selfish."

"No, I'm determined. So are you. It's what I–" Sweet paused.

Even Nikla's heart stuttered until he said the next word. She stopped moving until he finished his thought.

"It's what I like about you." Sweet padded toward her.

Nikla exhaled and threw on her bra. "Great. You like me. I guess that's a good thing. If you hated me, you would have buried me with Bobbi for that spot."

"I'm willing to compete for the spots in the right way. If you get the smaller unit, I will be bitter. I won't be any good for anyone that way."

"Guess what? I'm bitter now." She grabbed her purse. "I realize that as a Dominant that you're used to having things your way, but compromise must be a part of your makeup. I matter." Her voice broke at the end. "Thank you for a great evening and a really crappy morning."

"That's it? You're just going to walk away without us finishing this?" Sweet stalked her and met her at the doorway, careless of his nudity.

Nikla had to keep her gaze up to his face.

"Admit it. If I wasn't as ambitious as I am, you wouldn't find me attractive."

Nikla started to open her mouth but Sweet stopped her.

"I'm attracted to you for the same reason." He touched her head. "You have a brain in your head. You have goals. I don't hold it against you."

"Unless I get that spot, right."

Sweet gritted his teeth and flexed his jaw.

"What's sad is that you're exactly what I want and exactly what I don't want. You're nothing like my last boyfriend. But in some ways, you're exactly like my father. It's your way or the highway. No in between." Nikla's voice lowered.

"You're the one I want. I compete to win. I want it all."

Nikla chuckled. "So do I. One of us is going to be disappointed."

Sweet leaned in to kiss her, but Nikla jerked back and opened the door to leave. Not content to let her have the last word or action, Sweet hooked Nikla around her waist and pulled her close to his body.

"What are you doing?" Nikla put her hand to his chest.

"Kissing the woman who drives me crazy in all the right and wrong ways." Sweet kissed her.

As he kissed her, Nikla couldn't stop the tears from flowing. Sweet broke from the kiss long enough to wipe her tears.

"We are going to have to compromise." He framed her face in his large hands.

"Too bad compromise means one of us doesn't get what we want." Nikla pulled out of his grip. "I have a lot to think about. Maybe you do, too."

As soon as Nikla opened the door, Sweet saw Masaun coming up the stairs to his unit. The anger in his eyes couldn't be hidden.

"Excuse me." Nikla tried getting by Masaun.

"Oh, no. You wait right there. What I have to say involves the two of you." Masaun stood in the doorway.

Sweet didn't bother covering himself. No way would he leave Nikla with Masaun, even for a second. He had no idea what bee went up his ass this morning.

"What's going on?" Sweet glared at him.

"You want to put some pants on?" Masaun kept his stare on Sweet's eyes.

He pointed to Masaun. "Brother." Then he nodded down to Nikla. "Girlfriend."

"No, I'm not." She shook her head.

That news felt like a punch in the gut. Now Sweet felt exposed.

"Fine." Masaun threw a balled piece of paper at Sweet. "Thanks to your *girlfriend*, the health department is threatening to shut us down." He glared at Nikla. "They received an anonymous tip telling them that some sexual activity occurred in the vicinity of the kitchen and/or where food items intended for the general public is prepared. Now, I saw you two in the office."

Nikla gasped and looked up at Sweet. From the way she turned away from him just as fast, he figured she must have deduced that he knew about that bit of news, too.

Masaun continued. "I didn't know you two did it in the kitchen area." He stared at Sweet. "I know you wouldn't blab on yourself. That leaves one person." Masaun took a step toward Nikla.

Sweet stood in front of her.

"What I didn't understand is why she would want to take us down. I did my own research. Did you know her father owns–"

"Healthy Bites. I know." Sweet never suspected that she would use herself to take him down. Maybe that was the reason she stopped picketing. He hated himself for doubting her.

Masaun snickered. "And you weren't suspicious? Yeah, you know what? I'm done. I'm not going to buy you out. Why bother? When news about this comes out we'll be destroyed. Let's shut it down." He turned on his heel and stomped back down the stairs.

In the silence of the room, Sweet didn't know what to say. He blurted the first thing that came to mind. "Did you do that? Did you set me up?"

The look Nikla gave him felt like she'd shot him in the head and the heart. She covered her mouth with her hand. "Go to hell." Nikla ran down the steps to get to her car.

With her gone, Sweet stalked to his kitchen. He braced his hands on the counter before he picked up a glass and threw it against the wall, shattering it into a million tiny shards.

So much for Nikla's statement that at least he had his family. In one fell swoop, he'd lost it all, his woman, his business, his lifestyle. He glanced around his place. Without his business, he also lost his home.

Fuck.

Chapter Twenty-Nine

Nikla didn't want to cry. As soon as she got into her car, she sped away from the Decadent Treats parking lot as fast as she could until she could get to a spot to weep in peace. For some reason, that spot, again, happened to be in front of the two empty storefronts.

She couldn't blame Masaun for suspecting her. After what she and Sweet had been through, she had hoped that Sweet would have come to her defense and told his brother that Nikla would have never done anything like that.

Now she didn't have her man. How could she even think about opening a business with this suspicious activity looming over her head? She knew she hadn't said anything to anyone. She had to figure out who found out and would have told the health department.

Nikla's phone rang, forcing her to wipe her eyes with the back of her hand so that she could see the name or number on the screen. When she saw Sweet's name, she let out an exasperated sigh.

A small part of her wanted to turn off her phone and let the man suffer. A large part of herself had to hear what he had to say.

"Why are you calling me?" No hello. No pleasantries. Sweet needed to know that he'd hurt her.

"Come back. We need to talk." His gruff voice sounded like he had chewed glass before calling her.

"No, we don't. You said all you needed to say. You called me a liar." Nikla dove into her glove compartment to see if she could find some facial tissue or fast food napkins to wipe her eyes and nose.

"I never called you a liar. But you never answered my question, either."

Nikla snickered. "I shouldn't have to. I thought you would know me by now."

"I do know you." Sweet exhaled. "I would bet every dime I have that you're sitting in front of the empty suites. Am I right?"

Nikla closed her eyes. She wanted to hate him. How could he doubt her and be so familiar with her at the same time?

"Our arrangement is over. I learned everything I wanted to learn from you. We won't have to see each other again. Please, just leave me alone.

Goodbye." Nikla disconnected the call.

It didn't take long for Sweet to call her again. This time she didn't answer, and she didn't stay in her spot. Sweet knew where she'd gone. She didn't want to be there if he arrived.

He knew where she lived, too. Nikla couldn't take seeing him at her apartment. Any other time, she would have invited him in and let him have his way with her. If she saw him outside of her door now, she would slam the door in his face after some very choice words.

Where the hell could she go? If she went to her father's house, he would ask way too many questions. Deana would annoy the hell out of her, but at least she didn't have to be anyone but herself with her. Nikla would try her anyway.

After a brief argument with Deana after waking her up so early in the morning, Nikla headed to her friend's condo. Thankfully she'd packed a bag with a change of clothes. Going to her friend's place wearing a genie costume would be a conversation Nikla didn't want to have right now.

"What's up with you and your boy?" Deana asked as soon as she opened her door.

Nikla smiled. "Want to see my genie costume I wore last night?" All the sudden talking about the pink costume didn't seem like a bad thing now.

"You're avoiding the topic. What? For Halloween did he dress up like a little girl or something? Oh! Was he a clown? Clowns are freaky." As though one stood in front of her right now, Deana shivered and contorted her face. She wrapped her arms around her body. In her simple t-shirt and shorts, her petite friend looked like a teenager at a sleepover.

"No, nothing happened," Nikla lied. "Our arrangement is over. Time to get on with business."

"If everything is so cool, why aren't you staying at your own place? Why crash here with me?"

Nikla couldn't tell her friend. She didn't have the strength to explain. "Sleep. Let me get a couple of hours before I have to go to work."

Shit. Sweet knew where she worked, too. He could show up there as well. Since he knew her father's name, he could probably find his address, not that she would want to stay with her father. If Nikla didn't want to talk about Sweet with Deana, she for sure didn't want to do any explanations with her father.

Nikla pushed past Deana and headed toward her bedroom.

"Um, not there." Deana ran around Nikla to block her path.

A realization hit Nikla as she sighed. "Why did you invite me over if you had company?"

"You're my girl." Deana nodded her head behind her. "He's leaving."

"I can go." Nikla turned around.

"No." Deana put her hands on Nikla's shoulders from behind and guided her back down the hallway. "I have a pretty comfy daybed in my exercise room. You're welcome to it."

Deana opened the door to the spare bedroom. A large elliptical trainer machine sat in the middle of the room like an overgrown praying mantis. Behind it sat the daybed Deana described.

Right now Nikla could sleep on a bed of rocks. She dropped her overnight bag on the floor, walked out of her shoes, and plopped down on the bed. "Close the door on your way out."

"You're welcome on the room." Deana laughed. "Hey."

Nikla turned over to regard her friend.

"Truce?"

Nikla looked at Deana but said nothing.

"I've missed our talks and our lunches. I miss us." Deana padded to her. "Can we please be friends again? I'm so sorry for what I said. I'm a bitch. You can tell me that."

Nikla cocked a smile at the corner of her mouth. "You are a bitch. But I missed you, too." She sat up and opened her arms to embrace her friend. "Now let me sleep. I'll talk to you in a couple of hours."

"And then what?"

Nikla braced herself up on her elbow. "What?"

"After you get some sleep and we talk, then what will you do? You can't keep running from this guy forever. And you can't keep running from your problems."

Nikla shook her head. "Now you sound like him."

"And now I'm starting to like him." Deana walked over to the door, then turned to Nikla before she walked out. "If you truly don't want to see this guy, tell it to him face to face. That's the only way he'll get the message." She closed the door behind herself.

Nikla plopped back on the bed and allowed the tears she'd been holding back to flow. She didn't bother to wipe them away. For as bad as she felt, she knew the tears would keep streaming down.

As much as she didn't want to admit it, she knew both Deana and Sweet had been right. Nikla couldn't keep running. Right now she needed a break, and maybe not from her love life, either.

Nikla reached into her bag on the floor and pulled out her cell phone.

She hit the speed dial number for her job. Nikla had never called out sick to work. She figured being heartbroken counted as a major illness.

"Hey Big Tom. I hate to do this to you but I won't be able to come into work today." Then Nikla thought about it. "Actually this week."

"What?" Big Tom's voice boomed and it sounded like the man stood in the bedroom with her. "This is so short notice. You can't come in and push through just for today?"

Nikla shook her head as though he could see her. "No. I can't. I'm sorry. I'll call when I can come in." She disconnected the call and fell back on the pillows.

This time she had to bury her face in the pillows to muffle her cries. If love meant feeling this bad, Nikla hated it. She didn't need love. If only she could convince herself of that logic, she would be okay.

****

Sweet stormed down the stairs to his truck. As a Dominant, he'd never had a submissive not do what he wanted. As a man, he had never had a woman dismiss him like Nikla had. He felt a sense of betrayal more than anger. Only a small part of himself now thought Nikla had reported what they'd done to the health department.

"Hey!"

Sweet heard the scream behind him but didn't bother turning around. He could tell his brother's voice from a mile away.

"Where do you think you're going?"

This time Sweet did turn around. He found Masaun marching toward him. In his standard blue suit, he looked like a federal agent coming after him.

"I'm going to see Nikla. She has some explaining to do and she's not taking my calls." Sweet unlocked his truck and jumped behind the wheel.

Masaun held the door open. "If she doesn't want to talk to you right now, let her have her space. Maybe she feels some guilt."

Sweet glared at his older brother. He grabbed his door and pulled it shut.

Masaun knocked on the glass and motioned for him to drop the window. After starting his truck and waiting a beat, Sweet lowered his window.

"You know what the great thing is about being a Dom?" Masaun began. "Control."

Masaun nodded. "That's right. Control. That doesn't mean that you control every little thing. It means you control your environment. When you don't feel like playing, you don't. When you do play, you decide what you want to do. But you also have to be aware of your submissive and slave. You have to listen. You have to take care of them because of you don't, the scene can go badly." Masaun put his hand on Sweet's shoulder. "Your scene is going to go badly if you go over to wherever Nikla is. She's going to feel like you're not listening to her. To be honest, man, after everything that has happened, do you really trust her?"

Sweet kept his truck running. "I've been asking myself that question over and over and over again. My head and my–" Sweet looked at his brother. He didn't want to reveal that Nikla had stolen his heart already. "—my gut," he continued, "know she wouldn't have reported us." He chuckled. "Every time we did something, she would accuse me of having some hidden camera so that I could use it against her. She had a hard time being open in the lifestyle."

"I didn't know this, which is why it was so easy for me to accuse her of trying to destroy our business."

Sweet nodded.

"What was your excuse?"

Sweet stared at his brother.

Masaun said, "You knew her. Slept with her. Played with her. How could you second guess her unless you really didn't trust her?"

Or himself, Sweet wanted to supply.

"Give her and you some time." Masaun patted Sweet on his chest. "Maybe you need to think about how you really feel about her versus how you feel about your business. It's apparent the two cannot exist together. Not with her father in the mix. And you know what they say. Blood is thicker than water."

Sweet knew what his brother implied with his statement. Masaun wanted Sweet to do the right thing for their business, not fix the issues between him and Nikla. Maybe Masaun had a point. Between Melinda and Nikla, Sweet didn't have the right touch with submissives or with love. Damn if his heart didn't still smart over this loss.

Needing time to think, Sweet drove off to clear his head. His heart forced him to go by the empty suites. A small part of him hoped beyond hope that Nikla would be there waiting for him, ready to jump in his arms or at least ready to talk. When he found only vacant parking spots in front of the store, Sweet felt just as empty inside.

He had to see Nikla. He had to talk to her. If he could just look into her eyes, he would find the truth.

Sweet threw his truck in reverse and headed to Nikla's apartment, dismissing Masaun's suggestion to give her space. Space would kill anything he had with her.

What was he thinking? He did that by accusing her of betraying him and his brother.

"Damn." Sweet hated that aching feeling in the pit of his stomach that let him know he'd fucked up royally.

Once he got to her apartment, Sweet wasted no time in running up to the door and banging on it as hard as he could. "Nikla! Come on! We have to talk!"

After a few minutes when no one answered, Sweet headed over to the recreation center. He burst through the door and ran over to the workout room where he'd done yoga with her. Inside he found a classroom full of people doing some dancing exercise. The blaring music reminded him of being in a bar.

"You're not too late, sir. Join us in Zumba!" the instructor said without missing a step.

Sweet turned and went up to the front desk. To the bored-looking employee he said, "I'm looking for Nikla Dearwood."

"Who?"

Sweet pointed to the workout room. "Nikla. She normally does the yoga and Pilates classes. Where is she?"

"You're looking for Nikla?" a voice asked from behind him.

Sweet turned around and found an African-American man about his height but full of muscles behind him.

"Yeah, where is she? I've been calling her but, she won't answer me." Sweet tried not to sound frantic, but the urgent nature couldn't be missed.

"She called out sick," the big man answered.

Sweet nodded. Never figured the hard-working Nikla would have ever called in sick to work. Sweet figured her pain matched his.

"She called out sick the entire week."

Sweet took a step back.

"Do you know why she would be out for a week?"

Sweet didn't answer the man. He had one last place he could check. If he couldn't find her there, he would know Nikla wouldn't want to be found.

Once he arrived at Healthy Bites, Sweet had to take a breath before going into the establishment. The last encounter he had with Lawrence Dearwood didn't go smoothly.

He walked into the store. Aside from the three patrons sitting at various tables, he found Lawrence standing behind the counter putting out more muffins. When Lawrence's gaze fell on Sweet's, he smirked.

"Come here to rub it in my face about how well you did yesterday?" Lawrence wiped down the counter.

"I'm looking for Nikla. Have you seen or heard from her?"

Lawrence's face relaxed. "No. But that's not unusual for me."

"I tried calling her, going to her apartment, and going to her job. She called in sick."

Lawrence's eyes widened.

"For the week."

Nikla's father stumbled back. "She's never called sick for work, and certainly not for a full week." He came from around the counter. "What did you do to her?"

Ignoring Lawrence's accusatory inquiry, Sweet continued. "If you hear from her, please tell her I'm looking for her."

"I'm not a messenger." He pointed to the door. "I have no obligation to you. I have one with my child."

"I love her." To say it out loud freed his soul. Sweet wanted to tell Nikla that first, but in the moment, he needed to be completely honest. "If you care anything about Nikla, you'll tell her that a man who loves her needs her back in his life. You'll tell her that I'll let her be whatever she wants to be. You tell her Swithin loves her."

"Who?"

"She'll know." Sweet left the establishment thinking that his words fell on deaf ears.

He knew her father would never relay the message to Nikla. Sweet had to face facts that he might have lost Nikla for good.

Chapter Thirty

After a long car ride, Nikla found herself in Baltimore. If she had a chance to fix one relationship in her life, the one with her mother had to be first.

Sitting outside of a small cottage-style home, Nikla gripped her steering wheel. She felt her chest tightening and her breathing turning into shallow pants.

"No. Not now. Come on. No panic attacks now." Nikla tried taking deep breaths but found it getting harder and harder with each one.

She managed to pry her fingers from the steering wheel to employ a trick she'd seen Sweet do to himself. She pinched her hand in between her thumb and index finger.

Nikla concentrated on that sensation. If nothing else, the BDSM lifestyle got her to concentrate on herself more than practicing yoga ever did. She never knew thinking about the pain would make her whole.

When she could corral her breathing, Nikla let her hand go. She took another cleansing breath and grabbed her purse as she exited her car. No time like the present.

She went up to the front door. Before she could even ring the bell, the door opened.

"I wondered if I was going to have to go out and get you." Her mother stood on the other side with a slight smile. "Are you okay?"

Nikla stared at her mother. She didn't want to admit it to herself, but she did look an awful lot like her. From the skin tone to her nose to the brown eyes, they matched. No wonder her father found it hard to look at her.

"Hi, Mom." Nikla took another deep breath, confident of her decision to be there.

Her mother took a large step to the side. "Come on in."

After a beat, Nikla walked into her mother's home. The cozy place felt open and inviting despite what Nikla had assumed. When her mother left the family so suddenly, she thought she'd done it to sow some wild oats. She had expected to see a party palace with a bar, maybe even a disco ball in the center of the living room.

With the colorful artwork on the walls, the multicolored rugs on the floor, and t he multitude o f vibrant plants scattered a round t he p lace, it looked more like an artist's commune than a single's pad.

"I'm making tea. Would you like some?"

Nikla scanned her mother's appearance. In her floor-length caftan, she even looked like some hippie, earth-mother type, way different from how Nikla remembered her. Her mother had been a high-level executive at an electric utility company. Nicole Dearwood had been in power suits Mondays through Fridays. On the weekends, she wore khakis and crisp buttoned shirts. A great word to describe her would have been stiff. Now she looked loose and fluid, open like her home.

"Tea? Yes, that would be fine." Nikla followed her mother to her kitchen.

The light green room made the place feel like a garden.

"I don't know what it's like in Virginia, but I'm so glad the weather broke here. I hate a warm autumn." Nicole set a white kettle on a stove eye and opened a cabinet over it. She pulled out two different colored mugs. One had cats on it. The other had "World's Greatest Mother" emblazoned in red over it.

"Remember that one?" Nikla's mother smiled. "You and Junior gave that to me on Mother's Day twenty years ago."

Nikla remembered. She and her brother had combined their money to buy the mug and a necklace that she never saw her mother wear.

"Can't believe you kept it." Nikla pushed the mug away from her.

"I kept everything you kids gave me." Her mother put tea bags into each mug. "I didn't think it would take you this long to come see me."

"I would have thought you would have sought me out first."

The teakettle whistled, breaking up the tension in the room. Nicole turned off the stove eye and removed the kettle from it. She poured hot water into each mug. After she placed cream, honey, and sugar on the table for Nikla, she sat down at the round table next to her.

"You want to know why I left, right?" Nicole dunked her tea bag in the steamy water as she kept her gaze on it. She reconnected her stare with Nikla. "I never ever wanted to leave you and Junior." After flavoring her tea with cream and honey, she stirred it as she smiled. "For several years, I was ill."

Nikla froze.

"Depression." Nicole looked at her daughter. She looked completely vulnerable. "I felt helpless and alone. I tried talking to your father about it, but your father is, well–"

"Dad." Nikla completely understood what her mother meant. If he told Nikla to suck it up when she had her panic attacks, she could only imagine what he'd told her mother. He probably told her to get happy.

"He didn't see my depression as a big deal. He said, 'You have a great house, beautiful children, and a wonderful job. What else do you need?' I needed to be myself and your father didn't want to deal with anything. Stop crying, he would say. Suck it up, he would tell me. Snap out of it." Until Nicole picked up her mug did Nikla notice her mother's hand trembling. "I always argued with him when he made you feel bad about your panic attacks. I understood them." Her mother wiped her eyes with a napkin.

Nikla had to do the same thing.

"I was so determined to be a good mother and wife that when I found myself in the bathroom contemplating downing a bottle of sleeping pills, I knew I couldn't be any good to anyone. I asked your father for help. He said that I needed exercise and a good trip." She snickered. "That's when I knew I needed to help myself. I told him I would go to a place to get some help. He called me weak."

Nikla knew exactly what that felt like. Out of instinct and love, Nikla reached her hand out and held her mother's. The warmth of it radiated through her body.

"I waited until you had gone off to college before I did anything."

Nikla wiped her nose. "You waited to get yourself better because of me?"

Her mother shook her head. "Please don't think of it that way. I wanted to make sure you kids had a happy life before I handled my own. I wanted to stay. Your father didn't understand me or my condition. I went to the place where I knew I would get support. No place like home, right?" She blew her nose and smiled through her pain. "Is that the only reason why you're here, to get the answer of why I left?"

Nikla shook her head. "I met this guy. Our relationship is so, so complicated." She would leave out the details of him spanking her and how much she truly enjoyed it. "I tried so hard to be a good daughter to Dad. I did so much for him, things that I shouldn't have done. In the process, it made the man I cared about question my ethics and loyalty."

Nikla stopped talking when she heard her mother laughing.

She glared at her. "What's so funny?"

"My baby girl is still my little girl. After all this time, you still need me to help you with boy troubles." Her mother stood from her chair and embraced Nikla, who openly sobbed.

Her mother allowed her to cry for a while. Nikla's father would have never allowed her to be that vulnerable.

"I'm so sorry that I thought so many bad things about you." Nikla hiccupped as she talked to her mother.

"Don't. The whole reason I left after you kids left the house was so that you didn't hate your father. He was raised a certain way. He's a hard man. In certain aspects of my life, I liked that. But I also needed a man who could understand me and all my frailties."

Nikla had that in Sweet. Until her mother verbalized it did she realize that Sweet had not only changed her, but he had accepted her.

"Have you found someone?" Nikla asked.

Nicole shook her head. "I date here and there. I'm content being single for now." She pointed at Nikla. "But you, you're in love. I can tell. A man who makes you cry is the one you truly love."

Nikla smiled. "He's so dynamic. He's not afraid of anything. He's seen me at my worst and still wanted me. He's sacrificed a lot for me."

"Why are you here instead of being with him?"

"I have had so many bad relationships. I thought if I talked to you, I could understand myself better."

"You came home to get an understanding of yourself. Yep, I'd say you're my daughter for sure."

Nikla had to smile at that assessment. Years ago, hell, just yesterday, she wouldn't have had that same reaction.

"Are you going back home tonight?" Nicole asked.

"If it's okay, I'd like to hang around for a couple of days to get to know you. I'll get a hotel room nearby and–"

"Nonsense. You'll stay right here with me. I have the room. It'll be wonderful to have my child under my roof again." She framed Nikla's face and kissed her forehead.

Getting to know her mother would be a bonus. She wouldn't have to know that Nikla also needed a place to hide out from Sweet's prying eyes. She knew she would have to go home eventually. Right now, she needed this time for herself.

****

Three days had passed and Sweet hadn't seen or heard from Nikla. He'd spent his days camping out at her job just in case she felt "better" before the week ended, and his nights watching her apartment. Tonight wouldn't be any different.

He could hear his brother in his head telling him to give Nikla her space. Masaun would tell him that if Nikla truly wanted him, that she would come to him. Sweet didn't have that kind of time or patience.

Sweet paid no attention to his brother's advice. He went to Nikla's apartment. This time he found her vehicle outside. His heart started up as soon as he saw her gray sedan.

Sweet knocked on her door and waited a moment. When she didn't answer right away, he raised his fist again to knock. This time the door opened.

Nikla's face looked lifeless. Had he done that to her? Had being with him drained her of her power, her strength, her life? Ignoring the doubting voice in his head, Sweet pursued her.

Even in her oversized, loose-fitting t-shirt and baggy sweatpants he found her sexy. She had her hair in a messy bun at the top of her head.

"We need to talk." Sweet braced his hands on the doorframe.

"I think we've said enough to each other." Nikla wouldn't look him in his eyes.

That wouldn't stop him. Sweet pushed his way into her apartment and closed the door behind him.

"Please leave." Nikla put her hand to his chest.

The singular connection ignited the smoldering fire within him. He'd longed for her touch. Even angry, he would take her any and all of her attention.

"No. You've controlled what's happened between us for the last few days when you avoided my calls. Now you're going to hear me out." Sweet pinned her against the wall as she continued to press her hands against his chest. "I need you back in my life. Out of everything that's happened to me over the last week, you're the only thing that makes sense. I need for you to come with me to my place and–"

"No." She shook her head.

"What?"

"What? Would rather hear 'red'? Fine. Red."

Sweet pressed his body against hers. "Tell me you don't miss me." He brushed his lips against hers and immediately heard her breath catch. "Tell me you don't miss this." Sweet kissed her lightly at first, simply sweeping his lips against hers before he fully captured her mouth.

Sweet tasted her familiar honeyed flavor on her lips. He put his hands on her waist and moved them down to her ass. As soon as he gripped it, she snapped back to the situation.

"No, stop." Nikla broke from the kiss. She managed to duck under his arms and move away from him. "You come in here and tell me what you want and need. 'I need you to do this' and 'I need you to do that.' What about what I need?"

Sweet remained quiet as she spoke.

"I need to be with a man who's not going to question my ethics. I need to be with someone who supports me. I need to be with someone who listens to me. I don't think you're that person." She went to the door and opened it.

"I'm not going."

"Fine. I'll call the police. You haven't asked me where I've been or what I was doing. I realize you're a Dominant and all the focus should be on you, but I'm a person, too. I have a voice, and I want to be heard."

Damn. Sweet could hear his brother saying "I told you so" in his head.

"Okay, where were you these last few days? What's been going on while I've been worried about you, calling you day and night?" Sweet crossed his arms over his chest.

Nikla shook her head. "Goodbye, Sweet." She made sure to keep her face turned away from him as she held the door open.

Damn it. Sweet didn't want to go. After the turmoil he'd been through over the past week, he wanted to stay there with Nikla and fight the good fight. Couldn't she see that they needed to be together? Couldn't she tell that he'd been hurting without her? From just looking at her, he saw her pain. He also recognized that him standing there, saying the wrong things, doing the wrong things, gave her more anguish than he wanted.

Finally taking his brother's suggestion, he walked to the door. He stopped at it long enough to snake his hand around her waist and pull her close to him.

Sweet kissed the side of her face. "I'm not perfect. I'll give you your space, but know I still want you. I'll never stop trying to win you back." He took a deep breath before he said what he really wanted to tell her. "I love you." Sweet reached the door, but before he crossed the threshold, he stopped. He turned back to her. "Blue."

Nikla stared at him for a moment. "What?"

"You said if I was ever in trouble to use my safe word."

A look of recognition crossed her face. Nikla dropped her gaze to the floor.

Without another word, Sweet retreated, feeling like a failure.

How could he gain her trust again when she could barely look at him?

Chapter Thirty-One

After a quick shower and a restless night, Nikla changed into her normal yoga pants, sports bra top with a wraparound sweater, and some sneakers. She arrived at work early, hoping not to find Sweet waiting for her in the parking lot.

Work would be the only thing to occupy her mind right now. If she called in sick and sat at home alone with her thoughts, she would be driven crazy thinking about Sweet, his business and what could have been.

It still surprised her that Sweet had shown up to her apartment. It shocked her even more that she had the strength to refuse him although seeing him again, kissing him, and having him touch her brought her body back to some wonderful memories.

Then he said he loved her. Did he mean it? Had he only said it out desperation?

He'd even used his special safe word. For that, Nikla had almost accepted him back into her life.

As soon as he left, she'd gone to her freezer for that damn Snickers bar. One look at it, she knew taking even one bite wouldn't have solved her problems. She did something she should have done years ago. She finally threw that damn candy bar in the trash.

Nikla did her classes that day in a fog, something some of her students noticed.

"Are you okay?" Ashley asked after her class. "You seemed a bit out of it."

Nikla sighed as she gathered the supplies. "I am, but I'll be okay."

At the doorway to the workout room, Karen opened the door for Ashley.

"Oh hey, Nikki, uh, Nikla." Karen tucked her hair behind her ear. "Can I talk to you?"

Nikla looked up and saw Big Tom walking behind Karen. He glanced at her and nodded his head.

"Whatever you have to ask, you can do it here." Nikla secured her workout bag on her shoulder.

"Okay. I really need someone to cover my spinning class tonight. Can I count on you?" She chewed on her lower lip.

Nikla sighed. Honestly she had nothing else to do. "Sure." She felt so defeated.

Karen squealed and attempted to throw her arms around Nikla. Nikla held up her hand to stop the enthusiastic woman.

"I'm going out to lunch." Nikla walked by Karen and stared at Big Tom. "If that's okay."

Big Tom said nothing as she continued walking.

As usual, Nikla and Deana went to the same place for lunch. Nikla got her standard salad bar salad and stared at it as it sat on the table. She picked at it with her fork but couldn't eat any of it. Why did she even bother going out to lunch?

Nikla stared at a crouton on her salad. She picked it up and placed on the back of her hand. Like the jellybeans Sweet had put down her arms the very first time they played in his store, she focused on the feeling of that rye-bread crouton on her hand.

She closed her eyes and thought about every bump and grit over the crouton. Nikla concentrated on the connection to her skin. To her, the cube felt like a million pounds and would keep her in her spot. Coupled with the fact that she still wore her candy bracelet, Nikla knew Sweet still had her under his spell.

"Are you listening to me?" Deana asked, snapping Nikla out of her thoughts.

"No. I'm thinking about something else," Nikla answered honestly while still keeping the crouton on her hand.

"What? Your business?" The snarky way Deana said it bristled Nikla.

"Yes. You know, you've never been really supportive of me trying to open this studio. What's up with that?" Nikla dropped her fork on her plate.

"I have been. Are you kidding? I'm always talking about my smart, ambitious friend, Nikla Dearwood, who's trying to do her own thing."

Nikla wanted to believe that. Considering Deana had never lied to her, and Deana always spoke what was on her mind, she had no reason to doubt her.

"As a matter of fact, I saw that lying, cheating dog, Justin, a couple of weeks ago and I told him that you were going to have your own business and would crush him and his rich-ass family."

Nikla broke her stare from the food on the back of her hand to look at her friend. She could only imagine Deana yelling at Justin, who probably crumpled into a ball until she finished her speech.

"I even told him that you had met some hot-ass guy with a huge dick."

Nikla shook her head. "Deana."

Deana nodded. "I sure did. I said that you are getting it on the regular now."

Was getting it, Nikla wanted to add. Even though she didn't want to admit it to him, Nikla did miss Sweet. She glanced down at her wrist and noticed her candy bracelet. Damn. She pulled her sweater down to cover it.

"Yep, I even told that idiot that your man owns his own business and that he laid it down behind closed doors." Deana cackled, but Nikla realized what she'd said.

"You told Justin that Sweet and I had sex in his business?" Nikla asked. "Yeah. You should have seen his eyes. They got so wide. That'll teach him."

"I wished you hadn't done that." Nikla brushed the crouton off the back of her hand, then stopped their waitress to ask for her check.

"Why? He was a horrible boyfriend and a lousy lay. I let him off easy." "He went to the health department and told them what we did. Decadent Treats is in trouble now. Sweet and his brother talked about closing."

Masaun hadn't been wrong when he blamed Nikla. If she hadn't told her friend what she and Sweet had done, she wouldn't have blabbed it to Justin. She never figured Justin to be vindictive considering he cheated on her.

"I'm so sorry, girl. I didn't know the jerk would have—"
Nikla paid for her lunch. "What I tell you is between me and you. If you can't respect that then maybe we shouldn't be friends." She stood up. "You think about that. I sure will."

As she went to her car, Nikla felt like she had a purpose. She had to apologize to Sweet and Masaun, but she didn't know how to do that. She'd kicked him out of her place. If he didn't listen to her then, he wouldn't do it now.

****

Sweet sat behind the desk at Decadent Treats making calls and handling some business. When Masaun came into the room, Sweet didn't move.

"You haven't done enough?" Masaun crossed his arms over his chest.

Sweet pointed to the couch, the place he normally occupied. "Have a seat. Let's talk."

"Do you have pants on now? Have you already had sex on the couch?" Masaun goaded.

"Don't be a dick. I'm trying to talk to you here." Sweet pushed himself back from the desk.

Masaun plopped down. "Fine. I'm sitting. What?"

Sweet took a deep breath before speaking. "I'm signing over my half of the business to you."

Masaun's face went pale as he stared at his brother. "What are you talking about?"

"I fucked up. I'm admitting it." Sweet shrugged. "You're right. I get impulsive and I look for the immediate reaction. I did it at The Dollhouse. I tried doing that with Nikla. I did it here. My head isn't into business. Nikla called me selfish. She was right."

Everything about her was right. In the couple of weeks he'd been without her, his body ached for her. Kissing and touching her the other night whetted his appetite, but he wanted more.

Masaun leaned forward and braced his elbows on his knees. "Look, we can fix this. Between me and Kindle, we can work something out with the health department. There's got to be something for first-time offenders."

Sweet shook his head. "Handled. I contacted the agent on the form. I told him effective immediately I would be stepping down as candy maker, and only after a thorough investigation would we be allowed to reopen the kitchen. I have a name of a great pastry chef who can make you some incredible candies once the health department gives you the okay." Sweet stood from behind the desk. He handed his brother a piece of paper with the name of the pastry chef he'd met at The Dollhouse. "The other stipulation is that I would step down as owner. I did the offense. I need to get away from the business."

Masaun jumped up. "No. This was your idea. This is your baby."

Sweet chuckled. "If this was a real baby, I would have been arrested and put behind bars for neglect. You know the true ins and outs of this place. I'm just a distraction."

"But you love cooking and baking. What are you going to do?"

Sweet smiled. "You were right about something when you talked about me disciplining submissives. My heart wasn't into it. I had lost my passion. I'm still passionate about food. But I love something else more."

"BDSM?"

"Nikla." Just saying her name started his heart.

Masaun nodded.

Sweet moved around the desk. "I'm moving out, too."

His brother shook his head. "You don't have to leave."

Sweet laughed. "You weren't singing that tune weeks ago. Besides, if I stay here, I'll get depressed thinking about what could have been downstairs."

"You can move in with me until you find a place."

Sweet shook his head. "You and Kindle need your privacy."

"We have extra bedrooms in our house."

Sweet cocked his head. "I'll go from one apartment over the store to crashing with my big brother. I'm not a flunky college grad. I've saved some money. I've made some calls on some prospects. I'll be okay." He approached his brother. "I know I've made things very hard on you in life since I was kid. I'm so sorry. I will spend a lifetime making it up to you."

Masaun shook his head. "No, don't..."

"You need to stop feeling like you have to save me. Let me fail." He patted Masaun on his shoulder. "Trust me. It's made me stronger."

"What are we going to tell Connie and Hanson?"

"Tell them they'll have one less hard ass yelling at them." Sweet headed to the door. Before going back up to his apartment to pack up his items he turned back to Masaun, who looked defeated. "Are we good?"

Masaun ran his fingers through his hair. "Getting there." He grinned. "Hey, the least I can do then is to throw you a good-bye party. We can do it here after work on Friday."

"No, you don't have to do that."

"Kindle will kill me if I don't. Nothing special. Just the co-workers and us wishing you well."

"Okay." Sweet grabbed a couple of large shipping boxes and went upstairs to his apartment. With losing the business, he hadn't expected to feel renewed. The whole situation gave him clarity. He still had to figure out how to get Nikla back. He'd hurt her by accusing her of reporting them to the health department.

Deep down he knew she couldn't have done it. That niggling voice in the back of his head whispered poisoned words into his ear. He wouldn't be that weak again. With his newfound strength, he would get his woman back.

Chapter Thirty-Two

By the time Nikla arrived home at the end of her day, anger coursed through her body. She had some work to do. When her cell phone chimed that she had a new message, her body tingled for a moment hoping that maybe Sweet had contacted her. Even if the message said "Take off your panties" she would have done it. She missed him.

She looked at her phone and saw she had received a new e-mail. The e-mail came from the Zuberi Commercial Real Estate office.

Nikla sat down before opening it. The message simply asked that Nikla come to the office tomorrow afternoon. Her heart pounded. Maybe she had gotten the space.

She thought that that prospect would have made her happy. Instead, she felt like a failure. Without Sweet, she felt lost.

Nikla held up her phone, tempted to send Sweet a message or call him. She had to be strong. Plus, the idea of him rejecting her hurt worse than not hearing from him.

Time. They both could use some time apart.

A sleepless night didn't help Nikla. Every time she fell asleep she thought about Sweet or branching out on her own. Work would help her clear her mind.

As usual, Nikla arrived an hour before her class to get the room ready and to stretch. She didn't expect to see Karen bounding into her class so early in the morning. Had she known the flighty woman could bother to get up so early she would have asked her to cover some of her classes. What was Nikla thinking? Karen would never do that.

"Hey, Nikla."

"I told you I would cover you this Friday." Nikla crouched down to set up her iPod in the speakers.

"Yeah, I know. I was kind of hoping that you would also cover me this afternoon, too."

Nikla stood. Before she could refuse, Big Tom walked into the room like some bodyguard.

"I can't, Karen. I have plans this afternoon."

Big Tom cleared his throat. The sound raised the hairs on the back of her neck.

"No. I have plans." Nikla glared at Big Tom. "If you're not going to make her do her damn job, don't you dare guilt me into doing it."

"Come on, Nik. Be a team player." Big Tom strolled into the room.

Tired of this conversation and this whole situation, Nikla bent down and gathered her items. "I'm done. I give everything to my job. It's time I do that on my own." She hiked her purse on her shoulder. "I quit, effective immediately."

"You can't do that." Karen tugged on Big Tom's arm.

"Don't be hasty, Nikla. Let's talk about this." Big Tom went after her.

"No. You don't want to listen to me." She glared at Karen. "You want to fuck her and let everyone else cover her mistakes. Now you'll have two people to cover for. Good luck."

As she walked away, she heard Karen bawling behind her. The old Nikla would have run to her and taken back everything she'd said. Nikla felt too good to backslide. She smiled as she damn near skipped to her car.

Now that she had her day clear until her appointment that afternoon, she had to figure out what to do. She knew what she had to do.

Once she got home, she changed into a skirt and a simple knit top. No one else believed in her, but that didn't mean she didn't believe in herself.

Her first stop brought her to her father's store.

"What are you doing here so early?" Lawrence looked at his watch.

"I thought you'd be happy to see me. I came here without an invitation and everything." She kissed his cheek. "Besides, I'll have a lot of free time on my hands now."

Her father cut her a suspicious glare.

"I quit my job this morning." She would leave out the part that her supervisor and manager called her repeatedly since her hasty retreat.

Her father smiled, a strange reaction considering her father's staunch work ethic. The man always admonished her and her brother if they weren't doing something at every minute of the day.

"You know you can always work here." Her father tried handing her an apron.

Nikla shook her head. "Thanks for the offer, but I'm hoping to open my own place. As a matter of fact, I have an appointment this afternoon."

Lawrence slammed the apron on the counter. "You know, I don't know what I need to do to get you here. It's not enough that I got that other place shut down."

Nikla blinked and took a step back. "What?"

"Your boyfriend Justin came in here and gave me some information."

"Ex." Nikla processed the whole situation. "Justin told you that I had sex with Sweet and you used that against him. Essentially you used me. Did you think of that?"

From the way Lawrence's face softened, Nikla figured he hadn't thought of that. "Honey–"

"No, please don't say anything. Dad, I'm here for you. Even on days when I don't feel like it, I'm here. I've never turned my back on you. But I can't say the same for you. You want to keep me in your view but at arm's length. I can't have a relationship like that. If that's what you see between us, then this will be my last trip here." She turned to the door.

Nikla never suspected her father would have run after her. He pulled her into a hug and sobbed. He didn't cry or weep. Her Marine father didn't sniff back tears. She felt his tears hit the back of her neck. She assumed that this was the cry he needed to have when her mother had left him.

Nikla held her father until he composed himself.

"I never meant to hurt you," Lawrence said as he pulled back from her.

"You did. You can't control my personal life, and you can't go after a man I love." Nikla couldn't deny her heart. She couldn't go back to Sweet without being whole.

"I'm so sorry. I was so scared of losing you."

"I know." She held her father's hand. "I'll never leave you. I don't have to be stuck to your hip for you to know that." Nikla released her hold on her father. "And Mom didn't leave you, either." She watched Lawrence's face go still. "I saw her last week. She looks good. She looks healthy."

Lawrence wiped his eyes with the back of his hand, then dropped his gaze to the floor. "When did you get so smart and strong?"

Nikla smiled. "I've always been that way. You just refused to see it."

"I'm seeing it now. Maybe one day you'll bring your young man over when Junior comes home and we can all have dinner together."

A tear threatened to escape from Nikla's eye. "That would be nice." If only she had a man still.

"And Junior can bring his man with him, too."

Nikla knees nearly buckled under her. "How did you–"

"A father knows everything." He winked. "I'm not as stodgy or stubborn as you think."

"The next time you talk to him, let him know that." Lawrence nodded. "Can you help me out here?"

Nikla shook her head. "I have some things to do. I suspect you do, too, if you want to make things right with Sweet and his family. Those people didn't do anything to you."

"You're right. Man, you're rougher than any drill sergeant I've ever had."

"And don't you ever forget it." She winked at her father. "I also know the best way to increase your business."

"Oh, yeah? How's that?" Lawrence furrowed his eyebrows.

"Customers will be attracted to you and your business when you are your authentic self. For you, that means leaning on your military background." She smiled. "I shared on as many military accounts and forums about a great, military-led bakery." She peered over her shoulder when the door opened a four people in military fatigues entered.

"Looks like it worked. Hopefully, this is the start of a great turnaround." She kissed his cheek. "I'll call you. Love you, Dad."

"Love you, too." He gave her an official salute before she left.

Now that she could cross seeing Justin from her list, Nikla had time on her hands. She debated going to Decadent Treats, but her heart wouldn't allow her to go, wouldn't allow it to be subjected to a second heartbreak.

For now she would concentrate on herself. Her fingers brushed over the candy bracelet still on her wrist. If she wanted to heal, she would have to break clean.

****

The vibe in The Dollhouse felt different during the day Maybe because Sweet found it odd to see so many businessmen and women subjecting themselves to discipline.

When he went to the bar area, he noticed Juicy's eyes getting wide.

"What are you doing here?" She scanned the area.

"Don't worry. Zach knows I'm coming here. He's expecting me."

"You want something to drink?" Juicy wiped the bar down.

"I'm good."

"You sure, Sweet? It's on the house."

Sweet turned when he heard the gravelly voice behind him. When he saw the gray-haired man strolling up to him, Sweet extended his hand.

The fact that Zach had called him Sweet instead of Master Sweet didn't escape his notice. At least he knew the reason. Sweet had broken the rules and been formally ousted from the society. He didn't give up so easily.

"I was surprised to hear from you." Zach shook his hand.

Up close, Sweet noticed the deep spray of wrinkles around his dull blue eyes. He kept his hair loose around his face. Sweet had noticed on the rare occasion that he did play, Zach kept his hair in a ponytail.

"Is there somewhere we can go to talk?" Sweet kept his shoulders back and his chest out. He might be down, but he couldn't be counted out, not yet.

Zach walked toward the cage elevator that took him and Sweet up to a third level that only housed his office. Once inside, he flipped a switch on his desk that transformed the glass surrounding the office from translucent to black. Sweet wondered how the man got any privacy in an open office like he had.

"Aside from asking to come back, what can I do for you?" Zach sat behind his desk, which looked like a metal table that could be found in a mortuary.

"I want to buy The Dollhouse." Sweet never broke eye contact when he made his proclamation.

Zach stared at him for a moment before breaking into laughter. His graying moustache that went down the sides of his mouth framed the bottom half of his face nicely.

"You've got to be kidding. You break the rules and then you want to buy the place. Man, you've got brass balls on you." Zach reached into his desk and pulled out a pink bottle of Pepto Bismol and took a giant swig.

"Yes, I made a mistake. But who hasn't?"

"My place gets inspected on the regular. Vanilla folks always think I'm running a prostitution ring. I don't need you proving it by pumping some chick you've just disciplined."

Sweet balled his hands into fists. "Don't call her some chick. You don't know her."

"Easy. Everything in here is just play. I didn't know you caught feelings." Zach set his bottle on his desk. "For one thing, this place is not up for sale. If it was, what makes you think I would ever sell to you? I would sell to Hawk before I would let you have a crack at it."

"Despite what you may think, I love The Dollhouse. The recent series of events that have happened in my personal life made me reevaluate what's important to me." Sweet pointed down. "This place is what matters to me. I feel at home here. Maybe that's the reason I slipped up. I got too comfortable. I wouldn't do that as an owner. What I also see in here is a place to sell fetish toys, real ones. Good ones. If we do that, we can draw in more clients."

Zach stared at him for a moment. "You've been thinking a lot about this, haven't you?"

"You have no idea." Sweet couldn't believe the answer sat right in front of him. At his meeting with Zuberi this afternoon, he would tell them the same thing.

"I don't know. The members here have heard about you. They may not respect your leadership."

"Like in any relationship, I'll have to work on gaining their trust. Besides, it looks like this place is getting to you." Sweet pointed to the bottle.

Zach waved his hand at him. "Eh, now you sound like my old lady. Of course if she heard you, she would scream at me to sell. She's been wanting me to retire for years."

Sweet sat up taller. "I'm willing to work at it. Make me dungeon master. If I work out there, give me more duties in the business office. If that works out, let me put in the fetish shop. And then–"

"Stop talking, kid. I'll give you a shot, not as dungeon master, though."

Sweet held off jumping for joy until he heard Zach's proposal.

"You can buy in as a partner. If things don't work out, I'll buy you out. If they do, I'll sell you my share. What do you say?"

Sweet stood and put out his hand. "Deal. Will you have your attorney draw up the paperwork?"

"Yeah, I'll pull Juicy off the bar to do that."

Sweet peered down at the bar area and stared at the tattooed woman. "Juicy's an attorney?"

"The best. She loves working here more than defending scumbags."

Sweet glanced at his watch. "I have another appointment. I can come back later."

Zach waved a dismissive hand. "Whatever. I'm not going anywhere. But before you leave, I want to say something to you."

Sweet took a seat. In all the years he'd been to The Dollhouse, he never remembered having a conversation with Zach.

"You remind me a lot of myself at your age." Zach studied him for a while. "Yeah, full of piss and vinegar. You got a tiger by the tail, and you ain't letting it go, right?"

"I don't want to be rude, Zach, but I–"

"Listen to me. You're an okay Dom."

Sweet sat up taller, ready to defend himself.

Zach continued. "You have the technique down. No one can argue that. But in order to control someone else, you've got to learn to control yourself."

Sweet listened to the older man's words and let them sink into his head. "These subs and slaves look to a Dominant to have a handle on things, be a leader. They want you to be their rock. If you can't keep your shit together, then you're going to end up with a mess. You know why you and Honey Badger didn't work out?"

Sweet had almost forgotten Melinda's scene name. Almost.

He shook his head at Zach's inquiry.

"You two were one in the same, only you're dominant and she's submissive. You two are both spontaneous, whether you want to admit it or not. You need to be with someone who digs boundaries. You know why?"

"Why?" Sweet had to hear this.

"Because you like pushing them."

Sweet nodded. That would describe his relationship to Nikla perfectly.

"I didn't ask for this advice." Sweet stared at the older man.

"I didn't ask for that same advice when the previous guy who owned this place told it to me thirty-five years ago." He smiled. "But I thank God I listened."

Sweet extended his hand to Zach and coupled the sincere gesture with a nod.

"See you later, Master Sweet." Zach nodded.

With the use of his scene name, Sweet started to feel like life returned to some sort of order. The old Sweet would have dismissed Zach's wise words. As a man learning to rebuild, he respected his advice. Sweet hoped that with his new way of thinking that he could get Nikla back.

****

"I don't understand. Bobbi Zuberi said she was considering my business for that downtown unit." Nikla spoke to a middle-aged man who busied himself packing papers into several boxes within the office.

As Nikla surveyed the space, she noticed how empty it started to look.

"My mother really has no power or say so to lease those units."

Ah, so this guy was one of Bobbi's sons. She had only met the guy and she didn't like him.

"I called the number that was on the sign in the window." When Nikla recalled that moment, she also remembered meeting Sweet there.

She shook her head to get him out of her thoughts.

"I know. Did you notice the sign was down shortly thereafter?" her son asked.

Nikla nodded. "She said my business and another were on the short list to be picked. She told us we would hear something after Halloween."

"I apologize for my mother. Ever since my father passed away, she's been trying to continue what she's done in the past, which was lease out units. I have asked her not to do that because she really has no authority. But she likes meeting new people."

Nikla felt so deflated. She gave up her job in the hopes that this would pan out for her. The office door opened and Sweet walked through looking more handsome than ever. Her insides quivered the closer he moved toward her. She looked away to keep from crying.

"My name is Sweet Hawkes. I'm supposed to meet Bobbi here."

Bobbi's son extended his hand. "Edmund Zuberi, Bobbi's son. As I was explaining to Ms. Dearwood here, the units have already been leased. My mother had no right or authority to hold meetings about the units. I apologize for any inconvenience."

From her peripheral vision, she caught Sweet looking at her.

"I had actually come to withdraw my businesses from consideration."

Nikla brought her full attention to him. "What?"

Sweet nodded. "I've decided to go in a different direction with my business." He turned to Edmund. "I was just going to argue for Ms. Dearwood."

Nikla cleared her throat when it started to tighten. "I don't need your endorsement." She directed her attention to Edmund. "I need answers. If you had no intention of leasing the space, why have us come all the way out here? You could have told us this in the e-mail."

"We offer other office spaces around the Tidewater area if you're interested. I'd be more than happy to meet with you at our real office next door. This tiny eyesore will be torn down soon."

"Or maybe you thought if we saw you face to face that we wouldn't want to sue you." Nikla crossed her arms over her chest. The fire had been lit under her. She didn't want it extinguished yet.

"Sue us?" Edmund damn near choked back a laugh. "My mother may be unorthodox, but she is an excellent businesswoman. I guarantee you that she advised you to seek out other spots if you wanted to, right?"

Nikla remained quiet. Bobbi had on a couple of occasions told Nikla she could look for other units if she didn't want to wait for her. Bobbi wasn't so crazy after all.

Nikla still dug in her heels. "Your mother represented your company.

She kept us waiting for an answer. She had us jumping through hoops. For loss of potential revenue, I should–"

Sweet cut her off. "Thank you for your time." He put his hand out to Edmund. "I appreciated the opportunity." He glanced at Nikla. "I hope you feel the same way, too." He turned to the door.

Unsatisfied with his statement, she followed him. "What? That's it? You're not as angry as I am? I thought you really wanted the spaces."

Sweet stopped by his truck and turned to her. "I thought that's what I wanted, too. Then I met a crazy woman."

Nikla started to open her mouth to refute his statement.

"Bobbi."

Nikla kept her arms crossed until she heard his speech.

"If it wasn't for Bobbi, you wouldn't have pushed yourself to come train with me. And I wouldn't have gone to a yoga class. I wouldn't have gotten to know you."

Nikla's heartbeat slowed. She loved everything he'd said, but she couldn't be sucked into his vortex. She didn't want to lose herself. "That's great for you. But what about me? I quit my job, and–"

"You quit?" Sweet smiled. "Good for you."

She cocked her head.

"You needed to do something to push you to action. Bobbi pushed you."

"Out of a job."

Sweet shook his head. "You hated it. If you didn't, you would have done what you could to work it out." He dropped his gaze as though he'd realized what Nikla did. What he said applied to the two of them. "You're resourceful. You're smart. You'll figure something out."

"And you? What will you do?"

Sweet stared at her. He raised his hand as though he wanted to brush a curl from her face, but he stopped himself. "Do you want to be my submissive?"

Nikla never suspected he would ask her that question still, not now, not after all they had been through lately. "I can't answer that right now."

Sweet nodded. "I know I want to continue disciplining you. But I also know I've made a lot of mistakes. I should have never accused you of going to the health inspector. I can't apologize enough for that."

Nikla started opening her mouth again and, again, Sweet stopped her.

"Even if you did, it's still my fault. I should have enough restraint to respect you and my business." He took a step closer to her. "I apologize for what I did at your apartment. As a Dom, *I* need to learn discipline."

Nikla smiled and allowed him to finish.

"As a result of my actions, I'll be stepping down as owner of Decadent Treats."

"Because of me?" Nikla covered her mouth.

Sweet shook his head. "Now who's not listening?" He smiled. "Because of *me*." He glanced around. "You want to go for coffee? Just sit and talk?"

Nikla grinned. "I'd like that."

Sweet glanced behind them at the building. "I wouldn't leave your car here. Follow me."

Nikla did. She followed him to a lovely little coffee shop near the area. Even in his jeans and pullover V-neck sweater, he acted and treated her like he wore a tuxedo. He opened every door for her and pulled out her chair.

When it came time to order, like she'd done before, she'd told Sweet what she wanted and he ordered for her.

"After the incident between us, where did you go?" Sweet began.

"I drove up to Maryland and saw my mother." Nikla watched Sweet's expression go very cold and serious.

"Are you okay?"

She nodded. "Better than okay actually. I learned the real reason why she left. All of these years, I thought it had to do with me." She ran her hand over her hair. "I also discovered we have a lot in common. It was a great trip." Nikla took a sip of her coffee. The aroma of cinnamon tickled her nose. "You're different now."

Sweet looked pensive before speaking. "I'm learning to look before I leap. I was a man who thought and acted as though I had nothing to lose. Then I lost it all, my home, my lifestyle, the business," he looked at her, "you. I had to do some deep soul searching. Figure out my life. Maybe listen to some advice now and then. Listening will make me a better Dominant." He placed his hand on the table a few centimeters from hers. "I make no apologies for being a Dom."

When Sweet stared at Nikla, it felt like he dared her to disagree. Too consumed in hearing what he had to say, she remained quiet.

"I figured out a long time ago what I want in a submissive, in a woman. The last time I saw you, you said I only talked about what I wanted and needed. Damn right."

Nikla didn't expect that response. The more he spoke, the more she realized that maybe she should have.

The chattering around her in the coffee shop quieted in her head. Her full focus went into the words Sweet spoke. She stared at the shape of his lips, how they curled at the end the longer he talked. She even stopped her bouncing knee to concentrate on the man sitting across from her.

"I want a woman so sure of herself, she makes no excuses or apologizes for what she does for me. I want a woman who knows herself enough to know her limits, but still wants to push past them. I want a woman who would have no problem getting on her hands and knees and crawling to me if that's what I wanted her to do. I want a woman who needs me to be her man." Sweet leaned forward. He stared into her eyes so that she could catch his intent. "I need to be your man." He paused, took a breath, and said again, "I need to be *your* man, Nikla."

That last statement took Nikla's breath away. She could barely swallow.

"I miss you." He lowered his deep voice, forcing her to move in closer to him. "You know what I miss about you?"

Nikla shrugged. She kept her hands flat on the table as she listened to him.

"You probably think I'm going to say sex, especially with the way I approached you the last time. Or maybe you think it's the playing, which I do miss, but that's not it. I loved it when you called me when you needed someone to talk to. I missed you needing me, all of me."

Nikla imagined the two of them pressed against his truck kissing each other so hard that their mouths would become sore. She wanted him to take her right there at the table. She felt the heat coming from his hand.

Nikla licked her lips. Daring to break this intense scene, she inched her pinky finger closer to him. She didn't even bother dropping her gaze when her flesh touched his.

Sweet pulled back. "Acting impulsively got me in this mess. I can't keep being the way I was because I'm not getting what I want. I love you. I wanted to tell you that on the morning where it all came to a head. I should have, instead of accusing you of betraying me." He pushed his chair back from the table and stood. "I'll be at Decadent Treats until this Friday evening. You have my number. Call me if you want to talk."

Finding her strength to finally say something, Nikla spoke. "And that's it? You tell me you love me and now you're leaving?"

Sweet braced his hands on the back of the wrought-iron chair before nodding. "Yes. I know what I want. I've told you what I want. You need to decide what it is you want in life, in your relationship. Everything. You really need to think about it. The ball is in your court now." He winked.

Before she could argue against his new plan, Sweet left. When he disappeared from her view, Nikla exhaled. She put her hand to her chest to feel her pounding heart.

No man had ever spoken so passionately about her, about his need to have her. He'd given her a lot to contemplate. Could she bring him back into her life after all the pain he'd given her?

Chapter Thirty-Three

"To Sweet!" Masaun raised his glass of champagne along with everyone else at Decadent Treats once the placed closed down. "May he be a pain in someone else's ass."

"Here, here!" Connie and Hanson replied in unison.

Sweet laughed. "I can really feel the love in this room."

Hanson approached Sweet first. "Seriously, man, we'll miss you." He leaned against him. "Women came here to see you, and I would get your castoffs all the time."

"Hey, that makes me sound like a pimp or something." He punched his former employee playfully on his shoulder.

"Or something. You're going to have to share your secret on how you get women to fall all over you."

Sweet took a step back. "Do you see any women around me?" The glares from Connie and Kindle made him adjust his statement. "Besides my former employee and my brother's fiancée?"

"Oh, no. You've got to be kidding me." Connie sat her glass on the counter. "I can't believe she even comes here at night."

Sweet turned around and faced the locked door. He saw Nikla standing on the other side. The world around him froze as soon as his stare connected to hers. With the pitch darkness behind her, and the overhead light casting a white glow down on her body, she appeared like an angel. To keep his hands hidden and occupied, he crossed his arms over his chest.

"Hanson, will you open the door for her, please?" Sweet nodded toward the door.

"Are you kidding?" Hanson snickered. "The lone protester? You're going to let her–"

"Now!" Sweet barked.

As Hanson went to the door, Masaun stood next to his brother. "Do you know what this is about?"

Sweet kept his stare on Nikla as he addressed his brother. "I left her alone. That might have something to do with it."

Hanson opened the door. Nikla took one step into the store and stopped. The distance between her and Sweet felt like miles. He kept his gaze on her, hoping to draw her further into the store, closer to him.

"This is a private party," Connie began. "Don't come in here and ruin it for–"

"Connie, be quiet." Sweet maintained his same position although every fiber of his being wanted to rush to her and scoop her up in his arms.

"I need to first apologize to you and your brother." Nikla cleared her throat. "It was my fault about the health inspector. I told my best friend about me and Sweet. She told my ex-boyfriend, who then ran and told my father. My father was the one who made the call. For that, I'm sorry. I had no idea."

"Apology accepted." Masaun nodded and took a step back to stand with Kindle.

"Was that all?" Sweet asked, hoping she wanted more.

She shook her head. "To your employees, I'm sorry for my mini protest in front of your workplace. I should have never done that no matter the reason."

"Thank you," Connie said.

"You didn't bother me not one bit. You can come here at any time, day or night." Hanson lifted his arm to put around her shoulders.

"I wouldn't do that if I were you," Sweet said before his young employee could make contact.

"Okay, let me just go get my drink." Hanson went back to his original spot and picked up his champagne again.

"Anything else?" Sweet asked again.

Nikla cleared her throat. "For a long time, I've been living in fear. I was afraid of failing my father. I feared that because of me, my mother couldn't stand being home with us and had to leave." She stared at Sweet. "I was afraid of being my true self." Nikla took a deep breath. "I was afraid I couldn't be enough for you."

Sweet's heart thudded. Before he could refute her assumption, she continued.

"You pushed me to do things that brought me out of my comfort zone. For that, I'm no longer afraid. I figured out what it is I want."

"You have?" Sweet felt his heart pounding. He clenched his jaw as he waited for what she would say or do.

She nodded. Without a word, Nikla lowered herself to her knees, then dropped to her hands on the floor.

Sweet heard Kindle gasp behind him but he didn't turn away from the beauty crawling over the floor to him.

"What the hell is she doing?" Hanson asked.

Sweet ignored him. He kept his full attention to the love of his life exposing herself, showing what she would do for him.

Nikla made it to his feet and kept her head down as she sat on her haunches.

"Up," Sweet said.

Nikla rose to her feet but still kept her head down. "I need you. I need you to be my man. I need to be with you. I only figured out who I was after I met you."

"Look at me."

She brought her face up and stared at him. "I could never do that before, show someone how much I care without thinking of what others would think." Her voice sounded so strong and confident. As she had been instructed, she kissed his one cheek then his other before finally planting her lips on his in a tender expression, no lust, nothing scintillating. Perfect. When she pulled back, she stared into his eyes. "I love you."

This time Sweet heard Connie gasping.

Nikla smiled. "I love that you push me, and you make me uncomfortable in a good way. I love that you protect me but allow me to be me. I love that you're not afraid to try new things. I love that you now listen to me." She placed her hand to the side of his face. "I love that you didn't give up."

He smiled.

"And I love the new you. But there are parts of the old you I really miss." She held up her hand to show off her candy bracelet. "I still want to be your Sugar Baby."

Sweet reached up and held her wrist. His fingers twirled around the bracelet. In one hard snag, he ripped it from her arm, sending candy beads everywhere in the room.

"Oh, God!" Nikla started to turn to leave.

Sweet saw the tears cresting on her lower lids, but he refused to let her hand go. "Wait!" He pulled her back. When he dropped down to one knee, the room fell silent. "It feels like I have waited a lifetime for a woman like you. You're smart. You're funny. You're the sexiest thing on two legs. And you accept me for me." He reached into his pocket. "I've been carrying this around for a couple of weeks." He pulled out a tennis bracelet adorned with yellow, pink, white, and black diamonds. "Candy doesn't suit you. You need something more substantial. With these different colored diamonds, this is as close as I could get to candy." Before he wrapped the jewelry around her wrist, he asked, "Will you be my submissive?"

"His what?" Connie asked. "That didn't sound like 'wife.' What did he say?"

"Yes, I will." Nikla wiped her face with her free hand.

Sweet secured the bracelet around her wrist. "Good. It makes asking this next question so much easier." From his other pocket he retrieved a red velvet box. He opened it to reveal the matching engagement ring. "Nikla Dearwood, will you marry me? You've already made me the happiest Dom on the planet."

"Happiest what? Did he say 'man' or Don? Oh, God! Are you two in the mafia?" Connie asked.

"Yes, I'll marry you, Swithin Hawkes."

"Who?" Connie and Hanson asked in unison.

Sweet slipped the ring on her finger, stood, and wrapped his arms around her waist.

Before he could kiss her, she said, "I don't have a job."

"I don't care." He lowered his head.

"You marry me, you get my dad."

"I can deal with that." He continued lowering his head to connect to her lips.

"I'll want you to do yoga with me every day."

Sweet smiled and put his face next to hers to whisper in her ear, "I'll be sure to stretch you out daily." He felt her trembling in his arms.

Before she could say another word, Sweet kissed her. The intimate crowd behind him cheered in their approval.

"Looks like we'll have two weddings," Kindle said. "I'll get a sister."

"Me, too," Masaun said.

"And I get to make the wedding cake and the candy arrangements." Connie jumped up and down.

Sweet and Masaun looked at their employee at the same time.

"You two are doing a candy-themed wedding, right?" Connie furrowed her eyebrows.

"Connie, we're more than just candy makers." Sweet brought his gaze back to Nikla.

"You got that right." Nikla wrapped her arms around Sweet's waist. "Too bad we can't get married at The Dollhouse."

Sweet shrugged. "I don't know. Anything's possible."

"This calls for another toast." Hanson raised his glass. "To the Hawkes brothers. May this be the start of some great new beginnings."

"I'll drink to that." Nikla squeezed Sweet, who offered her his drink. She stood on her tiptoes and whispered in his ear. "Can we go upstairs?"

He shook his head. "My party. It would be rude of me to leave early."

She nodded.

"Plus, I don't live up there anymore. I'm renting a place for now while I look for a house." He kissed the shell of her ear. He held up his glass. "I need champagne."

Nikla glanced at the glass, then at Sweet. Now that she figured out what she wanted in her life, in her man, Nikla accepted the glass. "Anything for you."

Before Sweet, Nikla couldn't even hold hands with a man in public without feeling self-conscious. After Sweet's impassioned speech at the coffee shop a couple of days before, Nikla recognized her need to be with him, her need to serve him, serve her Master Sweet.

She poured more champagne into a glass and brought it back to him. "Your drink."

Sweet accepted it, brushing his fingers over hers. "Thank you." He wrapped his arm around her waist. Before taking a sip, he placed the glass to her lips and allowed her to drink. The sweet bubbles popped on her tongue as she held the amber liquid in her mouth a brief second before swallowing.

Downing the drink, Nikla realized that Sweet wouldn't be playing with her tonight. She knew how seriously he took to playing clear-headed. A small part of herself wanted to feel the sting of his whip, candy or real. Now that she had Sweet in her life again, she wanted the full experience.

Instead, Sweet transformed into the most cordial party guest. He introduced her officially to Hanson. Nikla had met Connie on Halloween night. Now that Nikla had plans to marry Sweet, the motherly woman talked Nikla's ear off on wedding plans and cake designs.

Nikla couldn't help but steal glances at her fiancé, her Dom fiancé. At a break in his conversation, Nikla excused him from his group of friends to get him alone.

"I wish we skipped drinking alcohol." Nikla fidgeted in her spot. "I need you, Master Sweet. You truly have mastered my body."

Now she knew how junkies felt. Her skin crawled in anticipation of the punishment he would inflict on her. The cane gave her the pop and sting that curled her toes. Her nipples hardened at the idea of Sweet squeezing them between nipple clamps. She would even endure a little anal play if he wanted.

"You have no idea what hearing that means to me. I love being your Master Sweet. I promise. You'll have me. There are other ways to play rather than the physical." He kissed her forehead.

After another fifteen minutes at the party, Sweet finally excused himself and Nikla.

"Leave your car here and come home with me." Sweet unlocked his truck and helped Nikla inside.

When Sweet got inside, she leaned against him. "You have changed."

Sweet wrapped his arm around her and held her close. "What do you mean?"

"The old you would have taken me to your old apartment and, well, you know." She smiled. She couldn't tell if the heat that filled her cheeks came from embarrassment or alcohol.

"Trying not to be so impulsive. Besides, a woman like you deserves better than sex in an empty apartment." Sweet patted her hip and gave her a possessive squeeze.

Yes, she certainly liked this new Sweet.

He brought her to a modest, three-bedroom, two-bath home in a quiet, older section of Virginia Beach.

He opened the door to his new home. Nikla found the sparsely decorated place a great match for Sweet. Like him, this house would be a work in progress.

In the corner of the living room, she spotted the egg-shaped hanging chair, the same one he had to take down in his apartment so that she could be strung up by Master Wasabi. Nikla ran her hand over the chair as she recalled those fond memories. She only snapped out of her trance when she heard Sweet clearing his throat.

Nikla found Sweet standing in the center of his living room.

"What are my rules?" He scanned her body.

Without a word, Nikla stripped out of her clothing. She threw the discarded items onto the couch. Nikla stepped out of her shoes and faced Sweet.

"Give me my greeting."

Standing on her tiptoes, she kissed both his cheeks, his lips, then she lowered herself to the floor.

"Good."

From her position, she watched him turn and stomp over the hardwood floor.

"Follow."

Nikla got on her hands and knees and crawled behind him to a room at the end of the hall. In the darkened room, Nikla tried staying in the light streaming from the hallway. When the light came on in the room, she gasped.

"I broke my promise, but I couldn't help it."

On the wall over Sweet's bed hung a large picture of her wrapped in ropes and suspended. Nikla covered her mouth with her hand as she stared at her image.

She turned her attention to Sweet. "Permission to speak."

Sweet nodded.

"Do you masturbate to it?"

He laughed so loudly, the sound vibrated the floor. "Up."

Nikla stood.

Sweet framed her face in his large hands and stared at her, kind of in the same way he did the very first time they'd had sex in his office. He studied her, staring into her eyes, and occasionally dropping his gaze to her mouth.

"I love you." He pressed his mouth to hers.

"I love you, too."

"Run a bath and get me undressed."

Getting commands from Sweet gave Nikla a sense of calm. "Yes, Sir."

After their bath, and Sweet made Nikla read him a chapter from *Wifey*, he pressed her body against his, wrapped his arm around her waist, and slept.

Nikla couldn't deny that she had expected hot, passionate sex. Getting a glimpse of what Sweet would expect of her as a wife and as a submissive had been better than anything she had imagined.

Waking in his arms gave Nikla a sense of security. Despite the November chill, Sweet's warm bed made her feel cozy. She snuggled under the blankets and against Sweet's hard, naked body.

Sweet growled. Nikla eased her backside closer to him and felt the result of his morning lust. She smiled.

With her back to him, she couldn't tell if Sweet had awakened yet. He cupped her breast and massaged it in his large hand.

Sweet turned her over to smother her in a soul-stirring kiss. When he broke from the kiss, he stared at her. "This is how to wake up in the morning."

Nikla smiled.

Sweet kicked the blankets off their bodies. "Ride me, Sugar Baby."

"Yes, Sir." She straddled his body.

Reaching down, she held onto his shaft as she guided herself down onto him, allowing him to fill her completely.

"Fuck!" Nikla rested her hands on his chest.

From that position, as she rose and fell on him, she spied her engagement ring and her matching bracelet. Sweet had called it her collar. Nikla would call it freedom, freedom to be herself, her real self.

She rotated her hips. That move got Sweet to groan. In response, he spanked her ass cheek.

"Yes!" Nikla leaned down and pressed her chest against his.

With one arm around her waist, Sweet kept her in her spot while he continued to spank her ass cheeks.

No one else would understand this treatment but her and Sweet. No one else mattered, and Nikla finally understood that.

In his ear, she said, "Yours."

"Again." He held her tighter.

Nikla felt his body trembling.

"Yours." She licked the shell of his ear, tasting his salty skin.

Sweet thrust his hips up to match her movements. "Yeah! Yeah! Nikla!"

"I'm yours!"

"Come now!"

Nikla gripped Sweet's shoulders and buried her face into the side of his neck. "Fuck!"

Sweet came deep in her as he continued holding her. "I'm never letting you go. Ever." He kissed the side of her face.

Gasping for air, Nikla could only say one word, "Yours."

Epilogue

"She is determined to make an appearance." Kindle cradled her protruding belly in her wedding dress as she spoke to Nikla and Lolli.

Nikla put her hand on her soon-to-be sister-in-law's hand on her stomach. "No hiding your pregnancy."

Kindle turned around. "Everything is happening so fast. But I am too excited on this next chapter of our lives." She held Nikla's hand."

"You will be missed at The Dollhouse," Lolli said with a smile.

"We will be back." Kindle winked at Nikla.

She'd become so close to Kindle that she felt like they had been separated at birth.

Nikla outfitted her with her veil then put the flowers in her hands. "Are you ready?"

Kindle nodded.

"Oh, wait! I need to do one thing." Nikla ducked into the bathroom and closed the door. From her purse she pulled out a pair of vibrating panties. She could not wait to see what Sweet had in store for her later.

"Let's go." Kindle held Lolli and Nikla's hands before they went out to the chapel. "Thanks to the both of you for being there for me."

"Of course," Nikla and Lolli said at the same time.

Kindle's father stood by his daughter as the wedding music began. The ring bearer and flower girl strolled down the aisle first. The groomsmen all escorted the bridesmaids next.

When Nikla spotted Sweet, her stomach flipped. He took her arm wrapped it around his. Then they started their slow march down the aisle.

"We could have something like this, you know. Very traditional," Sweet whispered.

Nikla shook her head. "There's nothing traditional about us." Before parting at the altar, she whispered to him, "I have on the panties."

It must have been loud enough for Masaun to hear. He cleared his throat. Sweet kissed her before they resumed their assigned spots. Lolli strolled down the aisle alone as the matron of honor. Nikla noticed the love in Razor's eyes as he watched his submissive make her way to the altar.

By the time Kindle made it down the aisle, not a dry eye existed in the church. She looked elegant and beautiful. Sweet and Masaun's parents beamed as Kindle strolled toward her future.

Nikla stared at Sweet, who kept his gaze on her the entire time until the preacher asked for the rings. He snapped out of his haze to do his one duty.

"I now pronounce you husband and wife. You may now kiss the love of your life."

Masaun framed Kindle's face and kissed her with such passion that even the preacher had to clear his throat to get them to break it up. A ripple of laughter went through the crowd.

When they broke from the kiss, Kindle wiped the red lipstick from his mouth. Then the duo turned to the crowd.

"I'm happy to announce for the first time Mr. and Mrs. Masaun Hawkes."

The crowd cheered as the two went down the aisle. Nikla linked arms with Sweet again as they went back down the aisle behind Lolli and the happy couple.

"I can't wait until this is us," Nikla said to Sweet through the roar of the cheers.

"Why wait?" Sweet asked as they got outside. "We could be on a plane to Vegas tonight."

Nikla squeezed Sweet's hand. "I love you so damn much."

"I love it when you curse." He laughed.

"I love my new family." She squeezed Sweet's hand. "And my new job."

Sweet had the brilliant idea for Nikla to do personal training at The Dollhouse for new submissives. Leaf became one of her best students. Ashley continued her yoga training with Nikla, and quickly started training as a submissive due to the location of her classes. After those two students came ten more. Business was good for both her and The Dollhouse, a business that Sweet now owned entirely.

"Let's get these pictures over with and let me do my toast. Then we can go." Sweet lined up with everyone else in the receiving line.

"Are we going home to change?" Nikla asked.

"No." He leaned down to her. "I want you to keep on the panties." He activated a remote in his pocket that started the vibrations.

"I won't make it through the reception."

"That's the idea."

Acknowledgments

Writing interracial BDSM stories has become a passion of mine. I knew to do it well, I had to do research. I do not mean Googling information. I met with local BDSM groups, asked them endless questions, watched them play, and attended play parties. I even swung a flogger or two, but quickly found I was not as well received as a trained Dominant. I wanted to make sure that when I wrote about characters hearing something at a play party or the smells and sights that exist at them that I was recalling something I had actually been through and not only using my imagination.

As a result of my in-person research, I hope my writing comes through as authentic. On the flip side, I sincerely hope that anyone in the Lifestyle sees my writing as my love letter to them. I have grown to appreciate the openness of each and every person who has shared their story with me and allowed me to be a voyeur into an intimate moment.

I must acknowledge the fact that due to the original publisher of this book closing, it forced me to push myself out of my comfort zone and take control of my work. I feel more of an ownership over my craft than I have ever felt.

The pandemic, though devastating to many people and families, forced me to slow down and return to the thing that made me fall in love with writing, which is reading. Reading not only reminded me why I loved books, but it helped me strengthen my writing.

Hope you loved this read and will read my other works.

About the Author

Best-selling author of interracial BDSM erotic romance, Bridget Midway has been published since 2005. The multi-award winning and award-nominated author has found her niche with readers with her scintillating interracial BDSM erotic romance including the 2008 EPPIE Award finalist, *Love My Way*, and 2010 Romance Slam Jam Steamy Novel of the Year finalist, *Corporate Needs*.

For more information on Bridget Midway, go to her website at
http://www.BridgetMidway.com/